THE GIRL WHO TOLD STORIES

THE GIRL WHO TOLD STORIES

A Joe Court Novel

BY

CHRIS CULVER

ST. LOUIS, MO

Other books in the Joe Court Series

1

Nicole had walked through her garden hundreds of times, and yet today felt like the first. A nervous energy ate away at her insides as the leaves of the marijuana plants brushed her shoulders and cheeks. When Hiram Ford hired her, he had led her to an open grassy field in the center of a dense wood and told her he wanted two hundred and forty mature female plants at the end of the season. For twenty grand plus expenses, she agreed without hesitation.

Nicole had never gardened before, but she dove into the project and researched everything she could—not just about marijuana, but also about the science of gardening. Hiram had provided the equipment, seeds, fertilizer, and protection. She provided ingenuity and sweat equity. Weeks before the last frost, she started her seeds in egg cartons full of soil in a sunny window in her bedroom. While they germinated, she tilled the site and nurtured the soil. After planting her seedlings outdoors, she strung poultry netting from stakes in the ground to keep the deer away from the tender young plants.

Nicole hadn't known it before, but she had a gift for gardening. She enjoyed smoking marijuana, but she loved growing it. Few activities had been so rewarding or relaxing. That the money her plants earned her would pay her way through college and help her leave her dump of a hometown made the job even more worthwhile.

Until Hiram's men had begun assaulting her co-workers, it had been the best summer job a sixteen-year-old girl could ask for.

She reached out and felt the leaves of a nearby plant. It was late September, and Hiram had already begun harvesting his fields, but he hadn't made it here yet. He never would, either.

"I won't be here too much longer, guys," she said. "The police will destroy you soon. Sorry. I wish I could help."

At first, she had felt self-conscious talking to her plants, but after spending eight hours a day for an entire summer with them, they had become almost like silent friends. Besides, the nearest road was a mile away through woods and bramble so thick a hiker couldn't see more than a hundred yards ahead, and the nearest home was at least two miles beyond that. She could have pranced around buck naked if she wanted, and nobody would have seen her in a million years. Because a big timber company owned the property, hikers didn't even come into this part of the county. She was alone but for her thoughts and her horticultural charges.

As she walked amongst the rows of plants, she checked for indications of disease or male buds. The male plants might be perfectly healthy, but they'd pollinate the nearby female plants, which would then produce seeds and decrease the overall yield. Nobody wanted that, so she pulled two likely plants and carried them to the burn pile beside her shed, singing a Lady Gaga song along the way.

Her boss, Hiram Ford, was an old man who owned gas stations and bars across the region. He gave her the resources to do her job and left her alone, which she appreciated. The cops who provided security for him, though, were sons of bitches who deserved to die slow, painful deaths. If she'd had the ability, she would have killed them all.

Hiram had fields all over the place, so Nicole wasn't his only gardener. He hired girls because he thought they were more responsible than boys, and he refused to hire anybody over eighteen. If the police caught a sixteen-year-old girl tending a field of marijuana plants, they'd arrest her for trafficking, but they'd charge her as a minor. She'd spend a few years in a juvenile facility, but then she'd get out and finish school. Hiram would even pay her for her time. Life would continue.

If they caught a nineteen-year-old girl with two or three hundred plants, she'd face twenty or thirty years in the North Carolina Correctional Institution for Women. With charges that serious, a deal to turn on her boss for reduced prison time became much more attractive. That was dangerous for everybody.

The plants she threw on her burn pile smoldered before their leaves caught fire on the hot coals. She didn't know what strain of plant she was growing, but the smoke was almost sweet.

"Hey, sugar," said a scratchy voice behind her. For a second, her breath caught in her throat, and muscles all over her body tensed. Then her shoulders relaxed, and she closed her eyes.

"Damn it, Hiram," she said, turning around. "I hate it when you do that."

As she turned and opened her eyes to see her boss, the hairs on the back of her neck stood on end. Hiram was a small man with thinning white hair, a bushy mustache, and skin that had grown leathery from the sun. He was harmless, but his companion was anything but. His name was Michael Grant, and he was a ranger with the North Carolina Division of Parks and Recreation. He wore jeans and a red T-shirt. A black pistol hung from a holster on his hip, and he carried two blue five-gallon gas cans.

"Hey, Nicole," said Michael, winking. "Been a while."

"It has," said Nicole. "After what you did to Monica, I had hoped you fell off a cliff and broke your legs."

He put down his containers, crossed his arms, smiled, and tilted his head to the side.

"If I had fallen, would you have rescued me?"

"No, but I would've spat on you and put some duct tape over your mouth so you couldn't scream," she said before looking to Hiram. "What's the story, boss?"

Hiram sighed and looked down.

"We've got a problem, hon," he said. "A journalist's been poking her nose around places it ought not go."

Nicole's skin tingled, and a fluttery feeling began building in her gut. Sweat dripped down her lower back, sending a cold chill across her skin, but she tried not to let her surprise or fear show. He shouldn't have known about

4

Sallianne yet. That wasn't part of the plan. This was bad. Nicole cleared her throat and looked down as a tremble passed through her.

"Oh, yeah?" she asked, crossing her arms. "You think my garden's compromised?"

"I know it is," said Hiram. "I put up a trail camera a week ago to catch her. She's been here and took pictures."

Nicole had contacted Sallianne three weeks ago, so the timeline made sense. She blinked. Her heart thudded against her chest so hard she was sure Hiram and Michael could see it through her T-shirt.

"What are you going to do?"

Hiram shrugged and looked to Michael.

"The reporter's dead now, so she ain't a problem," said Hiram. "This garden is, though. Michael brought some diesel. We'll do a controlled burn and take the field out before anybody else sees it. You've still got some gasoline in the shed, don't you?"

Nicole swallowed hard and blinked.

"Did you kill her?"

Hiram said nothing. Michael raised his eyebrows.

"You got any gasoline?" he asked. "Diesel's hard to light on its own. Gasoline makes it a lot easier."

Nicole's fingers shook, so she balled them into fists. Her guts twisted, but she forced herself to nod.

"In the shed," she said, coughing to cover up the tremble in her voice. "It's for the tiller."

Michael nodded and looked to Hiram.

"All right, girl," said the old man. "We're just going to

burn the whole lot. Shed, equipment, fertilizer, and plants. I hate to lose it, but I'd rather lose a garden than go to prison. Michael will tell you where to put the diesel so the fire doesn't spread. He'll put that forest ranger training to good work."

The two men smiled, but Nicole's legs felt so weak that it was hard to stand. She and Sallianne had only spoken a handful of times, but she had been a nice woman. She didn't deserve to die—not for this, at least. Nicole had gone to her for help, but she hadn't ever thought she'd get her killed. Her stomach roiled, and she felt like throwing up.

For the next fifteen minutes, Nicole's mind and body moved on autopilot as she and Michael spread ten gallons of diesel around the field. She didn't know where to put things, but Michael had done controlled burns before. All the while, Nicole's mind kept drifting back to Sallianne. She wasn't a part of this. She was just a journalist. Hiram hadn't needed to kill her.

Once she and Michael ran out of fuel, the two walked back to Hiram. The old man paced along the edge of the woods near the shed and avoided looking at either of them. He rubbed the back of his neck and kept his eyes on the ground. He almost looked nervous. Nicole would be, too, if she had just murdered someone.

"The diesel's spread out," said Nicole, hoping her voice didn't crack. Her eyes felt wet. She wiped away a tear. "Can I go home now? The fumes are making me feel sick."

"You're not even going to ask about payment?" asked Michael. "You worked hard for months, so you ought to get something for that."

She closed her eyes and began speaking, but her voice came out as a stutter. Then she took a deep breath and looked to Michael.

"I planned to ask about my payment later," she said, looking to Hiram. Her voice wavered for a second. "The boss has had a bad day. I don't believe in kicking a man when he's down."

"That's admirable of you," said Michael. "I'll remember—"

"You two shut up," said Hiram, interrupting the forest ranger. A chill passed down Nicole's back, and she felt her insides tremble as he shook his head and glared at her. "I know you contacted her, honey. I trusted you and paid you good money to do a job for me, and you stabbed me in the back."

She looked to Michael. He smiled, and slowly, anger began to burn through her pain. Her hands trembled as hot, vitriolic rage built inside her.

"Only because you let Michael and his douchebag friends hurt Monica," she said. "Who knows how many other girls they hurt. I never would have contacted her if you had done your goddamn job and protected us."

Hiram winced.

"I'm sorry for what Michael and his friends did to Monica," said the old man, "but that doesn't excuse what you did to me. He paid her, didn't he?"

"Monica signed up to tend a garden," said Nicole, her face growing hot. "You turned her into a prostitute. She didn't want that."

"But she took the money, didn't she?" asked Michael.

"Fuck you," said Nicole. "I hope you get AIDS and die."

Michael's back straightened.

"Monica have HIV or AIDS?"

Nicole smirked.

"You should have asked that before you and your buddy held her down," she said. "Maybe you could have avoided this whole mess."

"That's enough," said Hiram. "Kill her in the shed, Michael. The fertilizer will burn hot enough to cremate her body."

Michael grabbed her forearm before she could run. She tried to rip her hand away from him, but his fingers were like steel. He had at least fifty or sixty pounds on her, most of which was muscle. Monica said she had fought like hell to get away from him when Michael and his buddy raped her, but she hadn't gotten anywhere. Nicole had to be smart.

"I'm still valuable to you," she said, looking to Hiram. "I'll work for free. And I'll sleep with you. Whenever you want. You just call ahead, and I'll be ready. I'll even wear lingerie. Unlike Monica, I'll have a choice."

Hiram's eyes traveled up and down her body, but he shook his head.

"If you had asked me ten years ago, I would have

taken you up on that," he said. "But I'm too old for that shit now, and you lost my trust when you contacted a journalist and told her about our operation."

"I didn't want to do that," she said. "I had to protect the girls. Michael's a cop. So are his friends. They got drunk and raped Monica. Eventually they'd come after the others. They may have even come after me. You couldn't protect us, so I had to step in."

"That was a one-time thing," said Michael. "We wouldn't have hurt anyone else."

It was bullshit, and they both knew it. She looked at Hiram, but he turned away before she could speak.

"Please, Hiram," she said, crying now. "Don't do this. I'm a good worker."

"You're damaged goods," he said, looking to Michael. "Put her down in the shed."

Nicole's gut twisted, and her shoulders drooped. Her stomach felt as if she had just stepped off a cliff.

"This is wrong, and you know it," she said. "Don't do this, Hiram. You know my family. You know my daddy. Come on. Do the right thing."

Hiram turned, and Michael squeezed her arm hard enough that she knew she'd find bruises beneath her shirt —if she survived. She tried to pull away, but he was too strong. Then she stomped on his foot with her heel and tried to kick him in the balls, but he pulled her into his chest and wrapped both his arms around her. Then her legs left the ground as he tossed her over his shoulder.

She clawed at his back and neck, but she couldn't

reach any of his vulnerable areas. He just laughed.

"Men bigger than you have done far worse to me," he said. "You just hold on. This will be over soon."

The ground was uneven. She hoped he'd fall and trip, but she didn't expect to have that kind of luck. So Nicole writhed and squirmed, trying to kick him, but she couldn't do any real damage on his shoulder. When they reached the shed, he tossed her onto a pile of bagged fertilizer. He and his buddy had held Monica down on that same pile.

"You want this to go quick, or do you want me to shoot you in the belly so you bleed to death?"

Every muscle in Nicole's body trembled. She had to fight to keep the tears from her voice.

"Please just leave me alone. I'll do anything you want."

He considered her and then looked to his right. Hiram was off in the woods already. A smile lit his face, and he began closing the shed door.

"Turn over and put your ass in the air."

Monica had described Michael saying something similar to her. Nicole didn't plan to go quietly, and Michael had just given her the tools to fight back. She couldn't let him see that, though, so she forced herself to sob.

"Please don't hurt me," she said.

"I can't make that guarantee," he said, "but if you shut up, we both might enjoy ourselves. Now get on your belly and pull down your pants."

She forced her shoulders to tremble as she rolled onto her stomach. As Michael's belt buckle jangled, Nicole reached down between two bags of fertilizer for the garden knife she had stored there after hearing Monica's story. The weapon had a serrated edge for sawing tough branches and a sharp point.

The instant her hand touched the textured, rubber grip, she felt strength flood through her. Michael wouldn't get to hurt her the way he'd hurt Monica. His hands reached to her hips and pulled at the waist of her jeans, but the fabric wouldn't budge.

"I told you to pull your pants down," he said, reaching to the front of her hips and fumbling with the button on her jeans. She had waited for that moment.

"Fuck you, asshole," she said. Without looking, she pivoted her hips and whipped her arm around. She had hoped to stab him in the neck, but Michael must have felt her weight shift because he vaulted to his feet. She adjusted her strike at the last moment, so her blade thudded against his thigh and dug several inches into his muscle. Nicole ripped forward and pulled as hard as she could, cutting him as deeply as possible to maximize her chances of hitting an artery.

Michael screamed and swung his arms, backhanding her across the face. White flashed in her eyes, and she fell to the side, off the pile of fertilizer. Her ears rang, and she felt dizzy. Blood slicked her right hand, but the knife's textured grip had allowed her to maintain her hold.

"You little cunt," bellowed Michael, trying to push himself to his feet. The moment he put weight on his leg, he fell backwards. Nicole took a breath as the world stopped spinning. She had to move.

She pushed herself to her feet and sprinted toward the door. Michael grabbed her ankle, but the blood on his hands made his grip slippery. She kicked hard and ran into her garden. Michael screamed for Hiram to stop her, but the old man didn't stand a chance. This was her garden, and these were her woods. She knew them both well.

She sprinted through the plants, holding her breath to avoid the chokingly thick diesel fumes, until she reached an old deer trail that ran through the forest. Hiram tried to follow, but she lost him within minutes. When she was sure she was alone, she doubled back through the woods and sprinted toward the road where she had left her car.

Hiram and Michael had parked beside her Hyundai, so she stabbed all four tires on each of their vehicles before getting into her car and driving. Nicole refused to be a victim. If Michael and Hiram hadn't known it before, they sure as hell did now. She hoped to live long enough to piss on their graves, but first she had to escape and survive.

With multiple cops on Hiram's payroll, that was easier said than done.

2

It felt early to drink, but Ann was pouring, and I couldn't say no to a friend. My cell phone said it was two in the afternoon, which meant Cora wouldn't come home from her playdate for another hour. Until then, Roy, Ann, and I had her courtyard and surrounding lawn to ourselves. I let myself sink low into the cushions of my oversized outdoor seat as I closed my eyes and breathed in the still warm fall air.

"You look like you could fall asleep," said Ann. I opened my eyes long enough to see her smile and sip her wine. I let my eyes close again.

"It's been a nice few months," I said. "I'm not ready for it to be over, so I'm closing my eyes and pretending it's still August."

"Cora will miss you."

I opened my eyes and sat a little straighter.

"Who says I'm going anywhere?"

Ann tilted her head and gave me a soft smile.

"You're a great nanny, but I assumed you were looking for another job now that Cora's back in school."

I smiled and shook my head.

"Nope. I plan to ride this gravy train until it stops."

She laughed and raised her eyebrows.

"This gravy train never left the station. I don't pay you."

I shrugged and closed my eyes but said nothing. Ann

knew parts of my past, but I hadn't told her everything. Eight months ago, I had quit my job as a detective with the St. Augustine County Sheriff's Department and taken my dog for a tour of the country. Roy and I put twenty thousand miles on my car and saw parts of the United States I had never imagined I'd see. Then I settled in Cloverdale, North Carolina. I left my family, my home, my job, and my past behind and became someone new, someone anonymous.

When I walked down the street in Cloverdale, nobody stopped me and asked me for favors or to complain about their neighbors. The people here didn't know I had been a detective; they didn't know my foster father had assaulted me when I was a teenager or that I had killed him when he came after me again after being released from prison. They didn't know my biological mother was a drug-addicted prostitute or that my adoptive mother had been a powerful captain in the St. Louis County Police Department. To my new neighbors, I was just Joe, a woman with a man's name who kept to herself and had a big brown dog.

"You don't charge me rent," I said, "so we're even."

"I've been meaning to ask you about that," said Ann. "Are you okay with that arrangement? I don't mean to pry, but do you need money? You watched Cora every day this summer, and I didn't pay you at all."

I shook my head.

"I don't need money, but thank you."

Ann cocked her head to the side as if I were crazy.

"If you say so," she said, sipping her wine. I hadn't lied. I didn't need money. My biological mother had left me a trust fund that had already grown to almost seven hundred thousand dollars, and my friend Susanne had left me a beautiful piece of property when she died. When I left St. Augustine, I had sold that property for more money than I'd make in fifteen years, bringing my net worth to almost two million dollars. I could live on the interest for the rest of my life. "So what are you going to do since Cora's back in school?"

"I was thinking of taking up day drinking," I said, tilting my head to the side. "You know, as a profession."

Ann snorted and leaned back in her chair.

"You're on a bad influence on me," she said. I smiled to myself but said nothing. I enjoyed being a bad influence on someone. When I had lived in St. Augustine, I drank too much, but I had worked seventy or eighty hours a week and worried about what my family thought of me every day.

My life in North Carolina felt like a vacation. I rented a cozy apartment above Ann's detached garage. She called it her carriage house, and I didn't argue with her. I liked living there. Once I moved in, my entire world shifted and shrank. The gnawing, wrenching feeling in my gut disappeared. While Ann worked, I watched her little girl. We went to the park, we played with Roy, and we read stories. Cora and her mom accepted me for who I was. I appreciated that.

"Does the police department pay you?" Ann asked.

"You're kind of a cop."

Ann had never asked those kinds of questions before, but then again, she rarely drank in the early afternoon. I looked at her and smiled.

"I'm a volunteer reserve officer. They gave me a badge, but I only go in during emergencies. Thankfully, Cloverdale has few of them."

She nodded and started to say something but then stopped herself.

"Something on your mind?" I asked.

Again, she started to speak but stopped herself. Then she sighed.

"We're friends, right?"

"Yeah," I said, nodding. "We're friends."

"Good. I think so, too," she said. She paused and looked down. "Are you happy being a volunteer police officer and a little girl's volunteer nanny?"

She meant well, so I couldn't blame her for asking the question. I smiled at her.

"Happiness is a feeling, and I don't put much stock in feelings, but I'm proud of myself and the work I do. And I won't be a nanny forever. I'm going back to school this winter. UNC sent me the acceptance letter two days ago. I meant to tell you."

She leaned back.

"I'm glad. You'll do well in Chapel Hill."

I told her I hoped so and thanked her. We lapsed into a comfortable silence. When I was young and in the foster care system, I'd had all kinds of plans for my life. At one time, I had thought about joining the Navy and then using my benefits afterwards to go to college. Then, after I moved in with my adoptive parents when I was in high school, my plans changed. I went to college and majored in biology. I had thought about going to med school, but by the time I finished college, four years of med school and four additional years of post-graduate training didn't appeal to me.

So I became a cop, the same as my adoptive mother. I had loved helping people, but the job took a toll on me. Now I had a new plan. I'd go to graduate school and finish a master's degree in social work, and I'd volunteer as a reserve police officer a few days a month. Eventually, I hoped to work with kids in the foster care system and become the kind of advocate for them I had never had.

Then, once my life settled down, maybe I'd meet someone and have kids of my own. After taking care of Cora for a summer, I liked the thought of having children. For most of my twenties, I had felt like my life was on pause, and I was waiting for my real life to begin. Now, I felt like I had hit the play button. This was it, and I was ready. I couldn't wait.

For the next half hour, Ann and I drank wine and chatted and relaxed. Then, she left to pick up Cora from her playdate.

Ann and Cora lived in a brick, single-story L-shaped home with a big carriage house in back and a tall brick fence that walled off a central courtyard. It was a beautiful home, and I had enjoyed living behind it. As I went to get

Roy's leash to take him for a walk, though, somebody knocked at the gate. I hesitated before opening it and then smiled when I saw the two women standing outside.

"Hey, Joe," said Margaret Lloyd, the younger of the two. A tie held her brown hair from her oval-shaped face, while a delicate touch of makeup accentuated her cheekbones and lips.

"Hey, Margaret," I said. "Ann's picking up Cora from a friend's house, but you're welcome to hang out with me until she comes back."

"Thanks, but we're here to see you," she said, looking to her friend. "This is Tonya Cantwell. She's my sister-in-law."

I reached out and shook her hand.

"Mary Joe Court," I said. "It's nice to meet you."

"You, too," she said. Tonya was fifty or a little older and had dark hair with a part on the side. The sun had burned the pale skin on her neck and cheeks to a rosy pink, while coffee had stained her teeth a dull brown. The bags beneath her eyes made her look older than she probably was, and she moved at an almost leaden pace. Her clothes looked to be made of nice fabric, but her top and skirt had wrinkles. I didn't know the first thing about her, but I recognized a woman going through a hard time. For her sake, I hoped it was temporary.

"You guys want to have a seat?" I asked, stepping back and gesturing to the seating area on Ann's rear patio. The two women nodded and stepped inside. We sat at the table, and I gestured to the wine glasses. "I'd offer you a

18

drink, but I don't know where Ann put the bottle."

Margaret smiled and cleared her throat.

"Tonya is Sallianne Cantwell's mom. I'm her aunt."

I drew in a surprised breath.

"Oh. I'm so sorry," I said, straightening. "Your name didn't register at first. I listen to Sallianne's podcast."

"She's brilliant, isn't she?" said Tonya. She paused. "Margaret told me you were a cop."

I swallowed and nodded but didn't respond otherwise. Sallianne Cantwell was a minor celebrity in this part of North Carolina. She ran a true-crime podcast that focused on crimes in Appalachia. It was a great show, and she was a great storyteller. She used historic crimes to illustrate the region's diverse culture and history, its current problems, and its portrayal in popular media. According to news reports, she had disappeared a little over a week ago.

"I told Tonya you used to be a detective," said Margaret. "I had hoped you'd help us find Sallianne."

"I only know what I've seen on the news," I said, "but it looks like the police in Chapel Hill are doing everything they can to find her. They didn't find any signs of foul play, did they?"

"She had a fight with her boyfriend before she went missing," said Tonya. "The detective in Chapel Hill asked me not to tell anybody that. I don't know what that means."

I nodded slowly and tried to hide my grimace.

"The police probably asked you to hold that

information back because they're investigating the possibility that he hurt her," I said. "It sounds like they're treating this as a criminal matter. If they are, I can't get involved. I'm sorry."

Tonya looked up, blinking. Her makeup smudged as a tear formed in the corners of her eyes.

"But you're a cop, too, aren't you?"

"I'm a reserve police officer in a different town," I said. "I'm a volunteer who comes in during emergencies. That's it."

She stared at me for a moment.

"Sallianne spent a lot of time in Cloverdale," she said. "You're not in another town. You're right in the middle of it."

"What was she doing here?" I asked.

Tonya looked to Margaret and then to me.

"I don't know," she said, "but she came here dozens of times. I've got her credit card receipts. She bought gas here, she went to lunch here…she even bought groceries here a few times."

I considered and then looked to Margaret.

"Was she visiting someone?"

Margaret shook her head.

"Not that I know of. She didn't call."

I crossed my arms.

"And she never mentioned Cloverdale to you?"

"No, but we know she was here," said Tonya. Before I could respond and suggest that she might have had friends in the area, she continued. "The police think my baby's dead, but I don't believe it. If she had died, I'd know, right? That's what people say."

I started to say I didn't know, but Margaret interrupted me.

"It would mean a lot to Tonya and our family if you could just talk to the police in Chapel Hill for us," she said. "I'm a medical claims specialist, and Tonya's a nurse. Sallianne's daddy is a diesel mechanic. You know cops. You speak their language. We don't. They ignore us."

Facts were cruel, and no amount of tact could protect a family from difficult truths. The police probably couldn't share details with Sallianne's family because they hadn't cleared them.

"I'm sorry, but it's an active investigation. I have a badge, but it's not my case. The police can't talk to me without risking doing damage to that investigation."

"Please, Ms. Court," said Tonya. "She's my only child. I just need to know they're doing everything they can. I feel so powerless."

The pain in her voice caused an ache to grow in my throat. Unfortunately, nothing I could say would ever make her feel better. Experience had taught me that. I blinked and looked down.

"I'm sorry."

Tonya shook her head.

"She's my daughter. If you won't help me, I'll find someone who will."

That time, I didn't try to hide my grimace. The world was an ugly place, and I had no doubt she'd find an unscrupulous private investigator willing to take on her case. He'd tell her young people went missing all the time, that her daughter was probably fine, that he could find her —but only for a fee. He'd suck her bank account dry and then abandon her when she had nothing left to give him.

Worse than merely taking her money, though, he'd fill her with false hope that her daughter would come back. Sallianne had disappeared over a week ago, and her case had been all over the news. If she were still alive, she would have called her mom. Tonya didn't need hope, and she certainly didn't need a charlatan who told her soft, easy lies that gave her short-term comfort. She needed support and hard truth. Margaret and her family could provide the former. I couldn't do anything to make her feel better, but at least I could provide the latter.

"Don't hire anyone," I said. I paused. "I'll see what I can do. Okay?"

Tonya blinked. I could almost see the hope building in her eyes.

"You'll find her?"

"I'll make sure the police are doing their jobs," I said. She opened her mouth to say something but then tilted her head to the side and closed her eyes.

"Maybe someone kidnapped her," she said. "Or maybe she's lost. She likes canoeing and hiking. Maybe she went camping and doesn't have a cell signal."

"Those are all possibilities," I said, my voice soft, "but how likely is it she'd go hiking or camping in the deep woods without telling anyone?"

22

Tonya blinked and then closed her eyes.

"Maybe she's hurt. Maybe she didn't plan to stay long. Maybe she just fell and can't get up."

She was almost pleading with me. My stomach contorted, and my arms and legs felt heavy. I hated everything about this, but it'd only hurt her more in the long run if no one told her the truth.

"That's possible, but I don't think you should pin your hopes on it," I said. "I'll talk to the police. I doubt they'll tell me anything they haven't already told you, but I'll see what I can find."

Tonya considered me but then nodded.

"I'd appreciate that."

For the next few minutes, the two women gave me details of Sallianne's life, including some pictures and her address. Afterwards, both women hugged me before leaving. I shut the gate and considered my evening. I had hoped to take Roy for a long walk and then grab dinner at a bar within walking distance from Ann's house, but food would have to wait. My entire body felt heavy as I petted Roy's shoulder.

"Well, dude, it looks like I've got work to do."

3

Cora and Ann came home about ten minutes after Tonya and Margaret left. The moment Cora came into the yard, she ran toward me, so I knelt down and braced myself, ready for a four-year-old to hit me in the chest at full speed. Instead, she sidestepped me and wrapped her arms around Roy's neck. He jumped to his feet.

"I've missed you," she said, petting him and stepping back. The dog's lips curled upward, and he almost seemed to smile as he panted and licked her hands. I stood. Ann smiled at me as Cora whispered something to the dog.

"I'm sure she missed you, too," said Ann.

"I'm glad she likes Roy. It proves she's got good taste," I said, smiling. "Do you mind if I leave Roy with you guys for a while? I've got something I have to do tonight."

"Hot date?" asked Ann, raising her eyebrows.

I considered before answering.

"Police work," I said. "Margaret Lloyd and Tonya Cantwell came by. Tonya's Sallianne Cantwell's mother."

Ann looked to her daughter and Roy and nodded, her eyes distant.

"I heard about Sallianne on the news. I can't imagine what her mother's going through. If anything ever happened to Cora…" Her voice trailed off, and she looked to me. "We can feed Roy. Cora would love to keep him company."

I thanked her and made sure she knew where I kept Roy's food and water bowl. Then I headed out. Cloverdale was about an hour from Chapel Hill, the home of the University of North Carolina. As I drove, I called Cloverdale's chief of police and told him what I was doing. Everyone in the region knew about Sallianne, and the Chief said that he had planned to call the liaison officer in Chapel Hill for an update on her case anyway, so I'd save him some time by going myself.

The Chapel Hill police had a midcentury modern building with big glass windows, concrete walls, and a steel roof. It was all angles without curves, making me think of government research labs in bad horror movies. The building probably functioned well, but its concrete lines and steel contrasted with the natural landscape around it. Some people would find it attractive, but I didn't count myself among their numbers.

I parked in the lot out front and clipped my badge to my belt before stepping out of the car. It was a warm fall afternoon. I crossed the lot and pulled open the glass front door. The lobby had a front desk and some chairs and a television that hung on the far wall. Three civilians sat inside. One, a man, dozed, while the other two, both women, fidgeted and concentrated on their phones. I walked to the front desk and smiled at the woman behind the counter. She wore a khaki colored polo shirt with a badge embroidered on the chest. Her name tag said she was J. Wilcox.

"Hi, my name is Mary Joe Court, and I'm with the

Cloverdale Police Department," I said, taking my badge from my belt and showing it to her. "Do you have a public information officer I can talk to about the Sallianne Cantwell disappearance?"

She considered me and then drew in a breath.

"Do you have an appointment, Officer Court?"

"No," I said, shaking my head. "My boss asked me to get an update on the case. I'm just following orders."

That was partially true because Chief Tomlin wanted an update. If I mentioned Tonya Cantwell, though, they were more likely to shut me down than talk to me. Wilcox nodded and blinked and then cocked her head to the side.

"Since you didn't make an appointment, it may be a while," she said, already typing. "We're kind of busy today. I'll let Lieutenant Rathman know you're here. When he's available, he'll call you to his office."

"Sure, thank you," I said, nodding and turning toward the lobby. I sat but didn't plan to stay long. I hadn't realized the lead investigator was a supervisory officer. He probably oversaw forty or fifty officers, which meant his schedule wouldn't have room for impromptu visits.

About ten minutes after I sat down, I stood and told Officer Wilcox I'd set up an appointment at another time to talk to the lieutenant. After that I got in my car, pulled out my cell phone, and looked at the notes I had taken during my conversation with Tonya. Sallianne lived with a roommate named Angela Wolner. I called her number and waited for her to pick up.

"Hi, Ms. Wolner," I said. "My name is Mary Joe

Court, and I'm a police officer in Cloverdale. Tonya Cantwell gave me your number, and I had hoped to talk to you about Sallianne."

"Did you find her?" she asked, almost hopeful.

"No. Sorry," I said, shaking my head, my voice soft. "I'm just looking for background information. Can we talk in person?"

Her voice dropped and slowed.

"Sure," she said. "I'm at school."

"UNC?" I asked.

"No. I'm a kindergarten teacher. I'm putting some posters up in my classroom."

She gave me the address, and I headed out. It was a Saturday afternoon, so we had the building to ourselves. Angela met me at the door. She was twenty-five or twenty-six and had brunette hair that stopped just below her ears. Her oversized glasses made her thin face look smaller than it was. She wore gray jeans, sandals, and a long-sleeved green shirt. A lanyard with her name tag hung from her neck. I smiled at her and unclipped my badge from my belt.

"Hi, Ms. Wolner," I said. "Like I said on the phone, I'm Joe Court with the Cloverdale Police Department. Is there somewhere we can talk?"

She nodded and blinked.

"Sure," she said. "Let's go to my classroom."

She led me down a long hallway lined with green and yellow lockers to a brightly colored classroom. Bulletin boards adorned with the letters of the alphabet, numbers, and pictures of her students covered nearly every inch of the beige walls. Ms. Wolner's desk was at the front of the room near the window. We walked toward that.

"I'm sorry, but I've only got one chair for adults," she said, sitting down. I smiled.

"That's okay," I said. "I know you've talked to officers from Chapel Hill dozens of times now, but I hope you've still got a few minutes for me."

She nodded.

"Lieutenant Rathman warned me that people from the media would try to talk to me. Are you really a cop?"

I smiled and nodded.

"I am," I said. "If you'd like, I can give you my boss's phone number. He'll verify my identity. You can also call Tonya Cantwell."

She swallowed and shook her head.

"That's okay," she said. "I trust you. What do you want to know?"

I pulled a notepad out of my purse and sat on the low table behind me.

"As you know, Sallianne disappeared over a week ago. I've spoken to her mom and her aunt, but I haven't talked to anyone else. According to Tonya, you and Sallianne have lived together since you were undergraduates. You're one of her best friends."

She hesitated before speaking.

"We're roommates, and we go out some. I guess that means we're friends."

I cocked my head at her but said nothing. When I'd

first spoken to her, she had sounded genuinely disappointed that I hadn't found Sallianne. Not only that, she and Sallianne had lived together since college. Kindergarten teachers didn't make much money, but Angela likely could have afforded to live on her own. She stayed with Sallianne, though. Why she downplayed their relationship now, I didn't know, but it made me uneasy.

"What do you think happened to her?" I asked.

Angela licked her lips and looked down.

"I think she's dead. She would have called me by now if she were alive."

I furrowed my brow.

"If you were just roommates, why would she have called you?"

Angela straightened. Then she cleared her throat and crossed her arms.

"We went out together some," she said. "I guess we were friends. Does our relationship matter? You said you wanted to find Sallianne."

I forced myself to smile.

"I'm just trying to get the lay of the land," I said. Angela opened her mouth to respond, but I spoke before she could. "Do you think she had an accident, or do you think someone hurt her?"

She said nothing, so I repeated the question. Then she sighed.

"She and Ahmed have been fighting a lot lately," she said. "Ahmed's her boyfriend."

I nodded, hoping she'd continue. She pushed a stray

lock of hair over her ear but said nothing.

"Okay," I said. "What'd they fight about?"

She smiled.

"Like I said, we were roommates. We weren't friends."

So we were back to that. I needed information, so I'd let it go for now, but I made a mental note to return to it later.

"I asked if someone had hurt her, and you brought up Ahmed," I said. "Why? Has he ever hit her?"

"No."

"You sound certain of that," I said.

She rolled her eyes.

"I think I'd know if someone was beating up my roommate."

"Sure," I said, smiling. "What can you tell me about him?"

She shrugged.

"Not much to tell," she said. "She met him at school. She's a PhD student in the Department of Communication, and he's a graduate student in biomedical engineering."

I jotted down some notes.

"Did Sallianne and Ahmed fight often?"

She hesitated and then shook her head.

"They didn't use to, but now things are getting serious. They want different things out of life. Ahmed knows he's losing her."

"Has he ever been violent?"

She shook her head.

"Until three or four weeks ago, I had never even seen him lose his temper, but he's been a dick lately," she said. Then she paused. "Sallianne and I went for drinks a few nights before she disappeared, and he came to the bar unannounced and screamed at her. It was an ugly fight."

Already, I didn't like how this was turning out.

"How did Ahmed know you were at the bar together?"

She looked down and sighed.

"That was another problem," she said. "Sallianne found a tracking app on her cell phone. It's the kind of thing parents put on their kids' phones to know where they are. It was just crazy. Ahmed used to be a nice guy. Sallianne talked about marrying him, but now…"

Her voice quieted. I waited for her to continue, but she said nothing.

"How'd she react to finding the tracking app?" I asked.

She raised her eyes and snickered.

"Not well," she said. "She couldn't be with someone who tracked her movements. That's insane. Besides, their lives were going in different directions. She wanted to stay here and develop her podcast and write books. He wanted to get out of North Carolina and go to the West Coast for his career."

I nodded.

"Did he know she planned to break up with him?"

"I never asked, but probably," she said. "Ahmed was a

31

lot of things, but he wasn't a fool. He could see what was happening."

I nodded and wrote notes. If this were my case, I'd interview Sallianne's other friends and family next to better understand her mindset. Then I'd subpoena her phone records to see any text messages or emails she and Ahmed might have exchanged. Then I'd question him and compare his story to stories I had heard from Sallianne's friends and family. This wasn't my case, though. I was just here for information.

Angela and I spoke for about fifteen more minutes. The day Sallianne disappeared, Angela had gone into school early for a conference with the parents of one of her students, but Sallianne was alive and well when she left the house. Angela knew little about Sallianne's podcast or other work, so she suggested I contact Dr. Watts in the University of North Carolina's Department of Communication if I wanted to know more. It was a good lead.

At half after four in the afternoon, I got in my car and called the Chapel Hill Police Department. Lieutenant Rathman was still unavailable, so I set up an appointment to speak with him tomorrow morning. Then I started toward home. As I drove, my mind kept going back to Angela. She had downplayed her relationship with Sallianne, but for what reason, I didn't know. It didn't matter, anyway. Bullshit was ephemeral. Reality had a way of breaking through it every time, despite our best intentions. Still, I doubted she had killed her friend. It'd be hard to fake the worry in her voice when I first spoke to her. I'd figure out her story later, though. It was getting late, and I needed to walk my dog.

Lieutenant Rathman and I would talk tomorrow, but I had a feeling I already knew how this case would turn out. Sallianne fell in love with the wrong man, and he killed her when she tried to break it off. I had worked half a dozen similar cases over the years. We didn't know where her body was, but her death wasn't a mystery. It was just a tragedy. Hopefully, Lieutenant Rathman could make an arrest soon and give her family some peace.

4

Nicole waited for nightfall beneath a thicket of kudzu. She could almost feel the vines slithering and growing around her, entombing her in their suffocating embrace. She hated this, but she had no choice but to wait. The last time she had poked her head out, a cop had been waiting outside the woods with a view of her parents' front door. She had to be smart.

Crickets around her chirped, and some kind of small animal scurried through fallen leaves and debris on the ground. This whole day had been a nightmare. The moment she stabbed Michael Grant in the leg, she had sealed her fate. Hiram and his goons would never stop looking for her. Now she had to run and persuade her parents to run, too.

When it finally became dark enough for the night to conceal her, Nicole stepped out of her vine-covered hiding spot. Her lungs felt tight, and her legs trembled, but she wasn't far from her parents' house. The first step from her hiding spot was the hardest, but after that, each step became easier. She carefully placed each footstep on the ground to avoid roots, ruts, or leaves that might crinkle and give away her location. Progress was slow, but nobody noticed her.

Nicole's mom, Sherry, had planted a row of lombardy poplars at the edge of their property for privacy, so once Nicole pushed through those trees, she knew she had made it. The Johnson family lived in a modest brick ranch home that had been built in the late sixties. It wasn't pretty, but it was comfortable. After they had moved in, her dad had built a pond out back, and her mom had purchased and installed a life-sized resin statue of a topless woman. Sherry said a nice statue made the backyard feel like a Roman garden. It didn't. It was just fucking trashy.

Nicole hesitated in front of the statue and then shoved it backwards onto the grass. Her mom would make her dad pick it up, but at least she didn't have to see it for now. Then she opened the rear door and stepped into the living room. Her mom called it the Egyptian room because she had purchased a replica of an Egyptian pharaoh's mask and put it on the mantel above the fireplace. On the built-in bookshelves, she had then put other Egyptian "artifacts" she had purchased at Hobby Lobby. It was all crap. Hiram's men would do the art world a favor if they torched the place.

"Momma!" she called. "Where's Daddy?"

Sherry Johnson walked into the room with a champagne flute in her hand. She wore leggings and a silk leopard print robe. Sherry was thirty-two, but she told everyone she was twenty-five. She had brunette hair that she dyed blond at the beauty salon every four weeks, thin lips, and high cheekbones. She wore too much makeup for a woman who only left the house to shop and hook up with her boyfriend, but she was beautiful. Unfortunately, that beauty didn't extend beneath the surface. When

Nicole's daddy had knocked Sherry up in high school, he hadn't been thinking of his long-term future. If he had been, Nicole suspected, he would have kept some rubbers in the glove box of his old Toyota pickup.

"Daddy's working," she said. "What's bugging you, girl?"

"We've got a problem," she said, pushing past her mom and walking down the hallway to her bedroom. "I'll explain when we get in the car. We've got to get going, though. Pack a bag. I've got some money. We need to disappear for a while. And you need to call Daddy and tell him to get home. We've got to leave town."

Sherry put her champagne flute down and crossed her arms.

"What the hell are you talking about?" she asked, following Nicole into her bedroom. It was the only room in the house Sherry hadn't decorated herself. When she was a little girl, Nicole had loved her mom. Now she saw through her bullshit. If it hadn't been for her dad, she would have left town already.

Nicole grabbed her backpack from beside her desk and turned it upside down over her bed. Binders and textbooks tumbled out, and she glanced up to see her mom standing in the doorway.

"What are you doing?" Nicole asked. "I told you to pack a bag. We've got to go."

Sherry shook her head and crossed her arms.

"I'm not going anywhere," she said. "I just opened a bottle of wine."

Nicole balled her hands into fists and closed her eyes.

"Damn it, Momma, can't you trust me for once?" she asked, opening her eyes again. "I just stabbed a cop in the leg with a goddamn gardening knife because he tried to rape me in the middle of my marijuana field."

Sherry's mouth opened, and her eyes fluttered.

"What the hell are you talking about?"

"You never even wondered what my summer job was, did you? I left this house every morning at seven and came home at four in the afternoon covered in dirt and horse shit, and you never once asked me what I was doing all day."

Sherry opened her eyes wide.

"I thought you were playing with your friends or something."

"I'm sixteen. I haven't played in the dirt in a decade. I was growing weed for Hiram Ford so I could pay for college. Hiram's employees—cops—raped a girl who worked for him because they knew she couldn't go to the police. One of them tried to do it to me today, so I stabbed him in the leg. He was going to kill me afterwards."

Sherry opened her mouth as if she wanted to say something, but then she shook her head and held up her hand in a stop motion.

"I can't deal with this," she said. "You deal with your own problems."

"I didn't expect your help."

Sherry left without saying a word. Nicole shook her

head and stuffed two days' worth of clothes in her backpack before going to her bookshelf and pulling off the Harry Potter hardback books where she had hidden her money. She had almost nine hundred dollars cash tucked into the pages of each book. Together, it was well over six thousand dollars. She stuffed the cash into her backpack and zipped it up before leaving.

"Momma, call Daddy and tell him to come home. I'd do it, but I left my cell phone in my car," she said, walking down the hall toward the kitchen. The room had dark cabinets and the same wooden paneling found in the living room. Her mom had done little to decorate the space, mostly because she spent little time there. Sherry was pouring white wine into her champagne flute when Nicole entered. "I had to ditch my car so the cops couldn't track me. Where are your keys? We've got to get Daddy."

"He's at Hiram Ford's cabin, repairing his roof," said Sherry. "It was an emergency job."

Nicole closed her eyes and felt her legs grow weak.

"Fuck."

"Young ladies shouldn't use language like that," said Sherry. "It isn't becoming."

"Oh, shut up," said Nicole. "When you were my age, you were fucking half the football team and your English teacher. Mr. Wright still asks about you, by the way, so you must have done something right."

Sherry set the wine bottle on the counter but kept hold of her glass.

"I don't like you right now," she said.

"It's mutual," said Nicole, walking toward the garage. "Stay here. I'm getting Daddy, and we're leaving."

Sherry put her glass down and stepped in front of her daughter and crossed her arms. She opened her eyes wide.

"You're not going anywhere until you apologize to me. I'm your mother. You don't get to talk about me the way you just did."

Nicole would have just pushed past her, but somebody knocked on the front door before she could. A second later, the doorbell rang. Sherry tilted her head to the side and pointed to her daughter.

"This ain't over, Nicole," she said, before putting her wine glass beside the bottle in the kitchen. "You stay right here. We'll talk when I get back."

"Sorry, but I'm not interested in talking," said Nicole. "Get the door. I'm leaving."

"If you leave, don't come back."

"That's the plan, Sherry," said Nicole. "See you later. Good luck with your life."

Sherry shook her head and walked through the kitchen toward the entryway, while Nicole dug through her mom's purse for her keys. The front door's hinges squealed open a moment later. Nicole paused and listened. Sherry was trying to whisper, but she was too drunk and angry to keep her voice down. She called the guy at the door *officer* and told him Nicole was in the kitchen.

"You old, stupid cow," whispered Nicole, already

gliding down the hall toward her mother and father's bedroom. The cops must have been watching the house for movement. They had known she'd come home eventually.

When Nicole got into her parents' room, she went to her dad's nightstand for the semiautomatic .45-caliber pistol he kept there. It was a big gun, and it felt awkward in her hand, but she could compensate for that. She had her own pistol—a Glock 26—but it was in the gun safe in the basement with their rifles and shotguns. Nicole considered getting it, but she didn't like the idea of walking into a room with only one exit.

She checked to make sure her .45 had a full magazine before inching back into the hallway.

"I know you're in my room, Nicole," said Sherry from the entryway. "You're not as sneaky as you think you are. This cop wants to talk to you."

Nicole's heart sank, and her arms and legs felt ten or twenty pounds heavier than they ought to have. She pressed her back against the wall and crept toward the entryway. When she peeked around the corner, she saw her mother and a uniformed police officer standing near the front door. The cop held a familiar gas can.

"You come around the corner," said Sherry. "This cop says you tried to start a forest fire."

Nicole clenched her jaw and held her hand behind her back as she stepped out. She had seen the cop before, but she didn't know him. He worked for Hiram, though. She brought her finger from the trigger guard to the trigger on her pistol.

The officer held up the gas can.

"Have you seen this before, honey?" he asked. "We found it at the scene of an arson. It's got your fingerprints on it. I need you to come with me."

"Bullshit," said Nicole, stepping her right leg back and bringing the pistol to bear in front of her. She straightened her right arm and lowered her left elbow. It gave her a stable base to shoot from and should help with the recoil of her daddy's big pistol.

"Honey, put that gun down," said the cop, lowering the gas can to the ground and bringing his hand toward his weapon.

"Dude, stop talking and put your hands on top of your head before I shoot you," said Nicole.

"What the hell are you doing, Nicole?" asked Sherry, turning and throwing her hands out. She walked toward her daughter, putting herself between Nicole and the cop.

"Get out of my way, Momma. You don't need to get hurt."

"You won't shoot me," said Sherry. "Put the gun down."

Sherry was right. Nicole wouldn't have shot her. The cop, though, didn't hesitate. His hands moved so fast Nicole almost couldn't see them. He drew his weapon and fired three times, hitting Sherry in the back with each round. She stumbled forward. Nicole squeezed the trigger on her pistol the moment her mom went down. The round hit the cop in the shoulder. She squeezed the trigger again and then a third time, hitting him in the chest with both shots. The impacts from a .45 at twenty feet were like sledgehammer blows. His body rocked, and he fell backwards. The stink of burned gunpowder filled the air.

The cop may have been alive for the moment, but he couldn't survive with golf-ball-size holes through his lungs. Nicole knelt down in a growing puddle of her mother's blood.

"Momma!" she said.

Nicole's beautiful mother didn't move, though. Nicole reached down to feel her neck, but her mother's eyes never blinked. The life had already left them. Sherry had been a terrible mom, but she didn't deserve this. Nicole's chest and throat tightened.

"I'm sorry, Momma," she said, blinking back tears. "I can't stay to take care of you. I've got to go."

She ran to the garage and put her pistol in her backpack. The cops would look for her mom's car, so she couldn't take that. Instead, she grabbed her bicycle and rode into the night, wishing she had a plan.

5

I started driving to Cloverdale, but as I reached the outskirts of Chapel Hill, my phone buzzed. I didn't recognize the number, but I answered on the third ring.

"Hey," I said. "This is Joe Court."

The caller paused before answering.

"With a name like Joe, I expected a man."

"Sorry to disappoint," I said. "Who is this?"

"I'm Lieutenant David Rathman. You came to my station to ask about Sallianne Cantwell."

I didn't have anywhere to park nearby, so I just nodded.

"Yeah. Can I call you back in about an hour? I'm in the car."

"You still in Chapel Hill?"

"Close," I said.

"Then turn around and get me a grilled chicken panini at the Mediterranean Deli on Franklin Street. Consider it payment for a conversation."

I paused as my mouth popped open. I had worked with officers from jurisdictions across the country, but never before had one asked me to buy a sandwich before talking to me. It took me a moment to get over my initial surprise, but then I lowered my chin and furrowed my brow.

"You want me to buy you dinner?"

"It is dinnertime, hon, and I'm hungry."

I blinked a few times and then forced a sweet note into my voice.

"You want me to do anything else?" I asked. "Maybe I can pick up some groceries or a bottle of wine?"

"Dinner's fine," he said. "Thanks, though."

He hung up before I could respond. I tossed my phone to the seat beside me.

"Asshole," I said, looking for anywhere to turn around. I exited the interstate about half a mile away, turned around, and headed back to town. The deli wasn't hard to find, and the food smelled good. I ordered the lieutenant's sandwich and a second one for myself and then drove a mile and a half to his station.

The officer at the reception desk led me to the lieutenant's private office on the second floor. Rathman was fifty or fifty-five and had graying hair, a thin, angular face, and a goatee. His nose had a slight twist to it, like he had broken it and never had it fixed, and his gray eyes were dull and impatient.

"Ms. Court," he said, standing and nodding. "You get dinner?"

"Sure did," I said, trying to keep the annoyance from my voice. "It came with a Greek salad."

He nodded, so I opened the bag, removed my sandwich, and handed him the rest. He looked through it and then sighed.

"Where's my baklava?"

I balled my hands into fists but smiled.

"You didn't ask for it."

He grunted but said nothing as he pulled out his sandwich. Then he looked at me.

"You should sit."

My temper was building, but I tried to keep it in check as I sat on a chair in front of his desk to eat. My sandwich was delicious, so at least I had that going for me.

"So, I hear you're a reserve police officer," said Rathman.

I nodded.

"Yep. I enjoy helping my community."

He snickered a little.

"Sure you do," he said. "You got a boyfriend who's a cop or something?"

If he hadn't had information I needed, I would have walked out. Instead, I allowed my lips to go flat.

"No, sir."

He nodded and raised his eyebrows before sliding back from his desk and pulling a file from a drawer.

"We used to call girls like you badge bunnies," he said. I crossed my arms and forced myself to smile but said nothing. He looked at me and held up his hands. "That isn't a bad thing. Everybody's got a type. You happen to like cops. That's great."

I silently counted to ten in my head before speaking.

"I'm a sworn police officer who attended an accredited police academy. I'm also a twenty-nine-year-old woman, so I'm not a girl, and I'm not a badge bunny. If you need a title for me, you can call me Officer Court.

Clear, Lieutenant?"

He blinked a few times.

"You don't have to get your panties in a bunch. I'm doing you a favor here."

I could see why Tonya Cantwell had difficulty talking to him. My nails bit into the palms of my hands as I clenched my fists.

"I appreciate that," I said. "As I'm sure you've been told, I'm here to talk about the Sallianne Cantwell investigation. Sallianne's mother, Tonya, came to me earlier today asking if I could look into things on her behalf."

The lieutenant smiled.

"And instead of sending her to me, you drove all the way out here to talk to me in person."

I kept my expression neutral.

"Yep. Anything you can tell me about the investigation?"

He picked up his sandwich, took a bite, and chewed.

"It's ongoing."

I nodded.

"Anything else you can tell me?"

"Ms. Court, you are a reserve police officer," he said, leaning back and crossing his arms. "When you're not pretending to be a cop, what do you do? Are you a hairdresser or something?"

I wrapped up my sandwich, put it in my purse, and then matched the lieutenant's posture.

"Until she went to school, I watched a little girl

during the week while her mom worked."

He chuckled and shook his head.

"So you're a babysitter," he said. "Have you ever seen a murder victim, Officer Court?"

I smiled.

"A few."

"You ever worked a murder?"

I nodded and kept the smile on my face.

"A few."

He lowered his chin and gave me a disbelieving look.

"In Cloverdale? Between babysitting jobs?"

"I wasn't always a babysitter, and I haven't always lived in Cloverdale," I said, standing. "And I apologize for wasting your time. I'll just have my boss call you. Like you said, I'm a reserve officer. I'm volunteering to do this in my free time, and I prefer to work with professionals. You're a prick, and if your police work is anything like your conversational skills, I'd get more done working on my own."

He straightened and popped his mouth open but said nothing until I turned to leave.

"You interfere with my investigation, you'll find yourself in a jail cell."

I had held back my annoyance before, but now I didn't care.

"You do your job, and I'll do mine," I said. "I'm sure we'll be fine."

He may have said something else, but I didn't pay attention. I left the building and walked to my car, where I ate the rest of my panini. At least that was good. Afterwards, I pulled out my phone to call my boss. He didn't answer, and I didn't leave a message. Then I called Tonya Cantwell. She answered almost immediately.

"Tonya, it's Joe Court," I said. "How are you holding up?"

"I'm fine," she said. "Did you find anything out?"

"Sort of," I said. "I talked to Angela Wolner and Lieutenant Rathman with the Chapel Hill police. He's a jerk."

Tonya paused.

"Yeah."

Neither of us spoke for a moment.

"I'm not convinced that Lieutenant Rathman is up to the investigation," I said. "I'll continue looking into things, but I'm limited in what I can do."

She didn't hesitate before answering.

"Don't quit," she said. She paused and sighed. "I need your help. The lieutenant stopped answering my calls days ago. I need to know someone is trying to find Sallianne. She's my baby."

"I can't promise anything except that I'll do my best," I said, "but if you have questions, you can call me day or night. You have my cell phone number."

"Thank you," she said. Her voice wavered. "I've got to go."

I told her I'd talk to her later before hanging up. Lieutenant Rathman could be as abrasive as he wanted with me, but he should have taken Tonya's calls, and he

48

should have been patient with her. That he ignored her was unprofessional and cruel. Tonya was just looking for her daughter, and she deserved to know he was doing everything he could. Even if I didn't find Sallianne, I'd try my best, and I'd keep her in the loop. I'd treat her the same way I'd like to be treated were I in her position. In my world, that still mattered.

For now, though, I needed to go home. I had a dog to walk, reports to write, and an early morning meeting at the county courthouse. Sallianne would be fine for the night.

6

Nicole hadn't ridden a bike in years, but that didn't slow her down. She threw her leg over the side and pedaled. Her father had taught her how to ride when she was a little girl. He didn't go out as much as he used to, but he had loved getting outside and riding. If it were up to him, he'd spend every free hour he had on his bike. He even had a little trailer that could hold camping gear for weekends away from home.

Back when she was still a little girl, he and Nicole used to drive to Stone Mountain State Park, where they'd ride and hike and camp for entire weekends. Nicole's mom wasn't into that kind of thing, so she'd stay home. Sherry used to complain that she didn't enjoy being left alone, but even as a little girl, Nicole knew that her mother hadn't spent those weekends alone. It didn't matter, though; Sherry had her boyfriends, and Nicole and her father had each other.

Life with Sherry hadn't been all bad, though. She always made sure Nicole had clean clothes to wear to school, and Nicole never went a single day with an empty belly. A lot of kids at school didn't have it so good. When Nicole was real little, she had long hair that ran halfway down her back, and it used to get so tangled that she couldn't even take a comb through it. When Sherry saw that, she brushed it almost every night and taught Nicole how to take care of it.

And now she was dead.

The realization hit Nicole harder than she had expected. Now that she was away from the house, she couldn't stop thinking about what had happened or what she had done. Her ears still rang with the sound of gunfire, the smell of burnt powder clung to her clothes, and she could feel her mother's blood drying on her hands and knees.

She had been planning to ride to her boyfriend's house without stopping, but she pulled onto the shoulder. County work crews had dug a shallow drainage ditch in the soft ground beside the street. She got off her bike and fell into the cordgrass and ferns along the edge of the ditch. To her right lay thick woods. To her left lay the road that led to her house. Her legs trembled, and her stomach roiled.

She hadn't meant to kill that cop. She wouldn't have if he hadn't shot her mom. He didn't need to do that. He didn't even warn her. The moment he saw his chance, he shot her in the back like she was a dog. Before she could stop it, Nicole's stomach clenched tight, and she vomited on the grass. Then a tremble passed through her from her feet to her forehead as tears sprang to her eyes.

"Momma, you shouldn't have done that," she said. "You shouldn't have been there. You should have been out with Steven or Jason or whoever your new beau was. Daddy was working. I should have been home alone. You shouldn't have been there."

As if some unseen force had pulled her down, Nicole

found herself on her side with her knees brought to her chest. She cried as the red and blue lights of a police cruiser shot past on the road. Even if the cop had seen her, it didn't matter. He had places to be.

She stayed on the ground long enough for moisture to seep from the soil through her clothes. The days were still warm, but the temperatures at night dropped into the mid- to low sixties. With wet clothes, that'd get awful cold. She didn't want to dig into her stash of clothes this early, so maybe she could steal some pants from TJ's sister. Stephanie went to East Carolina University in Greenville. Even though she was a full-time student, she would have left a few clothes behind. She and Nicole were close to the same size, so something ought to fit.

Nicole closed her eyes and forced herself to breathe.

"You're okay, Nicole," she whispered. "You've made it so far. Now you've got to keep going."

She stood from the ditch and found her bike a few feet away. She had made it about half a mile from her house, but she could still hear the police sirens. Once they found the body of a cop in her house, they'd come looking for her. They'd probably even have search dogs. She had to move.

Once she was on her feet, she got back on the bike and rode another quarter mile along the road before turning into a trail through the woods. She had grown up in Cloverdale. When other girls her age were playing with dolls or dressing up as princesses, her daddy had been taking her out on bike trails through the woods. She knew them well, and she knew one that would take her to TJ's house.

The woods were black as pitch, so she pedaled just fast enough to keep the bike upright. About a quarter of a mile into the woods, her tires splashed through a rock-strewn creek and out the other side. If the cops brought dogs, that ought to slow them down.

Within twenty minutes of shooting the cop, Nicole emerged from the trees behind her boyfriend's two-story home. She and TJ knew each other growing up, but they weren't friends. It wasn't until high school, when their hormones went into overdrive, that they started seeing each other as attractive members of the opposite sex. She liked him well enough, but her future burned far brighter than his. He'd end up working as a mechanic like his daddy. It was a fine job, but he'd never leave Cloverdale. She wanted more from her life than to end up a housewife in a dead-end town in the middle of nowhere.

She ditched her bike on the edge of his lawn. The lights in the first floor were off, but the desk lamp was on in his bedroom. He was in. The Macon family's rear lawn sloped downward to the woods, giving the home a big walk-out basement with a sliding glass door. It was a pretty house on a nice piece of property. TJ's daddy owned the biggest auto body repair shop in the county and did pretty well for himself. TJ coasted through life, knowing he'd take over his daddy's business once Mr. Macon retired, but Nicole suspected he'd run it into the ground within five years. That'd be his problem, though;

she'd be long gone by then.

She didn't bother trying to open the back door because she knew it'd be locked. Instead, she did what she always did when she wanted to see her boyfriend: She climbed onto the deck railing, walked to the low spot in the roof, and jumped. TJ had taught her how to sneak in when they first started dating. Since then, late-night visits had been a regular occurrence.

She scampered across the roof. On a nice night like this, the family kept the windows on the entire second floor cracked for a cross breeze, making entry easy. Nicole popped off the screen outside Stephanie's room and climbed inside. The room was neat and mostly empty. It had a big dresser and a dark wood sleigh bed with four pillows near the headboard. Normally, Nicole would have called out for TJ to warn him she was inside, but covered in blood and with a pistol in her backpack, she thought it was best that she changed before doing anything else.

She opened the dresser drawers and checked the sizes on the clothes inside. Once she found some leggings and a shirt that would fit, she stripped off her own clothes and dressed. Her dirty clothes, she put in her backpack. After that, she felt a lot better. Since she didn't know how long she'd be gone, and since Stephanie had a lot of clothes, Nicole grabbed a few days' worth and stuffed them in her bag before going to the hallway.

Light spilled beneath TJ's door at the end of the hall. As she walked toward it, she heard bedsprings squeaking. Then she heard TJ's low grunting and a softer, feminine sound. Her skin felt hot as she reached for the doorknob.

"You've got to be fucking kidding me," she said, throwing open the door. TJ, her boyfriend, lay on the bed. Jeanette Jones straddled him and had her hands on his chest. The moment she entered the room, the two lovers stopped. Then Jeanette rolled to the side and covered herself with the bedspread. TJ swung his legs off the bed and held up his hands.

"Nicole," he said. "This isn't what it looks like."

She crossed her arms.

"You're having sex with Jeanette," she said. "There's nothing to be mistaken about."

"It was an accident," he said. She raised her eyebrows. "See, Jeanette goes to Chapel Hill, and she came home to see Stephanie, but Stephanie stayed at school for the weekend. My parents were out, and you weren't here—"

"I know Jeanette, and I know where she goes to college," said Nicole, interrupting him. "How does her coming home for the weekend lead to you putting your penis inside her?"

He started to say something but then shut his mouth. Jeanette pulled the bedspread tight across her chest.

"I'm real sorry, Nicole," she said. "I came to see Stephanie, and this just happened, okay? We didn't plan it. I guess we were lonely."

In other circumstances, she would have cared more, but now, she could only close her eyes and shake her head.

"I'm glad you got your loneliness fixed, Jeanette," she said. "TJ's an idiot, and you're a vapid skank without an independent thought in your head. You're a good match."

Neither of them had a response to that, so Nicole focused on TJ.

"Where's my phone?"

He pointed toward the ensuite bathroom.

"You ain't a nice girl, Nicole," he said. "Jeanette didn't do nothing wrong."

"I walked in on her having sex with my boyfriend," she said, walking to the bathroom. She grabbed a phone from the counter without looking at it. "And thank you for taking care of my work phone. I'll find a new spot for it."

"That's right, you will," said TJ, standing. He pulled the bedspread to cover himself and uncovered Jeanette. She yelped and grabbed at the blanket, pulling TJ back onto the bed. Nicole shook her head and left.

"Neither of you have anything I haven't seen before," she said. "Enjoy your lives together. I hope you both die alone of incurable venereal diseases."

Nicole walked out the front door and then around the house to get her bike. She had better things to worry about than an unfaithful boyfriend. Once she reached her bike, she turned on the phone and sighed.

"TJ, you fucking idiot," she whispered. Nicole had two cell phones, one for work and one for home. She kept her work phone, a prepaid burner, at TJ's house because his parents weren't as nosy as her mother. She hadn't picked up her work phone, though; she had grabbed TJ's iPhone. After entering TJ's passcode, 1-2-3-4-5, Nicole dialed her father's cell number. The phone went to voicemail. She swallowed hard.

"Daddy, it's Nicole. I'm on TJ's phone. Call me when you get this. We need to talk."

She hung up and waited for a few minutes before swinging her leg over her bicycle and pedaling. She got about a quarter mile up the road before her phone rang.

"Daddy?" she asked.

"Sorry, sugar. Your daddy's tied up right now."

Nicole shuddered as a cold chill passed over her. It was Hiram. She blinked and felt her fingers and hands tremble.

"Let my daddy go," she said. "He's a good man. He wouldn't hurt you."

"Your daddy is a good man," said Hiram. "I've always liked him. I used to like you, too, until you murdered my employee."

Nicole swallowed the lump in her throat.

"Your employee murdered my mom," she said. "He shot her in the back. That was after your other employee tried to rape and murder me in a garden shed. How's Michael's leg, by the way? Did I cut a major artery? I was hoping I'd kill him, too."

"No such luck, honey," said Hiram. "He's a little worse for wear, but he's alive. A nurse sewed him right up."

"That's unfortunate," said Nicole. "What now? Your men have tried to kill me twice, and now you've got my daddy."

"I was thinking we'd make a straight trade. You come to see me, and I'll let your daddy go."

Nicole tilted her head to the side.

"Nah. You'd kill me. Here's my offer: you let my daddy go, and I promise not to go to the police with everything I know."

Almost the instant she finished speaking, someone screamed on the phone loud enough that she had to pull it away from her ear. Nicole held her breath as her stomach tightened. She had never heard her father scream in pain before, but, somehow, she knew that was him. The sound was almost inhuman. Then, it stopped.

"What the fuck did you just do?" she asked, almost crying.

"A friend of mine cut off one of your daddy's fingers with garden shears and then stuck a ball gag in his mouth to shut him up. He's got seven more fingers and two thumbs. You want him to lose those, too?"

"You son of a bitch," she said, her voice barely a whisper. "I did what you wanted. I grew your stupid weed. You didn't need to hurt him."

"You told a reporter about my operation," he said.

"Only because your employees raped Monica."

"And for that," said Hiram, "I am sorry. Monica received a cash payment for her suffering."

"You can't pay to make somebody's memories go away, Hiram," she said. "What your men did was wrong. What you did was even worse."

"I suppose we have to agree to disagree on that," said

Hiram. "Now, listen up, girl: I've got friends in every police department in this state. You go to the police, and they'll turn you over to me. I'll torture your daddy to death in front of you and then shoot you in the head. If you turn yourself in, I'll let your daddy go."

"You'll kill me," she said.

"You stabbed one police officer and murdered another," said Hiram. "Your life's over, anyway. After killing a cop, every police officer on the Eastern Seaboard will be looking for you. If you turn yourself in, at least your daddy will live. If you don't, you're both dead. Think it over, honey, and call me back."

Hiram hung up. Nicole's stomach contorted, but she had already vomited out everything in it. This was her fault. She shouldn't have worked with Hiram. His money wasn't worth this. Somehow, she had to get her daddy back, but first, she had to survive.

She hesitated and then dialed a friend's number. Rose answered on the third ring.

"TJ?"

"No, it's Nicole," she said. "I've got TJ's phone. It was a mix-up. Don't ask. I need somewhere to sleep. My momma and I had a fight. I don't want her to know where I am. Can I crash at your place?"

"Yeah," said Rose, her voice bright. "My parents are cool. You can stay here."

Nicole shook her head.

"Your parents can't know," she said. "I'll just sneak in tonight and leave tomorrow morning. I don't want my mom to track me down. When she realizes I'm gone, my mom'll call my friends, and as soon as she does, your mom will tell her where I am. I need a night away from her."

Rose hesitated.

"Okay," she said. "Yeah. That's fine. Just come to my window. I'll let you in."

"Thanks, Rose," said Nicole. "I'll be over soon."

"Sure. See you soon."

She thanked her friend once more and then hung up. That was one problem solved. Now, she just had to figure out how to get her father out of Hiram's hands without getting hurt. Something told her that would be a lot harder than calling up her chemistry lab partner.

7

It was well after dark by the time I reached Cloverdale. I should have gone to the police station and written a report about everything I had done in Chapel Hill while the events were still fresh in my mind, but nothing I had learned would alter the investigation into Sallianne's disappearance. She was gone, Lieutenant Rathman was a dick, and the police in Chapel Hill would arrest her boyfriend in the next few days. I still planned to follow up on a few things for Tonya Cantwell, but I didn't have a big role to play in this investigation.

So I drove home and knocked on Ann's front door. Roy whined from inside but didn't bark. Ann opened a moment and held a finger to her lips.

"Cora's in bed," she whispered. "Everything okay?"

I nodded.

"The world's full of assholes, but yeah," I said. "I'm glad to be home. Was Roy okay?"

She looked to the dog and smiled.

"Sorry about the assholes, but Roy's great," she said. "Cora tried to brush his teeth, but he wasn't interested."

I patted Roy's shoulder.

"He's never had much interest in oral hygiene," I said. She laughed, and I paused a moment before continuing. "You ready for tomorrow?"

She nodded.

"Are you ready for tomorrow?"

"Wouldn't miss it," I said. "Everything will be fine. If you need anything, let me know. Otherwise, Roy and I will go for a walk, and then I'll go to bed."

"Good night, Joe," she said. "And thanks. This means a lot."

"It's what friends do," I said. I left her there and walked to the carriage house I rented, where I got a leash and flashlight. It was late, so Roy and I only stayed out long enough for him to stretch his legs and go to the restroom, but it was a nice walk. Afterwards, Roy and I went home, where I had a glass of wine and read a few chapters in a mystery novel. When my eyelids grew heavy, I went to bed, grateful that my evening had ended much better than it had begun.

Roy woke me up at about six the next morning by licking my face, which was typical for him. I went for a morning run and then left Roy in the courtyard to lay in the grass as I showered and changed into a gray skirt and short-sleeved white top. The outfit was nice but not so nice that it would draw attention. Plus, I'd feel comfortable wearing it even if the day grew hot. When I left the carriage house, I found Ann sitting on a lounge chair on her patio.

She gave me a tight smile.

"I just took Cora to school," she said. "Can I get you a cup of coffee?"

"The answer to that question is always yes," I said. She chuckled, and we walked through the back door into her kitchen. Cora's drawings covered the refrigerator and were thumbtacked to a cork board hung on the cheery yellow walls. Windows allowed in copious amounts of light. Ann poured a mug of coffee with trembling hands.

"It's okay to feel scared, but you'll do great," I said, my voice soft. "We've already called ahead, so we know there will be a sheriff's deputy in the courtroom. Jeremy can't hurt you, but if he tries, the deputy will arrest him. And if he says something rude, the judge will smack him down."

She nodded and took a slow breath before handing me a mug of coffee.

"I didn't think he'd contest the restraining order," she said. "He pushed me. I'm not asking anything from him; I just want him to leave me and Cora alone. Why would he do this?"

I considered and then looked down.

"He's trying to hurt you," I said. "He's an asshole, but after today, if we see him at the house again, I'll arrest him."

She didn't look convinced, but she nodded anyway.

"I hope the judge sees it the same way."

"I'm an armed police officer," I said. "If your ex-husband comes to this house and tries to hurt you or Cora again, I'll be here. If I can't arrest him, I'll shoot him, and then we'll bury him in the hills."

She laughed and looked down.

"You talk a big game, Joe, but we both know you couldn't shoot anybody," she said. "You're too sweet."

I sipped my coffee but said nothing, grateful that she

didn't know how wrong she was. After a few minutes of silence, I glanced at the clock on the microwave.

"We need to leave so we're not late."

She took a deep breath and nodded. Since Ann was nervous, I drove us both to the county courthouse, where we checked in with the court's clerk before sitting in the lobby. Jeremy, Ann's ex, arrived about five minutes later. He sat beside his attorney on the other side of the room, pretending we weren't even there. His lawyer had probably coached him. Ann's attorney arrived a few minutes later.

Dozens of people entered and left the waiting room as deputies called them into courtrooms around the building. I wasn't nervous, but Ann could barely sit still. Had we been related, I would have held her hand. Instead, I just sat beside her. Her lawyer sat on her other side.

At ten, the sheriff's deputy called us all into the courtroom. The judge sat behind the bench, having already heard three cases that morning. He welcomed us and called Ann and Jeremy to their seats. Both had brought lawyers, bringing an air of formality to the case it might not have otherwise possessed. Once everyone had sat down, the judge read through a document his clerk produced and then glanced to Ann and Jeremy.

"Okay, folks," he said. "According to my documents, Ms. Ann Pittman filed for an *ex parte* temporary protective order against her ex-husband eight days ago after an alleged domestic violence incident in her home. Mr. Jeremy Pittman was served this order two days later. We're here to see if there's adequate cause to extend that temporary order. I understand both Mr. and Ms. Pittman have attorneys?"

Both Ann and Jeremy said they did, so the judge nodded.

"Excellent. We'll start with Ms. Pittman. She'll tell her side of the story, and then Mr. Pittman will tell his side of the story. Please don't interrupt one another. Attorneys may object, but please use your objections judiciously. If I feel that you're trying to intimidate or badger a witness with your objections, it won't end well for you. Ms. Pittman, please introduce yourself and describe the events that led to your seeking a temporary protective order eight days ago."

Ann stood and introduced herself. She said she and Jeremy had lived together as husband and wife for four years and that they had a daughter together. She also provided police reports from three previous incidents of domestic violence, one of which should have landed him in prison for sexual assault. Ann was methodical and clear. Her lawyer had coached her well to establish the elements required for a protective order.

After the introduction, the judge asked her to describe the event that led her to file for a temporary order. She said that eight days ago, Jeremy had come for a scheduled two-hour visit with Cora, but he slurred his words and smelled like whiskey. Ann refused to let him in the house, but he pushed the door hard enough to knock her down. She fell to the ground, and he called for Cora. When she got up to block his path again, he shoved her against a table hard enough to leave bruises on her back.

She fell to the ground again, and he went into the courtyard. Since she didn't see what happened in the courtyard, that was the end of her testimony. The judge thanked her, and then gave Jeremy the opportunity to present his side.

He said he was sober when he showed up and that Ann had illegally refused him access to their daughter. He claimed Cora was in danger from Ann and me and that he acted to protect himself and his daughter. It was bullshit, but the judge listened with a neutral expression. Then it was my turn to take the stand. The judge swore me in and told me to explain who I was and what I had seen.

I pulled the microphone toward me.

"Good morning," I said. "I'm Mary Joe Court. Joe is spelled J-O-E, by the way. Just in case you have to write it down. Everybody spells it wrong. I rent the carriage house behind Ms. Pittman's home. We share the courtyard and backyard, and I babysit Cora."

The judge nodded and thanked me for the introduction before telling me to explain what I had seen on the morning in question.

"Obviously, I didn't see anything inside the house, but Cora and I were in the courtyard drawing on the patio floor with chalk when Ann shouted from inside the house. She sounded as if she were in pain. After that, a man called for Cora. I didn't know what had happened, so I picked Cora up and carried her to the carriage house. I locked her inside with my dog, got my pistol, and came out to make sure Ann was okay.

"When I came out, Mr. Pittman was in the courtyard. He screamed at me and demanded to know where his daughter was. I asked him where Ms. Pittman was, and he took a step toward me. Mr. Pittman was drunk and angry. I determined that he was a threat, so I removed my pistol from my holster and asked him to leave. He refused, so I aimed that pistol at his chest and told him I considered him a threat and would shoot him unless he left. He told me I wasn't worth it and left the courtyard through the gate.

"I then went into the house and found Ms. Pittman on the floor crying. She said Mr. Pittman had pushed his way into the house and then shoved her against a table. She lifted her shirt and showed me red marks on her back. I took pictures with my cell phone."

The judge looked to Ann's attorney and asked whether she had copies. She nodded and handed them to the sheriff's deputy, who then walked them to the judge. He looked through them and nodded before looking at me.

"Thank you for your testimony, Ms. Court," he said, before looking to the attorneys. "Do we have other witnesses or information to consider?"

Jeremy's lawyer leaned forward. He wore a navy suit, white shirt, and red and blue striped tie.

"Before you deliberate, I have a couple of questions for Ms. Court," he said. "May I speak to the witness?"

This wasn't an adversarial proceeding, so the lawyers

didn't automatically have the opportunity to cross-examine witnesses. It was up to the judge. He looked at me and asked whether I minded answering questions, and I said I was fine with it. The attorney looked at me and smiled.

"Ms. Court, you said you perceived Mr. Pittman as a threat and then pulled a firearm on him. Is that correct?"

I leaned forward and nodded.

"Yes."

The attorney nodded and smiled.

"Does your experience as a professional babysitter give you insight into the human psyche other people don't possess?"

I raised my eyebrows and leaned forward as I looked toward the judge.

"I'm not sure what he's asking."

The judge nodded and looked to the attorney.

"Please rephrase your question so it's a little more direct."

"Sure," said the lawyer, nodding. He smiled at me the way I would have imagined a snake to smile. "You watch children for a living. What makes you qualified to determine whether Mr. Pittman was a threat?"

I locked eyes with the lawyer.

"I heard Ann scream. Then I heard her cry. Mr. Pittman then showed up in the backyard. He looked angry. Those seem like threatening circumstances."

The lawyer nodded and smoothed his tie.

"Do you have a lot of experience with angry men?"

I snickered but said nothing. The judge told me to answer the question, so I leaned forward.

"More than you could imagine."

"Oh, really?" asked the lawyer. "Are you the victim of domestic violence yourself?"

"No, but in the past seven years, angry men have assaulted me on at least four occasions."

The lawyer lowered his voice and began pacing before giving me a sympathetic look.

"Do you think it's possible that your experience as the victim of violent crime has made you biased against men?"

"I've also been assaulted by women, so no," I said. "I'm not a fan of drunks, though."

The lawyer furrowed his brow.

"Why have you been assaulted that many times?"

"I spent six years in law enforcement, first as a uniformed officer and then as a detective with the St. Augustine County Sheriff's Department in St. Augustine, Missouri. During that time, I investigated crimes ranging from petty theft to homicide. I determined that Mr. Pittman was a threat to his ex-wife and daughter based on my years of experience investigating men and women who beat their spouses and children. Currently, in addition to my babysitting duties, I'm a reserve police officer with the Cloverdale Police Department."

The room went quiet. I smiled at the lawyer.

"Do you have any further questions, counselor?" asked the judge.

"No, sir," he said, already walking toward his client. Jeremy had closed his eyes.

Ann's attorney leaned forward.

"Can I ask Officer Court a question?" she asked. The judge nodded, so she stood. "Officer Court, you said you were a reserve police officer in Cloverdale. That's a volunteer position, as I understand it. What made you do that?"

I looked to Jeremy.

"Mr. Pittman," I said. "When I moved into Ann's carriage house, she told me that her ex-husband had a violent streak and that I should call the police if I saw him lurking about the house. She also warned me that the local police were sometimes slow to respond due to a lack of manpower. Since I had law enforcement training, I thought they could use the help. I volunteered."

The lawyer nodded.

"Had you not intervened on Ms. Pittman's behalf, what do you think would have happened?"

"I can't say for certain, but Mr. Pittman was drunk and had hurt Ms. Pittman multiple times in the past. In my experience, domestic offenders escalate unless the legal system intervenes. Given time, I think he would have killed her."

Jeremy's lawyer objected and claimed I was speculating. The judge sustained it, but nobody had further questions. He excused me and then drew in a breath.

"Based on the information presented today, the

plaintiff has proved with a preponderance of evidence that Ms. Pittman has a qualifying relationship with the defendant and that the defendant has perpetrated multiple acts of domestic violence as defined by North Carolina law. Mr. Pittman, I hereby order you to refrain from further contact of any kind with Ms. Pittman for the next year. You are to stay at least five hundred feet from her home and place of employment, and you will stay at least one hundred feet from Ms. Pittman at all times. Any violation of this order is a criminal offense for which the police will arrest you. If you have questions, your attorney can talk to my clerk."

Ann brought her hands to her mouth as the judge adjourned court and asked the sheriff's deputy to escort Jeremy from the building. I leaned forward from the gallery and put a hand on Ann's shoulder. She reached back and covered my hand with her own. She was almost trembling as she stood and turned to face me.

"Thank you," she whispered.

"It's what friends are for," I said.

Her eyes grew glassy as she looked to her attorney.

"So is that it?" she asked. "Jeremy can't bother us anymore?"

"If he does, he'll go to jail," she said. Ann blinked and smiled and wiped a tear from her eyes as she looked at me.

"Let's go celebrate," she said. "I owe you lunch."

"Wouldn't miss it," I said.

8

Ann and I had lunch at a little coffee shop near the courthouse. She didn't need to buy me lunch, but I rarely turned down free food. When she wasn't taking care of Cora, Ann was a librarian at the Cloverdale public library, but she frequently taught information literacy programs at local schools. So we talked about the students she ran into and her co-workers and the travails of working in the public sector in this part of North Carolina. I talked about my work as a reserve police officer in Cloverdale. When she asked about my previous work as a detective in St. Augustine, I paused and drew in a breath through my nose. Then I looked at the table.

"It was a long time ago. I'd rather not talk about it."

She considered me for a moment and then nodded.

"All right," she said. "If you ever change your mind, though, and need a friend to talk to, I'll listen."

I looked at her and smiled but shook my head.

"Some skeletons are best kept in the closet."

"Mysterious," she said, winking. I shook my head.

"More depressing than mysterious," I said. "Trust me."

"I do trust you," she said. For the next few minutes, neither of us said anything. Then my phone rang. I would have just let it go to voicemail, but it was Tonya Cantwell, Sallianne's mom. I told Ann I'd be just a minute before heading outside.

"Tonya, hey," I said looking around to make sure I had privacy. "It's Joe. What's up?"

"I just wanted to let you know that I got a phone call from Lieutenant Rathman," she said. "They've arrested Ahmed Ganim for murder. He was Sallianne's boyfriend."

My shoulders felt heavy.

"I'm sorry," I said. "Did they find her body?"

"No," she said. "Lieutenant Rathman said they had been watching him for a few days, and they knew he and Sallianne had been fighting. They arrested him at the airport. He had a one-way plane ticket to Dubai. The US doesn't have a formal extradition treaty with the United Arab Emirates, so they picked him up before he could escape. He was the last person to see Sallianne alive, and the neighbors reported that he and Sallianne had a blowout fight right before she disappeared."

I nodded but furrowed my brow.

"I heard they had been fighting. For what it's worth, he would have been my primary suspect, too. I'm sorry for your loss."

She paused.

"So this is it?" she asked.

"It looks like it," I said. "This is a hard case, and there's a good chance the prosecutor's office will try to work out a deal with Ahmed to avoid a trial. As part of that deal, they'll try to get Ahmed to reveal where he put Sallianne's body. If that happens, details about her last moments and her manner of death might leak to the press."

She sighed.

"But at least I'll have her body," she said. "I'll be able to bury my baby."

"There are still a lot of variables," I said, "but it's possible."

"I don't care what happens to him," she said. "I just want to know what happened to my daughter. This uncertainty is eating away at me. I can't stand it."

"Hopefully we'll have some certainty soon," I said, my voice soft. "I'm sorry I couldn't do more."

"That's okay," she said. "Thank you, Joe."

I wished her well and told her to call at any time if she needed anything from me. We hung up a moment later. When I got back to the table with Ann, things didn't feel quite so festive. I told her what had happened, and she sighed and told me she had to get back to work, anyway.

So we drove back. Ann left for work, and Roy and I went inside, where I grabbed a bottle of vodka from my freezer and poured myself a drink. I had no business drinking in the middle of the day, but the police had made an arrest in Sallianne's disappearance, the court had issued a restraining order against Ann's ex-husband, and I had a decent bottle of vodka and nothing else to do.

So I sipped and lounged and wondered what I was doing with my life. When I lived in St. Augustine, I had little free time to sit and think about my life and question my choices. Now I had lots of free time but few answers. About fifteen minutes after I came home, my phone buzzed, and I sighed when I saw the number. Then I answered and forced myself to sound chipper.

"Julia, hey," I said. "It's been a while."

Julia Green was my adoptive mother. I loved her, and I loved her family, but life had a way of complicating even simple relationships. Before I left St. Augustine, she and I had gotten into a big fight about a case I was working. A woman I was investigating wanted to hurt me, but she couldn't get to me directly, so she went after my adoptive brother, Julia's son Dylan. Dylan was okay, but he could have been hurt badly. Julia blamed me and then told me she needed some space. I gave it to her and left town.

"Hey, Joe," she said, her voice halting. "I hope it's okay that I'm calling."

"I'm glad you called. It's good to hear your voice," I said. "I've been meaning to call you."

Julia paused. I cleared my throat.

"How are Audrey and Dylan?" I asked.

Julia's voice brightened.

"They're good. Dylan started college a couple of weeks ago at St. Louis University, and Audrey's back in Chicago."

We spent about ten minutes catching up. The conversation was easy but superficial. That was how I wanted it. After a lull in the conversation, Julia cleared her throat.

"How are you doing, Joe?"

I looked at my half-empty glass, unsure how to answer.

"I've got everything I need."

Julia paused.

"Where are you?"

I smiled and hoped she heard it through my voice.

"We agreed that you wouldn't ask that question," I said.

"I know, but I miss you. You're my daughter. I need to know you're safe."

My smile slipped a little.

"I'm fine, Julia. It's perfectly safe here. Besides, I've got Roy with me all the time. He'd never let anyone hurt me."

"I'm glad you've got him," she said. "I know you needed some time away, but I wish you'd come home."

My throat tightened, and my mind automatically began forming excuses to hang up. Then I swallowed hard.

"I don't want to have that conversation."

"Okay," said Julia. "I understand."

The silence felt heavy, almost oppressive. I wanted to hang up, but I stuck it out.

"You're mad, aren't you?" said Julia, a moment later.

"Yeah."

"Was it something I did?"

I licked my lips and looked down.

"I don't know."

"Have you seen a doctor about it?" she asked. "I started seeing a therapist a couple of months ago. She's helped."

"This isn't the kind of thing a therapist can help with," I said. "I need to figure this out on my own."

We lapsed into another uncomfortable silence. Then Julia cleared her throat.

"Well, it sounds like you're busy," she said. "Thanks for taking my call. If you need anything, please call me."

"I will," I said, leaning forward for my drink. For a moment, neither of us hung up. I closed my eyes and drew comfort from the sound of her breath. The longer we stayed on the line, though, the more my lower lip trembled. Julia was my adoptive mom, but whenever I thought of her, my heart ached, my hands trembled, and I got so angry I could barely speak. Something inside me wanted to explode and scream at her, but I couldn't let it out because I didn't want to lose one of the very few people in the world I truly loved.

So I swallowed my pain and confusion and anger and hung up the phone before I did something stupid and lost another person important to me. Then I leaned back in my chair and drank my vodka. I didn't know why Julia upset me, but whenever I thought about her, I hurt even more. I didn't know how to deal with that, so I just closed my eyes and took deep breaths until my tears ran out.

"You're fine, Joe," I whispered. "You don't need her. You don't need anybody."

I stayed like that for a while, but then my phone buzzed with an incoming call. I wiped away my eyes and glanced at the screen, but I didn't recognize the number. It wasn't Julia, so I answered before the phone could ring a second time.

"Hi. This is Joe Court. What can I do for you?"

"Hey," said a woman's soft voice. "My name is Sawyer Cook. I'm a friend of Sallianne Cantwell's."

I leaned forward and nodded, drawing in a breath and hoping I didn't sound too frazzled.

"Okay. What can I do for you, Sawyer?"

"Angela Wolner told me the police arrested Ahmed for murdering Sallianne. She said I should call you. Ahmed didn't kill Sallianne. I thought you should know."

I paused before responding, hoping she'd elaborate. She didn't.

"Do you know for a fact that he didn't kill Sallianne, or is that speculation?"

"It's a fact," she said. "He didn't do it."

"And how do you know he didn't do it?"

"Because he was with me the night she went missing," she said. "And he's been with me every night since then."

I stood and walked to my purse to get a pen and notepad.

"You've got my attention," I said. "Tell me what's going on. From the beginning."

She drew in deep breaths.

"Ahmed and I have been seeing each other for the past six months. Sallianne has been so focused on her podcast that she and Ahmed would go days without speaking to each other. My fiancé teaches in the history department, and there's so much pressure to publish that he works twelve to fifteen hours a day. I hardly even see him."

I nodded.

"Okay," I said.

"Ahmed and I both work hard, but we're not like them. We love our partners, but sometimes it's just nice to sit on the couch with somebody and watch TV, you know?"

"I understand," I said, nodding and hoping she'd speed this up.

"So, one night when Sallianne and Lucas were working, Ahmed and I hooked up. It was stupid, but neither of us had had sex in weeks. We needed it."

"Tell me about the day Sallianne disappeared."

"It was a Friday," she said. "She and Ahmed had a fight. He thought if he could convince her to move, she wouldn't be as focused on that stupid podcast of hers. He wanted her to have a real career at a newspaper, and he wanted to get a job with a tech company."

I sat down at my small breakfast table and leaned back on the chair.

"Angela Wolner told me they fought some," I said.

"Yeah, they fought a lot," she said, her voice low. She paused. "After the fight, she kicked Ahmed out. He went to his apartment and called me and asked me to come over. He sounded upset, so I went over. We started kissing, and then one thing led to another. Unfortunately, Sallianne came in while Ahmed and I were in bed together. I think she meant to apologize, but she saw us and said we were both losers that nobody else could love."

I raised my eyebrows and tilted my head to the side as I jotted down a few notes.

"Ouch," I said.

"Yeah," said Sawyer. "Sallianne had a sharp temper, but she was my friend. At least I thought she was. That hurt."

I spent a minute writing notes and a few thoughts, but then I straightened.

"That would hurt. What happened after that?"

Sawyer sighed.

"Ahmed told Sallianne to leave, but we stayed in bed. I was crying, and he held me. He didn't kill her because he was with me."

The story made sense, but that didn't make it true.

"Have you told anybody else this?"

She sighed and paused.

"I didn't need to tell anyone else. Sallianne took care of that for me."

I raised my eyebrows.

"Tell me about that," I said.

"Ahmed and I were naked, so we stayed in bed," she said. "We thought Sallianne left the apartment right away, but she didn't. First, she dumped out my purse on the couch in the living room and stole my cell phone. She used it to call my parents to let them know Ahmed and I were having an affair. Then, she called Lucas, my fiancé, and left him a message that said I was cheating on him. Then she sent Lucas pictures I had texted Ahmed."

I straightened. This was new information, and it changed the case.

"So Sallianne had your cell phone?"

"Yeah," she said. "Ahmed and I screwed up, but she didn't have to do all those things. She ruined my life."

Sleeping with her boyfriend probably had something to do with bringing out her latent hostility, but I didn't comment on that.

"I need you to call Lieutenant Rathman in Chapel Hill and tell him everything. If Ahmed didn't kill Sallianne, you need to share this. It'll keep him from going to prison for a crime he didn't commit."

For a few seconds, she said nothing. Then she cleared her throat.

"Ahmed's mom lives in Dubai," she said. "He was just going home. Sallianne ruined his life. She ruined my life, too. Now Lucas won't talk to me, and my mom and dad are ashamed of me."

That she slept with her friend's boyfriend might have had something to do with the state of her life, but that wasn't my concern.

"I'm sorry for all that, but you can right some wrongs by talking to Lieutenant Rathman now. Okay?"

She agreed and hung up. I blinked and rubbed my eyes before writing notes. The story was tawdry, but if it were true, we'd find ample evidence. I couldn't blame Rathman for arresting Ahmed when he did, but we'd have to let him go. Hopefully his arrest wouldn't come back to bite us later.

No matter what Sallianne had done, she didn't deserve to die, and Tonya Cantwell didn't deserve to lose a daughter. Even if I searched for a hundred years, I couldn't guarantee I'd find Sallianne, but I'd do my best. And if my search kept me from thinking about my own problems with my adoptive mom, that was all the better.

9

Technically, fall would start very soon, but the trees looked as if they planned to hold their leaves forever. Nicole crouched behind the trunk of a thick shortleaf pine tree and checked her boyfriend's iPhone to ensure she had a signal. Green needles covered the ground, suffusing the area with the thick scent of tree sap. Around her, oak, black locust, and pine trees stretched to the horizon, creating a thick canopy above her head.

About two hundred yards ahead of Nicole in a hollow in the woods lay Hiram Ford's enormous log cabin. Her dad had worked on the initial construction and came away so impressed that he talked about it almost every night. The structure looked as if it had big timbers for walls, but it was mostly concrete with a wooden veneer on the exterior. The walls were ten inches thick and held miles and miles of rebar, while the windows and doors could withstand hurricane-force winds. Her dad used to joke that it could survive a direct hit from an A-bomb. Nicole doubted that, but she knew Hiram's little fortress could withstand anything she could bring to bear against it.

Smoke curled from one of the three chimney stacks, and she saw movement through the diaphanous white curtains covering the windows. Her father was in there somewhere, taken because of something she did. It made her gut hurt to think about it. She had to rescue him, but she didn't know how.

Hiram claimed he had officers in every county in the state, and so far, Nicole had seen nothing to make her doubt that. So even if she called the police and told them everything she knew, the deputy might just pull a gun and shoot her in the head. She needed a better plan than her hopes and prayers could give her, but to come up with something that would have even a remote chance of success, she first needed information. That's why she was here.

She pulled TJ's phone from her pocket and searched through the directory but found nothing that would help her. Then she opened a browser and looked for a pizza place that delivered. The first two restaurants she called refused to go all the way out to Hiram's cabin, but the third agreed as long as she paid an extra six-dollar service fee. Considering she didn't plan to pay for anything, she didn't mind.

She ordered two medium pepperoni pizzas and a salad big enough for a family of four. The driver said it'd take him at least forty-five minutes, but Nicole wasn't in a hurry. She hung up and munched on a granola bar her friend Rose had given her that morning. The food silenced her growling stomach but did nothing at all to eliminate the tremble in her fingers or the sweat that rolled down her back and belly.

When the pizza arrived, Hiram would answer the door and say he hadn't ordered a pizza. With luck, the driver would yell and scream, but even if he didn't, he'd give her the diversion she needed to look into the cabin's windows for her father. With that information, she'd figure out what to do.

She had a pistol, but that alone wouldn't cut it against Hiram's men. They were cops, so they spent dozens of hours a year at the firing range. Nicole could take them out at three hundred yards with a good rifle, but she didn't have one. No matter how she approached this, they had her outgunned.

Hiram was ruthless and careful, but he was still just a man. Even ruthless men had limits. If she could find out where in the building her dad was being held, maybe she could steal a car and rig it to run through the front window. Even if it didn't hurt anybody, it'd make a hell of a lot of noise and draw everybody's attention. When Hiram investigated, she could sneak through the back door.

Or, maybe, she could light the house on fire. If she burned enough of the building, they'd have to evacuate. They wouldn't leave her dad inside. She could pick them off with her pistol as they came through the front door. But if they left her dad inside, all the better. She'd call the fire department, and two or three dozen burly men with fire axes and hoses would come running. They'd find her dad tied up in the house, rescue him, and start asking questions.

Everything she did, though, hinged on surviving and finding her father. So she pulled her pistol from her backpack, slipped it into the pocket of her jeans, and hunkered down to wait for the pizza delivery man.

After about twenty minutes in which nothing happened, her shoulders relaxed. She had parked her bike in a ditch near the road and camouflaged it with fallen branches from a pine tree. It blended into the landscape and should keep any passersby from stealing it. She was fine to wait for a while.

"Nicole!"

As the voice echoed through the woods, Nicole's shoulders dropped, and she closed her eyes.

"You stupid son of a bitch," she said, her voice low.

"Nicole! I know you're here!"

It was TJ. She looked toward Hiram's house to see whether anybody had come outside. Nobody stirred.

"You stole my phone!"

Nicole clenched her jaw and looked around until she saw her ex-boyfriend in the shadow of a shagbark hickory tree.

"Get down, dumbass," she said, her voice a strident whisper.

"Where are you?"

TJ didn't lower the volume of his voice as he scanned the woods.

"I'm here," said Nicole, standing where he could see her. "Now shut up and hide."

"What the hell are you doing?" he asked, tromping through the woods and breaking every branch along the way. TJ was anything but an outdoorsman. Her dad had taken him hunting once to get know him better, and TJ's heavy footsteps had scared off every deer within a half mile before they even got to their camp. Neither of them had seen even a single squirrel, rabbit, or deer the entire day. "And why are we at Hiram Ford's house?"

"Because Hiram's got something I care about," she said. "And I told you to shut up and hide."

He crouched and stepped beside her, looking around.

"Why are we hiding?"

She glanced at him and rolled her eyes.

"Don't ask," she said. "And why are you here, anyway?"

"You stole my phone."

She screwed up her face and shook her head.

"I didn't steal a damn thing," she said, watching the cabin once again. "While you were getting syphilis from Jeanette, I picked up your phone by mistake. It was an accident."

"Well, I want it back," he said. "And you can forget about me taking you to the homecoming dance. That's off the table now."

"I'll get over the pain," said Nicole.

"I don't see what the big deal was," said TJ. "It was just sex. It wasn't even that good."

She glanced at him and then focused on the house, thinking she had seen movement somewhere but unsure where.

"Was it better than working one out on your own? Because that's all you'll have once the Department of Health reports you've got multidrug-resistant gonorrhea."

He crossed his arms.

"You always thought you were funny," he said, shaking his head and standing. "I hate to break it to you, but nobody laughs at your jokes."

She shrugged.

"I think I'm funny, and that's all that matters," said Nicole, glancing at him. She softened her voice. "I'm kind of in the middle of something, buddy. You were fun to be with, and you'll make some stupid girl real happy one day, but it's time we broke up. Why don't you pack it up and go home?"

"I want my phone," he said.

"And I want my virginity back, but we can't always get what we want. Now go home while you can, TJ."

A twig broke to Nicole's left, sending a shock through her body.

"TJ's staying right where he is," said a familiar low voice. Nicole swore under her breath as she and TJ turned. Michael Grant, the forest ranger who'd tried to rape her at her garden, stood not twenty feet away. He wore jeans and a polo-style shirt. A holster on his hip held a black semiautomatic pistol. His eyes locked on Nicole's. "I thought I heard voices out here. You guys are in some deep shit."

"TJ's not a part of this," said Nicole, stepping around a tree to hide her hands as she reached for the gun in her pocket. "Let him go. It's me you want. He's just a big dumb idiot who's looking for his cell phone."

"I've had about enough of you insulting me," said TJ.

"TJ, I'm going to count to three," said Nicole. "You should run. That douchebag with the gun will shoot you in the back, so zigzag and duck behind trees. I stabbed him in the leg recently, so he won't chase you."

Michael's hand hovered over his firearm.

"The moment you get to three," said the ranger, "I'll shoot you both."

Nicole didn't give him the chance. She pulled her weapon from her pocket and fired without aiming. Since she hadn't given herself time to get into a proper stance or to even grip the weapon with both hands, it kicked hard and nearly flew out of her hands. Michael dove to the ground. Nicole looked at TJ.

"Run!"

The moment she finished shouting, Nicole ran over the uneven ground, her heart pounding in her chest and sweat pouring down her brow and into her eyes. As she reached the road, she turned and looked over her shoulder. Michael and TJ were writhing on the ground, but Michael was the stronger man. As she watched, he overpowered TJ and began shackling his hands behind his back with cuffs. If she tried to help him now, she'd end up locked up beside him. Her best chance to save him was to escape.

So she uncovered her bike, threw her leg over the side and started pedaling. About two or three hundred yards down the road, she came to TJ's truck. She tossed her bike in the bed and dove into the cab. TJ had taken the key with him, but that didn't matter in his thirty-year-old truck. He had stripped the ignition lock cylinder, so any key would work. She reached into her backpack, grabbed her car keys, and stuck one into the ignition. The truck's engine turned over and roared to life, and she floored the accelerator, getting her breath back and squeezing the steering wheel hard. Now she had to save her daddy and her ex-boyfriend.

This just got worse and worse.

10

I still wore the outfit I had put on that morning when I testified, so I changed into jeans, a clean top, and a cardigan that covered the pistol in the holster on my hip. Then I checked Roy's water bowl to make sure he had something to drink. He whined when he saw me going to work, but he'd be okay. Cora would come home and play with him soon enough.

Cloverdale's police station was an old red brick building with big windows out front and surveillance cameras that filmed the street and adjoining parking lot. The crepe myrtle bushes beside the front door still had dense clusters of pink blossoms, while a pair of saucer magnolia trees anchored the corners of the building. Someone—probably Lorna, one of the town's uniformed officers—had placed a big water bowl with a dog's paw painted on its exterior beside the front door.

I parked in the lot and walked into the lobby. The room had a TV hung from a bracket in the corner, chairs, a coffee table, and houseplants beside the front door. Bobby Crosby sat behind the receptionist's window in the lobby. The harsh overhead lights glinted off his bald scalp. He was about forty and had five kids—all boys, and all under twelve years old. After watching Cora all summer, I didn't know how Bobby or his wife had the energy to get out of bed in the morning.

"Hey, Joe," he said, looking up at me and smiling.

"Didn't know you were coming in today."

"Wasn't planning on it, but I wanted to see the boss," I said, nodding toward the door that separated the private areas of the station from the lobby. "Buzz me in?"

He nodded and hit the buzzer. I opened it and stepped back.

"The chief's in his office."

"Thanks, Bobby," I said, already crossing the open bullpen toward a set of stairs at the back of the room. Cloverdale had six full-time uniformed officers, one chief, and one reserve police officer—me. Wayne and Charlotte worked the day and swing shifts, but I couldn't find them. They must have been out on calls.

The second floor looked like a traditional small office building and had one large hallway and private rooms that branched off from it. Thin navy blue carpet covered the floors, while fluorescent lights buzzed overhead. Pictures from important events in Cloverdale's past covered the walls. I walked to the chief's office and knocked on the door.

"It's Joe Court," I said. "You got a minute?"

"Come on in," said Chief Bryan Tomlin. I opened the door and walked inside. The office had plain white walls and a window that overlooked Fifth Street. The furniture was utilitarian and simple but functional. Tomlin sat behind his desk and typed at his computer before focusing on me and gesturing to a chair. "Have a seat and give me a minute. I'm almost done."

I nodded and sat while he finished whatever he was

doing. Chief Tomlin was twenty-nine years old, the same age as me. He was young to be the police chief, but he was the only person who applied for the job when the previous chief quit. I didn't know much about his background, but he kept the lights running and hired good people. After a moment, he looked at me and smiled.

"I'm glad you came in," he said. "I've got a job for you if you're up for it."

"Serial murderer or transnational drug gang?" I asked.

Tomlin furrowed his brow.

"Come again?"

I smiled and shook my head.

"I was just making a joke," I said. "Sorry it wasn't funny. Before you say anything about an assignment, I had hoped to talk to you about Sallianne Cantwell."

He leaned back and nodded.

"I hear the folks in Chapel Hill made an arrest," he said.

"Only because their suspect forced their hands," I said, nodding. "Ahmed Ganim was Sallianne's long-term boyfriend, and the police arrested him in the airport. He didn't kill her, though. He was with Sawyer Cook the night Sallianne disappeared. They were having an affair."

Tomlin picked up a pen from his desk and looked as if he planned to write something, but he didn't have any paper.

"So we've got a love triangle going on."

"There are four people involved. Sawyer has a fiancé," I said. "So it's more like a love rectangle. I don't know how that works."

Tomlin raised his eyebrows.

"I'm glad it's not our case."

"It still might be," I said. "Nobody's found a body yet, and according to her mom, Sallianne spent a lot of time in Cloverdale. Someone might have killed her for reasons separate from her love life, which is why I came to talk to you. If Rathman finds Sallianne's body in Cloverdale, it'll become our case, and we'll be days behind. Until they figure out why Sallianne visited Cloverdale so often, our department needs somebody on this case. I'm just a reserve officer, but I was a good detective, and I've worked a lot of homicides. I can do this if you'll let me."

He leaned forward and rested his elbows on his desk.

"I can't have a reserve officer working a homicide," he said.

"Then you need to work the case yourself," I said. "This young woman is gone. In all likelihood, she's dead, and it's possible she died because of something she did in Cloverdale. Her family deserves to know what happened."

He considered me.

"What would you say if I offered you a temporary position on my staff?"

"I'd start by asking what that temporary position entails."

He nodded and pushed back from his desk so he could open the center drawer.

"Cloverdale can't afford a full-time detective at the moment, but I've got more work than my regular team can handle. I can pay you eight hundred dollars a week for the next two weeks. You'll be a full-time detective, and you'll work Sallianne's homicide and other duties as assigned. It's meaningful work, and I need somebody to do it. Would you be interested in that?"

I didn't have to think long before nodding.

"If it'll let me work Sallianne's disappearance with the department's resources, you've got a detective."

He pulled a document from his drawer, signed it, and then slid it toward me. I skimmed it and glanced at him before signing at the indicated spot.

"How long have you had an employment contract with my name on it?" I asked.

"Couple of weeks," he said, smiling. "I knew I'd need you eventually, but you were busy with Ann Pittman's little girl. I didn't think I could pry you away from her."

"Cora's in pre-school now," I said. "Good timing."

I handed him the paper, and he looked through it before slipping it into his desk and standing. I stood and shook his hand.

"Glad to have you on staff," he said. "You already know everybody, so I won't introduce you around. Our morning briefing is at eight o'clock every weekday, and the coffee's in the break room. In the meantime, I need you to call Officer Maddox. Gas station out on Eleventh Street got robbed about an hour ago. You're the lead detective. Maddox handled the initial call and will fill you in on the details."

I considered before speaking.

"With all due respect, Chief, Sallianne's case is a murder," I said. "Is a gas station robbery that important?"

"This is fifth station robbed in the past six weeks. We believe it's the same team each time, and they get more violent with each robbery. If we don't stop these guys, they will kill somebody. You've got your orders. If you don't agree with them, we can tear up your contract right now. It's up to you."

I straightened.

"No. I'm a team player, and I get it," I said. "I'll call Brady."

Tomlin's expression softened.

"Good luck, Joe," he said. "I'm glad you're onboard. And make sure you keep your receipts. Cloverdale will reimburse you for gas and wear and tear on your car."

"Sounds good. Thanks," I said. Tomlin nodded and got back to work on his computer. I took the stairs to the first floor and nodded to Bobby as I left the building. Once I reached my car, I called Officer Brady Maddox's cell number. He answered quickly. "Hey, Brady, it's Joe Court. How do you feel about taking orders from a woman?"

He paused.

"I'm married, so I'm used to it," he said. "The boss step down and make you chief?"

"No, but he gave me a temporary job," I said. "I'll be working this robbery with you. I'm on my way, but do me a favor before I get there and pull any surveillance video you can."

"So you'll be in charge, huh?"

"Yep," I said, nodding and turning my car on. "Is that a problem?"

"Nope," he said. "We need help."

I paused.

"Is it bad?"

"Get over here and see for yourself."

I put my car in gear.

"I'm on my way. See you in a few."

I hung up and tossed my phone to the passenger seat. Sallianne could wait. I had a serious felony to work, and hopefully I wasn't too rusty.

11

The gas station was on Cloverdale's main drag across the street from a shuttered fast-food place and beside a cheap motel. The sun was bright and still high, forcing me to squint even with my sunglasses. A single marked police cruiser had parked between the station's convenience store and a two-stall brick car wash. No cars pumped gas, washed their vehicles, or remained in the spots beside the building. I pulled into the lot and parked.

Brady Maddox and an older man in black slacks and a white button-down shirt emerged from the store a moment later. Brady wore a navy Cloverdale police officer's uniform. The sun glinted off both his silver badge and his forehead. He was forty-five or fifty and had graying black hair and intelligent green eyes. I hadn't worked with him a lot, but he seemed like a good officer. I nodded to him as I opened my door.

"Officer Maddox," I said, first focusing on Brady and then the civilian. "Sir, I'm Detective Joe Court with the Cloverdale Police Department."

The civilian nodded and shook my hand. He had a calloused palm and a strong grip.

"Dustin Crane," he said. "I'm the owner."

"It's nice to meet you, Mr. Crane. I know Officer Maddox has done some good work here, but I'll be taking over the investigation," I said, reaching into my purse. When I first became a reserve officer in Cloverdale, Chief

Tomlin had given me a hundred generic business cards with the station's contact information on them. Each card had a blank line where I had written my name and cell number in case somebody needed to get in touch with me. Now, they'd come in handy. Crane took one from my outstretched hand and glanced at it as I continued speaking. "I'll talk to you in a few minutes, but first I'd like to get an update from my officer. So if you'll excuse us, I'd appreciate that."

Crane nodded and stepped back. I put my hand on Brady's elbow and led him toward his cruiser. Once we were out of earshot, I took a notebook and pen from my purse and raised my eyebrows.

"What have we got?"

Brady looked toward the gas station.

"The station received an emergency call twenty-five minutes ago. I was the nearest responder, so I drove over, arriving seven minutes after the phone call. The convenience store didn't have any customers, but the clerk was in the bathroom in significant pain. She had burns on her face and neck, so I called for paramedics. They arrived fifteen minutes after my call and checked the young lady out. Because she was in so much pain, they gave her a sedative and took her to Eastview Medical Center with the lights and sirens going."

Eastview was the local hospital. It had a small ER and a fair number of doctors, but most serious cases would have gone to UNC Medical Center in Chapel Hill. I nodded and wrote down the information.

"Tell me about these burns," I said. "Any idea how she got them?"

He looked down and then raised his eyebrows.

"The perps threw something at her face," he said. "I don't know what it was, but I called for a hazmat unit just in case. They're coming in from Greensboro."

"So it's a chemical burn," I said, grimacing. "Jeez."

"Like I said, it's ugly."

I nodded and wrote that down.

"This isn't the first gas station robbery lately, is it?" I asked. He said it wasn't. "Did the others involve chemical attacks?"

"No, ma'am," he said, shaking his head. "We've had five robberies so far, and the violence has escalated with each robbery. First one happened about six weeks ago. Our suspects have hit a new store about once a week. They always wear black ski masks, and there are three suspects in each robbery. Before robbing a store, they wait until all the customers leave. Then they go in."

I wrote down the pertinent details.

"Are they armed?" I asked, glancing up.

"Yep," he said, nodding. "At least two of them have semiautomatic pistols. It's hard to tell from the surveillance video, but they look like the same guns at each robbery."

"And you think it's the same perps each time?" I asked, lowering my chin.

"Based on their body types and mannerisms, yeah," he said. "And I'm pretty sure the suspects are male. We never see their faces, but one of them's got a big Adam's apple, another has hairy forearms, and the third guy just has big shoulders, a small waist, and large hands and feet. They always wear dark pants and dark shirts."

"This is all good information," I said, glancing toward the shop owner. He was on a cell phone. I'd talk to him soon. "What can you tell me about the robberies themselves?"

"They're fast," he said. "The perps walk through the front door wearing ski masks. One guy holds the door open, and the other two go inside. In each instance, they grab the clerk and pull him or her out from behind the counter. One of the bad guys holds the clerk at gunpoint, while the second robs the register. If the store's got liquor, they steal a few bottles, too. Total take on each robbery is between two hundred and three hundred dollars plus the cost of stolen merchandise."

I furrowed my brow. This was a lot of risk for three hundred bucks a pop, especially when it was split between multiple perpetrators. If they wanted money, they could have gotten legitimate jobs and made a whole lot more with much less risk. That made me wonder whether they did it because they liked it. It was a disturbing thought.

"So they burned this clerk with a chemical. Have they attacked anybody else?"

"The first two robberies, no," said Brady, shaking his head. "They pulled the first two clerks out from behind the counter, pointed guns at them, and made them lie facedown on the ground until they left. They pistol-whipped the clerk in the third store and broke his jaw. Fourth guy, they punched and kicked. This is the fifth one."

I grimaced again. When I got up that morning, I had expected to speak at Ann's hearing and then work on Sallianne Cantwell's disappearance. Now I could see why the boss wanted me working the robbery instead. These guys would kill somebody unless we stopped them. I considered what I wanted to do and then glanced at Mr. Crane, the store's owner.

"I assume the store had surveillance cameras," I said. Brady nodded and motioned me toward his vehicle.

"The camera streams the video to a cloud server, so Mr. Crane can access it anywhere," said Brady, opening his cruiser's door. I climbed in the passenger side while he spooled up a video on his cruiser's built-in laptop. Crane had installed a good system because the picture was as clear as looking through a window.

On the video, three men wearing black ski masks and dark clothes entered the shop. Two of the men wore long-sleeved black shirts, while the third wore a short-sleeved shirt. The man wearing short sleeves had hairy forearms but no visible tattoos. Two of the men, one stocky and one thin and wiry, sprinted inside. The man in short sleeves held the front door open and acted as a lookout.

The moment she saw the bad guys come in, the clerk reached beneath the counter to set off the security system, but by then, it was too late. The stocky man reached across the counter and pulled her forward as easily as if she were a child. Once she reached the other side, she held up her hands. The wiry man threw something at her. The video didn't have sound, but her mouth opened, and she brought her hands to her face as she writhed on the ground. Then the stocky man ran around the counter and cleared out the register while the wiry man ran to an aisle and picked up an armful of liquor. After that, both men left. The entire robbery took under three minutes.

Brady and I watched the video four times, but I saw little that would help me identify the suspects. Finally, I looked at him.

"Do we have other cameras?" I asked. Brady nodded.

"A couple on the exterior. The suspects approach the building from the rear and escape in the same direction. They never show their faces, and we never see a getaway car."

"And what's back there?"

He thought for a moment.

"Hotel parking lot and then a field. If they had parked their getaway car in the hotel's lot, we would have seen it on video. We didn't."

"So they escaped through the field, then," I said, nodding. "What do the other stations look like?"

"They don't have fields behind them."

"What do they have behind them?"

He paused.

"I don't know off the top of my head. I didn't pay that much attention."

"Okay," I said. "Call Chief Tomlin and tell him we

need a supervisory officer here to watch over the scene until hazmat comes in. We also need somebody capable of collecting forensic evidence. Do we have anybody on staff?"

"Technically, everybody has forensics training," said Brady, "but Bobby's the best we've got."

"Then bring him here, too."

"Will do," said Brady. "If the boss asks, what will you and I be doing?"

"We're going to the other stores," I said. "I want to see what we're up against."

12

Kit Jameson and his friends had just robbed their fifth convenience store. It was the stupidest thing Kit had ever done, and, truthfully, he didn't even know why he and his friends had bothered. In five robberies, they had collectively earned twelve hundred dollars. To some people, that was a lot of money, but to Kit and the other boys, it was nothing. It wasn't even pocket change.

He gripped the steering wheel of his Land Rover and tried to avoid vomiting as he watched two police officers, one female and one male, work the scene. Two months ago, he had walked onto the campus of Newman-Rothschild University without knowing a single person. He had been eighteen and a little lonely. He had wanted friends and thought he had found some at the Theta Ki Nu fraternity. The young men he met weren't friends, though. Kit didn't know what they were to each other, but he knew enough about friendship to know the men with him in that car knew nothing about it at all.

"The blond cop is hot," said Rory. "I wouldn't kick her out of bed."

Rory was a junior political science major. His unkempt curly brown hair framed an oval-shaped face that a lot of girls who didn't know better fawned over. Those who had the misfortune of spending time with him, though, kept their distance.

"You wouldn't kick a golden retriever out of bed,"

said Max, a senior English major and the fraternity's pledge trainer. Everybody but Kit laughed. The sound was almost animalistic. It sent chills up his spine to think people could laugh after what they had done.

"A man's got needs, and if the goldie's willing, who am I to kick her out?" asked Rory.

That brought about fresh howls of laughter. Kit looked in the rearview mirror.

"We should get going," he said. "Eventually, somebody's going to ask why four guys in an SUV are staring at a crime scene."

"Not around here," said Trystan, the fraternity's president, shaking his head. "We're in Cloverdale. Nothing happens here. You see two cops standing outside a gas station, you know something's up. Half the town's probably watching."

Kit swallowed and nodded. Trystan may have been right. They had parked in the lot of a fast-food place about half a block from the gas station, and every car that passed on the road seemed to slow down to watch the two police officers.

"The girl is new," he said. "Should we be worried about that?"

"She's probably just some bimbo slobbing the chief's knob," said Max. "Not that I blame him. She looks like she'd be good at slobbing knobs."

"You know what I like about you?" asked Rory, looking to his friend. "You're classy."

"Don't I know it," said Max, laughing and looking

out the window. "Goddamn, do I need a drink. Did you hear that chick scream when I hit her with the acid? I didn't know she'd be that loud."

"Or that it'd smell that much," said Rory. "That was some rank shit."

The first time Kit, Trystan, Max, and Rory had robbed a gas station, Kit hadn't known what they were doing. Trystan had asked him to drive to the station and wait in the car while they got booze. He didn't realize until his friends ran back to the car with ski masks on their faces that they were robbing the place and that he was the getaway driver. By then, it was too late. He had already committed felony armed robbery.

"That woman is probably blind now," he said. "I don't know if that's the kind of thing you should laugh at."

Rory and Max went silent. Then Rory leaned forward.

"What's with you, man?" he asked. "You've never even met her. She worked in a gas station. My taxes pay for her welfare. If we had killed her, we would have saved the country hundreds of thousands of dollars."

Kit shook his head and swallowed hard.

"She's a human being, and you threw sulfuric acid at her."

Rory shook his head and crossed his arms.

"You're not even worth talking to," he said. "Just shut up."

"Kit's right," said Trystan. "The acid's attracting attention."

"Are you talking about Barbie?" asked Rory. "The blond cop? She's nothing. Just look at her car. It's a Volvo station wagon. Her station won't even give her a real cop car. Trust me, we don't need to worry."

"It's a change," said Trystan. "When things change, we have to pay attention. One day, we will lead the rabble, but for now, we're vulnerable to them."

Trystan talked like that a lot. He wanted power and didn't care how he got it. Once he finished college, he planned to go to law school and then clerk for an influential appellate court judge or a justice on the Supreme Court. After that, he'd either practice law for a few years to build contacts and amass a nest egg, or he'd go to work for a state legislator. Eventually, he'd run for office and work his way up to governor of North Carolina. From there, the world was his.

Max and Rory robbed the stores because it gave them a thrill. Kit went along with them because he wanted friends. Trystan robbed the stores because the robberies gave him leverage over people he found useful. He was a sociopath, but so were Max and Rory. Kit wished he had never met them.

"Rory's right," said Max. "She's hot, but she's a cop in Cloverdale. Think about that: Cloverdale. It's North Carolina's asshole. If she were any good at her job, she'd be working in Charlotte. We're fine."

Trystan shook his head.

"We're not fine. Even if she's just a pretty face, this shows that the locals realize they're not up to taking us down on their own. They're learning and bringing in extra help. We've got to show them how dangerous that is before they bring in the feds. We need to kill her."

"Bad idea," said Rory, shaking his head. "They send you to the chair for killing a cop."

"You threw acid on a woman's face," said Trystan. "If you're caught, your life's ruined, anyway. If we're proactive and kill the blonde, we can stop her investigation before it gets started. That's the choice we've got: We sit on our asses, do nothing, and go to prison, or we take action and save ourselves. What do you want to do?"

The car went quiet. Kit's heart raced, and he felt almost dizzy even though he was sitting still. He gripped the steering wheel hard and swallowed but tried to keep his feelings from his face, even as his insides roiled. They had been stupid to rob a convenience store and even stupider for hurting the clerks. If he had known what he was getting into, he never would have done either. Killing a cop, though, was on another level.

"It's the only way," said Max, after a pause. "I'm in."

"Me, too," said Rory.

Kit held his breath. He could almost feel sweat bead on his upper back.

"How about you, Kit?" asked Trystan. "We need a driver."

He squeezed the steering wheel.

"I won't kill anybody."

"We're not asking you to kill anybody," said Trystan. "We're asking you to drive. I need you on my team."

Kit blinked but said nothing.

"Think about your future," said Trystan, his voice low. "You've got so much potential. We can do so much together."

The knot in Kit's stomach tightened. To Trystan, murder was a team-building exercise. If he told Trystan no, Kit knew the other guys would go through with it, and he'd end up with a murder weapon in his closet or hidden beneath the floorboards of his room. Then, late one night, the police would get an anonymous tip. They'd search his room, find the gun or knife, and make an arrest. He'd go to the gas chamber, and Trystan would go to the White House or the state capital, accompanied by two friends bound by a secret none of them could divulge.

He swallowed the bile that threatened to rise in his throat. Maybe he could warn the cop somebody was after her. To do that, though, he had to know what his friends were planning. He needed time to think and plan, and that meant he had one option. He nodded.

"I'm in," he said. "Let's do this."

"All right," said Trystan. "Drive us home. We'll take care of her later. Meanwhile, we've got some booze and free time. Let's celebrate."

Kit put the car in gear, hoping he hadn't just made the biggest mistake of his life.

13

About twenty minutes after I arrived at the crime scene, a bright yellow hazmat truck slowed and then parked beside the gas pumps. Since the hazmat team didn't know what kind of hazardous agent it was dealing with, the guys set up a tent outside the store in which they could change into their protective yellow suits in relative privacy. They'd clean up the shop and determine what the bad guys had thrown on the clerk, which I appreciated, but to do that, they'd destroy evidence. That would make things hard.

Brady and I answered a few questions, and then the hazmat guys got to work. About five minutes later, Chief Tomlin's marked SUV pulled into the lot. I told him what Brady and I had found so far, and he scowled and hemmed and hawed. He didn't seem happy that we had called him away from whatever else he was doing, but we had all had jobs to do, and this was his. He'd get over it. A moment later, Bobby Crosby arrived in a cruiser to take care of the forensic evidence.

With the crime scene sorted and supervised, Brady and I headed out. Since we had driven in separate cars to the scene, I followed his cruiser in my Volvo. For a brief while, I noticed a white Land Rover in my rearview mirror that seemed to be following us, but it turned away before I could see its driver.

Our first stop was at a convenience store and gas

station about a block from Walmart. Crepe myrtles ringed the parking lot, while deep, thick woods owned by a logging company lay to the south. Brady and I parked near the building.

"So how'd this one go down?" I asked, walking to my partner's cruiser and crossing my arms. We were behind the station near an employee break area. An employee must have been out there recently because the butt of a cigarette still smoldered in an ashtray on the pine picnic table.

"Similar to all the others," said Brady. "Three perps entered the building through the front door. All three wore ski masks. They had firearms, but in this station, they didn't hurt anybody."

"And how'd they get away?" I asked.

"That's the question," said Brady. "I've watched the surveillance video half a dozen times. They walk from the rear of the building, along its side, and to the front door. After the robbery, we've got a video of them leaving the store through its front door and returning to the back, but we lose them here."

"And, I'm assuming, we don't have a video of any vehicles entering or leaving the parking lot at the time of the robbery."

"Correct," said Brady.

I nodded and looked around. The woods to the south looked dark and thick, like a wall of living greenery. A north-south road on the western side of the parking lot led to Walmart, while the east-west road to the gas station's north led to town and, eventually, the interstate. If they had taken either of those roads, surveillance cameras would have seen them.

I hesitated and then walked toward the woods. From two hundred yards away, the tree line looked solid, but as I got closer, I found a dark, rutted trail about six feet across cut through the timber. Thick, gnarled roots crisscrossed the forest floor. Brady stood beside me and crossed his arms.

"Huh," he said, grunting.

"Could a car make it through that?" I asked.

He raised his eyebrows.

"It'd be tight," he said. "I wouldn't want to do it in my cruiser, but I bet a pickup could make it."

"Or a Land Rover."

As I glanced at him, he tilted his head to the side.

"Land Rover'll run you, what, sixty or seventy grand?" he asked.

"I guess," I said, shrugging. "Never looked into it."

"Either way, they cost more than most people earn," he said. "Not too many dentists knock off convenience stores."

I nodded and focused on the woods.

"I thought I saw one following us earlier."

"Sure he wasn't just driving to Walmart?"

I looked at him and nodded.

"I'm just being paranoid," I said. "This is how they escaped, though. When we're done here, we'll look the area up on Google Maps. If we can't see the trail on their satellite imagery, we'll call the timber company and see what they say. In the meantime, let's go to the next store."

We spent the next two hours driving across Cloverdale and visiting convenience stores. The next gas station we visited was beside a shuttered tool and die factory. At one time, that factory would have had night watchmen and surveillance cameras, but it hadn't turned out a product in years. It was a waste. The station after that was nestled between a commercial agricultural business with enormous grain silos and the interstate. The perps had parked somewhere near the silos, outside the view of the gas station's surveillance cameras. After beating up the clerk and robbing the store, they ran to their car and disappeared without ever appearing on film.

The last gas station and convenience, though, was located off Cloverdale's main strip. The perps had punched the clerk, but they hadn't injured him permanently. Since then, he had recovered well and returned to work. I didn't talk to him long, but I interviewed him about what had happened. He said his attackers were men, and they wore the same pine-scented cologne. Unfortunately, he saw no faces, and it happened so quickly, he couldn't even remember whether they were black or white or any shade between.

After our brief interview, Brady and I left the store and walked down the side to the rear. A thin strip of grass and a tall wooden fence separated the commercial strip from a middle-class neighborhood. I could use that. I walked toward the fence, grabbed the top, and jumped so I could see the street beyond. Cookie-cutter houses lined a road that stretched several blocks ahead. A few cars had parked on the street, but most of the residents used their garages. Once I found a street sign, I dropped to the ground, rubbed my hands, and looked to Brady.

"Get your car and find Locust Street. I'll walk."

He looked toward the neighborhood and furrowed his brow.

"You think our perps live there?"

"They may have parked on it," I said. "Since we've turned our suburbs into surveillance states, we might get lucky."

He nodded.

"All right," he said. "Good luck. I'll see you in a few minutes."

I thanked him. Once he went around the building, I grabbed the top of the fence and pulled myself over. My landing on the other side wasn't graceful, but I didn't hurt myself. I was in the backyard of a two-story home with beige siding. The wind whistled through the branches of a redbud tree and a cedar play set. A swing swayed in the breeze. I hung my badge from a lanyard around my neck and headed up the side of the house to the front.

Every home on the street had two stories, a narrow lot, and a big front porch. One had a bright yellow front door and navy blue siding, while most of the others had a more sedate, neutral color scheme. Many of the homes had children's toys on the front lawn and in the flower beds. It was a family neighborhood. That'd help me.

I knocked on a couple of doors myself, but none of

the homeowners could help. Then Brady joined me, and we kept knocking. Finally, we got lucky when we came across a homeowner with a surveillance camera built into his doorbell. We knocked, and a man wearing a bathrobe came out. He was tall and had a goatee, and he carried a cup of coffee. His bloodshot eyes narrowed in the light. He looked stoned, but he smiled when he saw us.

"Hey," he said. "Can I help you?"

"Yeah, I'm Detective Joe Court. My partner is Officer Brady Maddox. We're with the Cloverdale Police Department. You have a minute?"

He sipped his coffee and nodded.

"I hope so," he said. "But who knows what'll happen five minutes from now? A meteor could strike us down."

I would have thought he was trying to be funny, but his lips were thin and straight, and no amusement shone in his eyes.

"Very true," I said. "We're here because of a robbery at the gas station up the road a couple of weeks back. The clerk got beaten up pretty badly."

He sipped his coffee again.

"I heard about that," he said. "He okay?"

"Yeah," I said. "Other people aren't, though. The perps hurt a woman during a recent robbery. We need to stop them before they kill somebody."

The stoner straightened. He was in his mid-forties. Despite his slovenly appearance, the home behind him was clean.

"Jeez," he said. "I didn't know it was that serious."

"It is," I said. "I noticed you've got a surveillance

camera on your doorbell. You keep the footage?"

"Oh, yeah," he said. "It's all backed up on the cloud in case I have to use it in court. Some of my fans get crazy."

"Fans?" I asked, cocking my head to the side.

"I thought that was you," said Brady, nodding. "You're Sir Lancelot."

The stoner bowed.

"Guilty as charged."

I raised my eyebrows.

"Sir Lancelot?"

"In my younger days, I starred in several hundred adult films," he said. "Now, I run a small production company out of the house. You guys like a tour of our facility? We film elsewhere, but I do the cutting and editing here. I used to work in California, but I moved to live closer to my mom. She needs help."

"We don't have time for a tour, but thank you," I said before Brady could say anything. I gave Sir Lancelot the date we were interested in, and he left to get his iPad. Then I looked at Brady and raised my eyebrows. His face reddened.

"I've never seen this guy's movies," he said. "He's famous, though. I try to know famous people who live in Cloverdale."

"I see," I said, nodding. "Any other famous porn stars in town?"

"Not that I know of," he said.

I smiled and nodded but said nothing. His face grew

redder and then even redder until I looked away. Sir Lancelot came back a few minutes later with his iPad. We spent about ten minutes looking at the screen as he searched for the time of the robbery.

And then three men wearing black appeared on the screen, heading toward the convenience store. None looked toward the house, but they were white, and they looked young. None wore a ski mask. Sir Lancelot's camera didn't catch their car, but this was the first lead we had. Once the men passed, we fast-forwarded fifteen minutes for their return. This time, they sprinted, but, again, we couldn't see a car. They must have parked nearer the neighborhood's entrance.

"Can you email this video to me?" I asked. Lancelot nodded.

"Can do," he said. "You need anything else?"

I shook my head and thanked him. He then closed his door while Brady and I headed toward his cruiser.

"Can we ID the suspects from that video?" he asked.

I shook my head.

"No," I said. "So here's what you'll do: put a list together of every convenience store and gas station within ten miles of Cloverdale. Your list will be sizeable, but we can't help that. Contact each store and tell them to look for young, white men. If a clerk sees three or four young white men wearing black, he or she should call the police.

"Once you make those calls, I want you to rewatch the surveillance footage of each of the robberies. This time, pay attention to the parking lots out front. The store's been empty in each robbery. That tells us our perps have a lookout hanging out near the store who tells his buddies when the customers leave. I want you to look for cars and civilians.

"If you see the same car at two scenes, arrest the owner. We'll charge him with everything we can think of and convince him we've got enough to send him to prison for life. He'll roll on his friends, you'll close the case, and I'll retire from law enforcement a hero."

Brady considered and then nodded but said nothing until we reached his car.

"So you weren't a hero in St. Augustine?"

I snorted and shook my head.

"Nope," I said. "I overstayed my welcome and became the villain. I'm not making that mistake again."

He opened his door and then reached across to unlock mine.

"You're a good cop," he said as I opened my door. "Sorry it didn't work out for you in your old place."

"Me, too," I said, sitting down. "Now, if you don't mind, drive me back to my car. I'm going to go home and walk my dog and think. We've got this case in hand. I need to think about a missing girl and how to find her."

14

Brady drove me back to my car at the gas station, and I drove home. The moment I parked in the driveway, though, I knew my walk with Roy wouldn't happen soon. Tonya Cantwell sat on the back steps that led to my rooms in the carriage house. Her eyes looked bloodshot, and she held her head low. A heaviness crept into my chest and arms, and the energy that had flowed through me while working the convenience store robbery ebbed into cold nothingness.

No matter how many murders I investigated, I had never gotten used to seeing that kind of pain. It should hurt to see a mom grieving for her daughter, though. It proved that I was still human.

I forced a tight, comforting smile to my lips as I stepped out of my car.

"Tonya," I said, nodding to her. She stood and wrung her hands in front of her. "Can I help you?"

She looked down. Her shoulders heaved, but she said nothing.

"Would you like a drink?" I asked.

Tonya licked her lips and shook her head as she shuffled her feet.

"The police in Chapel Hill released Ahmed."

"I thought they might," I said, nodding. "Sawyer Cook and I spoke. She and Ahmed were together the night Sallianne disappeared."

Tonya nodded and then exhaled a slow breath as she blinked glassy eyes.

"Is Sallianne alive, or is she dead? She's my baby, and I don't know. Every day brings some new, horrible surprise. I just want to disappear. I don't even know if I should cry for my daughter or if I should get in my car and look for her. Nobody can tell me anything, either. I just want to know. Don't I deserve that?"

My throat tightened, but I couldn't comfort her. That wasn't my place. Instead, I looked down, considering my words.

"The police are doing their best," I said. "They wouldn't have arrested Ahmed except that it looked like he was fleeing the country. He was a good suspect, and they had a strong circumstantial case against him. Unfortunately, it fell apart."

"Is she even dead?" asked Tonya. "I need to know. I can't go on like this."

"I've worked missing-persons cases where the missing person shows up weeks or months later, but they're rare. Sallianne probably isn't coming back. I'm sorry."

She nodded.

"That's what Lieutenant Rathman said." She paused. "He wouldn't tell me what he plans to do next."

He probably didn't know what to do next, but hearing that would only upset her, so I kept my mouth shut.

"I've found someone willing to look for her," she

said. "He's not a detective, but he was in the Army. My brother-in-law knows him. He's not cheap, but he's a good man. He's resourceful, you know? I trust him."

I tried to hide my grimace. Tonya's friend meant well, but if Lieutenant Rathman couldn't find Sallianne with all the resources at his disposal, I doubted a civilian could, either. He'd just give her false hope. It'd be well-intentioned cruelty, but it'd be cruel all the same.

"Before you call in your friend, give me some time," I said. "I'll call Lieutenant Rathman again and see what other leads he might have. I'll see what I can find, too. We won't give up."

She crossed her arms and nodded.

"Okay," she said, her voice so small I almost couldn't hear it. I stepped forward and put a hand on her shoulder. She hesitated and then walked closer. I held her in the driveway, and she cried on my shoulder. We barely knew each other, but we shared the intimacy of grief. I wished I could take that from her.

About twenty minutes after I arrived home, Tonya gave me a key to Sallianne's apartment, hugged me one more time, and then left. My rooms seemed far away, and the steps seemed impossibly steep. I didn't think I could climb up them on my wobbly legs, so I went into the courtyard instead. Ann and Cora must have been in the house or off running errands, but Roy seemed happy to see me. He was lounging on the grass when I walked in, but then he rolled onto his back and put his paws in the air.

I petted his belly and let my mind wander. Tonya Cantwell needed help, and she had come to me for it. There had been times in my life when I had needed help, too, and the people I turned to had barely lifted a finger. They put me in a foster home headed by a monster who had raped the girls under his care. His wife had turned out to be even worse. Neither would hurt anyone else again, but only because I killed him and sent her to prison.

If people had helped me when I needed help most, my life would have been different. Maybe I would have gone to medical school, maybe I would have joined the Navy, maybe I would still be able to trust people…I couldn't say. I deserved help that never came. Tonya needed help now, and I'd be the world's biggest asshole if I didn't do everything I could to find her daughter.

Unfortunately, I wouldn't find anything by reading Lieutenant Rathman's reports. He didn't think like I did, and I didn't think like he did. To find Sallianne, I needed to do my own legwork. I looked at the key Tonya had given me. Sallianne may have spent time in Cloverdale, but the information I needed was in Chapel Hill.

I fed and watered my dog, got in my car, and drove an hour to Sallianne's townhouse. She and Angela Wolner lived in an upscale development about two miles from the University of North Carolina's campus. Each townhouse had its own two-car garage and small outdoor area. The grass was trimmed, and tall shrubs gave the residents privacy. In the parking lot, a little girl rode a bicycle under her father's watchful eye. Both smiled when they saw me. I wondered whether they'd be that cheerful if they understood the grim task ahead of me.

I parked outside Sallianne's condo, hung my badge from a lanyard on my neck, and called Angela Wolner. She answered before her phone finished ringing once.

"Ms. Wolner," I said. "This is Detective Joe Court. We spoke recently about Sallianne Cantwell."

"I remember," she said.

"Good," I said. "I'm outside your apartment now. Tonya Cantwell, Sallianne's mother, has given me permission to search her daughter's room, but I wanted to call you first to let you know I was here."

"Oh, okay," she said. "Thanks, I guess. I'm at my parents' house. Do you need me to let you in?"

"No," I said. "I've got a key. Just wanted to let you know I plan to search the common areas, but I will not touch your room. Sound good?"

"Yeah, but I think you're wasting your time. Lieutenant Rathman already searched, but he didn't find anything."

I nodded and forced a smile to my lips.

"I know, but I'd like to look all the same."

"It's your time to waste. Good luck."

I kept the smile on my face.

"Thank you. I appreciate that," I said. "Just to settle my curiosity, did you know Sawyer Cook and Ahmed Ganim were having an affair?"

She didn't respond for at least half a minute.

"I didn't think it was any of your business."

"I understand your trepidation, but I'm a police officer working a homicide. Everything becomes my business when there's a body on the ground."

Angela paused again.

"Did you find a body?"

"No."

"Then what's the point of this phone call?"

I gritted my teeth before speaking.

"I guess there is none. Have a good one, Ms. Wolner."

I hung up and glowered before opening Sallianne's front door. My search of the apartment took twenty minutes, nineteen of which were wasted. The women had a nice place, but I found no blood, drugs, guns, cash, or anything else interesting at all. Then I went into the home office where Sallianne produced her true-crime podcast. I had known she did her own investigative work for the show, but I hadn't realized how thorough she was from only listening to her podcast.

Based on the files in her cabinet, she must have spent dozens of hours investigating each case she discussed on her show. Sallianne had two dozen files in her cabinet, and each file represented a major unsolved felony she had investigated. Everyone who investigated crime made enemies, and Sallianne had investigated a lot of crimes. Any number of people could have wanted her dead.

This could be a very long night.

15

Since Sallianne had so many files, I drove by an office supply store and purchased cardboard banker's boxes to keep everything organized. After that, I gathered everything and drove home, where I walked and watered my dog and started organizing the files so I could better search them. According to Tonya Cantwell, Sallianne had spent a lot of time in Cloverdale. I didn't know whether her visits were connected to her death, but they were a starting point.

After an hour of reading, I found Sallianne's first mention of Cloverdale in a thick file. Unfortunately, the work was incomplete and disorganized, so I didn't know who or what she was investigating. She did, however, include a topographic map of West County with several locations marked with Xs and interview notes written in shorthand. The file taught me very little, but it gave me a name: Nicole Johnson. Sallianne mentioned her half a dozen times in separate documents. She might have even interviewed her, but I couldn't decipher her shorthand.

I called Chief Tomlin on my cell phone. He answered after four rings.

"Chief, it's Joe Court," I said. "Sorry if I'm interrupting anything, but do you know the name Nicole Johnson?"

The chief paused.

"I realize Cloverdale's a small town, but you don't

expect me to know everybody, do you?"

"No, but I expect you to know the troublemakers," I said. "Before she disappeared, Sallianne Cantwell spent time in Cloverdale. I don't know what she was doing, but her notes mention Nicole Johnson several times. You ever arrested her?"

He chuckled.

"No, but I do happen to know her. She's a kid. Her dad built my deck and some Adirondack chairs He's a good man, but he's a Patriots fan, so we don't get along this time of year."

I shook my head and furrowed my brow.

"What do you mean he's a Patriots fan?"

The chief paused.

"The New England Patriots. They're a football team. Around here, we're good God-fearing folk and cheer for the Carolina Panthers, not those cheating savages from up north."

"Oh," I said. "Okay."

I didn't know what else to say, so I let the conversation lapse into silence. The chief cleared his throat.

"If you're looking for Nicole, I'll swing by her dad's house tomorrow morning and see if I can find her. It's getting late now, and she's got school tomorrow. I don't want to keep her up unless it's an emergency."

"How old is this kid?" I asked, furrowing my brow.

"It's been a while since I've seen her, but she's sixteen or seventeen now. Something like that."

I wouldn't have called a young woman that age a kid, but it made sense.

"This isn't an emergency, so she can wait until tomorrow," I said. "Brady and I spent most of the afternoon working on the convenience store robberies, so he should have an update for you tomorrow morning, too. Sound good with you?"

The chief said yes and then thanked me for my call. I hung up a moment later and stretched my arms above my head before looking to the dog.

"You ready for bed?"

Roy said nothing, which was typical. He was a dog of few words. As he went to the bathroom outside, I opened my laptop and searched for Nicole Johnson on Facebook and Instagram. I didn't find a lot, but I saw a picture of her. She was a pretty girl, but she hadn't posted anything for several weeks. Hopefully the boss would find her.

I closed my laptop, let the dog inside, and went to bed. Within moments, Roy was snoring, but my mind kept traveling back to Sallianne. She had been a pistol, but she had also been smart and driven. If I had met her when she was alive, I probably would have liked her. Even if I hadn't liked her, though, I would have respected her. True integrity was rare, and Sallianne seemed to have had it.

I wondered what people would say about me if I had disappeared as she had. Sallianne had left deep footprints wherever she went. A lot of people loved her. When news of her disappearance had hit the internet, podcast fans from across the country had posted well wishes on her

Facebook page and Instagram account.

I wondered how long it would take for people to realize I was even gone if I disappeared. I had spent the better part of a year trying to erase every track I had ever made. Some days, I thought I had made a mistake, but most of the time, I knew my choice to come to North Carolina was for the best.

I had my dog, my health, and enough money to live on for the rest of my life. One day, if I worked hard enough, maybe I'd even be happy. Until then, I could fake it. That worked for me.

**

Nicole's legs felt so weak she wasn't sure they'd support her if she tried to stand, and her chest felt so heavy, it was almost hard to breathe. Even still, she gripped the pickup's steering wheel and forced her eyes to stay open. She hadn't stopped moving since leaving Hiram Ford's house, and her exhaustion was overcoming her watchfulness. She needed food, water, and eight hours of sleep, but she'd settle for a can of Red Bull and somewhere safe to close her eyes for a few minutes.

She squeezed her steering wheel tight and clenched her jaw as she flicked on the turn signal to enter Braxton Park.

This was Sallianne Cantwell's fault. If that journalist had just done her job and gone to the police, none of this would have happened. She had claimed to have had friends in law enforcement willing to protect her and investigate. If she had called them, they would have found

Hiram's weed and drying barns and arrested him and all the cops who worked for him. The good cops would have gotten promotions, the bad cops would have gone to prison, and Sallianne would have had a hell of a story for her podcast.

Instead, she'd investigated on her own. She had wandered all over Cloverdale and gotten caught on Hiram's trail cameras. It was stupid.

Gravel crunched beneath the truck's tires as the asphalt gave way to stone. Braxton Park was just a big bog on the edge of Cloverdale. Trails crisscrossed the wooded grounds and led to a small, picturesque lake in which locals sometimes fished. She pulled TJ's truck onto the gravel parking lot and maneuvered it into the darkest corner. When cars passed on the main road, their headlights would light up the surrounding woods, but her truck would look like a shadow amidst the trees. She'd be as safe there as she'd be anywhere.

She killed the truck's engine, closed her eyes, and sunk deep into the vinyl seat. Tears trickled down her cheeks despite her best attempts to hold them in. Nicole wanted to blame Sallianne, but in her heart, she knew this whole mess was on her. Sallianne had made a mistake trying to investigate on her own, but she hadn't broken the law. The original sin lay with Nicole. She had brought the monster into the house. She had to deal with it.

Gradually, her breath became easier as exhaustion began to overtake her. Her eyes fluttered shut, and she drifted into darkness.

Then lights lit up the interior of her pickup as a car pulled into the park.

"Shit," she said, sitting upright and reaching for her keys. The newcomer was a cop in a marked cruiser. She stuck a key in the ignition, but before she could turn her wrist, the cop turned on his police lights. She closed her eyes and swore.

The cop parked behind her, blocking her exit, and stepped out of his cruiser. Nicole didn't recognize him, but he didn't draw his gun right away. Instead, he pulled out a flashlight and shone it in the bed of her truck. Then he flashed it in the cab at her. She covered her eyes, and he motioned for her to roll the window down.

"Evening, miss," he said. "There a reason you're parked here this late?"

She considered and then tilted her head to the side.

"Just a nice night," she said. "Thought I'd go stargazing."

"You couldn't do that at your own house?"

The cop was in his forties and had thinning gray hair. He was old enough to see through it if she tried to flirt with him. She needed another tactic.

"My momma and I had a fight," she said. "I just needed some time away. I'm better now. If you move your car, I'll just head home."

The cop nodded.

"This fight get physical?"

"No," said Nicole, shaking her head and smiling. "She doesn't like my boyfriend. You have kids?"

The cop nodded.

"I do," he said. "Can I see your license?"

She tilted her head to the side and forced herself to smile.

"See, that's part of the problem, Officer," she said. "I don't have it on me. Mom and I got into a fight, and I left so quickly I didn't even have the chance to get my purse."

"That is a problem," said the cop. He sighed and looked around. "You got a cell phone on you?"

Again, she shook her head.

"Sorry. It's in my purse," she said. "Which is at home. Mom wouldn't answer, anyway. She's mad at me."

The cop nodded again. His smile was tight, but he nodded.

"I'm sorry to hear you and your mom had a fight," he said, "but I can't let you stay out here in a truck all night— especially if you don't have a license. What's your name and phone number? I'll call and see if I can smooth things over for you. I'm good at talking to moms and dads."

Nicole clenched her jaw. She appreciated that the cop was looking out for her safety, but she didn't need this. If she gave him her name, he'd look her up, and she'd be in handcuffs in moments. It surprised her that he didn't recognize her right away. She had left two bodies—one a cop—in her house. The police should have been there by now, and they should have circulated her picture.

"I don't have to give you my name, do I?"

"It'd be a little hard to call your mom without it," he said, smiling. "If you're not comfortable talking to a man,

I can get a female officer out here. If you're not safe, we can help you. Just let me know."

Terrific. The nicest cop in North Carolina found her hiding out from a drug dealer's hired thugs in a city park, and she couldn't even tell him her name for fear of being arrested for murder. This was a crappy day.

"I'd like to exercise my Fifth Amendment right against self-incrimination."

The cop chuckled.

"I only asked for your name."

"And I've told you all I want to say," she said.

The cop sighed.

"All right, hon," he said, reaching to his belt for a pair of handcuffs. "Step out of the vehicle. The park closed at sunset. I'm arresting you for trespassing."

She cocked her head to the side.

"Can you do that without knowing my name?"

"Yes, ma'am," he said, nodding and reaching for her door handle. "We'll book you as a Jane Doe and take your fingerprints. We will find out who you are."

She swallowed and nodded.

"You already know who I am," she said. "Jane Doe."

The cop sighed and shook his head.

"You're going to force me to fill out a lot of paperwork, honey," he said. "Whatever you're running from, I hope it's worth it."

If it bought her time to think in relative safety, hell yes, it'd be worth it.

"Do I get dinner in jail?"

"If you're hungry, I'll get you something," said the cop, pulling open her door.

"Sign me up," said Nicole, swinging her legs out. "I surrender."

The cop grumbled something, but Nicole couldn't understand what he said. She didn't know how she'd get out of this, but it didn't matter, anyway. She needed a break, and jail seemed like a fine place to spend the night. At least she wouldn't get shot there.

16

My cell rang at a little after midnight, startling me awake. Roy shifted at the end of the bed but resumed snoring. I rubbed my eyes and took a deep breath, hoping to wake myself up before rolling over and reaching to the end table. The caller was Lenny Henderson, a uniformed officer in Cloverdale's department. Prior to becoming a police officer, he had been a youth minister at a Southern Baptist church in town. I didn't know what ended his ministerial career, but he was a good cop. He had a gentle way about him that allowed him to defuse domestic situations before they escalated to violence, and he was great with kids. I couldn't remember him ever calling in the middle of the night.

I cleared my throat and ran a finger across my phone to answer.

"Hey," I said, my voice still soft. "What's up?"

"Hey, Joe," he said. "Sorry to wake you up, but I hear you're working with us full-time now."

I nodded.

"For now," I said. "What's going on?"

"I've got a young woman here I was hoping you could talk to. She's fifteen to eighteen years old, and she looks healthy and well dressed. She's not desperate, and she's not crying. It's kind of weird. She seems happy to be in jail. I got her a sandwich, and she's sleeping now in the holding cell. She won't talk to me, but I thought she might talk to a woman."

I nodded and swung my legs off the bed to sit upright.

"If she's a minor, we need to talk to her parents. Have you called them?"

He drew in a low breath.

"That's the problem," he said. "She refuses to give me her name. She told me she was pleading the Fifth."

I smiled despite the situation.

"She must be a hardened criminal if the mere mention of her name is incriminating."

He laughed.

"She said she had a fight with her mom, but I'd like to make sure there's nothing else going on. Better safe than sorry."

I nodded.

"I agree," I said, blinking sleep from my eyes. "Give me fifteen or twenty minutes. I've got to get dressed."

"Will do," he said. He thanked me and then hung up. Roy raised his head from the bed but didn't otherwise move as I stood. I dressed and brushed my teeth before heading out. The dog would be fine inside for a few hours. He wouldn't even move from the foot of the bed.

When I reached the station, the lights were low, and someone had locked the front door. Lenny let me in.

"She's in the interrogation room now," he said. "And I'll warn you right away: she's a grump."

"I am, too, at this time of day, so I'll forgive her," I said. "Have you done any paperwork on her?"

He shook his head.

"Not yet. I left her pickup in the park. It's registered to Annabelle Macon, but I know her husband, and their daughter's in college now. This isn't her."

"Okay," I said, nodding. "I'll talk to her and see if I can get her name. If I can, I'll take her home. Sound good with you?"

He nodded.

"Sounds like a plan," he said, already heading deeper into the station. As Lenny went to the front desk to wait for incoming calls, I walked through the bullpen to the empty office the department used as an interrogation room. In it, I found a young woman with dark hair sitting with her head down on a heavy wooden desk. I cleared my throat, and she looked up. Then I sighed, having recognized her.

"Hey, Nicole," I said. "I'm Detective Joe Court. I was hoping to talk to you, so I'm glad to meet you."

Nicole opened her brown eyes wide.

"How do you know my name?"

"I'm a detective. I know everything," I said. "How's life treating you?"

Her face paled, and she licked her lips. Her shoulders looked stiff, and her hands trembled. Something had terrified her.

"Did Hiram send you?"

I furrowed my brow and then shook my head.

"Who's Hiram?"

Her mouth opened, but no words came out. Then

she straightened and cocked her head to the side.

"Nobody."

I nodded. We'd circle back to Hiram later.

"Officer Henderson found you in a pickup truck. Was it yours?"

She considered me and then sighed.

"No."

"Whose truck was it?"

She rolled her eyes.

"It's my boyfriend's."

I crossed my arms.

"So your boyfriend is Annabelle Macon?"

The corners of Nicole's lips curled upward.

"Mrs. Macon is my boyfriend's mom. My boyfriend is TJ Macon," she said. She paused and then tilted her head to the side. "I guess he's my ex-boyfriend now that I caught him fucking another girl."

"You must have left an impression on him if he let you use his truck after that."

She pushed back from the table and crossed her arms.

"I deserved compensation for what I saw," she said. "TJ agreed and let me use his truck."

"And if I called him, that's what he'd tell me?"

She shrugged but said nothing. I'd get back to that, too.

"You know Sallianne Cantwell?"

For a split second, every muscle in her body went rigid. The trembling in her fingers stopped, and she held her breath. Then she shrugged, and her shoulders relaxed. I didn't know what her reaction meant, but the name meant something to her.

"I've heard her podcast," she said. "And she's been on the news."

"Have you ever spoken to her?"

Nicole glanced at me but then looked at the table without saying a word.

"Do you know her?" I asked. "Personally, I mean."

Nicole raised her eyebrows.

"She's got a blog," she said. "I've left a comment or two. Does that make me a fan?"

"Maybe it does," I said, nodding. "Would it surprise you to hear that Sallianne seemed to know you well?"

"I'm memorable," said Nicole, tilting her head to the side.

"I see," I said, locking my eyes on her. "She's dead, you know."

I said it to get a reaction, but Nicole didn't even flinch.

"I know," she said. "It sucks."

"You don't seem too broken up about that," I said, pulling out the chair opposite her and sitting at the desk. Nicole tilted her head to the side.

"I'm sorry she's dead, but death is a part of life."

I nodded.

"How'd she die?"

Nicole hesitated and then shrugged.

"I wish I knew," she said. "Her family deserves to

know, I mean."

"They do," I said, nodding. "Her mom asked me to investigate her disappearance. We're not positive she's dead, but the statistics say she likely is. Are you positive she's dead?"

Nicole looked at me and narrowed her eyes.

"What are you asking me?"

"Have you seen her body?" I asked. Nicole pushed herself away from the table and shook her head.

"I didn't kill her. I liked her. She was a nice woman."

I leaned forward, intentionally violating her space.

"If you knew she was nice, you must have known her well," I said, nodding. "How'd you meet? And don't lie and tell me you just commented on her blog."

Nicole closed her eyes and pulled away.

"I don't know her," she said. "I'm just basing my opinion on what I've seen."

"Did you kill her?"

"No," she said, furrowing her brow and shaking her head.

"Did Hiram?" I asked, remembering the name she had brought up earlier. She paused and then shook her head again.

"I don't know anybody named Hiram."

"You mentioned him earlier," I said. "You asked if he sent me. It's odd that you'd mention him if you don't know him."

She paused.

"I mention men I don't know all the time," she said.

"Ask my friends. They'll tell you. I talk about Chris Hemsworth every day. I've never met him, but I'd love to bear his children."

I allowed my lips to curl into a smile.

"Do you want to bear Hiram's children, as well? Is that why you talk about him?"

She considered me and then looked away.

"I've had about enough of this conversation," she said. "It's late, and I'm tired. Plus, I'm a minor. Aren't there rules about interrogating minors this late at night?"

"This isn't an interrogation," I said. "This is a conversation. Did you commit a crime?"

"No."

"You didn't steal your boyfriend's truck?"

She rolled her eyes.

"No. He lets me use his truck when I need to."

I reached into my purse for my cell phone.

"What's your boyfriend's number?"

Nicole drew in a slow breath and then shrugged.

"Off the top of my head, I don't remember."

"I bet Officer Henderson confiscated your phone when he picked you up," I said, pushing back from the desk to stand. "I'll just go get it, and you can look him up."

She shook her head and raised her eyebrows.

"I won't call him. It's late."

"So you refuse to cooperate with my investigation."

She scoffed and shook her head.

"This is a bullshit investigation, and you know it. I

did nothing wrong. I was just trying to relax in the park when your officer picked me up. Going to a public park isn't a crime, is it?"

"Not when the park is open, but Officer Henderson caught you there after it closed. That means you were trespassing."

She screwed up her face and shook her head.

"You can't trespass at a public park. That's what makes it public."

"Just like you can't go to the library when it's closed, you can't go to a public park when it's closed," I said. "You trespassed and refused to give the arresting officer your name. Lenny's a nice guy. He would have just driven you home if you had told him your name. You didn't, so now you're sitting in jail facing charges. And you've got a choice to make: you can continue to lie to me, or you can tell me the truth and go home to sleep in your own bed."

She looked away.

"I don't have a home."

"Where did you sleep last night?" I asked.

"My friend Rose's house."

I nodded and crossed my arms.

"Do you sleep there often?"

She considered.

"No. I stay at my mom and dad's house most nights, but they're not home."

"Can you contact them?" I asked. She shook her head, so I sighed. "I'm going to level with you: Our station isn't set up to house a juvenile overnight. Do you have any relatives we can call?"

She leaned forward.

"Can't you just let me go?"

I shook my head.

"You're a minor, so no," I said. "If you don't have an aunt or uncle who can take custody of you for the night, here's your other option: You can stay on my couch, and we'll talk tomorrow morning about Sallianne Cantwell, Hiram, this fight you had with your mom, and why you were sitting inside your boyfriend's truck in the parking lot of a public park. That's the best I can do."

She narrowed her eyes.

"Shouldn't you talk to your husband about taking a strange girl home with you?"

"I'm not married," I said. "The couch will be all yours."

"All right," she said. "You've got a deal. You give me a place to stay, and we'll talk tomorrow."

She held out her hand for me to shake. I took it and squeezed hard.

"I'm glad to help you out," I said, "but if you run, I'll hunt you down and turn you over to the police in Chapel Hill as a person of interest in Sallianne Cantwell's disappearance. They will not be as nice as I am. Clear?"

She nodded.

"Clear."

"Okay," I said, standing. "Come on. Let's get going. It's late, and I'm tired."

17

I got Sherry Johnson's phone number from Chief Tomlin and called, but she didn't answer. I left a message on her voicemail to let her know I had her daughter in custody and that I needed to talk to her as soon as I could. After that, Nicole and I climbed into my Volvo and drove home. Neither of us had much to say until I parked in the driveway and glanced at her.

"You hungry? I've got some bread and lunch meat if you want a sandwich."

"The old guy bought me dinner from Wendy's," she said. "It was the only place open."

Lenny was about forty-five, so I wouldn't have called him old, but I nodded anyway.

"Good," I said, turning off my car and nodding toward the garage. "I live in the carriage house."

She followed me up the stairs to my place but then stopped and gasped when Roy barked and jumped up. He put his paws on the window and panted excitedly.

"You've got a dog?"

"He's friendly unless you wake him up in the middle of the night by trying to escape," I said. "Then he gets cranky."

"Good to know," she said, nodding and raising her eyebrows.

Roy seemed excited at the prospect of having a houseguest—especially one who smelled like food from

Wendy's—but Nicole wasn't used to having a big dog around. She'd get over it, though. As long as she didn't leave, he wouldn't bother her.

I made a bed on the sofa and got a pillow from my bedroom. Nicole had claimed she was fine, but she started snoring the moment I turned off the light. Whatever she was into, she was in over her head. Hopefully she'd talk to me about it tomorrow morning.

I went to bed, slept fitfully, and then woke up at a little after six when Roy whined and stretched on the end of the bed. I let him outside so he could use the restroom. Nicole was still asleep on the couch, so I tried to make as little noise as I could while I made coffee.

Unless something happened with Brady's investigation into the convenience store robberies, Roy and I would spend the day in the woods, checking out the sites that Sallianne had marked on the maps I took from her room. We might even find her body. I didn't relish the thought of finding her, but I had to prepare for it.

While Nicole slept, I read through the documents I had taken from Sallianne's apartment again. At a little after seven, Roy stood and walked to the hallway and whined. A moment after that, Nicole knocked on my doorframe. Despite sleeping overnight, she looked as if she could have slept another eight or ten hours and still been exhausted. I smiled.

"Morning," I said. "There's coffee in the kitchen. How are you feeling?"

"Fine," she said, crossing her arms and looking

around the room. "So this is where you live?"

"Temporarily," I said. She nodded.

"It's cozy," she said, smiling. "Is there somewhere I can shower?"

"Of course," I said. "The hallway has two doors. The bathroom's on the left. You can get a washcloth and towel from the linen closet on the right."

"Thank you," she said, ducking her head and turning.

"Once you're done, I'd like to talk to you about Sallianne," I said. "Then I'll run you by your house. I'd like to talk to your parents, too."

She nodded but didn't turn to look at me.

"Sure."

She shut the bathroom door, and I grabbed my coffee and went to the living room. Nicole had already folded the blanket and sheet I had given her last night and stacked the pillow on top. Roy followed me into the kitchen and then looked at his bowl and back to me again.

"You've already eaten, buddy," I said. "You can't convince me you didn't."

He sat beside his bowl and locked his eyes on me. I sighed, but I couldn't help smiling on the inside. Some dogs loved belly scratches, while others loved toys. My dog loved food. It didn't matter whose food it was or whether it was bread, meat, fruit, or vegetable. If it had calories, my dog wanted it.

"You want a cookie?"

He shot to his feet and panted. I snickered and then opened a bag of peanut butter dog cookies I kept in the freezer. The treats had four ingredients: pumpkin puree, peanut butter, eggs, and coconut flour. They were grain-free and healthy, and Roy loved them. I wasn't a big cook, but they made the dog happy, so I made a batch once a month.

I made him sit again, and his tail swished back and forth. When I held out my hand with a cookie, he took it and then ran off as if he feared I'd take it back. Roy was just a dog, but he was one of the few steady presences in my life. Our friendship was simple: I gave him food, and he loved me. I wish all my relationships could be that easy.

I freshened up my coffee and grabbed the documents from my bedroom so I could plan my day. Roy sat outside the bathroom with his head cocked to the side as he listened to Nicole inside. At first, it was kind of funny, but then he didn't move. The water was running, so at least Nicole wouldn't have heard him panting outside.

"She's in the shower," I said, my voice low. "Leave her alone, you perv."

Roy looked at me but then focused on the door again with his tongue sticking out as he panted.

"Do you do this when I shower, too?" I asked. This time, Roy didn't pay attention to me at all. He cocked his head to the side and furrowed his brow as if he were curious. I sighed and walked toward him, intending to grab him so he wouldn't scare Nicole when she came out of the shower. Then I heard a clatter from inside. I hesitated and then rapped on the door.

"You okay, Nicole?" I called. "I heard something."

She didn't answer, so I knocked again.

"Nicole?" I asked. Again, she didn't answer, so I knocked a third time. "If you don't answer, I'll open the door to make sure you're okay."

The water was running, but she should have heard me. I sighed and looked to the dog before trying the doorknob. She had locked it—which wasn't surprising—so I grabbed a small screwdriver from the kitchen and popped it open. The moment I got into the bathroom, my stomach fell, and I clenched my jaw.

"You little brat," I said, reaching into the shower to turn off the water. Nicole had disappeared. I lived on the second floor, which I had assumed would discourage anyone from trying to climb out the window. And maybe it did for most people. Some kids—like Nicole—were too smart for their own good, though, because she had pulled the curtain rod from the shower and used it as a cross brace over the window. She had then thrown the shower curtain outside and used that to climb down. When she let go, the curtain rod must have fallen, making the clatter that had drawn me inside.

I sighed and stuck my head out the window, but she was gone. At least she hadn't stolen my car. I shut the window, left the bathroom, and called my station to let them know what happened. My boss planned to go by Nicole's house that morning, anyway, so he said he'd look out for her.

After that, I clenched my jaw and swore a lot before

mopping up the water on the floor and getting my bathroom back in order. I had been nice to Nicole and given her the benefit of my doubt, but that wouldn't happen again. The next time I saw her, she'd sleep in an orange jumpsuit in jail.

Before leaving, I put up my shower curtain again so I could rinse off. Then I ate a bowl of cereal, glowered a lot, and loaded Roy into my Volvo and set off. I had six sites around the area to examine, and all of them looked remote and wooded. At least I'd get some exercise.

18

Detective Court had seemed like a nice lady with good intentions, but people like her had paved the road to Hell. Or something like that. Nicole couldn't remember the exact quote. It didn't matter, though. She had to move.

The detective lived about three blocks from a Methodist church with a big sign out front that announced a pancake breakfast and prayer service from eight to eleven in the morning. The lot held a dozen cars, most of which were too new for her purposes. Toward the far end, though, she found an older model Ford. The owner was a trusting sort because she hadn't locked it. Or maybe she suspected no one would steal a twenty-five-year-old Taurus. It didn't matter. Nicole hurried toward the vehicle and peered around the lot before pulling the door open.

Her heart thumped in her chest, and her fingers trembled. Thick grayish-blue velour covered the vehicle's seats and interior door panels. Where most vehicles of that vintage had rusted wheel wells, chipped paint, and an interior decorated with Diet Coke cans and dirt, this one was clean. It was probably an old lady's car, one she drove to church and bridge club and back home again.

Nicole put her backpack on the passenger seat and pulled out the small pocketknife she kept inside. TJ may have been a lousy boyfriend, and he may have had difficulty keeping his fly zipped around pretty girls, but he knew more about cars than she ever would. When her daddy bought her a car, TJ had shown her how to take care of it. He had also showed her how to break in and start the engine in emergencies if she lost the keys.

She opened her pocketknife and leaned down to unscrew the plastic panel beneath the steering wheel that held the ignition wiring. Then she stopped when her eyes caught the glint of something metal beneath the front seat.

"You've got to be kidding me," she said, reaching down for the key ring hidden there. She straightened, put the key in the ignition, and twisted her wrist. That was easier than she expected. She returned her pocketknife to the backpack and reversed out of her spot.

As she drove, Nicole drummed her fingers on the steering wheel. Her gut didn't feel right, and she kept biting the inside of her lip. The stolen Taurus had a full tank of gas, and she had a lot of money in her backpack. She could drive to Florida and start a new life. She still had TJ's phone, so she could use that to find someone willing to make her a fake ID. She'd pretend to be eighteen and work as a waitress. Then, in a few years, she'd go to community college. They let everybody in, so they wouldn't check her high school transcript and find out she had run away from home.

If she left, though, she'd leave her dad and TJ for dead. She loved her dad all the way. He didn't deserve to die in Hiram Ford's basement. Neither did beautiful, stupid TJ. He may not have had an ounce of common sense or a single industrious bone in his body, but he had abs you could wash your clothes on, and one day— probably in the not-too-distant future—he'd impregnate some vapid young lady and make her small-town dreams come true by marrying her. His life would be like a John Mellencamp song. He didn't deserve to get mixed up in her mess.

Nicole drove two or three miles and then pulled into Walmart's parking lot, where she called Detective Court's cell phone. The detective let it ring and go to voicemail. She was probably still at home, trying to figure out why Nicole was taking such a long shower, so she called back. This time, the detective picked up on the third ring.

"Hey, Detective," said Nicole. "It's Nicole. I bet you're wondering how I'm calling you from the shower."

Detective Court grunted.

"That question never crossed my mind," she said. "If you're in the mood to make calls, contact a lawyer, not me."

"Am I in trouble?" she asked.

"You tore my shower curtain and got water all over my floor," said the detective. "Aside from that, I was thinking of swearing out a warrant for your arrest."

"On what charge?" she asked, her voice strident.

"At the moment, you're my primary suspect in the disappearance of Sallianne Cantwell. Now go kiss your boyfriend, because the next time you see him, you're both going to have white hair and wrinkles."

She clenched her jaw for a moment.

"My boyfriend is being held captive by the same man who murdered Sallianne."

Detective Court paused.

"Okay," she said. "Tell me more. What's going on?"

Nicole's hands trembled, but she fought to keep the quiver from her voice. She drew in a breath.

"You're looking for Hiram Ford. He's not who you think he is. He looks like a nice old man, but he's a real shit bag. And he's got a lot of cops who work for him, so you've got to watch out."

The detective paused.

"If I ask around about Hiram Ford, what will people tell me?"

"I don't know. I'm just telling you how it is. The guy is dangerous, and he's got my boyfriend and my daddy. And he murdered my momma. That's why she didn't answer when you called. Momma was a bitch, but she didn't deserve to die like that."

Again, the detective paused. Nicole gripped the steering wheel and held her breath.

"If you're lying to me, I will send you to prison."

Nicole clenched her jaw.

"I'm not lying," she said. "This is why I didn't tell you earlier. You wouldn't have believed me."

"I believe you're a young lady who got into something over her head," said the detective. She paused. "Please turn yourself in. It's not too late to do the right thing and talk to me."

"Fine," said Nicole. "If you want me, you'll find me

at Hiram Ford's house. That's where my daddy and boyfriend are, too. You'll see."

She gave the detective Hiram's address and then hung up, hoping she had done the right thing. Hiram was dangerous, and his goons had guns, but she had warned Detective Court. That was all she could do. Surely, she'd bring backup.

Nicole pulled out of the lot, drove toward Hiram's cabin, and then parked on the side of the road in the spot in which TJ had parked when he went looking for her. She locked the doors and pocketed the keys before hurrying through the woods toward Hiram's house. She didn't know how Detective Court would handle this. If she went in with guns blazing, Hiram's men would overpower her. That'd be bad, but it'd bring in a lot of other law enforcement agencies. They'd forget all about her.

If Detective Court went in tentatively, though, Hiram's goons might shoot her before she had the chance to draw her weapon. Detective Court didn't know it, but she needed backup. Nicole would do what she could.

She crept toward the big cabin but slowed as she neared it. The last time she had been there, Hiram's truck had waited in the driveway, and smoke had curled from the chimney. It had looked like a comfortable home in the woods. Now, it looked abandoned.

Nicole hid and waited, a sinking feeling in her gut. About ten minutes after she arrived, a Volvo pulled into the driveway. Detective Court stepped out and cast her eyes around the woods, but nobody came from the home.

Hiram must have left.

"Shit," said Nicole, beneath her breath. She needed to escape before the detective found her, so she hurried back through the woods as Detective Court pounded on the cabin's front door. As she reached her stolen car, her phone rang. She answered without looking at it.

"Nicole," said Detective Court, her voice sweet. "Did you lie to me about Hiram Ford?"

"Sorry," she said. "Situations change. You seem like a nice lady, but I've got to find my dad and TJ."

"Running from me is a bad idea, Nicole," said the detective.

"I know," said Nicole. "But I don't have a choice. Good luck."

She hung up and tossed the phone beside her as she turned the car on and put it into gear. Now Nicole would have Hiram and the police after her. It was only a matter of time before one of them caught her, but it didn't matter. She had family and an ex-boyfriend to save. Her future could wait.

19

So that pissed me off.

By calling me to Hiram Ford's house and then disappearing, Nicole had intentionally wasted my time. Even though I worked in a small town, I had two major cases to work: the convenience store robberies and Sallianne Cantwell. I had shit to do. Driving across town to random cabins in the woods did not fit into my schedule.

When I got back to my car, I clenched my jaw tight and then called Chief Tomlin. He answered on the second ring.

"Boss, it's Joe Court. I just got a call from Nicole Johnson. She told me to meet her at a cabin owned by Hiram Ford. She wasn't there, but I thought you should know."

"Sorry to hear that," said Tomlin. "Did Hiram at least offer you a cup of coffee? He's got a lot of fancy stuff."

"Good for him," I said. "He wasn't home, either. I pounded on his door, but nobody answered. What do you know about him?"

"What do you mean? He's Hiram. He's an old man."

I allowed myself to sink into my seat and focus on Nicole.

"Nicole told me Hiram had murdered her mother and abducted her boyfriend and father."

For a second, the boss said nothing. Then he laughed

aloud.

"Sounds like Nicole's having fun with you," he said. "Hiram is a lot of things, but he's not a murderer. He's a rich old man who lives alone."

I nodded and drew in a breath.

"You know him well?"

"Well enough," said the boss.

"Why would she tell me he's a murderer?"

The boss paused.

"Are you at his house right now?

"Yeah."

"Then do me a favor and look around," said Tomlin. "Describe the area."

I gritted my teeth, looked around, and sighed.

"It's a cabin. There are a bunch of trees. What else do you want me to say?"

"That's plenty," said Tomlin. "Hiram lives in the middle of nowhere. Nicole lured you out there so she could escape. She and her boyfriend are probably out having a good time and laughing at you right now. Teenagers suck."

I gritted my teeth and nodded.

"Little brat used my shower curtain to climb out my bathroom window this morning."

The boss laughed.

"You seem surprised," he said. "Weren't you ever a teenager?"

I forced myself to smile.

"A long time ago," I said. "I'm trying to forget it."

"Well," said the boss, drawing in a breath, "I'll tell the guys to be on the lookout for Nicole. You have other work to do?"

"Yeah," I said, nodding and looking over my shoulder to Roy, who was lying on a hammock strewn over the rear seats of my Volvo station wagon. The dog perked up at my gaze and seemed to smile, but he didn't stand. "I'm searching for Sallianne Cantwell. She had a map in her home office that had locations around Cloverdale marked off. I'll check them out. Maybe we'll find her body."

Tomlin drew in a breath.

"Sounds good. I'm sorry about Nicole, but I'll let you know when we find her. And good luck on your search. Part of me hopes you don't find Ms. Cantwell, but a bigger part of me hopes you do. Her family ought to be able to bury her properly."

I agreed and thanked him before hanging up. Nicole had pissed me off, but my colleagues could deal with her. I had better things to do, so I put the car in gear and headed toward my first search location. It was a clear day, and the woods beside my car when I parked were dark but inviting. The air smelled clean. If nothing else, the dog and I would get some exercise.

I brought a leash, but Roy was well trained, so I didn't put it on. He trotted by my side as I walked through virgin forest. A thick layer of pine needles and leaves covered the ground. Little vegetation grew between the trees to trip us up or slow us down, so we made good time.

Every few minutes, I stopped to look at my cell

phone to make sure we were on the right track. As we neared the location, Roy started stopping every couple of feet and lifting his nose as the wind shifted. About a quarter mile later, I caught the first acrid whiff of smoldering leaves and burning pine needles. Then, I recognized another smell: marijuana.

Eventually, Roy and I emerged in a small forest glade of two or three acres. Trees ringed the clearing, but fire had blackened the ground and burned nearly every plant inside. The charred remnants of a shed protruded from the earth to my right. Roy and I followed the tree line around the burn and found areas where the ground had been dug, presumably to prevent the fire from spreading. This was no accident. The person who burned this field knew what he was doing.

I took pictures of everything with my cell phone. Near the remnants of the shed, I found a path that someone had beaten through the woods. That led to the road on which I had parked. Tires had crushed the greenery down on a makeshift parking lot, but rain had washed away any tracks that would help me identify the vehicle of whoever tended the field. I followed the road to my car and called my boss. Unfortunately, his phone went to voicemail.

"Chief, it's Joe Court. I took a walk through the woods and found a marijuana field. Someone torched it. I don't know how you want to handle this, so call me back."

I waited a moment, but the chief didn't call. So I checked out the second location, another glade deep in the woods. It, too, had once contained marijuana, and it, too, had been burned. I took a couple dozen pictures before heading to the third site, where I found another field. The boss called as I drove back to town. I pulled onto the side of the road before answering.

"Hey," I said. "I found two more fields. Someone torched them both."

The chief paused and then sighed.

"Did you find Sallianne, too?"

"No," I said. He drew in a breath and sighed.

"You sure they were marijuana fields? People sometimes burn their fields to clear them to make gardens."

"No, they burned marijuana," I said. "The smell is pretty distinct. I took pictures of everything."

The boss sighed yet again.

"Okay. We'll bring in the State Bureau of Investigation. Send me what you've got, and I'll forward it to the right people. If someone's growing that much marijuana in Cloverdale, we'll need their help."

"Will do," I said. "I've got a couple more locations to check out. Based on the pictures I've seen on Google Maps, at least one of them looks like a building out in the middle of nowhere."

The chief swore again and then wished me luck.

"You find Nicole Johnson yet?" I asked before he could hang up.

He grunted.

"Sorry, no," he said. "I've been on crowd control at a

residential fire all morning. A family lost their house out on Jackson Road. It looks like a grease fire that got out of control."

"I'm sorry to hear that," I said, pausing. "Since I'm on the clock, I'll check out a few more locations, and then I'll swing by Nicole's house. With luck, she'll be there. She owes me a shower curtain."

He chuckled.

"Good luck, Joe," he said. "I'll call my contact at the SBI. I hope your shower curtain dreams come true."

"Thanks," I said. I got back on the road, but this time, I didn't drive far before coming to my location. It was much closer to the road than the earlier spots had been, and it had a driveway that ended at an old wooden barn. There was no house nearby, but I parked and walked around the structure. Like the other locations, it was private and remote.

I walked into the open building and found ropes hung from the rafters. Even with major cracks in the clapboard siding and no doors, the interior smelled almost overpoweringly of marijuana. There were leaves and a few buds on the ground, and empty burlap sacks and bags of fertilizer stacked in the far corner. They must have grown the weed in the fields, dried and bagged it here, and then sent it elsewhere for further processing before selling it on the streets.

I snapped pictures with my cell phone before getting back in my car with the dog. I'd talk to the boss when I got back to my station. Until then, Nicole Johnson had a lot of questions to answer.

I drove to her home. No car waited in the driveway, and no light shone from inside. I didn't hold out a lot of hope that anyone would be home, but I got Roy out and knocked on the front door, anyway.

"Nicole! You in there?"

No one answered, so I peered through the glass panel beside the door. Blood pooled on the floor in the entryway. Drag marks led deeper into the house. I unholstered my weapon and stepped back before grabbing my phone and calling Chief Tomlin again.

"Boss, it's Joe Court. I'm at the home of Nicole Johnson. There's a significant quantity of blood on the ground and a trail that leads deeper into the house. I'm going in to make sure we don't have anyone injured inside. Please send me some help."

"I'm on my way. I'll bring everybody I can find."

"Thanks."

I hung up, put my phone in my purse, and then kicked the door near the handle. The frame and structure shuddered but held. Then I kicked again, and the wood around the deadbolt cracked. When I kicked a third time, the door swung open. The house smelled putrid, but I couldn't focus on that.

"Police officer!" I shouted. "Anybody home?"

Roy and I went in. He sniffed and bounded deeper into the house. He was a trained cadaver dog, and I suspected he had just put that training to good use. If he had run into somebody alive, he would have growled, but he remained silent.

"Police officer!" I shouted. "If you can hear me, come to the entryway."

Nobody came or shouted, so I crept through the house. As expected, Roy had found a body. It belonged to a woman in her early to mid-thirties. She lay on her belly in the kitchen and had multiple gunshot wounds on her back. It looked as if she had crawled there. I cleared the house before going through a rear door to the backyard. A statue of a naked woman lay on the ground, but I couldn't find signs of forced entry.

Roy and I walked around the house to the front and waited in the driveway. Charlotte Matthews arrived in a cruiser about ten minutes later. The chief arrived about a minute afterward. Each of them took one look inside and said they'd rather wait until the house aired out some before going in. I couldn't blame them. It smelled foul.

"You found a body," said Charlotte. "Was she an attractive woman with blond hair? Maybe a little older than you?"

I nodded, and Charlotte looked to the boss.

"Sounds like Sherry Johnson."

The chief looked toward the house and sighed. Then he focused on Charlotte.

"We need Bobby," he said. "He's got the most forensic training of anyone on staff. And call the county medical examiner. I'll call the State Bureau of Investigation." He paused and looked at me. "Unless you think we can handle this one in-house?"

I shook my head.

"No. We need all the help we can get," I said. "The killer shot the victim in the back and dragged her down the hallway. Nicole Johnson told me Hiram Ford had murdered her mom. You think he could have done this?"

Tomlin shook his head.

"He's an old man who owns a bunch of gas stations and bars and things like that," he said. "He also gives a boatload of money and food to the county food bank. Without him, families would go hungry."

"So how do you want me to handle him?" I asked.

"Do you have anything connecting him to this murder except Nicole's word?"

I shook my head.

"No."

"Do you trust Nicole?" asked Tomlin.

"No," I said, "but even if she's lying, why would she pick Hiram's name? She could have picked a teacher, her vice principal, or anyone she disliked. She didn't even have to give me a name."

The chief sighed.

"Hiram's a businessman, so he hires and fires a lot of people," he said. "For all we know, he might have fired one of her friends. It doesn't matter, though. Your job is to follow the evidence, and you don't have any against Hiram except Nicole Johnson's word."

"Let's find her, then," I said, nodding. "And update the sheriff's department and Highway Patrol and whoever else you've notified about her. Now she's a suspect in a murder."

20

Kit had known very little about the other convenience stores he and his friends had robbed, but today was different. Trystan had woken him and the other guys up at a little after eight and forced Kit to drive everyone to a little house in Cloverdale. Paint peeled off the clapboard siding, and the wrought-iron handrail on the concrete steps out front tilted to the side. As they drove past, a woman in jeans and a T-shirt struggled to get a little boy with blond hair into a Kia sedan in the driveway.

"That, gentlemen, is Nancy Fowler, and she works at the gas station on Fifteenth Street in Cloverdale. Her son has autism. The boy's dad is no longer in the picture. We're going to rob her store this morning."

Kit rolled the Land Rover past the home but didn't slow. He glanced at the small, stooped woman and then looked in the rearview mirror to Trystan.

"Why'd you take us by her house?"

"To show you she's not a threat," said Trystan. "She's a single mom, and she'd do anything for her little boy. She won't fight back."

An empty feeling began to grow in the pit of Kit's stomach, and his skin tingled.

"Don't hurt her," he said, his voice soft. The other guys laughed.

"Grow up, Kit," said Trystan, still chuckling. "Rory, Max, you know your jobs. Kit, turn right and pull over. I'll be taking your keys. You have an active role today."

Kit's shoulders tensed, and the hairs on the back of his neck began lifting. His gut felt as if he had just stepped off a building.

"No," he said. "If you want to rob the store, that's on you. I'm just the driver."

"Time for the baby bird to flap his wings," said Rory. "Giddy up, motherfucker. You're popping your cherry today."

"Last time we did this, you said I'd just be the driver," said Kit, looking in his rearview mirror to Trystan. "I like driving. I'm good at it. Besides, this is my car."

"You're a fine driver," said Trystan. "And today, you'll be a fine door holder. That's your job. You're like that guy on *Game of Thrones*. Afterward, I'll drive us into the sunset, and we'll all get drunk. If you do well, I'll introduce you to Mia and get you laid."

"Nancy Fowler hasn't done anything," he said. "She's just a checkout girl at the convenience store."

"Sounds like Kit's got a crush," said Max. "You like older women, buddy?"

"I won't let you guys hurt her," he said. "That's it. End of story. And I'm not pulling over."

Before he realized what was happening, the car went quiet. Something hard jabbed the back of Kit's neck.

"Re-evaluate your position," said Trystan.

Kit reached behind him to slap away whatever Trystan had pushed against him. His hand brushed against the barrel of a firearm. His entire body stiffened, and he drew in a sharp breath. A wave of dizziness washed over him.

"What the fuck are you doing?" he asked gasping. "You don't need to do this. Put the gun away."

"Beg, motherfucker," said Rory. "You want to live, beg for mercy."

"Now, now, Rory," said Trystan, his voice soft. "This is Kit's choice. Don't antagonize him."

Kit's heart raced, and his eyes were wide. His arms felt so heavy he could hardly grasp the steering wheel, and then his vision started growing dim at the periphery. It was like he couldn't get enough air. His lungs felt tight.

"Just breathe, dude," said Max. "You pass out while driving, you'll kill us all."

Kit nodded and forced his lungs to suck in air.

"It's time you earned your spot on the team," asked Trystan. "This is an opportunity to help yourself. You're either with us, or you're against us. What's it going to be?"

"I'm with you," said Kit. "Just put the gun away."

The pressure on his neck abated.

"Good," said Trystan. "Now you've just got to prove it."

Kit looked in the rearview mirror and watched as Trystan slipped the pistol into his pocket. He felt sick. There was a big oak tree beside the road. Rory was in the front seat, and he wasn't wearing a seat belt. If Kit rammed that tree hard enough, maybe Rory would go flying through the window. Even if it didn't kill him, that'd put him out of commission for a while. It'd also end their misadventures for the day.

Kit wasn't like Trystan, though. He didn't have the guts to hurt anyone. So he drove past the tree without stopping.

"What do you want me to do?" Kit asked.

"Drive to the gas station on Fifteenth and find a hiding spot," said Trystan. "You, Rory, and Max are going to rob the store. You just have to hold the door. You won't even have a gun. Rory and Max will do all the hard work."

"Will I have a mask?" he asked.

The guys chuckled. Trystan nodded.

"Yeah. You think we want to get caught?"

"I don't know," he said. "Maybe you want me to get caught."

"No. I've got big plans for you," said Trystan. "You're too valuable to lose now. So drive. If you do your job, this will be just fine. But if you try to do something stupid, I'll shoot you in the back of the head, set your car on fire to destroy the evidence, and then I'll introduce Rory to your little sister at your funeral."

Kit sat straighter and looked to Rory. He grinned.

"My sister's a kid," said Kit. "Stay away from her."

"I like 'em young," said Rory. "I'll be gentle and break her in slowly. Don't worry."

Kit slowed the car and pulled to the curb. Everybody had a breaking point. Trystan had found his. Kit looked at Rory before turning and handing his keys to Trystan.

"If I ever see any of you near my sister, I'll kill you

and have my father's security team hide your bodies."

They laughed. Trystan reached forward and squeezed his shoulder.

"I'm sure you would," said Trystan. "Now get out of the car."

Kit did as Trystan ordered. After that, Trystan drove. Then they parked and waited. Nancy made coffee and walked around the small store, tidying up the aisles. It was a lousy job, but she did it with a smile on her face. Somehow, he had to keep the other guys from hurting her.

At about ten, the morning rush abated. Trystan drove to a side street two blocks away. Rory, Kit, and Max got out of the car.

"There's a camera behind the register," he said. "Get in and get out. I'll be here waiting for you. Approach from the rear and wear your masks. I'll tell you when to go."

"We know the drill," said Max, reaching into a backpack and pulling out four ski masks and handing them to each of the young men in the car. Then he pulled out a green bottle of cologne and sprayed it on his neck, hands, and chest before handing it to Rory, who did the same. A pungent pine scent filled the car.

"What's with the cologne?" asked Kit, taking the bottle from Rory's hand.

"Just put it on, shitbag," said Rory. "Do as we say, and you won't get caught."

Kit hesitated and sprayed some on the exposed skin of his neck. It burned, indicating it had a high alcohol content. At least it would dissipate soon, so he wouldn't have to smell like the inside of a taxi all day.

"When your body sees or feels something, the sense information is first routed through your thalamus before being sent to other parts of your brain," said Trystan, glancing in the rearview mirror. "Smell is different. It skips the thalamus and proceeds to the olfactory bulb, which is connected directly to the amygdala and hippocampus. That's why you can smell your grandma's perfume and feel like she's sitting beside you even if she's been dead for years. By putting on cheap aftershave, we overpower the senses of everyone in the store so their memories aren't tripped if they see and smell us later."

"Who would have thought paying attention in Dr. Jacobson's neuropsychology class would pay off?" asked Rory, chuckling. Everyone but Kit laughed. His heart pounded.

"You okay, Kit?" asked Max. "You look like you're going to puke."

"I'm fine," said Kit, breathing in deeply and slowly.

"Good. Because if you puke and leave DNA evidence behind, we'll shoot you," said Rory. "So hold your vomit like a real man."

Max and Trystan laughed. They sounded like jackals.

"Everybody get in position," said Rory. "Remember your job, Kit. Hold the door and watch for people."

"Got it," said Kit.

"Relax. You'll do fine," said Trystan. "Good luck."

Kit nodded, but he couldn't have relaxed even if he

had wanted to. Rory didn't give him time to think about what lay ahead because he opened his door and hurried down the street, already pulling his mask over his head. Max followed a second later. Kit ran to keep up.

The convenience store wasn't far. They stayed outside for a few minutes until Trystan gave them the signal. By then, Kit had so much adrenaline flowing through him he felt almost nothing. Nancy stood near the rear of the store beside a display of cigarettes, dirty magazines, and liquor bottles. Kit held the front door open while Rory and Max ran inside. Unlike on previous trips, Max had a backpack. Rory had a gun, which he pointed at the woman. She held her hands up and opened her eyes and mouth wide.

"Get the fuck out!" he screamed. Nancy seemed rooted in the spot. Her face grew paler. "Fucking move!"

Max vaulted around the end of the counter and grabbed her by the arm and pulled. That seemed to wake her from her stupor. She stumbled forward and crouched low.

"Don't do this," she said. "Please, don't do this. I've already called 911."

"Get the fuck out," said Rory. Max shoved her from behind. She caught herself on the counter, knocking over a plastic stand full of lottery tickets. Max slung his backpack off his shoulders. Nancy didn't move toward the door. Rory would kill her if she didn't leave, so Kit grabbed a rubber wedge from the sidewalk outside and shoved it beneath the door to hold it open. Then he went in and grabbed Nancy's arm.

"Come on," he whispered. "You've got to go, or they'll hurt you."

"But I can't…"

"Run," said Kit, pulling hard. When they reached the front of the store, he shoved her toward the pumps. "If you don't move, they'll kill you and orphan your son."

Her eyes narrowed, but then she turned and ran with her hands over her head. When Kit turned and looked inside the store again, he found Max pulling a bottle with a rag stuffed in its neck from his backpack. Rory lit the rag with a cigarette lighter and then ran toward the door as Max tossed the Molotov cocktail at an aisle with motor oil and other automotive supplies.

The glass shattered, and flames covered the display. Rory grabbed Kit's arm as he ran past.

"Run, dude!"

Kit didn't need the encouragement. He followed Rory toward the rendezvous point with Max a few feet behind them. When they reached the car, all three of them dove inside, and Trystan pulled away from the curb as if he were out for a Sunday drive. Max and Rory laughed.

"Did you see that chick's face?" asked Max. "She almost shit herself."

"I thought I'd have to shoot her," said Rory. "If Kit hadn't grabbed her, there'd be a lot of charred townie right now."

Trystan looked at them from the rearview mirror.

"You left your post?" he asked, looking at Kit.

"He read the situation and did his job," said Rory. "You would have been proud of him. He propped the door open and grabbed her before she could call the cops."

Trystan considered him and then nodded.

"Good. We'll double back in a few minutes to watch the place burn. You feel good, Kit? Sounds like you saved that townie's life."

"Yeah, I'm good," he said, still sucking in deep breaths. He swallowed and considered what they wanted him to say. "We should have grabbed some liquor before we left. They had it behind the counter."

"I like how this guy thinks," said Rory. "We should have grabbed the booze."

"We'll get drunk later," said Trystan. "First, we've got work to do and a cop to kill. Stick to the plan, and we'll all be fine."

Trystan paused and looked in the mirror.

"And Kit, I'm proud of you. I'm introducing you to Mia tonight. You've earned her."

Kit didn't know how he felt about a girl being offered as a reward for service, but at least no one had died. He had kept Nancy safe. That wouldn't keep him out of prison, but it'd keep him from death row for now. That had to be enough until he figured out how to stop these guys from killing a cop or hurting his family.

21

The blood spatter in the front entryway and floor had given me exigent circumstances to walk through Nicole Johnson's home and search for anyone hurt inside, but it didn't give me the legal right to open drawers, move furniture or collect evidence. So, after clearing the house and making sure it was empty, Chief Tomlin, Charlotte, and I left. The chief then went to talk to the county prosecutor and get a search warrant, leaving me and Charlotte to secure the scene and body inside.

The nearest home was about a quarter of a mile away. A woman who was a few years younger than me sat on the front porch with a book in her lap while her young son played with big yellow trucks in the mulch in her flower beds. The little boy smiled and waved at me and Roy before his mom noticed us. She was polite, and her little boy was adorable, but she hadn't seen or heard anything out of the ordinary. When I asked whether she had ever heard Nicole and her mother fighting, she asked whether I had ever fought with my mother when I was a teenager. I took that as a yes, so I thanked her and walked to the next few houses. Unfortunately, nobody else was home, so I walked back to Nicole's house.

It was probably seventy-five degrees, but the ever-present humidity made it seem hotter. By the time I reached the Johnsons' home again, sweat beaded on my brow, and Roy panted. The chief had come back and was talking to Charlotte, so I led Roy to my car and gave him some water in a cheap plastic bowl. Once the dog had his fill, he plopped down in the shade on a bed of pine needles near my car. If I'd had any other dog, I would have put a leash on him and tied it to a low-hanging branch. Roy, though, wasn't going anywhere. The boss waved me over after that.

"Roy and I visited the neighbors," I said. "Nobody was home to the east, but the lady who lives in the house to the west hasn't seen or heard anything unusual for the past few days. Did you get the search warrant?"

"The prosecutor's getting it signed now," he said. "In the meantime, I need you to get to the Qwick Stop on Fifteenth Street in Cloverdale. Brady's on his way now. I don't have details, but it was just robbed."

I swore under my breath and nodded.

"They kill anybody this time?"

"They let the clerk go," said Tomlin. "She called 911."

"Okay," I said, sighing. "If you find anything interesting here, keep me informed."

"You, too," he said. "Good luck, Detective."

I thanked him and then hurried Roy into the back of my Volvo. Since I didn't want to drag a dog around to a crime scene, I dropped him off at home before heading toward the gas station and convenience store. Even miles away, though, I knew we had a problem: a black plume of smoke rose from the ground, and as I grew closer, I smelled the greasy stink of burning building supplies. Then I saw the flashing red and white lights of a fire truck.

"Shit," I said, pulling to a stop in the parking lot of a shopping center about a block from the store. I took out my phone and dialed Brady's number while I jogged to the address. "I'm parked by the Family Dollar, and I'm running toward the building. What's going on?"

"I see you," he said. "I'm across the street outside the apartment building. No need to run. The fire department is keeping people away in case the gas tanks catch. The perps torched the place."

I looked across the four-lane street in front of the store to an apartment complex with brown siding and a lawn that had more brown spots than green. Brady waved at me from beside a marked police cruiser in the small parking lot out front. I told him I'd be right over before slipping my phone into my pocket and checking the traffic for an opening.

"What happened?" I asked once I reached my partner on the case. "Chief Tomlin didn't have a lot of details."

He grimaced and looked toward the gas station. It had six gas pumps and a brick storefront. Advertisements for cheap beer and cigarettes covered the windows, while a rack of propane tanks covered the wall nearest the front door. The fire department had covered the ground in a foot of white fire-retardant foam, while they fought to contain the fire that had already consumed most of the store. A pair of paramedics had parked an ambulance on the edge of the property, but they weren't moving to help anyone.

"They've graduated to murder."

I looked down and blew out a long breath before furrowing my brow and looking at him again.

"I thought they let the clerk go."

Brady nodded toward his cruiser. A young woman sat on the backseat. Tears streamed from her puffy, red eyes, and she held her arms tight across her chest.

"That's Nancy Fowler," he said. "She's the store clerk. About two minutes before the robbery, she spotted three men in black clothing and ski masks trying to sneak up behind the building on a closed-circuit camera system. A woman and her son were buying sodas inside, so Ms. Fowler hurried them to a back office, where they'd be safe during a robbery. She then came out and called 911.

"When the bad guys came in, she tried to tell them she had already called 911, but they pulled their guns and told her to get out of the store. One robber then grabbed her and shoved her. He said that if she didn't leave, they'd kill her and orphan her son."

That got my attention. I cocked my head to the side.

"Does she have a son?"

Brady nodded.

"Six-year-old boy. He's in kindergarten at the special school."

I brought a hand to my face as I thought.

"So they not only scouted the store out, they scouted her," I said. "What about the people she hid inside the office?"

"That's the problem," he said. "Ms. Fowler doesn't

know what happened, but she ran out to the road called 911 again. The call went to the county sheriff's department, but the nearest deputy was at least ten minutes away. I was closer, so I came with my lights and siren going. When I got here, the building was burning, and she was on her hands and knees, crying. She told me what happened."

Their deaths weren't Ms. Fowler's fault, but the tears made sense now. My chest felt heavy, and my face had grown warm.

"Is there any chance they're alive?"

"Fire department tried to go in, but the roof collapsed on them," said Brady. "Nobody in that office is still alive. The fire burned through the building in minutes."

I brought a hand to my face and swore aloud.

"And you said it was a mom and her kid?"

Brady nodded. No matter who the victims were, they didn't deserve to die. The muscles of my shoulders, back, and jaw tightened, and a knot began growing in the pit of my stomach. I didn't have kids or a husband, but I couldn't imagine losing my spouse and my child on the same day like that.

Neither Brady nor I said anything for a few minutes, and gradually, cold anger began to overcome my initial shock. Intentional or not, these assholes had murdered a child. Hell had a special place for people like that.

"You okay, Joe?" asked Brady a moment later. I glanced at him and tried to banish my melancholy thoughts.

"I'm fine."

He nodded and drew in a breath.

"You have kids?"

I thought of my brothers, Ian and Dylan, and my sister, Audrey. Then I thought of Ann and Cora. Then I shook my head.

"No."

"Your eyes kind of went dark there," said Brady.

"The world's a dark place. I fit in," I said, forcing myself to look at anything but the gas station. "Okay, so we'll work this assuming the two victims inside are deceased. I need you to take Ms. Fowler to our station for a formal, recorded interview. Make sure somebody picks up her son from school, too, so he doesn't feel like somebody's forgotten him. Do we have any idea who the victims inside are?"

Brady jotted down notes on a notepad but shook his head.

"I interviewed Ms. Fowler, but she said they weren't regulars. She didn't know their names."

I sighed and looked toward the gas station, considering.

"There's only one car in the station's lot," I said. "I can't see the plate from here, but have one of the firefighters write down the license plate number. Unless the victims walked there, that should be their car. We can send Lenny Henderson by their house to do the next-of-kin notification."

"He's good at those," said Brady. "He's got ministerial and bereavement training, so people respond to him well. The chief usually goes with him."

"Good. Get Tomlin, too," I said, nodding. "We'll need people to canvass this neighborhood. I want surveillance footage from the traffic lights and every business around here with cameras. And someone needs to check out Ms. Fowler's neighborhood. The perps know her well enough to know she's got a son, so we need to ask around and see if her neighbors have noticed anybody lurking around."

Brady wrote notes and focused on his notepad for a second before glancing at me.

"We need help," he said. "You mind if I call the county sheriff's department?"

"Will they take orders from a woman?"

Brady paused and straightened.

"I'll make sure they know you're in charge," he said.

That wasn't what I had asked, but it didn't matter. As long as they listened to someone and did what they were told, we'd be fine.

"Good. You know what to do," I said. "This is a homicide investigation now. Call your wife and let her know you won't be coming home soon. We've got work to do."

22

Kit, Trystan, Max, and Rory sat, transfixed and silent, as the convenience store burned. Kit had been a felon since the first robbery, but this one felt different. His heart thudded against his rib cage, he felt breathless, and skin all over his body tingled. He felt more alive than he had ever felt in his life. His hands trembled, and he almost felt giddy. He had smoked weed and gotten drunk, but the feeling coursing through him was better than any artificial high he had ever experienced.

"I think the kid liked getting out of the car for once," said Max, nodding toward Kit. "He's smiling like he just got his first blow job."

The guys laughed. Kit tried to hide his smile, but his lips refused to listen to his brain.

"Shut up," he said. The guys laughed again.

"First time feels the best," said Rory. "When I did it the first time, I smiled for a week."

"You still talking about armed robbery?" asked Max.

"Nope," said Rory, laughing. Even Kit snorted with laughter. And why shouldn't he laugh? Nobody got hurt, they didn't get caught, and the gas station's insurance company would pay for the damage. It was a victimless crime.

"So what now?" he asked. "Do we just stay here? Do we celebrate somewhere? What do we do?"

Rory and Max looked to Trystan, who was still sitting

in the driver's seat. Their leader had a somber look on his face. The smiles left everyone's lips.

"I'm glad you guys are having fun," he said, "but that's not why we're here. Don't forget: This is work. We're here for the blonde. If she's on this case, she'll show up soon."

That brought Kit back to reality. He had almost felt proud of himself for getting Nancy Fowler out of the convenience store, but he hadn't done anything worthy of pride. The robbery was part one of a reconnaissance mission. Trystan wanted information on the detective who was working the case so they could kill her.

The car went silent. After the robbery, the guys had piled into Kit's SUV, and Trystan had driven them two blocks from the gas station to watch. This time, Trystan had brought two pairs of binoculars. The fire had started small, but it engulfed the entire station within moments. If Kit hadn't seen it happen, he wouldn't have believed a fire could spread that quickly.

By the time the fire department arrived, the roof had already started collapsing. They tried to go in, but a big section of roof fell before they could get more than a few feet inside. After that, they hosed down the exterior and then focused on spraying foam over the parking lot so that it looked almost like a puffy, white cloud.

A few minutes after the fire department arrived, Trystan pointed up the road.

"She's there," he said. "She parked by the dollar store, and now she's running."

Rory perked up.

"I could watch her tits bounce as she runs all day," he said, focusing the second set of binoculars on the cop. Kit and Max both snickered. Trystan didn't crack a smile.

"She stopped running," said Trystan. He paused. "Now she's going across the street. There's another cop there."

Kit didn't feel as if he needed a play-by-play, but he said nothing. For the next few moments, Trystan narrated as the blond cop spoke to a uniformed officer. For a while, nothing happened. Then, a minivan pulled into the parking lot beside the two cops. Kit couldn't see it well, but both Trystan and Rory sucked in a breath.

"Fuck," said Rory, his voice low.

"This changes nothing," said Trystan.

Kit wanted to ask what they saw, but neither he nor Max said anything as the scene unfolded. A guy in a blue jumpsuit got out of the minivan's driver's seat and opened the rear door. He pulled a gurney from the back, and Kit felt his stomach fall.

"Shit," he whispered.

"Is that the fucking medical examiner?" asked Max.

"It's fine," said Trystan. "We left nothing behind they can trace to us. Even if somebody died, nothing changes."

Kit's hands started trembling again, but this time, it wasn't because of his adrenaline. His stomach roiled, and he almost felt as if he was going to vomit. He hit the button to roll down his window to get some fresh air. For a moment, nobody said anything. Then Kit realized something. He furrowed his brow and looked to Trystan.

"You said the store was clear," he said, his voice low. "You said the customers had left."

Trystan looked back.

"It doesn't matter."

"Yes, it does," said Kit. "You knew what Rory and Max would do, but you told us the store was empty. It wasn't. There were people in there."

Rory shifted but said nothing. Trystan's gaze went cold as he looked at Kit.

"Max and Rory wouldn't have done anything if you hadn't held the door," he said. "You dragged Nancy out. This is on you, not me."

"This is why you wanted me on this job," said Kit, shaking his head. "You wanted to be the lookout, so you'd know customers were in the store when we robbed it. You wanted people to die."

Trystan considered and softened his expression.

"I wanted witnesses for the cops to interview," he said. "I didn't think anybody would die. I thought they went out the back."

"That's bullshit," said Kit. "You wanted them in there. You wanted them to die because you thought that'd bring the girl cop."

Trystan put the binoculars back to his eyes and focused on the crime scene again. The air in the SUV felt thick. A heavy weight seemed to press on Kit's shoulders. He felt ill.

"If Trystan says he thought they went out the back,

he means it," said Max. He hesitated. "Right, Trystan?"

Trystan said nothing. The car plunged into an uncomfortable silence.

"You're a fucking murderer," said Kit. "And I want you out of my car."

Trystan turned and lowered the binoculars.

"I didn't go into the store, I didn't hold the door, and I didn't drag anybody out," he said, shaking his head. "That was all you. You're the murderer, Kit. Nobody forced you to do anything. This was your choice."

Kit's mouth opened, and he blinked.

"You son of a bitch," he said. "This morning, you put a gun to my head and told me that if I didn't go along with your plan, you'd shoot me, burn my car, and introduce Rory to my sister at my funeral. How was any of this my choice?"

Rory snickered and shifted on his seat, but Trystan didn't react.

"I don't remember doing any of that," he said before looking to Rory and then Max. "Do you remember that?"

Both guys hesitated before shaking their heads.

"No," said Max, his voice soft.

"I don't, either," said Rory, reaching back to run a hand over Kit's cheek. Kit pulled away, and Rory smiled. "I wouldn't mind meeting your sister, though, especially if her skin is as soft as yours. Do you moisturize?"

"Fuck you," said Kit. He shook his head. "Fuck all you guys."

Trystan lifted his binoculars again and focused on the

crime scene.

"I appreciate that you're upset, but we're partners now," he said. "This is a war, Kit, and in war, people die. The blond cop is our enemy and our target. Make no mistake: She wants us dead. If we give her even a single iota of a chance, she'll take it and gun us down in our sleep. If we don't kill her, she'll kill us. It's simple logic. Now are you with us?"

Rory and Max locked their eyes on him. Kit didn't want to answer, but he knew he had to. They'd kill him otherwise. So he nodded.

"Yeah, I guess I am."

"Good," said Trystan. "Now pay attention. You have a role to play in the job ahead, and none of us can afford you fucking it up."

23

It looked as if the fire department had the fire under control, so I waited for a break in traffic and crossed the street. Cloverdale had a volunteer fire department that handled most emergencies around town, but these guys were the professionals from the county. A balding man in a navy fireman's uniform walked toward me with his hand outstretched. He was fifty or fifty-five, and unlike most of the other men, he didn't carry a helmet or compressed air tank on his back.

"I'm Detective Joe Court with the Cloverdale Police Department," I said, shaking his hand. "Is it safe to be here?"

"Yeah, we're good now," he said, nodding and looking over his shoulder. "I'm Lieutenant David Blackburn with the West County Fire Department. We've got the fire controlled, but it's still too hot to go in there without protective gear."

"That's all right," I said. "I'm sure Officer Maddox told you, but the store clerk told us there were two people inside."

Blackburn sighed and ran a hand across his brow as he nodded.

"We heard," he said. "Before we could go in, the roof started collapsing on us. We tried cutting through the wall behind the store, but that collapsed, too. You should arrest the contractor who built this place for negligent homicide. There's not even a fire block to prevent the fire from igniting the ceiling rafters. This building was a disaster waiting to happen. I'm glad there weren't more people inside when it went up."

"That's something to be thankful for," I said. "Can you tell me about the fire itself? Could it have been an accident?"

He hesitated.

"It's possible, but I doubt it," he said. "The fire spread too quickly. Based on what my guys saw inside, the fire started near a shelf containing automotive supplies. Motor oil has a flash point of somewhere between four hundred and four hundred and fifty degrees, so it takes a lot of heat to get it started. Once it lit, though, the fire burned hot enough to ignite antifreeze and brake fluid. From there, it hit the ceiling rafters and started burning the insulation. No one in the office stood a chance. Once the place cools down and I have the chance to examine the crime scene firsthand, I'll have more concrete answers."

"I'd appreciate that," I said. "I won't take more of your time. Good luck."

"You, too, Detective," he said, nodding. I left the gas station and walked back across the street. Brady was on the phone, but he finished his call and looked at his notepad.

"Hey, boss," he said. "The county is sending me two uniformed officers and two detectives. Unless you have other thoughts, I plan to send the two detectives to Ms.

Fowler's neighborhood, and I'll have the uniformed officers canvass the street here. If anybody has surveillance cameras or saw the robbery, we should know soon enough. Chief Tomlin's trying to track down Lenny. Meanwhile, I was planning to take Ms. Fowler back to the station to interview her in front of a camera."

"Sounds like you've got everything under control," I said. "Do we have the surveillance video from the other robberies somewhere?"

He nodded and told me where I could find it on the department's cloud server.

"Sounds good," I said. "You take care of Ms. Fowler. I'll wait here until the county officers arrive. Once they do, I'll meet you back at the station to put together a video montage we can show Ms. Fowler. I want to see if she recognizes the perps from the other robberies."

"But they never show their faces."

"True," I said, nodding, "but you can tell a lot by their movements and how they interact. We don't need enough for an ID in court; I'm just looking for confirmation that the guys who robbed her store robbed the other stores, too."

He said he understood and wished me luck. I watched the unfolding scene across the street as he and Ms. Fowler drove off. The fire was out. It'd be awhile before anyone could get in, but already a van from the state medical examiner's office had arrived, and a technician had removed a gurney from the vehicle's back. That brought everything into focus again.

A woman and her child had died in that fire.

Before moving into Ann's guest house, I had spent little time around children and hadn't given them much thought. I'd always assumed that somewhere along the line, I'd get married and maybe have a few kids of my own, but those plans were abstract and nebulous. Now, after living near and babysitting a wonderful little girl every day while her mother was at work, the plans didn't seem so far off, and the child who died in that fire didn't seem so abstract.

As I waited, my phone rang. I answered without looking at the caller ID.

"Hey, it's Joe," I said. "What's up?"

"Hey, honey," said a familiar, feminine voice. "It's your mom… it's Julia Green. How are you?"

I hadn't expected to hear her voice. A tight knot began forming in the pit of my stomach. I licked my lips.

"Hey, Julia," I said, softening my voice. "I need to keep this line free. I'm working, and I expect my boss to call me any moment."

"Oh, you're working," she said. "I didn't know you had a job. I thought you were just touring the country."

"It's temporary," I said. "Roy and I were driving for a while, but we're settled for now. Everything's okay."

Julia said nothing for a few moments. Then she drew in a breath.

"What kind of work are you doing?"

I forced a smile to my lips and hoped she heard it through my voice.

"Police work," I said. "For the past couple of

months, I've volunteered as a reserve officer, but now I'm taking a temporary full-time assignment as a detective. The town needed help with some convenience store robberies and a missing-persons case. Now, my robbery case has turned into a double homicide investigation. A woman and her child just died in a fire. It's awful, so I need to get going."

Julia paused.

"That's awful. I've got something to tell you, but I'll just call you later."

I looked up and down the street but couldn't see any marked patrol vehicles from the sheriff's department.

"I can give you, maybe, two minutes," I said. "Is everything okay?"

She paused.

"Yeah. Everybody's healthy. We're all good."

I nodded and sat in the front seat of my Volvo.

"Your voice doesn't sound okay," I said.

"I'm nervous," she said. She paused and drew in a breath. "I've been seeing a therapist for the past couple of months. She's been encouraging me to make this call."

My stomach tightened just a little.

"Okay," I said. "What's going on?"

"I love you," said Julia. "You're my daughter. We come from different worlds, but you're special to me. You know that, right?"

The tightness in my gut traveled upwards to my throat. I nodded and looked down.

"Yeah. You're special to me, too."

Julia paused.

"I can't keep going like this. When you left, you broke my heart, and since then, you've pushed me away every time I've tried to get close to you. I didn't even know you had settled down somewhere, and apparently you've been there for months. You're working a double murder, and I didn't even know had a job. Where are you? Are you even in Missouri?"

My eyes felt wet, and every muscle in my body felt heavy. I wanted to tell her I was angry at her, but I didn't know why, that I had thought about the situation but hurt every time, and that I had finally stopped picking at old wounds to let them heal. I loved Julia. She had rescued me when I needed rescuing. I wished I knew why I couldn't talk to her now.

"I'm at the scene of a double murder, and a state medical examiner is waiting outside a gas station so he can wheel out a woman and her child," I said. "We'll talk when I've got less on my plate."

"I'm sorry life hasn't been kinder to you, sweetheart," said Julia. "I hope you get to see some nicer sides of life, too."

I swallowed a lump in my throat.

"We'll talk later, okay?" I said. "I love you."

"I love you, too."

I hung up a second later and stayed still in my car. For months, I had avoided thinking about the reasons I left St. Augustine, but my past had a weird way of invading my present. I didn't want to think about it now, but I couldn't turn my back on it forever. Eventually, it'd catch up to me. But not today. I had too much shit to do.

I waited another ten minutes for a pair of detectives from the county sheriff's office to arrive. After introducing myself and filling them in on the situation, they agreed to canvass Ms. Fowler's neighborhood to see whether her neighbors had seen anything strange. After that, I drove to my station and settled in front of a computer screen. I had a lot of footage to view, but as I played it, I kept thinking of my conversation with Julia.

She was right: I had pushed her away, and I didn't even know why. Julia was my mom. She hadn't given birth to me, but she had raised me and taken care of me when I needed her. Before I'd had the strength to care about anyone else, she and her husband had loved me.

I didn't want to lose her, but it hurt to think of her. Maybe one day I'd understand that, but I didn't just yet. It didn't matter, though; I was a cop, and I had a murder to investigate. My personal life could wait.

24

I spent the next two hours watching every video we had from the robberies. So far, I had focused on the videos from the exterior, hoping they'd show us the robbers' getaway vehicles. They didn't, though. The real break came from a video taken from a surveillance camera at the third robbery. The owner of that store worried that his employees would steal from the register, so he positioned two very high quality surveillance cameras directly behind it.

One of our bad guys wore a ring imprinted with some kind of logo on his right index finger. I zoomed the video in as tight as I could and then adjusted the contrast to better see the emblem imprinted on the silver. It was a snake wrapped around a sword. Above that was a circle with a line across its center.

I leaned back in my chair and heard it creak beneath me. I hadn't seen that exact symbol before, but I had worked in a college town long enough to recognize a fraternity's seal. That circle with the slash through it didn't represent a zero; it was the Greek letter theta. Our murderers were college kids.

I pulled out my keyboard and opened a web browser to search for fraternity emblems. Within five minutes, I was staring at the home page of the Theta Chi Nu fraternity. The fraternity had over a hundred chapters, mostly in southern colleges and universities, four of which were in North Carolina. I minimized my browser and opened another video from another robbery. The resolution was poor, but it looked like two robbers had Theta Chi Nu rings.

I went back to the fraternity's web page. Theta Chi Nu had chapters at Duke University, Davidson College, Wake Forest University, and Newman-Rothschild University. All four schools were private and expensive, and all four were within a two-hour drive of Cloverdale. We could use this.

With so many young people living together, college campuses had unique public safety concerns, so most colleges—both private and public—had their own police forces, most of which had the same powers of arrest as regular law enforcement officers.

I got the phone numbers from each of the schools, but before calling their public safety offices, I called Brady.

"Brady, it's Joe Court. I've got a lead on our bad guys. At least two of them are college students in the Theta Chi Nu fraternity."

"So you've ID'd them?" he asked, sounding impressed.

"Not yet, but I'm getting close. I need you back here."

He paused.

"Give me a few minutes. I just dropped Nancy Fowler off at her house. Her parents were there already with her little boy, so she's squared away. Did Officer Hoxie call you yet?"

I shook my head.

"No. Never even heard of him."

"He's a uniformed officer with the West County Sheriff's Department. He and his partner walked up and down Fifteenth Street to look for surveillance cameras and got video from the liquor store at the corner of Fifteenth and Robert E. Lee Drive. It's about two blocks from Qwick Stop, and it shows four men wearing black in a white SUV two blocks from the store a few minutes after it burned."

I might have dismissed it had I not seen a white SUV following me a few days ago.

"They didn't get a license plate, did they?"

"Nah," he said, "and the video's so grainy they can't even get the make of the vehicle. It's big, it has four doors, and it's white."

"It's good enough," I said. "Tell Detective Hoxie I owe him a bottle of scotch. Get back here. With any luck, we'll make some arrests tonight."

"Will do," he said. "See you in a few."

I thanked him and hung up. Then I started calling the public safety offices at the colleges with Theta Chi Nu chapters. Most of the schools were helpful. Almost two dozen students at Duke University had registered white SUVs, but the public safety office didn't have a fraternity directory. They said they'd get in touch with the student affairs office and see what they could find. Wake Forest University was about a third the size of Duke and only had four white SUVs registered to students, none of which were registered to members of the Theta Chi Nu fraternity. The guy at Davidson College told me its chapter of the Theta Chi Nu fraternity had closed three years ago for multiple and egregious violations of the student code of conduct, particularly its sections against hazing. The public safety office at Newman-Rothschild University didn't even answer the phone. We'd circle back to them later.

When Brady arrived, I showed him the video. He seemed impressed.

"How'd you know that was a fraternity ring?"

"St. Augustine was a college town," I said. "I arrested a young woman from the college after she murdered a guy in a fraternity. He wore a similar signet ring."

Brady frowned and nodded.

"That little town of yours doesn't seem like somewhere I'd want to send my daughter to college."

I tilted my head to the side and shrugged.

"I wouldn't, either," I said. "That's life, though. No matter how much shit you shovel, somebody's always making more. Sometimes it's better just to move on."

"I'll take your word for it," he said. "The security guys at Duke get back to you yet?"

I shook my head.

"Nope, but I think they will," I said. "What do you know about Newman-Rothschild?"

He considered me and then straightened.

"I went to East Carolina University in Greenville," he said. "Newman-Rothschild was way out of my price range."

"So it's expensive," I said.

"My parents and I were broke, but yeah, it was expensive," he said. "Tuition plus room and board'll run you fifty or sixty grand a year. They didn't give too many scholarships, either. That was their trademark. They wanted to keep the riffraff out."

That tracked with some of my thoughts about our bad guys earlier. At each robbery, they had hit the register for whatever cash it held, but they had never asked about a safe or vault in the back office. Instead, they stole liquor. These guys weren't after money; they robbed and hurt people because they thought it was fun. I'd enjoy seeing their faces when I put them in prison.

I looked to Brady.

"We're driving to Newman-Rothschild University. Let's put the fear of God into some rich kids."

**

The school was ninety miles west of Cloverdale in the foothills of the Blue Ridge Mountains and had the almost cookie-cutter Georgian architecture common to many private liberal arts universities with money. Had I been a high school student who saw those buildings on recruitment brochures, I would have found the campus charming, maybe even beautiful. Knowing what I did about the school, I found its imposing brick walls and wrought-iron front gate disquieting.

Brady had driven, while I navigated. Neither of us knew anything about the campus, so it took fifteen minutes of aimless driving to find the residential section of campus and then the Theta Chi Nu fraternity house. Thankfully, it was time well spent. The moment we pulled into the fraternity house's parking lot, we found a white Land Rover SUV with a student's parking pass on the back window.

Without saying a word, Brady stopped behind the vehicle and typed the license plate number into his cruiser's laptop.

"The car is registered to Jameson Investments, Inc.," he said. "They're based in Charlotte."

"Not as helpful as I had hoped," I said, nodding. "Check to see if it's been involved in any arrests."

"Already on it," he said, continuing to type. "The car's been pulled over twice in the past six months. Once on suspicion of drunk driving and once for going seventy in a fifty-five mile-per-hour zone. Driver on both occasions was Kit Jameson. He's eighteen."

I crossed my arms and nodded.

"So if he's here, he's a freshman," I said. "Let's see what the Office of Public Safety has to say about him."

Brady nodded and drove. The Office of Public Safety occupied a Cape Cod style home that had been painted a stark white. Lavender plants lined a brick walkway to the bright yellow front door. Even at night, it looked cheery. It would have been a little small for a family with kids, but I could imagine a young professor and her husband living there quite comfortably.

Brady and I walked toward the door and knocked

before sticking our heads inside. Dark gray slate covered the floor and fluorescent lights buzzed from the ceiling, casting the entire room in an almost eerie bluish-white light. A female uniformed officer sat behind a dark wooden desk. She blinked when she saw us and shut the novel she had been reading.

"Can I see some ID, please?" she asked.

I smiled and unhooked my badge from my belt.

"I'm Detective Joe Court with the Cloverdale Police Department. With me is Officer Brady Maddox, also of the Cloverdale Police Department. We're here because we're investigating a double homicide, and we'd like to talk to one of your students."

I had expected her to gasp or at least sit straighter. Instead, she blinked and raised an eyebrow.

"Do you have an arrest warrant?"

"No," I said, shaking my head. "Our investigation is still in its early stages. We're just here to talk. I don't plan to make an arrest unless something drastic happens."

She nodded. Her lips curled into a tight smile, but no goodwill reached her eyes.

"When you're closer to the tail end of your investigation and have a court order, we'll cooperate. Until then, please leave the campus. This is private property. I'd hate to arrest you for trespassing."

I smiled and ignored her request.

"We'd like to talk to Kit Jameson," I said. "Can you give us his phone number?"

She shook her head.

"I'm not allowed to do that," she said, already typing at her computer. She looked up a moment later. "I've got the name of his family's attorney, though, if you'd like to talk to him."

I opened my eyes a little wider.

"Do you stonewall all investigations into students on campus, or is that a service you only provide to those students whose parents have money?"

The officer smiled and blinked but didn't take the bait.

"Kit Jameson is a person of interest in a double homicide," I said, speaking slowly. "He burned a mother and her child to death."

"Can you prove that?" asked the officer, leaning forward and raising her eyebrows.

"Not yet," I said.

"Then my hands are tied," she said, standing and nodding toward the door. "You're standing on private property. Please leave."

"I need to talk to him," I said.

"Unless you have a warrant, that won't happen on our property. Now please leave."

If I had thought it would get me anywhere, I would have asked to speak to her supervisor. She didn't order me off campus on her own authority, though. She was taking orders from someone else. I looked to Brady.

"Okay, Officer Maddox," I said. "I guess we're out of here."

He nodded, and we left the building. As we walked

toward his cruiser, he glanced at me.

"What now?"

"We improvise," I said. "It'll be a long night."

25

Hiram had stash houses, drying barns, and marijuana fields all over West County, and he could have hidden TJ and Nicole's dad at any of them. Every spot she had tried so far, though, had been empty. Now, dirt caked her arms and face, her back ached, the sun had been down for hours, and her feet seemed to grow heavier with every step she took.

This never should have happened. Hiram had grown weed for years, and he had never hurt any of his girls. He had been a good boss. That was why the local public pool never had enough lifeguards, why the ice cream shop out on Twelfth Street never had enough help in the summer, and why moms and dads had to pay girls from Greensboro big money to drive to Cloverdale to babysit in the summer.

In any given summer, Hiram hired fifteen to twenty girls to grow and process dope for him and another twenty or thirty high school kids to work in his legitimate businesses. Hiram sucked up all the local talent and had paid the college tuition of half the girls in West County. In a town like Cloverdale, where the local high school only had a hundred and forty kids, that was a big deal. The jobs he provided became the lifeline that lifted a lot of young people out of poverty. Nicole had trusted him. Now, she wanted him dead.

She stopped and leaned against a tree. Not a single

cloud blotted the night sky. Stars stretched from one end of the horizon to the other, and the moon, heavy and white, cast long shadows on the ground where the overhead canopy of leaves grew thin. Even with the big Maglite she had found in her stolen car, she could barely see the trail anymore.

Nicole leaned forward and rested her hands on her knees and breathed in the night air. The sun had set hours earlier, and the night had started to grow cool. She needed to start thinking about shelter before it got too much colder.

She should have gotten a job watching kids at the pool or folding laundry at Soap 'n Suds. Her paycheck would have been small, but the job wouldn't have left her skulking through the woods, looking for her dad and cheating boyfriend. Instead, she'd taken a job that paid well, and now her mom was dead, and she had murdered a cop. The cop deserved what he got, but her mom wasn't a bad person.

Nicole swallowed the lump in her throat and pulled TJ's cell phone from her pocket. According to her map, she was a quarter mile from one of Hiram's smaller fields, but unlike the previous fields she had scouted, she couldn't smell smoke yet. Maybe this one was still intact.

Nicole sighed and straightened and kept walking. She had made the trip to her own garden so often she had known every tree, shrub, and gnarled root on the path from the shed to her car, but she had only walked to this field once, and that had been to show Claire Stockton around. Hiram had ultimately decided to let the field go fallow for the season, but Claire was a good worker elsewhere. Hiram had been lucky to hire her.

Gradually, the woods around Nicole thinned as she walked, and more starlight fell to the ground until she emerged in an open field with waist-high grass and an old wooden shed on the far end. No one had planted a thing on the property, and nobody stood guard outside the shed. She didn't expect to find her daddy or TJ in that shed, but she crossed the field anyway and peered inside.

Nothing.

Nicole sighed and opened her phone to search for the next property. It was a drying barn about a mile away through the woods.

Nicole had never considered herself an outdoorsy person, but she had grown to love the woods after working inside them for the summer. They were peaceful. Even after fighting with her mom or arguing with TJ or worrying and talking to her dad about college, she could walk in the woods and feel the leaves caress her skin and hear the birds sing and feel the insects buzz past her as they flew on their way, and she'd know her problems didn't matter. The trees around her had germinated and grown before her own parents even hooked up in the back of her daddy's pickup, and they'd survive long after she went into the earth. The entire world was like that. Compared to something that big, she didn't matter at all.

Nicole crossed the field and entered the woods beyond. A narrow, rutted trail led from the field to the drying barn, but it was so dark, she had to use her phone and flashlight to search and make sure she was on the right track every twenty or thirty yards. Then, the woods parted, and she saw the old barn in front of her.

When TV shows and movies took pictures of old barns, they were almost always painted red and white, and they looked pristine and cute. More often than not, they had a basketball hoop and a big sliding door that led to a cavernous, clean interior. This barn, though, was an A-frame building constructed with timbers that had aged to a dark gray. Rust streaked the metal roof, and the windows on the west side were all broken. The east side, she couldn't see. No one stood outside, and no lights came from within. It could have been in a horror movie.

Nicole left the comforting darkness of the woods and cast her eyes around the field that surrounded the barn. Hiram's men were police officers, so all of them had weapons training. Even if they only had pistols, they could pick her off at fifty or seventy-five yards. Her mouth felt dry. She rubbed her hands up and down the legs of her pants and licked her lips.

"God, please don't let them be here."

God was the silent type, though, and didn't answer, so she crouched low to minimize her profile before darting forward. As she neared the barn, the wind shifted, and she smelled raw marijuana. She hadn't expected it to be as strong as it was, so it almost knocked her back.

Hiram must have harvested a few fields and hung the product up to dry before burning everything. She looked around again. Nothing moved, and no one jumped out of the shadows, so she turned on her light. The powerful beam illuminated a barn filled with row upon row of cut marijuana plants that had been hung upside down from the ceiling and from every exposed beam.

Nicole's mouth popped open. Hiram had enough weed in that barn to keep West County high for years. After Sallianne disturbed his other sites, keeping the product there was a risk, but if he could bring the contents of this barn to market, he'd earn half a million dollars or more. The weed didn't matter, though. Neither her dad nor TJ were inside.

Muscles all over Nicole's body ached from the day's work, but she took out her phone and searched for the next location, anyway. She had to find them. Hiram never would have taken them if not for her. They were her responsibility.

"You like weed, little girl?"

Nicole's breath caught in her throat the instant she heard the voice. Muscles all over her back, legs, and chest tightened as a flashlight illuminated her from behind. She had a gun in her backpack. If she could sling that off her shoulders and reach inside, she could take this guy out before he could hurt her. Of course, if he had a gun, he could shoot her well before that happened.

She raised her right hand while lowering her left shoulder to slip the bag off.

"I'm lost," she said. "Think I could use your phone?"

"You've got your own," he said. "I've been watching

you for a while. Now take off your backpack, toss it to your right without opening it, and put your hands on the barn. I'll pat you down for weapons. I've got a .45 pointed at your back, and my partner's got a thirty-aught-six pointed at your head from the tree line. You start something, he'll paint your brain matter all over my nice barn."

"I guess we wouldn't want that," said Nicole, lowering her voice. She slipped the backpack off and put it on the ground beside her. "Like I said, I just got lost hiking. If you take me to the highway, I won't tell anybody about your harvest. You can even blindfold me."

"Put your hands on the barn," he said. She did as he asked and held her breath, expecting him to grope her. Instead, he put his hands on her shoulders and delicately —and professionally—patted her down. As his hands reached her waist, she squeezed her hands tight into balls to prevent them from trembling.

"If you let me go, you can do more than pat me down," she whispered, her voice sultry and low. "You can do whatever you want to me. Just let me go."

He chuckled a little.

"I bet that pretty little mouth of yours has all the high school boys tied in knots, but you're not my type, Nicole."

She drew in a sharp breath. Her legs felt weak.

"You know my name."

"Yep," he said. "Hiram came by yesterday looking for you. We told him we hadn't seen you."

She swallowed a lump in her throat.

"You work for Hiram?"

"Turn around, sweetheart," he said. She turned. Her captor wore jeans and a khaki jacket with a white shirt beneath it. Gray streaked his beard and unkempt hair. He was thirty-five or forty and handsome in a rugged way. He looked like a lumberjack. His eyes traveled up and down her, but he wasn't checking her body out. She didn't know what he was doing, but his eyes made him look almost disinterested.

Then she got it.

"You're one of them, aren't you?" she asked. He raised his eyebrows and cocked his head to the side. "You're part of Hiram's gay army."

He smiled.

"Is that what he calls us?"

"No," she said, shaking her head. "That's just the nickname I gave you in my internal monologue. He likes you guys. He says you're hard workers."

"I appreciate that assessment," he said. "Word around town is that Hiram's having a problem with his workforce. One of his girls went to the press, forcing him to burn down some fields. You know anything about that?"

"I hear the problems with his workforce stemmed from his inability to prevent his security team from raping his gardeners."

The man grimaced, nodded, and then sighed.

"That happen to you?"

"To a girl I know," she said. "It didn't stop him from trying to kill me, though."

"Sorry to hear that," he said. He paused. "If it were up to me, I'd let you go with my blessing. It isn't up to me, though. I've got to take you home and see what my partners say."

She forced herself to smile.

"Sure I can't just give you a blow job to let me go?"

He laughed and shook his head.

"Nope," he said, scooping up her backpack and squeezing her upper arm. "Now come on. You hungry? Kevin made a big pot roast. It's a little heavy on the rosemary, but it's good."

Nicole pulled her arm back, but he squeezed before she could pull away.

"Just checking your grip," she said. Her captor grunted and pulled her forward. She came along, wondering how she'd get her backpack and escape. "What's your name?"

"I'm Greg," he said. "You'll meet Wayne in a minute."

"Just so you know, I think you the gays have done great things for the world," she said. "My boyfriend and I watched *Queer Eye for the Straight Guy* on Netflix a couple of weeks back. It changed TJ's whole life. I almost convinced him to wear a pink shirt the other day."

Greg chuckled.

"You think he's looking for you now?"

"Nah," she said. "I caught the big dumb ox sleeping

with some college girl. Then Hiram caught him lurking about in the woods outside his house. This is a rescue operation."

Greg squeezed her arm and pointed to a root in front of them with a flashlight. She thanked him for not letting her trip.

"Rescue's not going so well, huh?"

"It was going okay until just now," she said. "You sure you can't just let me go?"

"Yep," said Greg. "Like I said, your fate isn't my call. I'll do what I can to keep you safe, but that barn you found has almost a million dollars' worth of weed in it, which means you gave my partners about a million reasons to want you dead. That's not even counting the reward Hiram would give us for turning you in."

She tried to laugh, but it sounded more like a whimper.

"Please don't hurt me," she said, her voice almost a whisper.

Greg stopped walking. So did she. If she had any tears left, she might have cried. Her throat felt tight, and a tremble passed through her, weakening her legs.

"If the vote's against you, and we have to kill you, it'll be quick. I won't let anybody hurt you. That's the best I can do."

"That's great," she said, trying to keep the tremble out of her voice. Greg squeezed her arm again and then resumed walking. Another man joined them a minute later. He had a hunting rifle slung across his back, and he took Nicole's other arm. With every step they took, she found her strength leaving. For the third day running, she had just experienced the worst day of her life. At least it couldn't get much worse from here.

She hoped.

26

Brady and I left the campus and drove to the local police station, a modern brick building constructed in the side of a sloping hill. The bottom held a massive six-car garage and a big slab of concrete for parking, while the top of the hill held administrative offices and a bullpen for the uniformed officers. Since neither Brady nor I had ever been there, we had to drive around the building twice before finding the visitor parking lot and main entrance.

"This little town has some money," said Brady, upon parking. "A lot nicer than Cloverdale, huh?"

I nodded.

"Always makes me uneasy when I see these little towns with multimillion-dollar police stations. Makes me wonder where the money came from and how the locals earned it."

Brady opened his door but didn't step out.

"You're kind of a cynic, you know that?"

I opened my door and considered him.

"I've got an honest assessment of humanity based on years of experience seeing it at its worst," I said. "If you keep your eyes open long enough, you'll be a cynic, too."

"If you say so," he said. We got out and walked to the station's front door. The interior was bright, clean, and open—more like the lobby of a midrange hotel than a police station. A uniformed officer sat behind a thick, lightly stained wooden desk built into the right wall, while empty chairs filled out the rest of the room.

"Hey, folks," said the officer. "Can I help you?"

I unhooked my badge from my belt.

"I'm Detective Joe Court with the Cloverdale Police Department. This is Officer Brady Maddox. Can we speak to your watch commander?"

The officer reached to pick up her phone but put it to her chest without hitting a button.

"Is this official business?"

I nodded.

"Yeah," I said. "We're working a double homicide, and our primary suspect goes to school at Newman-Rothschild."

"Gotcha," she said, hitting a button on the phone. She paused and then spoke softly before hanging up. "Lieutenant Dudeck will be out shortly."

I nodded and thanked her. Brady and I stepped away from the desk, but we couldn't go far before a bald, heavyset man in a navy blue uniform hurried out toward us with his hand outstretched. He was a shade under six feet tall, and he had broad shoulders that stretched his uniform. Brady and I both nodded to him and shook his hand.

"Lieutenant Andy Dudeck," he said, looking to the receptionist. She stood. "I see you've met Grace."

"Nice to meet you, Lieutenant," I said. "I'm Joe Court. This is Brady Maddox."

For the next few minutes, I briefed the lieutenant on our investigation. He asked a few questions but kept quiet otherwise. When I finished, he crossed his arms and leaned against the receptionist's desk, nodding and considering us.

"How much did you tell the folks at Newman-Rothschild?" he asked.

"Not a lot," I said. "Their officer shut us down the moment we informed her we needed to speak to a student."

He nodded.

"That's typical," he said. "More than likely, they called the kid's parents and the school's attorneys to coordinate a legal response the moment you left. If you need to talk to him, we can work with you. I'll pass out the kid's information to my uniformed officers, and we'll look for him. The moment he parks illegally or rolls through a stop sign, we'll pull him over. If we can see something in his car in plain sight, we'll make an arrest."

I crossed my arms and sighed.

"Thank you, but I don't know if I've got that much time," I said, looking down and thinking. "He's a freshman at the school, and he's in a fraternity. Were you guys in a fraternity in college?"

I looked up to see Dudeck and Brady both shaking their heads. Grace, the officer working the reception desk, perked up.

"I was in a sorority," she said. "Alpha Delta Pi. It made college so much more fun."

"Any hazing go on in your sorority?"

"Oh, no," she said, shaking her head. "Our girls were

216

great. They made us feel like genuine sisters."

"But a freshman will be the low man in a frat, right?"

She hesitated and then shrugged before nodding.

"Maybe," she said. "A lot of frats were like that, but we didn't hang out with them too much."

Good. I could use that.

"Does the college publish a telephone directory?"

The lieutenant looked to Grace. She pushed back from her desk and searched through a drawer before pulling a spiral-bound directory from the bottom drawer. She handed it to me. The first thirty or forty pages contained the phone numbers of professors and office staff, but toward the back were the phone numbers of each of the dorm rooms and fraternity houses on campus.

I searched until I found the listings for the Theta Chi Nu fraternity. The fraternity house had almost fifty residents, most of whom were listed as upperclassmen. I got the name of the house's pledge trainer—Max Linsenmayer—and then pulled out my phone. According to the directory, Kit Jameson, the owner of the white Land Rover, lived in the Union Street Residence Hall. Hopefully he had slept at home tonight.

I called his number and waited through six rings before it went to voicemail. I held my breath and hoped my acting was better than my luck lately.

"If you're there, pick up the phone, shitbag," I said. I hung up and waited before calling back. This time, I hung up before leaving a message. When I called the third time, a groggy voice answered on the second ring.

"What?"

"It's Mary," I said. "And we're at the bar waiting."

Kit paused.

"Who are you?"

"Mary. I'm Max's girlfriend, shitbag," I said. "And we're at the fucking bar. They're closing, and I want to go home, but Max is too drunk to drive. He sent you, like, a thousand text messages."

Kit cleared his throat.

"I don't know what you're talking about. I didn't get any text messages."

"This is Kit Jameson, right?" I asked. "That's who I'm fucking calling in the middle of the night, right?"

I looked up. Lieutenant Dudeck and Brady both looked amused.

"Yeah, this is Kit," he said. "But I didn't get any messages."

"You're getting one now," I said before pausing, expecting him to say something. He didn't, so I continued. "Will you pick us up or not?"

He sighed.

"Tell Max I've got class tomorrow. He can call Rory or Trystan. They can even use my car if they want."

"You got that white Land Rover, right?" I asked.

He drew in a breath.

"Yeah," he said. I smiled and nodded. We had the right guy.

"I'll tell Max you don't want to pick us up, but he won't be happy. If you can't even be bothered to pick up a brother when he asks, are you sure you've got what it takes to be a member of your fraternity? I'm just asking. No judgment."

Kit paused and sighed.

"If this is such a big deal, why isn't Max calling himself?"

"He's puking in the bushes," I said. "Like I said, he's drunk. He had a long day."

I waited for a few seconds, expecting him to hang up or tell me no. Then he sighed again.

"Fine. I'll pick you up. Where are you?"

I held my thumb over my phone's microphone and looked to the lieutenant.

"Where would a college kid get drunk in this town?"

"Dara's Tap House," said Grace. "We pick up a lot of them there."

I nodded and moved my thumb.

"Dara's. You know where it is," I said. "We'll be in the parking lot. You can't miss us. Max will be the one with puke on his shirt."

"I'll be there as soon as I can," he said. "I've got to get dressed."

"See you soon," I said. I hung up and looked to Brady. "Let's go to the bar."

**

The bar was about half a mile from campus, and thankfully, we got there before Kit arrived. Brady let me out and then parallel parked on the street about two blocks away in case Kit made a run for it. It was 3:00 A.M., and the bar was closed. I sat on a bench beside the front door. I had graduated from college seven years ago, but I could pass for a graduate student. Kit would wonder where my supposed boyfriend was the moment he saw me, but hopefully he'd still pull into the lot. Even if he didn't, though, Brady would pull him over.

So I sat and waited. About ten minutes after I arrived, I saw the bluish-white headlights of Kit Jameson's Land Rover sweep into view. It slowed and then pulled into the empty parking lot. Immediately, Brady pulled away from the curb with his lights flashing. The kid looked around before slumping over the steering wheel. I smiled, walked toward him, and knocked on the glass. He hesitated before opening the window.

"Kit Jameson?" I asked. He looked at me and sighed.

"Mary?" he asked. I nodded and unhooked my badge from my belt. "Max isn't here, is he?"

"Nope," I said, showing him my badge. "I'm Detective Mary Joe Court from the Cloverdale Police Department. Do me a favor and turn off your vehicle. You know why we're here."

He turned off his car and then returned his hands to the steering wheel.

"I have nothing to say," he said.

"That's your right," I said, nodding. "You should talk to us, though. You ever been to Cloverdale?"

He said nothing. Brady, meanwhile, stepped out of his car but left the lights flashing. Brady pulled a flashlight from his utility belt and looked in the rear windows.

"Do you have any weapons on you, Mr. Jameson?"

Jameson looked at me and shook his head before looking over his shoulder at Brady.

"He can't just look in my car like that."

"Actually, he can," I said. "You're a person of interest in a double homicide, and he's looking to make sure you don't have any guns or other weapons at hand that could hurt us."

"Oh," he said, closing his eyes and sighing. "I guess that's okay."

Brady cleared his throat and motioned me toward the rear of the vehicle.

"Put your hands on the steering wheel and stay still," I said, walking and nodding to my partner. "What've you got?"

"A pair of ski masks like the ones worn in the robberies."

It was good evidence, but it didn't close the case for us. Still, we could use the ski masks to get search warrants for his car and his dorm room. Since he didn't live in his fraternity house, we wouldn't be able to get in there without more information, but this was a good break. I nodded and walked to the driver's side door.

"Mr. Jameson, open your vehicle's door and step out. You're under arrest on suspicion of armed robbery and murder."

He reached for the door handle.

"I want a lawyer."

"Good call," I said. "Now get out of the car."

27

Brady and I had a long night ahead of us, and it started almost the moment we put Kit Jameson in handcuffs. Officer Maddox walked Kit to the back seat of our cruiser, while I sat in the passenger seat and called Chief Tomlin in Cloverdale to let him know we had a suspect in the convenience store robberies and that we'd need a warrant to search his vehicle as soon as possible. The chief and I had barely begun talking when a black four-door Mercedes drove by the front of the bar, honking and flashing its lights.

I glanced to Brady and held my phone to my chest so the boss wouldn't hear me talk.

"Go check out the Mercedes."

Brady nodded and started walking toward the edge of the parking lot while I told Chief Tomlin what we needed. Kit sat in the back seat but paid me little attention. That was fine by me. I returned to my conversation with the chief.

"We've got Brady's cruiser, so we've got a laptop," I said. "I can type the search warrant's affidavit, but I'll need you to get it signed."

The boss sighed and cleared his throat.

"That sounds like a plan," he said, yawning. "This is good work. Type it up and send it to me. I'll wake up the prosecutor and see…"

He said something else, but I couldn't hear him over

the sound of honking. The Mercedes had parked in the lot, and two young men stepped out. A third man stayed in the driver's seat with one hand on the steering wheel and another pointed at Brady. This was getting out of hand.

"Hey, boss," I said. "Something's going on. I'll call you back."

I hung up before he could speak. Then I walked toward the melee while calling the local police station for backup. They knew where we were and said they'd be there within five minutes. I put my phone in my pocket and unbuttoned the strap that held my firearm in its holster so I'd be ready in case somebody did something stupid.

"Everybody get back in the car and leave," shouted Brady, holding out his arms. "This is none of your business."

"This is a free country, old man," said a mean-looking guy with curly brown hair. He was in his early twenties and had about six inches on me, putting him at six feet tall or more. He was in good shape, too. I couldn't take him in a fight if it came down to that, so I held my hand over my firearm.

"We're armed police officers, and we're on the job," I said, my voice clear. "I'm feeling threatened right now. For your own safety, please leave."

A bigger kid with a buzz cut straightened and put up his hands as he took a step back toward the Mercedes. The driver, a young man with blond hair swept to the side and cold, blue eyes, stopped honking the horn and stuck his head out the window.

"There's no need for threats, officers," he said. "We're here to register our displeasure at the illegal detainment and arrest of our friend."

"Don't fucking say anything, Kit," shouted the curly-haired kid.

I reached for my phone and looked toward the curly-haired kid. He stared at me with malevolent eyes as I snapped first his picture and then his friends in the car.

"I'd be careful about what you say, buddy," I said, slipping my phone into my pocket. "You're very close to interfering with a police investigation. Get back in your car and leave."

His eyes traveled up and down me.

"We appreciate the advice, but we'll stay," said the blond. "I want to make sure you don't waterboard our friend."

"We won't do that," I said, looking up as I caught the distant sound of a siren. "You ever been to Cloverdale?"

The kid's eyes narrowed, but he said nothing. His friends slunk back toward the car as Brady walked to me. With the situation defused somewhat, my partner and I stepped back.

"You think they're our guys?" he asked. I nodded.

"Oh, yeah," I said. "Now, we've just got to find enough evidence to nail Kit Jameson and then convince him the best way to stay off death row is to name his accomplices."

Brady smirked.

"Is that all?"

I glanced at him and gave him a tight smile.

"Few things worth doing are ever easy," I said, waving toward the first police cruiser to arrive at the scene. It pulled to a stop on the street, and a uniformed officer stepped out. The boys in the Mercedes climbed back into the car but didn't leave.

Over the next twenty minutes, I typed a search warrant affidavit and sent it to my boss in Cloverdale. He took it to a local circuit court judge, who signed it and sent it back. At a little after six, we opened the SUV's back door. Unfortunately, the car was clean. We found a ski mask wedged beneath the driver's seat and a second on the floorboards behind the front passenger's seat. There were no guns, knives, or other weapons and nothing else that would show Kit had driven this vehicle to a robbery. We also found two empty plastic liquor bottles rolling around in the back.

Brady and I bagged what we could and laid it out on the trunk of his cruiser. My partner looked at me.

"Is this enough?"

I grimaced and shook my head.

"Not to charge him with murder," I said. "It's good evidence, but the ski masks aren't distinctive enough to tie anyone to the robberies."

"What about the liquor bottles?" asked Brady. "We know they stole booze when they robbed the stores."

I raised my eyebrows.

"If they had stolen something expensive enough to have a unique serial number, we'd nail them, but this is cheap stuff that they could have purchased anywhere. We'll keep the ski masks and the bottles to see if we can get DNA on them, but we can't hold Kit on this. It's not enough."

He looked over his shoulder at the SUV and the kids in the Mercedes.

"So what next?" he asked. "Do we just let him go?"

I considered and then nodded.

"For now. Write down the license plate number of that Mercedes and then let Kit know he and his friends are free to leave. I'll fill out the paperwork for the stuff we've seized."

Brady nodded and then looked down.

"I'm not a fan of letting murderers walk without a plan."

"We don't have a choice," I said. "We'll crawl into Kit's life, see where he's weak, and then use that to break him. Until then, we'll do our jobs the best we can with the tools we have available. Sound good?"

He straightened and drew in a breath.

"It sucks, but yeah."

"We're in agreement," I said. "Now tell them they can go. The sooner you do that, the sooner we can get home. I need to feed my dog."

He nodded and did as I asked. For the next twenty-five minutes, I filled out paperwork, and Brady talked to the locals. Once we finished, we drove back to Cloverdale, where we stored our evidence and informed Chief Tomlin of our findings. He said he appreciated our work, but he was disappointed we hadn't found anything. Brady and I were, too.

I got home at a little after nine in the morning. Roy seemed happy to see me, which was always nice. He followed me to the carriage house, where I found two handwritten notes on my door. The first said Cora and Roy had slept in her room. Cora wondered whether he could do it again. Beneath that note, I found one from Ann, which said Cora had found Roy out in the courtyard at eight on her way to bed and couldn't bear the thought of him spending the night outside alone. Ann hoped I didn't mind if her daughter treated my dog as a stuffed animal for a while.

Even after a disappointing night, the notes made me smile. When I had lived in St. Augustine, I tried to avoid taking work home, but it always followed me anyway. At times, I had so many files in my living room that I didn't even have anywhere to sit. I had surrounded myself with death and misery twenty-four hours a day, and it had made me miserable and lonely.

Cloverdale was far from perfect, but misery and death had no hold over me here. As soon as I walked through the gate and into the courtyard, work disappeared. Cora, Ann, Roy, and the home we shared became my entire world. Roy was just a dog, and Cora and Ann had been strangers a year ago, but I cared about them all and I looked forward to seeing them every time I came home.

They made my life brighter. I couldn't ask for more from my friends.

I turned the lock and stepped inside. Roy ran in and went to his bowl in the kitchen. I gave him some food and made sure he had water. Then I went to bed. As I slept, I dreamed of Julia and Doug Green and their kids, Audrey and Dylan. I used to braid Audrey's hair every Wednesday night, and I used to share giant bowls of Cap'n Crunch cereal with Dylan every Saturday morning while we watched cartoons. In my dreams, we were a family again.

Some days, I wished I could sleep forever.

28

The room was still dark when Nicole opened her eyes. Of course, it'd be dark forever. Greg had left her in the farmhouse's partially finished basement. A pair of dirty casement windows along the ceiling allowed a little light to filter inside, but the big boxwood bushes along the home's foundation prevented them from brightening the interior.

Nicole didn't understand how the group worked, but Greg and five other men lived in a big old farmhouse about five miles outside Cloverdale. When she, Greg, and Wayne arrived last night, they had introduced her to a few of the other fellows as if she were a houseguest instead of a captive, and then Greg led her down to the basement, where she'd sleep. He even put a sheet on the old black futon and gave her a bowl of vegetables—they had eaten all the meat—from a pot roast Kevin had made for dinner. It was downright hospitable.

After dinner, she showered in the basement's bathroom, and the group's cook—Kevin—came down with a big stack of wedding magazines and some of his sister's clothes that he thought would fit. Kevin and his fiancé—Greg—planned to get married, but Greg wanted to do it at the courthouse. Kevin wanted a blowout party with carriage rides for all the guests. He wanted to feel like a prince on coronation day.

For an hour and a half, she and Kevin had talked about Jane Austen novels, high school, college, and her troubles with TJ and her mother. Kevin talked about his mom and sisters. Afterwards, Kevin French braided her hair, just as he had done to his little sisters before he'd gone off to college, and then he took her empty bowl upstairs, wished her goodnight, and locked the door so she couldn't escape.

It was the strangest kidnapping Nicole had ever heard of. If she had met Greg and the others under other circumstances, they might have become friends. Aside from locking her in the basement, they seemed like nice guys.

And now it was morning. She stood from the futon and stretched. Nicole wore a pair of red flannel pajama pants and a pink long-sleeved top that Kevin had given her. The clothes were bigger than she was used to, but they were clean. After traipsing around in the woods and running from Hiram and the police, she had almost forgotten how good clean clothes felt.

For a while, she had luxuriated in the feel of clean cotton, but then she started thinking about her dad and TJ. They were prisoners, too, but she doubted Hiram was treating them as well as Kevin, Greg, Wayne, and the others were treating her. She would have loved to stay and relax, but she had to escape.

So she stood on the futon and tried to open the window, but it didn't budge. The boys would give her breakfast, and they'd give her silverware. The end of a spoon might be strong enough to break the window if she hit it hard enough. They'd probably give her napkins she could wrap around her hands to protect her skin. It was worth trying. Once she broke the glass, she could shimmy her way out and escape.

Then again, she had nowhere to go. Hiram had businesses—legitimate and otherwise—all over West County. He could have taken TJ and her dad to any of them. Or maybe he had cut his losses and run. He could have killed them already. Nicole had no way of knowing. Maybe she should just turn herself in. It might give her dad and TJ a chance.

She lowered herself from the window and then sat on the futon to think. Her options were poor. As much as she had enjoyed growing weed, and as much as she had appreciated the money it had given her, she wished she had never met Hiram Ford or the stupid thugs who worked for him.

After about ten minutes of silence, she changed into some fresh clothes in the bathroom and climbed the stairs. The door was locked, so she knocked until somebody answered. It was Kevin, and he smiled at her.

"Hey, honey," he said. "You have everything you need down there?"

"It's set up real nice," she said, nodding. "Can I get breakfast?"

"Of course," he said. "You go back down. You want some eggs, or do you want oatmeal? We've got both, but the eggs are fresh from our chickens."

She forced herself to smile and wondered whether she could kill him if she had to. When she and Greg last spoke, he hadn't given her many details, but he alluded to a house vote to decide her fate. If it went against her, she'd die.

Nicole hated violence, but she'd protect herself. Kevin, Greg, and their friends, despite their superficial friendliness, viewed her as a threat. They may have disagreed about the magnitude of threat she posed, but they wouldn't let her go. They'd turn her over to Hiram. The old man would pay them a reward, and they'd sell him the weed they had in their barn. She'd die, but they'd all profit.

Everything came down to money and power. As long as people kept smoking weed, people like Hiram and Greg and the boys would grow it. They didn't deserve her mercy because they'd never show her any. So yeah, she could kill Kevin. And Greg. And Wayne. And everyone else in that house. They'd do the same to her.

First, though, she had to figure out how to escape. She smiled at Kevin.

"I would love a big bowl of scrambled eggs," she said, turning her head so he could see her hair. "That braid you gave me last night's still holding. It's so cute."

"You are adorable, honey. We've got to get girls here more often," said Kevin, winking. "I'll get you those eggs right away. You just go have a seat downstairs."

"See you later," she said, stepping back. He closed and locked the basement door. As she walked down the steps, she felt for any loose treads, hoping she could find a nail jutting out. A single nail wouldn't be much of a weapon, but given the circumstances, she'd take any advantage she could. Nicole didn't know how, but the next time Kevin tried to braid her hair, he'd die. So would everybody else in this house.

It was the only way she'd survive.

29

I slept until Roy whined to go outside at about one in the afternoon. I let him out, but I tossed and turned after going back to bed. Brady and I had done solid work on the convenience store robberies, but we needed something that definitively tied Kit Jameson to them. Once we had that, we'd use DNA extracted from the mouth of the liquor bottle or from sweat from the ski masks we found in Kit's car to nail his accomplices. We knew who the bad guys were and what they had done, and we even had a road map to send them to prison. I was pleased with that case.

My investigation into Sallianne Cantwell, though, had me worried.

I swung my legs off the bed and walked to the kitchen to make coffee. As it brewed, I paced the length of my living room. Sallianne was a journalist, and she had been investigating marijuana fields in Cloverdale. She hadn't stumbled upon these marijuana fields on her own, either; someone had given her the locations. Somehow, Nicole Johnson was involved, too, but I didn't know quite how.

It was possible Nicole was Sallianne's source, but that raised all sorts of new questions. Either way, Sallianne was gone, Nicole had escaped my custody, and Nicole's mother was dead. Nicole's father was missing, too. Those were my facts, and they all worried me.

After pacing for almost ten minutes and coming up with nothing, I drank some coffee, showered, and then checked to make sure Roy had water before driving into work. When I arrived, Chief Tomlin was in his office with the door open, enjoying a late lunch. I knocked on the doorframe to get his attention. He smiled at me.

"You mind if I join you and pick your brain for a few minutes, boss?" I asked. He shook his head.

"Not at all," he said, gesturing across his desk to a seat. "You get some sleep after your late night?"

"A bit, but my dog woke me up," I said, nodding and sitting. "I was hoping to talk to you about Nicole Johnson and Sallianne Cantwell."

The chief put down his sandwich and leaned back.

"Okay," he said. "What have you got?"

"Nothing," I said. "And that's the problem. I searched Sallianne's apartment and found notes she had taken about a case she was investigating, and those notes led me to both Nicole Johnson and a lot of fields in which someone had grown marijuana."

"And I called the State Bureau of Investigation about the fields," he said. "They referred them to the DEA. Their agents will investigate."

"Good," I said. "We also found Sherry Johnson, Nicole's mom, dead in her house. We don't know where Trevor Johnson, Nicole's father, is."

The chief crossed his arms and nodded.

"Sounds like we're on the same page," he said. He looked toward his desk. "And just so you know, I've contacted the State Bureau of Investigation, the State Highway Patrol, the West County Sheriff's Department, and the police stations in Raleigh, Greensboro, Chapel Hill, and half a dozen other places. I've also put in a request with her bank. If Nicole tries to use her debit card, we'll get a call. She's in the wind so far, but she can't disappear forever."

"She told me Hiram Ford killed her mom. You think Hiram's just a patsy, though. Do you think Nicole killed her?"

Tomlin exhaled through his nose.

"I'd say she's a person of interest," he said. "Trevor Johnson is a real stand-up guy, but Sherry Johnson wasn't a big fan of motherhood."

"What do you know about Sherry?"

"I hate speaking ill of the dead, so this should stay between the two of us," he said. I nodded and leaned forward. "Sherry's been a handful her whole life. I moved out after college, but I grew up in Cloverdale. Sherry's mom and dad couldn't keep up with her, so she ran wild in high school and dated a lot of people. She was, maybe, sixteen or seventeen when she and Trevor got pregnant. They married and kept the baby, and they've been together ever since."

"We know anything about their home life?" I asked.

He shook his head and then leaned forward to type. He spent a minute at his computer before looking to me again.

"As best I can tell, nobody in the Johnson household

has ever called us to report domestic violence or other issues, and no one has ever called in a complaint about them."

I gave myself a moment to think before asking my next question.

"You said Sherry was a handful her whole life," I said. "How well do you know her?"

The chief considered his words.

"Between the two of us?" he asked. I nodded. "I went to school with her younger brother. If he knew how well I knew her, he'd beat me up."

I lowered my chin.

"Do you have an ongoing relationship with her?"

"That's none of your business," he said. "I didn't kill her, though, and I don't know who did. It wasn't Trevor, though. He knew what he was getting into when he married her."

I leaned back.

"Are you going to recuse yourself from her murder investigation?"

"No," said Tomlin. I waited for him to clarify his position, but he said nothing. If he was sleeping with her, that'd be a problem in court, but he could argue with the prosecutor about it. I was a temporary employee. If he wanted to imperil a prosecution before it started, that was on him.

"Is it possible Sherry and Trevor were growing marijuana and their daughter found out about it and told Sallianne?"

He considered.

"It's possible, but I don't know how likely that is," he said. "It wouldn't explain why she'd go to Sallianne instead of us, either."

I didn't have an answer to that.

"Did you find any firearms in the Johnsons' house?" I asked.

He nodded.

"Quite a few in the gun safe, but none of them match the rounds found in Sherry Johnson. She was shot with a .40-caliber round. The Johnsons had a nine-millimeter pistol, .38-caliber revolver, two shotguns, and two hunting rifles."

I nodded.

"The killer could have taken the murder weapon with him."

The boss nodded.

"That's certainly possible."

I nodded, considering the chief for a moment.

"The evidence is scarce, but based on what we've got, you're the best suspect we've got in Sherry Johnson's murder."

The boss furrowed his brow.

"Excuse me?"

"I suspect you were having an affair with Sherry Johnson. Maybe things got heated, maybe she threatened to tell your wife and break up your marriage. However it happened, you killed her to stop that from happening."

He laughed and shook his head.

"Sherry didn't care that I was married."

"But it's plausible," I said. "Every defense attorney worth a damn will make that same argument the moment we arrest anybody but you."

He paused and sighed.

"You really want me off this case, don't you?"

"You have an obvious and serious conflict of interest," I said. "If you were a plainclothes officer, I would have already written you a letter of reprimand. Since you're my boss, that's tough."

He shook his head and rubbed his eyes.

"Did your previous boss think you were a pain in the ass, too?"

"Among other things," I said.

He took his hand from his face.

"Fine," he said. "I'll recuse myself from the case and bring in the county sheriff's department. Anything else?"

"Yeah," I said. "You knew Sherry Johnson pretty well. Do you know Nicole?"

He lowered his chin.

"You accusing me of something?"

"No. As far as we know, she's still alive, and I want to find her. You know anything about her?"

"I've barely met her," he said. "She rarely came up while her mother and I were together."

"Okay," I said, standing. "I'll track down Nicole Johnson."

He grunted and looked at his computer.

"If you find her, try to avoid accusing her of

committing a crime unless she did it."

I smiled and left. Tomlin was pissy, but he'd get over it. And if he didn't, it didn't matter, anyway, because I was a temporary employee. I went back to my desk and read through my notes. When I met Nicole the first time, she had been driving her boyfriend TJ's truck, which meant we needed to talk to him.

I called the high school to make sure TJ was in and to let them know I needed to interview him, but the receptionist informed me he wasn't there and hadn't been for several days. Given the circumstances, that was a serious problem. I walked back to the boss's office. He sighed the moment he saw me.

"You need me to recuse myself from another case?"

"No," I said. "I just called the high school. TJ Macon, Nicole Johnson's boyfriend, hasn't been to school for several days."

The boss crossed his arms.

"What do his parents say?"

"I haven't called them yet," I said. "I wanted to make sure they haven't filed a missing-persons report before I talked to them."

The boss nodded and tilted his head to the side.

"Annabelle Macon—she's TJ's mom—works in Charlotte," he said. "She's in some kind of finance. Her husband, Tom Macon, runs Macon Motors. He's a good mechanic."

I considered him and then smiled.

"You know everybody in this town?"

He closed his eyes and leaned back.

"They didn't make me chief of police for my good looks."

"I guess I'll head down to Macon Motors, then."

The chief nodded and gave me directions. The garage wasn't far, so I just walked over. New tires hung from racks on the walls in the office, and the air held the pungent odor of engine oil, rubber, and just a hint of gasoline. A salesman in a striped shirt stooped behind the counter and nodded at me.

"Afternoon. I'm Leon," he said. "What can I do for you?"

I showed him my badge and asked to see Tom Macon. Leon nodded and said he'd find him. A few minutes later, a man in his early fifties entered the office. He was tall and had shoulders so broad he almost had to turn sideways in the doorway. An easy smile came to his face as he held up massive, grease-covered hands.

"Leon said you were looking for me. I'm Tom Macon. I'd shake your hand, but you wouldn't like the result."

"That's okay," I said, smiling. "I'm here to talk about TJ if you've got a minute."

Tom sighed and put his hands on his hips.

"What's that knucklehead done?"

"Nothing, but I'd like to talk to him about his girlfriend," I said. "She's missing."

He nodded and rolled his eyes.

"That sounds about right. I love my boy, but he's

seventeen and does most of his thinking with his penis. I figured he and Nicole were holed up somewhere. Hopefully they don't come back pregnant or married."

I nodded.

"Can you call him?" I asked. "It's very important I talk to them."

"Let me wash my hands," he said. "I've been trying to get in touch with him, but you know how it is: boys will be boys. I'll try again."

I wondered whether he'd take the same laissez-faire attitude if he had a girl, but I didn't ask. Instead, I thanked him, and he disappeared down a back hallway. A few minutes later, he returned with clean hands and an iPhone. He put it on speakerphone and dialed, but TJ's phone went to voicemail.

"Does your son have an iPhone, too?" I asked. Tom nodded. "Do you have the Find my iPhone app?"

"Yeah, but I told him we'd only use it in an emergency," he said. "Is this an emergency?"

I raised my eyebrows and nodded.

"Yeah."

He ran his finger across the phone to open the app and then glanced at me.

"You talked to Sherry and Trevor about this?"

"Nicole's parents?" I asked. Tom nodded. "I've reached out to them."

Tom blinked and considered.

"Did you call Nicole? She's responsible."

"I've got officers across the state looking for her," I

said. Tom nodded and focused on his app for a moment. Then he held up the phone.

"It says TJ's phone is offline," he said, smiling. "Young love isn't always responsible. That's how you get grandkids, I think."

I forced myself to smile and nod as I reached into my purse for a business card with my contact information on it.

"If TJ calls you or comes home, let me know right away."

He looked at my card and then to me, his face drawn.

"You wouldn't have gone to all this trouble for two missing high school kids unless there was a problem. Should I worry, Detective?"

I considered my answer. If I told him the truth—that Sherry Johnson was dead and her husband was missing—he'd panic. That wouldn't help anyone. Honesty mattered, but so did prudence.

"Just call me right away if you see either TJ or Nicole," I said.

He looked at my card and nodded, his face paler than it had been when I went in. As I walked back to my car, I hoped my next visit with Mr. Macon wouldn't be for a next-of-kin notification.

30

The students at Newman-Rothschild University knew their school owned vast tracts of land in the Blue Ridge Mountains, but few of them had likely traipsed across the property the way Kit, Trystan, Rory, and Max were. The university owned fifteen thousand acres. It was twenty-three square miles, a bigger landmass than the island of Manhattan. But where Manhattan had over 1.6 million people, Newman-Rothschild's campus held fewer than three thousand. They hadn't seen a single person since entering the forest three hours earlier.

"This sucks," said Max, holding out a hand for Rory to pull him to his feet. The landscape around them rose and fell in what appeared to be gentle hills from a distance. When walking across them, though, the boys recognized them for what they were: the remnants of ancient mountains that time and erosion had worn down but never tamed. Creeks, thick with slick rocks and some quite deep, crisscrossed the landscape, creating obstacles to ford every few miles. It was hard trekking, but they didn't have a choice. The police were watching the college's other exits.

"Max is right," said Kit, slapping a black fly that had landed on the back of his neck. It flew away before he could reach it. "This is too hard. We should just head back. She's not worth this."

"Stop talking," said Rory, holding onto the thin trunk

of a scrub oak tree and reaching down to help his friend
to his feet. Around them, the land sloped downward to a
narrow valley between two massive hills. Leaves and
branches covered their heads and kept the sun off them.
Rory pulled Max upright and then looked to Trystan.

"None of us want to be doing this, but it's
necessary," said Trystan. "You understand that, right?
We're like NATO. You attack one of us, you attack us all.
This bitch came after you. That means we've got to take
her out."

"This is a bad idea," said Kit. "If we kill her—and
that's what we're talking about—the cops will look right at
us. Rory and Max, you guys want to be lawyers, right? And
Trystan, you want to become governor one day. This kind
of shit will stain your life."

"Prison's a lot worse," said Rory. "Unless you're into
that sort of thing. You want some prison loving?"

Kit shook his head, but Trystan spoke before he
could say anything.

"Now, now, Rory," he said. "It doesn't matter what
way Kit swings as long as he plays ball when the time is
right."

"I'm not gay," said Kit. His voice sounded small and
defensive. He hated that. "And even if I was gay, it
wouldn't matter. This would still be stupid."

"Okay," said Trystan, crossing his arms. "What would
you have us do?"

Kit hesitated but then shrugged.

"I don't know."

"And that's the problem," said Trystan. "Before this chick showed up, we could do whatever we wanted. We hit four stores. They didn't have a goddamn clue who we were. Then this chick shows up, and fucking bam! She called you up in the middle of the night and pretended to be Max's girlfriend. She knew she couldn't reach you any other way. This detective is putting pieces together. As long as she's around, she's a threat."

"There are better ways to respond," said Kit. "We can get rid of the guns, we can get rid of all the liquor we stole, and then we can throw away the other two ski masks. If she had evidence, she would have arrested us last night, but she doesn't know anything. She just got lucky."

"She's a cop, dumbass, and she's coming after us," said Rory. "She doesn't need evidence. Whatever she doesn't have, she'll just make up. That's what cops do. Don't you watch TV?"

"Even if we take her out, this won't go away," said Kit. "You understand that, right? It doesn't make her findings disappear. And who do you think they'll blame once she dies? If we kill a cop, this shit's over. If you think this chick's bad, wait until you see who they bring in. It won't be some county detective looking at us. It'll be, like, an FBI agent or something."

Trystan smiled and shook his head while laughing.

"Listen to you," he said, shaking his head. "You're so worked up, you're not even thinking straight. Even if the cops think it's us, there won't be any evidence. We've worked this whole thing out. We'll steal a car, go to her house, and shoot her in the head. Then we'll get rid of the gun, burn the car, and go back home. There won't be any evidence. And here's the other thing you're forgetting: they think we're on campus. There are cops outside the gates. That's the best part of this. Those cops are the best fucking alibi we could ask for. We're covered, dude."

Trystan put a hand on Kit's shoulder and looked him in the eye. If Kit hadn't looked away, he wouldn't have seen Trystan put his other hand over the pistol tucked into his waistband. Kit's heart pounded even harder in his chest, and he licked his chapped lips. They were miles from campus in a valley between two enormous hills. That deep in the woods, Trystan, Rory, and Max wouldn't even have to bury his body. They'd just let nature take its course. His corpse would decompose and disappear.

"Are you with us, or are you against us, buddy?" asked Trystan, his voice so low it was almost a whisper. "I need you on my team. Don't say no."

Kit's entire body shook, but he forced himself to nod.

"Okay," he said.

"Good," said Trystan, smiling and straightening. "Let's go, boys. This bitch is dying tonight."

**

After meeting with Tom Macon and learning very little, I drove back to my station. Brady sat at his desk in the bullpen, drinking a cup of coffee and typing at his computer. When he saw me, he nodded and smiled.

"Hey, Joe," he said. "Boss says you've been in for a while."

"Yeah. My dog woke me up early. He's an asshole," I said. "Since then, I've been trying to track down a local teenager named Nicole Johnson. She's got some questions to answer about a murder."

He looked at his computer.

"The chief likes to keep you busy, doesn't he?"

"He does," I said, walking toward the break room, where I poured myself a cup of coffee before sitting at the desk beside Brady's in the bullpen. "You here for the free coffee, or are you working?"

He smiled but didn't turn his head from the computer.

"I'm filling out paperwork," he said, "but if you've got a minute, I've got updates."

I leaned back and sipped my coffee.

"Go for it," I said.

"First thing, I've got a report from the hazmat team who worked the attack at the Stop 'N Go station. They found sulfuric acid on the floor and clinging to a glass bottle at the scene. That's what our bad guys threw at the clerk. It's nasty stuff."

"Jeez," I said. "Do we have any word on the victim?"

He nodded.

"She's still in the hospital and still being treated for severe chemical burns. I don't know if she's able to speak. She aspirated the chemical, and it's burned her lungs. She's in rough shape."

I blinked and drew in a breath and then swallowed hard.

"I hope she recovers," I said. "How about the most recent robbery? How's the clerk there?"

Brady raised his eyebrows.

"At least there we've got some good news," he said. "I talked to her mom just a little while ago. Ms. Fowler is at home with her son. Since the robbery, she's started showing signs of PTSD, but she's alive, and she's got a support network. We've also ID'd the victims who burned to death in the office as Susie and Dean Hillerud. Chief Tomlin and Lenny did the next-of-kin notification."

I nodded and sipped my drink. A mom and her son. I couldn't imagine how awful that would be on the family. For about a minute, neither Brady nor I spoke. Then Brady cleared his throat.

"I've also got a report from the state crime lab in Raleigh," he said. "The arson investigator found the ignition point and believes the fire was started by a glass bottle containing gasoline, laundry soap, and ethyl alcohol. When they're mixed, they form a sludge that's easy to ignite and hard to extinguish."

I nodded but said nothing as my mind processed that.

"So it's basically napalm?" I asked. "The kind of stuff the army used in Vietnam."

"I guess," said Brady, shrugging.

"Would it take special equipment to make?"

"I don't think so."

I furrowed my brow.

"How the hell would a rich college kid from North Carolina know how to make it?" I asked.

"I can't help you there," said Brady. "But the kid's lawyers called to ask us to stop harassing their client. They claim he was studying with friends at the time of the most recent robbery."

"Let me guess," I said, "his study buddies are members of his fraternity?"

"Yep," said Brady, nodding. "I've got three names. They claim they were studying together in the fraternity's basement."

"So we can definitely trust that," I said, nodding.

Brady's lips cracked into a tight smile.

"If there's one thing I've learned in law enforcement, it's that you can always trust the word of criminal defense attorneys."

"Work the alibi and see if we can break it," I said. "Once you find someone who denies they were in the fraternity basement, put a search warrant together for their phone records. Text messages won't lie."

He typed a note for himself at his computer and then looked to me.

"Will do," he said.

"Good luck," I said. "I'm beat, so I'm going home for the day. We'll regroup tomorrow and see where we are. Sound good?"

He nodded and said it did, so I thanked him and left the building. It wasn't even five in the afternoon, but I was so tired, I could barely think straight. Instead of going straight home, though, I went by the grocery store and bought two bottles of white wine and some fancy raspberry candy for Cora. Ann and Cora had taken care of Roy last night without me even asking, so they deserved a thank you. Plus, I liked the excuse to spend time with my two favorite people in North Carolina.

As I drove home from the store, I looked forward to my evening. I had rarely felt that way when Roy and I lived alone in St. Augustine. Maybe I should let more people into my life.

31

Ann must have been running late because her windows were dark and her car wasn't in the driveway when I arrived. I stretched, grabbed my grocery sacks, and went upstairs. Before I could open the door, Roy barked at me from inside. I smiled and let myself in. When the dog saw me, he wagged his tail hard, but then sat down, almost trembling with excitement.

"Stay, buddy," I said as I carried the bags to my small breakfast table. His tail wagged even harder, and he licked his nose. When I looked at him again, I smiled. "Okay. Come here."

Roy vaulted to his feet and licked my hands and forearms as I petted him and scratched his ears. My job forced me to see the world at its worst, but every time I came home, my dog reminded me the world had good sides, too. Whenever I had a bad day, Roy sat by my side and let me know I wasn't alone. And when I had a good day, he became a friend with whom I could share my triumphs.

I was a dog person. I hadn't known that until I had one, but I couldn't imagine my life without one now. Roy would never replace a human being, but he was part of my family all the same. He was my uncomplicated friend, and I loved him.

Since he had been cooped up inside for a few hours, I let him into the courtyard so he could use the restroom.

While he did that, I grabbed his harness and leash. I locked the door behind me and walked down the steps toward the courtyard. The dog waited for me at the bottom.

"Hey, dude," I said. "You want to go for a walk?"

He jumped up the moment I said *walk* and then bounced on his front legs with excitement. Once I got him to stand still, I put the harness over his shoulders and chest and then put the leash on. He'd be okay without a leash, but he was still a dog. Roy rarely chased things, but I didn't want the first time he took off after a squirrel to end with him in the middle of a busy street.

I patted him on the side. He seemed to grin at me.

"Okay, buddy," I said. "Let's go see the world."

**

The vinyl seat creaked as Kit shifted his weight. They were in an old red Dodge Caravan that Max had bought off a guy months ago in the parking lot of a Costco in Springfield, Virginia, for nine hundred dollars cash. Originally, they had purchased it to use in a recruiting event for their fraternity. They had planned to get some sledgehammers, push the minivan onto a big tarp, and then let the freshmen have at it on their fraternity house's front lawn. It would have been mindless mayhem, but it would have been fun. Afterwards, they planned to grill steaks, smoke cigars, and tell the freshmen about the Theta Chi Nu fraternity.

Then an asshole in the school's residence life office heard about the plan and decided it was beneath the dignity of Newman-Rothschild's young men to participate. Mindless destruction of property, they argued, sent the wrong message to those off campus who might have been looking at the university.

It was just harmless fun, though. Nobody would have gotten hurt, and the brothers would have cleaned up afterwards. Besides, the car had four hundred thousand miles on its engine, and it barely ran. It'd cost more to fix it than it was worth, so it'd go to the junkyard anyway. Beating it with sledgehammers wouldn't change its fate. Despite the fraternity's argument, the school didn't relent, and the fraternity had to cancel the event. That left them with a crappy old minivan in a storage center five miles from campus. Now, they finally had a use for it.

Trystan sat in the driver's seat and wrinkled his nose.

"Did you fart, Kit?" he asked, glancing to his right.

"I think it's just the car," he said.

Trystan nodded and focused on the road. Everybody agreed that Detective Court was a problem, but they disagreed on how to deal with her. Their plans made Kit sick.

"We should just run," he said. "The police couldn't stop us. Everybody in here has a trust fund. Our parents would understand, too. We could be in Mexico by tomorrow before the cops even know we're gone."

Nobody responded.

"This is stupid," said Kit. "We have options, and we're picking the stupidest one."

Trystan glanced at him.

"You robbed a convenience store and murdered a young mom and her kid," he said. "You think your parents will fund your Mexican dream vacation once they learn that?"

"We didn't know they were in the store," said Kit. "That's on you, Trystan."

Trystan glanced in his rearview mirror.

"That true, guys?"

Max considered.

"I take responsibility for my actions," he said. "We wouldn't have done it without Kit holding the door and escorting the clerk out, though."

"He's right," said Rory. "You can't blame anybody for what you did, Kit. Sorry, but it's important for a Theta Chi Nu brother to be accountable for his actions. We have to solve our own problems."

"Fine," said Kit. "I take responsibility. Pull over and let me out."

Trystan shook his head.

"We're in the middle of nowhere, buddy," he said. "I'd be derelict in my duties as your fraternity brother if I abandoned you out here."

Kit's throat tightened, and he clenched his hands into fists.

"I hate you guys," said Kit. "I didn't want to do any of this."

Rory and Max laughed, but Trystan said nothing. Kit thought about jumping out of the car, but he didn't relish the thought of hitting the pavement at eighty miles an hour. Even if he survived the initial fall, Trystan would stop the car and shoot him in the head. He was fucked. Worse, he had done it all to himself.

As they reached the outskirts of Cloverdale, Trystan slowed the minivan.

"You guys know the plan," said Trystan. "We've scouted the house and surrounding area already. Kit and I will stay in the car to act as lookouts. Rory and Max, you'll go to the detective's house, knock on her door, and shoot her in the head as soon as she opens. Then we'll leave. Once we've hit Siler City, we'll ditch the van and clothes and set those on fire. Then we'll disassemble our firearms and put them in dumpsters around town. After that, we'll take an Uber home and be there before the police even know we've left campus. It'll be easy."

Trystan always thought his plans were easy and that he had anticipated every eventuality. At first, Kit had believed him. Now, his eyes were open, and he could see dozens of problems. Detective Court knew their faces. She had seen them at Dara's Tap House. The moment she saw Rory and Max on her doorstep, she'd know something was up. She'd probably pull her gun. Kit hoped she did. He hoped she'd shoot them both. They deserved it.

But even if Rory and Max killed her without getting hurt, the neighbors would hear the gunshots. Everybody had cameras on their phones now; they'd be lucky if only half a dozen people took videos of them leaving the scene. This was stupid. They deserved to get caught after this.

Trystan navigated Cloverdale's streets as if he were a local and pulled into the back alley that ran behind a row of houses two blocks from the carriage house in which the detective lived. Since few of the residents in Cloverdale had money, their decrepit minivan fit in well.

"Now we're just waiting until nightfall, boys," said Trystan.

"Smoke 'em, if you've got 'em," said Rory, reaching into his pocket for a bag of weed. "We may be here for a while."

He lit up and passed the joint to Max, who took a deep draw before passing it to Trystan and then Kit. The weed was potent and relaxing. Even after smoking, Kit still hated their plan, but he no longer felt like fighting about it. As the sun grew lower in the sky, he closed his eyes and let himself sink into the seat.

"Well, I'll be damned," said Trystan. "We may have just gotten lucky, boys."

Kit opened his eyes in time to see an attractive blond woman walking a big brown dog at the end of the alley. It was her. Trystan turned on the car.

"Change of plan, guys," he said. "Sit up. We're going to run her down."

He put the car in gear and accelerated before Kit could say a word.

32

Cloverdale didn't have a rush hour like a major city would, but when people drove to and from work or school, its streets filled more than usual. I paid none of the cars notice until a gray Honda sedan pulled up beside me on the road. The window rolled down.

"Hey, stranger," said Ann. "It's been a while. You've been busy."

"I have been," I said, smiling at her and then Cora. She waved. "Have you guys had dinner yet? I'm not a great cook, but I'm a world-class picker-upper of Chinese takeout."

"Haven't had Chinese for a while," said Ann, looking in the rearview mirror to her daughter. "How's that sound to you?"

"Does Roy like Chinese food?" asked Cora.

I looked at my dog and smiled.

"He likes all food, but his favorite—"

Before I could finish my thought, tires squealed to my left. The sound jarred me from the conversation, and I stood straighter. A red minivan had pulled out of an alley near us and careened almost on two wheels as it turned. For just a brief second, the sun beat against its windshield, blocking my view inside. Then the angle shifted as the van rolled on tired old shocks. The driver and front passenger both wore ski masks.

The van hit the sidewalk at thirty or forty miles an

hour and bounced. It was heading right toward us. It was so surreal I almost didn't believe what my eyes were seeing. Then my mind caught up with the world, and I knew I had to move. Muscles all over my body felt tight, alert, and ready to spring.

The nearest house had a tiny strip of yard but nowhere for me to hide if the driver of that van was intent on running me down. About twenty feet in front of me, a thick Douglas fir telephone pole protruded from the sidewalk. I had been a police officer for long enough to have worked dozens of car accidents where careless drivers had wrapped their vehicles around similar objects. That wouldn't be perfect, but it'd give me more protection than anything else on the street.

"Ann, drive!" I shouted, hitting my fist on the top of the vehicle. Ann chanced a look over her shoulder and then floored the accelerator. Her car leaped ahead, and I sprinted with Roy beside me toward the telephone pole. The minivan was so close I could smell the motor oil it was burning. Once I reached the telephone pole, I crouched down and gripped Roy's leash hard so he couldn't run away.

At the last moment, tires screeched. The van spun to the left. Ann's car careened around a corner about a block away. I didn't know where she was going, but I hoped she had called the police.

The van skidded to a stop about twenty or thirty feet from me, and its rear sliding door opened. Two guys jumped out of the back. Both held pistols, and both wore pantyhose over their heads. They raised their weapons as I dove to the ground.

The first shots rang out as I scrambled backwards, looking for anywhere to hide. One round slammed into the sidewalk near my foot, while a second hit the sidewalk about a foot from my face. Grit hit me on the cheek.

Without thinking, I dropped Roy's leash and reached for the firearm on my hip while rolling onto my back so I could see my attackers. As I pulled out my weapon and sighted down my body, Roy darted forward. Two more rounds hit the sidewalk near me before the shooters noticed my dog. Roy may have been the laziest dog I knew, but he weighed a hundred and ten pounds, most of which was muscle, and he could outrun everyone I had ever met. These guys didn't stand a chance.

He sprinted toward the shooters and crossed the ground between us before I could draw a breath. The shooter he attacked didn't even have time to brace himself before Roy's jaws locked around his arm near the shoulder. The shooter screamed as he and the heavy dog tumbled to the ground.

That was the opening I needed.

With the second shooter's attention focused on his partner, I shot to my feet and raised my weapon.

"Drop it!" I shouted.

He looked at me and then fired twice. The rounds buzzed past me, narrowly missing. Then he turned and ran toward the minivan but kept his gun pointed at me. I squeezed my trigger three times.

He was moving, so my first two shots hit the side of the minivan behind him. The third struck him in the shoulder, though, and seemed to pass straight through him before shattering the minivan's rear window. A third masked figure from the passenger seat jumped out and grabbed his friend.

"Police! Stop!"

The man in the ski mask pushed his friend into the open sliding door of the minivan. Then the tires chirped as the driver accelerated and hurtled down the street. I ran forward to see the guy on the ground. His firearm was on the sidewalk, so I kicked it away.

"Roy, release!"

Roy relaxed his bite and then stepped away to sit down. I held my firearm on the guy in front of me. He grabbed his shoulder and tried to sit up.

"Don't move," I said. "I'm a police officer, and you just tried to kill me. If you threaten me, I'll shoot you. Take the pantyhose off your face. I want to see you."

He didn't move at first, so I repeated the command. Then he reached up and peeled the pantyhose up to expose his face, confirming something I had already suspected.

"You're a friend of Kit Jameson's, aren't you?" I asked. He said nothing. "It's okay. I took a picture of you at Dara's Tap House with my cell phone, so I know you were there. You feel dizzy?"

He nodded but said nothing.

"I'm going to step back now and call for backup and

an ambulance," I said, glancing to my dog. Roy had lain down with his head between his paws. His tail thumped cheerily behind him. At least one of us had enjoyed the excitement. I looked to my captive again. "If you move or try to run, my dog will chase you. He will then catch you, and I will let him have his way with you. Do you understand?"

He clutched his shoulder and nodded.

"Good," I said, taking a step back. I took my phone from my pocket and called Chief Tomlin's cell phone. He answered on the second ring. "Boss, it's Joe Court. I'm on Cedar Avenue. Four assholes tried to kill me, and I've got one of them bleeding on the sidewalk. I need backup and an ambulance. I also need every cop in the county looking for a late-model red Dodge Caravan. It has bullet holes and at least one shattered window. It will have blood in it, too. Then I need you to call every hospital in the area. I shot one of them, and he'll need medical help to stop the bleeding and infection."

Tomlin paused.

"Shit," he said, his voice low. "Are you all right?"

"I'm fine," I said. "I've discharged my weapon, though, and I've got a guy bleeding on the ground. Send me some help."

"I'm on it."

I hung up the moment he acknowledged my request. Then I called Ann.

"Joe," she said, her voice breathless. "Are you okay?"

"Yeah," I said. "Roy and I are fine. I've got help

inbound. Are you home?"

"Yeah," she said. "Cora and I are hunkered down in the car. I didn't know if it was safe to go inside."

I considered my answer before sighing and looking at the guy on the ground.

"Give it a few minutes, but you should be okay," I said. "A lot of cops are rolling in."

"What happened?" she asked. "One minute, we were talking, and the next minute, a minivan was driving right at us. Then I heard gunfire. I just took off. I didn't even have a plan. Does this kind of thing happen to you a lot?"

I considered my answer before shaking my head.

"No, I don't think anyone's ever tried to run me down with a minivan before."

"Good," said Ann. Our conversation paused. A siren blared somewhere distant, but it was coming closer.

"By the sound, we've got help incoming," I said. "Unless you see a red minivan on the street, it should be safe to go inside. Just lock the door behind you. The police will need to talk to you, so don't be surprised if a uniformed officer knocks on the door within the next hour."

"Okay," she said. "We'll go in."

"And hey, Ann," I said. "Sorry about dinner. We'll get Chinese takeout some other time."

She paused.

"Yeah. Okay. You want a drink?"

Despite the situation, I smiled just a little.

"I rarely turn down a drink," I said, glancing up as a

black and white cruiser turned onto the street. "I've got to go, but I'll text you tonight. And give Cora a hug for me."

"I will, Joe," she said.

I thanked her before hanging up. As I slid my phone into my pocket, the guy on the sidewalk groaned and tried to crawl away but then stopped and started hyperventilating when Roy stood and bowed in front of him as if he wanted to play. That made me smile. He was a sweet dog.

"Tell him to stay away," said the young man, his voice wavering.

"He won't hurt you," I said. "I can't say the same about your future cellmates, though. You just tried to murder a police officer and got caught. My dog is the least of your worries."

33

My evening was long and dull. The Cloverdale Police Department had original jurisdiction over the shooting, but since I had fired my weapon in the line of duty, Chief Tomlin handed the case off to the West County Sheriff's Department. Over the next half hour, the West County sheriff and almost a dozen uniformed officers descended on Cloverdale. I didn't know anyone in their department, but they seemed competent.

The guy Roy attacked was named Max Linsenmayer, and he was the pledge trainer at the Theta Chi Nu fraternity at Newman-Rothschild University. By happenstance, I had pretended to be his girlfriend to lure Kit off campus just the night before.

The paramedics looked at his arm where Roy had bitten him and recommended that he go to the emergency room for treatment, which seemed prudent. A pair of uniformed officers drove him to the ER, where a doctor patched him up and gave him antibiotics. The moment the officers started asking him questions, though, he invoked his right to remain silent and requested they call his attorney. That ended that interview before it began.

Meanwhile, back on Cedar Avenue, three different detectives interviewed me over the next three hours. They also took my firearm, swabbed my hands for gunshot residue, and had me take a breathalyzer test to ensure I was sober at the time of the shooting. Ann corroborated my story, which was helpful. Every cop there understood why I had done what I had done, but they had to follow procedures, anyway. With wealthy suspects—one of whom was bitten by my dog—those procedures would prevent us from being sued down the line.

By about nine that evening, I was so tired I fell asleep in the back of a West County deputy's cruiser. When a deputy saw me, he and another officer escorted me and Roy home. We only lived two blocks away, and the bad guys were likely long gone, so it was unnecessary. Still, I appreciated the courtesy.

When I got home, I let the dog into the courtyard and texted Ann to let her know I was safe. She said she and Cora were already in for the night and wished me well. I wished her and Cora likewise. After Roy used the restroom, we climbed the steps to the carriage house I rented. Finally, I slept and dreamed of better times.

**

My morning started at a little before eight when my cell phone rang. Roy must have been tired because he barely lifted his head before rolling over and going back to sleep. I grabbed it from my end table and looked at the screen.

Rathman, D.

I cleared my throat before answering.

"Hey," I said. "This is Joe Court."

"Officer Court," said Rathman. "This is Lieutenant David Rathman with the Chapel Hill Police Department. How are you doing this morning?"

I almost told him I was better before he woke me up, but I held my tongue and blinked.

"Fine," I said, squinting in the morning light. "What can I do for you?"

"I heard a rumor you were involved in a shooting in Cloverdale," he said. "You okay?"

"I'm fine," I said, clearing my throat. "If you're calling about Sallianne Cantwell, I don't have much to tell you. Before she disappeared, Sallianne had contact with a young woman from Cloverdale named Nicole Johnson. Nicole is a suspect in a related homicide, but she's in the wind. We believe Sallianne was investigating marijuana cultivation in West County, but we haven't found a body or a murderer yet."

Rathman paused.

"I read something about those marijuana fields you guys found," he said. "You made any headway on finding out who owns them?"

"No," I said, shaking my head. "My boss turned the case over to the State Bureau of Investigation. They turned it over to the DEA. I haven't heard an update."

"Good work," he said. "I'm not calling about Sallianne, though. Tell me about your shooting."

"Sure," I said, wondering when the lieutenant and I had become close enough to have these kinds of chats early in the morning. "Four young men approached me in a minivan. Two young men got out and shot at me, but thankfully, they were bad shots. My dog took out one, and I shot the other guy. The man I shot made it back to the minivan, and he and the two men inside escaped. The young man my dog bit is in a West County Jail holding cell. You know anything about it?"

"I can't help you with the minivan, but a college student named Rory McDonald stumbled into the ER at UNC Medical Center in Chapel Hill last night. He had blood all over his shirt and said he had been in a car accident. Doctors cut away his clothes and found what appeared to be a through-and-through gunshot wound on his shoulder. You know anything about that?"

I sat straighter and almost smiled.

"Is Mr. McDonald a student at Newman-Rothschild University?"

"He is," said Rathman. "We found a student ID in his wallet."

I nodded.

"I assume you've got him in custody?"

"He's in a hospital bed at the moment," said Rathman. "He lost a lot of blood, so the doctor wanted to keep him for observation. One of my detectives tried to talk to him last night, but he refused to say who shot him."

I rubbed sleep out of my eyes as I thought.

"Who brought him to the ER?"

"He walked in but said he took the bus earlier," said Rathman. "There are protocols that kick in if a bus driver picks up a passenger he or she thinks is having a medical emergency, so there'd be a lot of paperwork if that were true. My guess is that his friends dropped him off a couple of blocks away so the hospital surveillance cameras wouldn't see their car, and he stumbled to the building."

It made sense, so I nodded.

"Okay," I said, drawing in a breath. "Thanks for the call, Lieutenant. If you can, keep him at the hospital. I'll swing by with a partner. If this is the guy I shot, I suspect he's also involved in a double homicide in Cloverdale."

"Double homicide. I'm glad I called."

"Me, too," I said. "We'll head to the hospital as soon as we can, and we'll go from there."

I hung up a moment later and called Brady Maddox's cell phone. He answered before it finished ringing once.

"Hey," I said. "You've got Max Linsenmayer in custody, right?"

Brady paused.

"He's in the West County Jail," he said before pausing again. "I heard about the shooting. You okay?"

"Yeah, I'm fine. It's not my first time being shot at," I said. "I just got a call from Lieutenant David Rathman in Chapel Hill. One of Mr. Linsenmayer's fraternity brothers is at UNC Medical Center with a suspected gunshot wound to the shoulder. He refused to speak with Chapel Hill detectives and tell them who shot him, but I thought he might talk to us if we give him the right incentive. You want to pay him a visit with me?"

"Uh, sure, I guess," he said. "Should we call the West County Sheriff's Department and let them know?"

"After we arrest him for murdering Susie and Dean

Hillerud," I said. "He and his buddies burned a mom and her son alive. I want to see his face when we put handcuffs on him."

"You're not in the office," said Brady. "You at home?"

I said I was and then gave him directions. It wouldn't take him long to get here, so I dressed, brushed my teeth, and pulled my hair back with a tie before leaving. Cora was setting up a tea party in the courtyard. Ann came out a moment later carrying a little tray with cups. Cora asked whether I'd like to join, but I told her I had to work. After the scare yesterday, Ann had taken the day off work and planned to keep her daughter home. I couldn't blame her. They said Roy would be okay with them, so I left him in the courtyard and met Brady in the driveway.

Our drive to Chapel Hill wasn't difficult. We arrived at nine and were standing in Rory McDonald's hospital room at nine thirty. He looked at me and sat straighter, his face growing pale.

"It's you," he said. "Are you going to shoot me again?"

I looked to Brady.

"That was easier than I expected," I said. "Did that sound like a spontaneous declaration of guilt to you?"

"He said you shot him," he said, keeping his eyes on Rory. "Which means he was involved in the attempt on your life."

"Oh, shit," said Rory, sinking into his pillow. "I need a lawyer."

Considering Rory was probably on half a dozen different drugs for pain, I doubted the admission would make it to court, but it gave us an excuse to hold him. I'd take that.

"Yeah, a lawyer would be helpful," I said, nodding. "Rory McDonald, you're under arrest for the attempted murder of a police officer. We'll talk later, but for now, just enjoy that bed. The ones in prison aren't that nice."

34

The doctors discharged Rory about an hour after we arrived, and we drove him to the West County Jail. Since we needed information from him, I went to the watch commander's office with a special request while Brady filled out the paperwork.

"Morning," I said. "I'm Detective Joe Court with the Cloverdale Police Department. You got a minute? I need to talk to you about a young man I brought in."

The watch commander, a middle-aged woman with a picture of three dogs and a balding middle-aged man on her desk, leaned back and nodded.

"You think he'll be a problem?"

"Not to your staff or the other inmates," I said. "He's rich, and he's an asshole, and we've got circumstantial evidence tying him to a double homicide and the attempted murder of a police officer."

She raised her eyebrows.

"You want us to keep him isolated?"

"No," I said, shaking my head. "I want you to put him in an interrogation room with Max Linsenmayer and turn on your recording equipment. These jokers tried to kill me. I'm hoping they'll talk and try to put together a story if we put them in a room together."

Her lips curled into a tight, disbelieving smile.

"Are they that stupid?"

I considered.

"They're arrogant and overconfident," I said. "They think they're smarter than us. If we put them in a room together, I'm willing to bet they'll think it's a mistake and try to take advantage of it. We'll use that."

She tilted her head to the side and drew in a breath.

"Okay, Detective," she said. "We'll put them together and see what happens. Understand that I won't put my staff in any compromising situations, though."

"I wouldn't ask you to," I said, nodding. "Thank you."

She wished me luck, and I went to Brady, who was in the jail's lobby waiting for me.

"You get everything sorted?" he asked.

"Yeah," I said, nodding. "If you don't mind, drive me home. I'll get my car. We're good with this case for a while, but I've got a lot of work to do before my temporary assignment runs out."

Brady knew the situation, so he nodded but said nothing. He drove me home, and I checked on Roy. He was good, so I got in my Volvo and started driving to my station. About halfway there, my phone rang. It was Chief Tomlin, so I pulled to the side of the road in a residential neighborhood and answered.

"Hey, boss," I said. "I'm driving into the station now. If you give me five minutes, I'll be in your office."

"You sitting down?"

I almost reminded him I was in my car, driving into the station, but I held my tongue.

"Yeah," I said.

"A kayaker found the body of Sallianne Cantwell in the Haw River about an hour west of Cloverdale. It's near Burlington."

For a split second, the world seemed to stop moving.

"What's her condition?"

He grunted.

"I don't have details, but she's been in the water," he said. "A pathologist from the state medical examiner's office is on site, and so are two SBI agents."

"Give me the location again," I said, reaching for a notepad in my glove box to write the information down. The boss described the area and said he got the call from Lieutenant David Rathman in Chapel Hill. I wrote the pertinent details down and then cleared my throat.

"Have they called Tonya Cantwell yet?" I asked. "She's Sallianne's mom."

"That, I don't know," said Tomlin. "The SBI is working the case. You'd have to talk to their agents."

"Okay," I said. "Looks like I'll be driving out to Burlington."

"Drive safely," he said. "We'll hold down the fort here."

I thanked him and hung up before looking up Burlington on my GPS. Looked like I had a long day ahead of me.

**

The road to Burlington was two lanes of black asphalt that wound through a forested section of the state. For most of it, I got stuck behind an old pickup that didn't dare come within ten miles of the speed limit unless I tried to pass him. Then, the driver opened the old girl up and gave her some gas. If my car had lights or a siren, I would have pulled him over, but since my Volvo didn't, I was stuck. It was frustrating, but at least the scenery was nice.

Burlington was bigger than I had expected and had a cute historic downtown. From what I could see, its parks looked nice, too. I paid attention to those kinds of things. I liked public parks, but I liked towns that gave public parks priority even more. Since I grew up in the foster care system, and since I gave most of my foster parents a hard time, I switched homes all the time and rarely stayed in one spot long enough to join the local T-ball or soccer team. Sometimes, the local park was the only place where I could relax and have fun. Public parks and playgrounds made my difficult childhood easier, and I appreciated every city that provided those for its residents.

Sallianne's body was northeast of town on a wooded stretch of the Haw River. Growing up on the Mississippi, when I thought of a river, I imagined massive waterways capable of transporting barges that held thousands of tons of coal and other cargo. The Haw was smaller and rockier. Back home, we probably would have called it a creek. As I crossed a bridge near the roadway, I noticed a man in galoshes standing in the middle of the river. The water barely reached his thighs.

I followed the road until I came to a group of about a dozen cars parked on the shoulder. Trees and scrub brush separated the roadway from the river, but through thin spots in the greenery, I saw men and women in uniform huddled along the river's rocky banks. I parked behind a marked cruiser from the North Carolina State Highway Patrol and clipped my badge to a lanyard, which I then hung around my neck.

As I got out of my car, a uniformed Highway Patrol trooper walked toward me.

"You need some help..." He furrowed his brow and looked at my badge. Then he looked at me, apparently not recognizing the badge. "Miss?"

"I'm Detective Mary Joe Court with the Cloverdale Police Department," I said. "I was told a kayaker found the body of Sallianne Cantwell."

"That's right," he said, nodding. "Is the case an interest of yours?"

"It is," I said. "Sallianne spent quite a bit of time in Cloverdale before she disappeared. Let your CO know I'm here and that I need to talk to him."

"Yes, ma'am," he said, nodding and turning. He walked toward the tree line, but before he could reach it, a man in gray pants and a navy blue T-shirt with SBI printed on the chest stepped through a thick curtain of vines and brush. The SBI agent had curly black hair, dark stubble on his chin, and a bit of a paunch. The trooper held a hand for him so he wouldn't fall, and the two spoke for a moment before the trooper pointed toward me. I waved, and the SBI agent nodded as he came toward me.

"Detective Court?" he asked. I nodded, and we

shook hands. "Special Agent Chase Gray. Interest in Ms. Cantwell ranges far and wide, I see."

I nodded and explained who I was, how I had gotten involved with the case, and what I had found so far. He listened and nodded and asked pertinent questions, most of which, unfortunately, I couldn't answer. When I finished, he looked toward the river and sighed.

"Sounds like this may be harder than I expected," he said. "Let's walk and see what we've got."

"Sure," I said. So we stepped through the bramble and down to the rocky shoreline. Two burly men in SBI T-shirts and big rubber galoshes hauled a bright yellow backboard out of the river. Strapped to it was a cadaver bag. As I watched them struggle, my throat tightened, and a heavy feeling began pressing down on me as I thought about Tonya Cantwell. I had told her to prepare for news of her daughter's death, but nothing could truly prepare anyone for a child's death.

"You all right, Detective?" asked Agent Gray.

I swallowed hard and nodded.

"Yeah. I know the victim's mother. I didn't expect this to hit me so hard."

The SBI agent nodded.

"You ever worked a death investigation?"

I looked at him and felt my lips curl into a smile. In Missouri, my reputation had preceded me wherever I went. Anonymity still felt novel.

"Yeah," I said, nodding. "I've worked a few."

He looked toward the river.

"You ever worked a floater?" he asked.

"Yep," I said, nodding.

"So you know what you're getting into by volunteering to be here."

"Yep," I said again, still nodding. "This won't be fun."

He looked to the river and nodded.

"It most certainly will not be."

35

Water made death investigations tough. It washed away hairs, fiber evidence, and skin cells from the victim's body, limiting the amount of forensic data we could glean from a cadaver. Moving water made it even harder because the current could have carried her miles from the dump site. And even after she came to a rest, the water would break down the soft tissue of her body and disarticulate the bones, starting with her fingers, wrists, toes, and feet, then moving to the larger bones of the head and jaw.

"Are we sure this is Sallianne Cantwell?"

Gray glanced from the river to me.

"Her picture's been on the news," he said. "We'll confirm with dental records, but it's her."

I nodded and furrowed my brow.

"So she's intact enough that you're able to recognize her," I said.

"Yeah," he said. "We got lucky."

"No, we didn't," I said. "She's been missing for several weeks. If she's been in the water that long, her skin and fat should be decomposed. We shouldn't be able to recognize her."

"If she hasn't been in the water, where has she been?"

"That's a good question," I said. "Who's the medical examiner?"

"Dr. Turley," said Gray, pointing to a thin, young man

with brown hair and a goatee. He stood alone on the bank and watched as two men carried the back brace and body over the rough ground. I walked toward him and waved. He nodded to me.

"Dr. Turley?" I asked. He nodded, and we shook hands. "I'm Detective Joe Court with the Cloverdale Police Department. Have you seen the victim yet?"

"Briefly," he said, nodding. "We'll be conducting a full autopsy and tox screen, so we'll have more details in the coming weeks. I'll make sure you get a report."

I forced a smile to my lips.

"What can you tell me now?" I asked. "I realize she's been in the water, but was she shot, stabbed, hung, drawn and quartered, hurt in other ways? Does she have her fingers and toes? What are your initial thoughts?"

He considered me and then looked upriver to a group of men and women in black inner tubes lashed together to form a floating platform. The current carried them past us. There were about ten people, and they all wore bathing suits. They sat up when they saw us. Most of them held beers, and I noticed a black trash bag floating behind them. A few waved at us. I waved back without thinking. Once they were downstream a bit, they started talking and laughing.

I looked to the doctor.

"Are there many people on the water?"

He nodded.

"Yeah," he said. "It's a well-used river."

"So our victim can't have been in for long," I said.

"People would have seen her."

"If I had to guess, she's been in for twelve hours at most," said the doctor. "And her body's intact. She's got all her fingers and toes, and her skin hasn't fallen off yet."

"How'd she die?" asked Agent Gray.

"Her skull's caved in, and her right arm and right hip are fractured, but I can't determine if the injuries are peri- or postmortem. She has soft-tissue bruising on her right side, but no other obvious signs of trauma."

"Good," I said, nodding. "Was she wearing clothes?"

He nodded.

"She had on blue jeans, a blue top, and tennis shoes."

"Okay," I said, nodding and trying to think through this. "Thank you."

I looked to Agent Gray.

"What's around here?" I asked.

He considered for a moment.

"As far as buildings or business, not much, but we need to get a look at everything we can all the same," he said, turning and waving toward another SBI agent closer to the shore. She walked toward us. "Tracy, this is Detective Joe Court. Detective Court, this is Special Agent Tracy Corbin. Do we have a search and rescue drone?"

"Nice to meet you, Detective," she said, looking to me. Then she looked to her partner. "The drone's in the truck. You want me to get it?"

"Yeah," said Gray. "There's not a lot around here, so I doubt Ms. Cantwell walked out here. Let's find her car."

Agent Corbin nodded and hurried toward the road. I

waited and chatted with Agent Gray. He was a North Carolina native and lived with his wife and two kids in Greensboro. We didn't talk long, but he seemed like a nice man. He also seemed competent, which was far more important in our present circumstances. Agent Corbin came back a few minutes later with a thick hard case. Inside was a drone with four rotors and a big control unit. Within moments, we were in the air, watching video shot by the drone's camera.

Agent Corbin was a good pilot and kept the drone steady above the tree line. For about ten minutes, she followed the river upstream. We saw a lot of people on inner tubes, including a young couple who had joined their tubes together and tied themselves to a branch overhanging the river. The surrounding water rippled.

"Zoom in on those two," said Agent Gray, squinting at the controller's small screen. "What are they doing? Are they dumping something in the water?"

"Don't zoom in," I said. I pointed to the screen. "That's his rear end bouncing up and down. They're having sex."

Agent Gray tilted his head to the side.

"You'd think they would have noticed the drone flying overhead."

Agent Corbin snickered a little.

"Not if he's doing it right."

I might have laughed, but we were standing not forty feet from a coroner's van that held a young woman's body.

"Let's move on," I said. Corbin kept flying. The countryside was pretty, but I was wasting my time staring at a screen with two other investigators. Instead, I walked about two hundred yards downstream. A group of four canoers had beached their canoes on a stretch of flat, rocky shoreline.

I flashed my badge at them.

"Hey," I said, walking toward the group. There were two couples, one in their twenties and the other in their late forties or early fifties. "I'm Detective Joe Court. You guys have a minute?"

"Sure," said the older of the two men. The woman with him was around the same age, though her black hair had fewer grays, and her skin had fewer wrinkles. "I'm Henry. This is my wife, Fiona."

The younger woman stepped forward.

"I'm Whitney," she said. "Henry and Fiona are my parents. Bryce is my husband."

The young man shook my hand. It looked like a nice family outing. I hated to interrupt it with a murder investigation.

"You guy stop for a reason, or did you get tired of paddling?" I asked.

"Some of us are tired," said Fiona, patting her husband and winking. "What's going on? If we can ask."

"We're working a homicide," I said. "You guys didn't see an abandoned car on the shoreline, did you?"

Fiona covered her mouth. Henry cocked his head to the side. The younger two blinked but said nothing.

"No," said Whitney, after a moment. "I mean, we weren't looking. You can't see the road from the river well."

It made sense, so I nodded.

"Where did you guys park?" I asked. "Assuming you didn't paddle here from your house."

Henry laughed and pointed downstream.

"There's a tour operator about six miles that way," he said. "We parked there, got on a school bus, and then rode to a landing where the company keeps the canoes about ten miles upstream. That way we float right back to our car. We don't have to haul canoes halfway across the state."

"Are there a lot of cars there?"

Henry nodded.

"It's a big outfit," he said. "They've got canoes, kayaks, and people on inner tubes. It's a good time."

It was worth checking out, so I thanked them and wished them a nice rest of the day before walking back to Agents Gray and Corbin.

"You guys find anything?"

"Just drunks on inner tubes," said Agent Corbin. "You?"

"A tour operator downstream," I said. "They've been busing boaters up and down the river all day. Somebody there might have seen something."

"Good idea," said Agent Gray, reaching into his pocket for a business card. "This has my contact information on it if you find anything."

I thanked him and headed out as he and Agent Corbin continued flying their drone. The tour operator had signs up and down the road, so it wasn't hard to find. It had a big pavilion with picnic tables and another building with bathrooms and showers. Other cedar-sided buildings held offices and equipment. Four families ate lunch at the picnic tables, and two staff members in khaki shorts and aquamarine colored shirts were picking up litter in the yard.

I focused on their gravel parking lot. It was a couple of acres at least and must have held two hundred cars. According to the Department of Motor Vehicles, Sallianne drove a 2011 Infiniti FX35. It was a medium-sized luxury SUV, which our records showed she had purchased used in 2017. I had the license plate written down on a notepad.

I walked up and down the aisles of cars and then stopped once I reached the edge of the lot. Parked on the grass beside a crepe myrtle was a gray Infiniti SUV. The interior looked clean, and the exterior lacked blood spatter, scratches, dents, or broken windows. There was no sign at all why its former occupant lay dead four miles upstream.

I pulled out my phone anyway and called Agent Gray. He answered quickly.

"Hey," I said. "It's Joe Court. I found Sallianne's car at the tour operator's place. We better get some people up here."

He paused for just a second.

"I'm on my way. See you in a few."

I thanked him and hung up before focusing on Sallianne's car. This made no sense. The tour operators ran day trips up and down the Haw River. They didn't have overnight trips, so if they found a car in their lot overnight, they should have freaked out. It would have told them they still had guests on the water. Moreover, Sallianne had been missing for weeks. Had this car been in the lot for days, dust would have covered it, but it was clean.

We may have found Sallianne's body, but we hadn't found any answers. If anything, we had more questions. Hopefully one of them would lead us to something helpful because I still had no idea why this young lady was dead.

36

About five minutes after I called Agent Gray, Agent Corbin pulled a black SUV into the gravel parking lot. I stepped away from Sallianne's vehicle and looked around, expecting more cruisers to follow. They didn't. As Agent Corbin walked toward me, I furrowed my brow.

"Where's your partner?"

"We found some glass and bits of plastic on the shoulder about a mile back," she said. "He's checking it out now. So you found her car, huh?"

"Yep," I said, nodding. Since the dead didn't have privacy rights, we didn't need a warrant to search the vehicle. Agent Corbin got a rubber wedge from her SUV and slid that into the top of the driver's door on Sallianne's Infiniti. That created a gap between the door and frame big enough that we could slide a metal shim into. She fished her shim around until she hit the power door lock and unlocked the vehicle. The interior smelled like marijuana.

"Whoa," said Agent Corbin, taking a step back and looking at me. "That's powerful."

"It is," I said, nodding and snapping a pair of blue polypropylene gloves onto my hands. "Open the back. I'll start searching there. You look in the cabin."

Agent Corbin searched the dash for a button to open the rear power lift gate. As soon as she hit the button, the car beeped, and the back door started opening. Since she drove an SUV, Sallianne didn't have a traditional trunk. Instead, she had a space behind the rear seat big enough to hold several weeks' worth of groceries. Unfortunately for us, it was empty save a plastic handle used to lift the floorboard.

I pulled up on the handle, and immediately the marijuana smell grew stronger. Beneath the floorboard, I found the vehicle's spare tire, jack, and an open gallon-sized Ziploc bag full of smaller Ziploc bags of marijuana. They weren't the best containers, but Sallianne probably didn't intend to keep her drugs long. A typical user wouldn't have this much weed, and he wouldn't package it like this. This was a dealer's stash, one intended to be sold.

I held up the bag so Agent Corbin could see it.

"I found the drugs," I said.

"And I found some money," said Corbin, holding up a roll of cash. "It's mostly twenties."

I carried the Ziploc bag to the front of the car and watched as Agent Corbin counted out the money on the hood. Then I handed her the bag and counted the cash to confirm her numbers before we bagged and tagged it. Normally, she would have bagged evidence herself without my input, but when dealing with cash, multiple people had to witness and sign everything to minimize the chance that someone would steal it. Sallianne had died with five hundred and seventy dollars cash in her glove box and a big bag of marijuana in her trunk.

We bagged what we had and continued searching the

vehicle. She had a combination ice scraper and snow brush beneath her front passenger seat, but as I picked it up, the ice scraper twisted. With a little force, the scraper head popped off. Inside the plastic handle, were two dry, twisted joints. They smelled moldy, which was unsurprising if they had been inside the ice scraper's handle for any length of time.

I bagged the evidence and then put it on the hood beside the big Ziploc bag. Then I looked to Agent Corbin.

"If she had this much weed in the back, why would she hide two nasty, ruined joints in her ice scraper?"

Agent Corbin tilted her head to the side.

"Maybe she put them in there a long time ago and forgot about them," she said. That was possible, so I nodded.

"You remember when cars last frosted over?" I asked. Agent Corbin drew in a breath and thought.

"Sometime last year."

I didn't know whether it would help, but I mentally filed the information away and continued searching. As I looked under the car and in the wheel wells, Agent Gray arrived in a white Dodge Charger. Agent Corbin filled him in on what we had found, and he listened, nodded, and opened his eyes wide when he saw the bag of weed. Then he surprised me with a question.

"How much gas does she have?"

I looked at Corbin. She furrowed her brow and looked at the dash and then shrugged.

"According to the gauge, the tank's empty. It might

just say that because the car's not on, though."

Agent Gray nodded and popped open the exterior gas tank door. Then he leaned down and smelled.

"I can't even smell fumes."

I crossed my arms.

"What are you getting at?" I asked.

"I'm forming a theory," he said. "Imagine this. You're Sallianne Cantwell. You're a communications graduate student at the University of North Carolina, and you sell drugs to make ends meet. Suppose you get a call from somebody asking you to meet for a big buy. The catch is that they want to meet you somewhere safe and free from prying eyes."

"I'm with you," I said.

"She chooses here," he said. "It's remote, and the tour company only works in the day, so she knows there won't be witnesses. Maybe she even took a canoe trip here. We'll have to check with the company."

"We can do that," I said. "Go on."

"So Sallianne comes and waits. Maybe she didn't realize she was low on gas, or maybe she just forgot to fill up. However it happened, her tank went dry. Instead of calling AAA and asking them to come out to a drug deal, she decided to walk to the nearest gas station. The road's dark, and it's surrounded by trees. While walking, I think, she got hit by a car and fell into the river and died. The driver may have even stopped alongside the road to look for her. With as many deer as we have around here, he may not have even realized he hit a person. He might have thought he hit an animal."

The theory fit the evidence well and explained the glass alongside the road, the abandoned vehicle, and Sallianne's injuries, but it left me with more questions than it explained.

"If that's true, where's she been?" I asked. "She and her mom were close. Surely she would have called her mom once she saw the news reports about her."

"I can't answer that," said Agent Gray. "I can only tell you what the evidence indicates. We'll see if we can trace the glass on the road to a specific car, but if Salliane's injuries are consistent with a car accident, we might have closed our case."

I nodded and grimaced.

"You don't seem convinced," said Agent Corbin. "You see something we don't?"

"No, you're seeing the same evidence I am," I said. "This just doesn't feel right. It's too convenient. Why'd she show up now? Why not last week? Why not the week before when the news started running her story? And if she's been lying low, why didn't she call her mom? If she were alive, it seems awfully cruel to let her mom think she was dead."

"All good questions," said Agent Gray. He paused and crossed his arms. "Tell you what: You know the victim's mom, and you've interviewed some of her friends. How about you go back to your station and work on your questions, and we'll work the scene here? When Dr. Turley finishes his preliminary autopsy report, we'll have a conference call and see where we're at."

I considered him.

"Is that a nice way of blowing me off?"

Agent Gray said nothing, but Agent Corbin looked down and smiled.

"If Chase was blowing you off, he'd send you on an errand to track down Chinese glass manufacturers that don't really exist," she said. "He's not subtle. If he sent you off to waste your time, you'd know it."

Agent Gray smiled and mouthed *sorry* to her before turning to focus on me.

"I pride myself on the quality of the busywork I assign," he said.

They seemed serious, so I sighed and nodded.

"All right," I said. "I'll go home. Good luck with the scene here and Sallianne's body."

"Just so you know, we already notified Ms. Cantwell about her daughter," said Corbin. "If we had known you had a relationship with her, we would have included you. She seemed to be expecting the phone call."

"The last time we spoke, I told her to be ready for it," I said. I closed my eyes and tilted my head to the side. "Not that anybody can be ready to hear their daughter died."

The group went quiet until Agent Gray cleared his throat.

"Well, good luck, Joe," he said. "I'm going to call my office and see if we can get a forensics team to pick up Sallianne's car. We'll print it and vacuum for fibers in a controlled setting."

It sounded like they had things under control, so I wished them luck and drove home. Along the way, I called Brady Maddox to ask about our experiment with Max Linsenmayer and Rory McDonald. Brady and I didn't speak long, mostly because we had little to say. The West County Jail had put them in a room together, but in almost six hours, neither said a single word. It was almost like they had planned for that eventuality. That was disappointing. I thanked him and wished him a good night before hanging up.

As I got home, I found an old brown pickup in the driveway beside Ann's Honda Accord. She must have guests. I parked on the street and took the stairs to the carriage house but stopped when I found a sticky note on my door asking me to stop by Ann's place. I went inside for the wine I had bought yesterday before going down to the courtyard. Roy and Cora were outside. Cora played with a doll, while Roy sat beside her on the grass. I petted his back and gave her a hug before going through Ann's open back door.

"Hey," I called into the living room. "It's Joe."

"We're in the kitchen," said Ann. I walked to the eat-in kitchen. I didn't know how she kept it so clean with a kid at home, but the kitchen was pristine. A scruffy-looking old man leaning against the island looked considerably less photogenic.

He straightened when he saw me. Ann leaned against her refrigerator with her arms across her chest. Her face had a ruddy complexion, as if she had been exercising. Her eyes looked flinty.

"Joe," she said. "This is Hiram Ford. He said he wanted to talk to you."

I recognized the name, so I nodded and looked at him.

"You know a young woman named Nicole Johnson, Mr. Ford?"

He blinked, considering his answer, before lying to my face.

"Not ringing a bell," he said. "I own a couple of businesses in town. She work for me?"

"I suspect she does," I said, glancing to Ann to make sure she was okay. She gave me a tight smile, so I focused on him again. "How about you and I take a walk and get out of this nice lady's kitchen?"

"That'd be just fine," he said, nodding to Ann. She clenched her jaw as Hiram left the kitchen and started walking toward the front door. I lowered my voice and asked if she was okay. She drew in a deep breath and nodded before mouthing that she was sorry. I didn't know what she had to be sorry for, but Hiram clearly had her on edge.

Whoever Hiram was, he scared my friend. Ann was a strong, intelligent, and capable woman, but she came from a civilized world where people didn't threaten or hurt one another. Hiram may have been some kind of local boogeyman, but I had made a career of facing down monsters...and sometimes putting them in the ground. If

Hiram thought he could intimidate me the way he intimidated Ann, he was in for a long, frustrating evening.

37

Since I wanted to take Roy for a walk anyway, I grabbed his leash and led him through the courtyard's gate to meet Hiram in front of the home. He was in his sixties or early seventies, and the sun had baked his skin so it looked like the amber-colored leather of a new baseball glove. He had yellow, ratlike teeth, likely stained by coffee or cigarettes, and the beady eyes of a snake. His mustache almost seemed to tremble as he spoke.

"Sorry we haven't been introduced before this," he said. "I have an interest in law enforcement."

"I suspect many law enforcement officials have an interest in you, too."

He snickered and then gestured down the street.

"Let's walk," he said. "I can hold your dog's leash. I love puppies."

"If you come anywhere near Roy, he'll bite your penis off."

Hiram lowered his arm and took a small, stuttering step back.

"You train him to do that?"

"It came naturally to him," I said.

He grunted and began walking. For about half a block, neither of us said anything. He didn't seem like the kind of person who needed to build up gumption; he was waiting for me to say something and set the tone of our conversation. I could do that.

"So," I said. "You scare Ann. What do you have on her?"

He snickered.

"Ann's a good woman," he said. "Her husband and I go way back."

"Ex-husband," I said.

He shrugged and tilted his head to the side.

"What the Lord has put together, no man should tear asunder," he said. "Ann and Jeremy were good together, and they share a wonderful little girl. I don't believe in divorce, especially where the divorce is predicated on misunderstandings and miscommunication."

"It's a good thing nobody gives a shit about your beliefs," I said. "He hit her on multiple occasions, and they're divorced. That's it. Now what do you want?"

"I just thought we could talk," he said. "I've got friends in lots of police departments in this state, and yet I hardly know the first thing about you. Why are you in North Carolina, Ms. Court? You seem like a Missouri girl through and through."

"If you know I'm from Missouri, you know more than most people," I said. "And I'm not a girl. I'm an adult. Please treat me with the same respect you'd treat a twenty-nine-year-old man."

He chuckled.

"I didn't mean any offense. Most women find me charming."

I glanced at him and then slowed as Roy stopped to smell a streetlight that another dog had likely peed on.

"I'm sure women tell you that," I said. "What do you want?"

He stopped walking and considered me before narrowing his eyes.

"A kayaker found Sallianne Cantwell's body in the Haw River this morning."

I nodded and smiled.

"I didn't know that made the news."

He shrugged and started walking as Roy finished sniffing.

"Like I said, I have a lot of friends in law enforcement," he said. "They tell me a car hit her while she was trying to sell some weed. It just breaks your heart, doesn't it?"

I started walking again.

"Your friends in law enforcement must like you if they're willing to divulge theories about an active investigation."

He looked at me and smiled.

"I don't mean to brag, but my business successes have left me with excess resources I'm more than willing to invest in organizations that benefit law enforcement officers and their families. My foundation even set up a scholarship for young men and women with law enforcement aspirations at the University of North Carolina. One of your colleagues told me you plan to go back to school there next year."

My insides went a little colder, and I drew in a slow breath.

"I wish my colleagues had kept that to themselves," I

said. "But yeah. I plan to go back to school."

"Social work," he said, smiling. "It's a fine field for a young woman like yourself. For anyone, I should add. You'll do good."

This guy had connections. I could see why he scared Ann, especially if he knew Jeremy.

"That's the hope," I said. "What do you want?"

"Like I said, I have a large scholarship fund for young men and women," he said. "I doubt you need money, though, do you? You must have resources the average woman doesn't have. You watched Cora for free all summer, after all."

My body felt tense. He probably got that tidbit from Ann's ex-husband, Jeremy, but he still knew far more than he should.

"Is there a point to this conversation?"

He shrugged and waved to an older woman sitting on her porch at a nearby home. Then he looked at me.

"I just wondered what was next for you," he said. "Ms. Cantwell's case is closed—or will be soon—and you've made arrests in the gas station robberies. You've done good work. The people of Cloverdale owe you a debt. I was just wondering how you want that debt paid."

I glanced at him.

"Just offer me cash."

He furrowed his brow and stopped walking. Roy and I kept going, so he hurried to catch up.

"Excuse me, Ms. Court?"

I glanced at him again.

"If you're going to try bribing me, don't beat around the bush. Just offer me cash so I can arrest you. Otherwise, this conversation is a complete waste of my time and yours."

"I'm not here to offer you anything," he said. "Are you looking for Nicole Johnson? You mentioned her earlier."

I looked at him but said nothing. He nodded and settled into the walk again.

"Old towns like Cloverdale have secrets," he said. "And sometimes it's best if those secrets remain hidden. We don't need outsiders unearthing our skeletons. Nicole Johnson is a troubled young woman. Her family doesn't need her sins broadcast for the world to hear. She and her momma used to fight like cats and dogs. I bet she snapped and killed her. She might have killed her daddy, too. Or maybe she and her daddy escaped to Mexico or Canada. They're gone, either way. It's a tragedy, but it's one best kept under wraps. Do you understand?"

"I understand your concern," I said.

We walked for another ten feet before he narrowed his eyes at me.

"You're shifty," he said. "Like a lawyer or a politician."

"I'm hardly the shifty one here. In fact, you remind me of a politician I once knew," I said. "His name was Darren Rogers, and he was a county councilman in St. Augustine County, where I used to live. He was a piece of shit, too."

Hiram snickered and shook his head.

"I appreciate your candor," he said, "but I'm just trying to help you out. People can get hurt when they meddle in affairs they don't understand."

I raised my eyebrows and stopped walking. We had come to the street where Max Linsenmayer and Rory McDonald had attacked me. Hiram stopped near me.

"You really do remind me of Darren," I said. "He warned me against investigating certain crimes, too."

"Did you listen to him?"

"Nope," I said, shaking my head.

Hiram narrowed his eyes and tilted his head to the side.

"Did that work out in your favor?"

"Nope," I said. "I lost friends and alienated people I cared about. It was the right thing to do, though."

He blinked and nodded.

"You're naïve, honey," he said. "But you're welcome to enjoy everything Cloverdale offers. I will warn you, though: People around these parts don't like it when strangers cause trouble."

I nodded and pointed up the street.

"You see that telephone pole?" I asked.

He nodded.

"I hid behind that as four young men tried to kill me the other day," I said. "They came out of their car with guns. Roy protected me and bit one of them, disarming him. That saved his life. If he hadn't dropped his firearm, I would have killed him. I shot his friend in the shoulder."

Hiram looked around and then raised his eyebrows.

"Sorry to hear of your troubles."

"I didn't say it because I wanted your sympathy," I said. "I said it because I wanted you to understand something: People who threaten me end up hurt. It is a bad idea to come after me or the people I care about, Mr. Ford. Now get out of here before I get upset."

He considered me and then drew in a breath.

"Understand that this might mean war, Ms. Court."

"If it does, it'll be short."

"Oh, I guarantee that," he said, nodding and winking before turning. "Good day, Detective."

As he walked away, I sighed, wondering what the hell I had just gotten myself involved in.

38

Roy and I walked home in the dark. Ann came into the courtyard as soon as I opened the gate. Cora must have been inside the house.

"Everything okay?" she asked.

I nodded.

"Mr. Ford and I talked," I said. "If he bothers you again, let me know."

"What'd he want?"

I considered my answer a moment. Ann looked down.

"You don't have to answer," she said.

"I think he was trying to intimidate me," I said. "It takes more than one crooked old man to scare me, though."

"He's got a lot of friends," said Ann. "Just be wary. I don't want you getting hurt."

"Don't worry," I said. "I've played this game a long time. Mr. Ford isn't half as scary as he thinks he is, and his friends won't be as loyal as he expects once I bring out the skeletons in his closet."

"I hope you're right," she said.

"I am."

She nodded and wished me luck before telling me she had to put Cora to bed. That was just as well. I had things to do. Roy and I took the stairs to my apartment, where I made myself a peanut butter and jelly sandwich for dinner. It wasn't much, but it tasted good. Afterwards, I pulled out my phone and called Tonya Cantwell. Agents Gray and Corbin had already notified her about Sallianne, but I wanted to make sure she was okay and to answer any questions she might have.

We spoke for a few minutes. Now that we had found Sallianne's body, Tonya could grieve for her daughter and plan for her burial. I told her again how sorry I was for her loss, and she thanked me for my work. After ten minutes, I hung up.

My stomach felt heavy, and my throat felt tight. For a few moments, I stayed at my kitchen table just thinking. Roy came over to me and sat beside me, and I ran a hand along his back. Sallianne was almost my age. I wondered what would have happened if I had died when Max and Rory came after me.

Brady and Chief Tomlin and my other colleagues at work would probably go to my funeral if I had one. Ann would come, too. Hopefully Cora would stay with her grandparents. I didn't know whether Julia and Doug Green or my siblings would show up. Then again, I doubted I'd actually have a funeral. None of my relatives knew where I lived, so no one would claim my body. The medical examiner's office would probably cremate my remains and then put me on a shelf in a warehouse beside the other cremated bodies of the unclaimed.

I stood and grabbed a bottle of vodka from my freezer. Since moving to North Carolina, I had kept my drinking in check, but at the moment, I didn't care about restraint. I poured myself a shot and drank it in a gulp. It felt good as it burned down my throat. Then I poured a second, drank that, and then poured a third. In quiet moments like that, I missed my family and my old life. I wished I were strong enough to go back home.

I drank more that night than I had in the previous six months combined and woke up the next morning at a little before seven with a pounding headache. As Roy went out to the courtyard to do his business, I drank two glasses of water and took some ibuprofen. Then I walked the dog before showering and going to work.

My head throbbed as I logged into my computer to check my email, but I deserved a headache. As I deleted emails from every store in the world I had ever shopped at, Brady Maddox walked toward my desk with a cup of coffee.

"You look tired," he said. "Long night?"

I took the coffee from his hand and nodded.

"That's kind of you," I said. "Thank you."

"Well, you deserve some kindness after what I've got to tell you," he said. "We had to let Rory McDonald go."

I put my coffee down and sighed.

"You're kidding me, right?"

"No," said Brady, shaking his head. "Like I told you yesterday, we tried tricking him into talking to his buddy in the interrogation room yesterday, but neither of them said a word in six hours. We found Max at the crime scene with a smoking gun in his hand, so we've got him. We'll throw the book at him. Rory, though, we had nothing on.

Your round went right through him, and we haven't been able to recover it from the crime scene, so we can't tie him to your shot. We checked his clothes for GSR and found some, but that only proves he fired a gun, and that's not a crime.

"Our case against him is circumstantial. He's a member of the Theta Chi Nu fraternity, and he had a gunshot wound. He first told the nurses at the hospital that he was hurt in a car accident, but he now claims he got that gunshot wound after cleaning his firearm. He says he was confused by the blood loss. That's all we've got."

My face felt warmer than it should, and I squeezed my jaw tight as I exhaled through my nose.

"When he saw me, he asked if I was going to shoot him again," I said. "Implying that I had shot him the first time, which would mean he was at the crime scene with Max."

Brady closed his eyes and nodded.

"The prosecutor doesn't think the admission will hold up," he said. "She said Rory was on so many painkillers, he didn't know what he was saying."

I clenched my jaw. I had feared this outcome, but the prosecutor knew the law, so if she didn't think it would hold up, it wouldn't. It pissed me off, but we had to deal with reality. We weren't politicians; we couldn't live in fantasy land and pretend it was real.

"Okay, fine," I said. "We've got Max. Let's get a warrant and search his fraternity. We might get lucky."

He drew in a breath.

"I hope you don't mind, but I already thought of that. Newman-Rothschild considers each room in the fraternity house to be a separate residence, which would require a separate search warrant. By their reasoning, we can only search Max's room. The lawyers are arguing it now, but it's not looking good for us."

My headache started pounding anew. I closed my eyes, trying to think this through. We needed a new approach.

"Okay, fine," I said. "The crime lab said the Molotov cocktail used in Susie and Dean Hillerud's murder contained laundry soap, ethyl alcohol, and gasoline. Max and Rory learned that recipe somewhere. Get in touch with Newman-Rothschild's IT department and ask if anybody has used the university's network to search for information on making napalm or thickening gasoline."

"I'd need a warrant for that," he said.

"Then get one," I said, allowing my exasperation to come through. "I can't do everything. You're a smart man. Figure it out. Okay?"

Brady forced a smile to his face and straightened.

"Yes, ma'am," he said. He left a moment later, and I sighed and sipped my coffee. I didn't have a right to be mad at him, but my feelings didn't always follow the rules. For a few minutes, I just stared at my computer, unsure of what to do next. Then I sighed as I realized why I was mad. The case pissed me off, but I had enough experience to deal with minor hiccups in a case. Brady and I would find something to send Rory McDonald to prison for the rest of his life; of that, I had no doubt.

My anger came from something much simpler: My time in the Cloverdale Police Department was ending. Chief Tomlin had brought me in to assist with the convenience store robberies and to work Sallianne Cantwell's disappearance, and we were very close to closing both cases.

When I left St. Augustine, I had been so angry, I didn't think about my future. I had needed a break, and I took the first one I could find. I had needed time to heal, and now that process had started. My world wasn't perfect, and it probably never would be, but it got better every day. I missed my mom and dad and my old house and my old colleagues. I missed my old life. Until I had picked up Sallianne's case, though, I hadn't realized how much I missed being a detective. And soon, I'd have to move on from it and lose that, too.

I opened a word-processing program on my computer. Eventually, Max Linsenmayer would go to court, and I'd have to testify. I needed to get my notes into order so I'd remember what I had done and why. So, for the next hour, I sat and typed and thought and compared the notes on my screen to the notes in my notepad.

Then, I felt a presence beside my desk. I looked up, expecting Brady. Instead, I found Charlotte Matthews, a uniformed officer, smiling at me.

"Hey, Joe," she said. "Sorry to interrupt, but we've got some civilians in the lobby who'd like to see you about the Sallianne Cantwell investigation."

I leaned back and furrowed my brow.

"Did they say what they needed?"

She shook her head, so I sighed and stood.

"Okay," I said. "I'll talk to them."

She led me to the lobby, where I found a woman in her mid-forties and her teenage son. Both of them had very dark skin, dark hair, and brown eyes. The woman smiled at me when I introduced myself but then turned a more severe look to her son.

"I'm Gina Stone. This is my son, Demetrius. He has something to tell you about Sallianne Cantwell."

I nodded and crossed my arms.

"Okay," I said, nodding. "Now that we've found Ms. Cantwell's body, the North Carolina State Bureau of Investigation is taking over that case, but if you have something to tell us, I'd be happy to forward a report to the agent in charge."

Demetrius looked to the ground and moved his jaw but said nothing. His mother prodded him forward.

"Tell her, Demi."

The boy looked at me and licked his lips. His throat bobbed up and down, and he rubbed his hands up and down the front of his shirt. He looked nervous, so I smiled.

"It's okay," I said. "Unless you're about to tell me you killed her, you're not in trouble."

His eyes snapped up.

"I didn't kill her," he said.

"Good," I said. "We think she died in a car accident.

Did you see it?"

Demetrius looked to his mom and seemed to shrink. She pushed him forward once more.

"It wasn't a car accident," he said, looking at the ground again. "She got hit in the head by a baseball bat. Someone murdered her."

I straightened and opened my mouth in surprise. Then I closed my eyes and tilted my head to the side as I thought.

"Let's go sit at my desk. We should talk."

39

Demetrius and Gina followed me back to my desk. I grabbed two chairs from surrounding desks so they could have somewhere to sit and I smiled at them.

"Would you guys like a drink? Coffee, water, soda?"

Demetrius's eyes opened wide.

"You got any donuts?"

"Demi," said Gina, narrowing her eyes at her son and lowering her voice disapprovingly. I smiled to show her it was okay.

"Sorry, but no," I said. "Police stations on TV shows always have donuts, I know, but we rarely have them in real life. We've always got bad coffee, though."

Demetrius nodded and looked to his mom. She smiled.

"We're fine, but thank you, Detective," she said. I pulled out my chair, sat, and took my cell phone and a notepad from my purse.

"Okay," I said, picking up my phone and opening a recording app. "Like I said, I'm Detective Joe Court. Do you guys mind if I record this conversation for my own notes?"

"Go right ahead," said Gina. Demetrius nodded.

"Great," I said, starting the app. "So, Demetrius. Your mom says you've got something to tell me."

He leaned forward and held his face about six inches from my phone.

"I saw Sallianne Cantwell's murder."

I smiled.

"You can lean back," I said. "It records pretty well."

He nodded and slouched in his chair.

"You saw Sallianne Cantwell murdered," I said. "When was this? Be as specific as you can."

"Maybe midnight. It was about two weeks ago."

Which was right about the time she went missing. I'd try to nail down the precise date and time later. He also needed to explain why he hadn't come forward earlier, but for now, I just wanted him to talk.

"Okay," I said, nodding. "Where was this, and what happened?"

"It was here," he said. "In town, I mean. At the old Miller Furniture warehouse. Me and some friends were there."

I didn't know the area, but I nodded as if I did.

"What were you doing there?" I asked.

He looked to his mom. She raised an eyebrow.

"He and his friends were smoking marijuana."

I straightened and looked at Demetrius.

"I see," I said, nodding. "How old are you, Demetrius?"

He said nothing until his mom cleared her throat. Then he looked up.

"Sixteen," he said, his voice low.

"Then you understand how the world works," I said. "Marijuana's illegal, but so is murder. If you witnessed a murder, that means you likely left forensic evidence at the scene of a murder. That means fingerprints, cigarette butts, beer bottles, just about anything you touched. You do not want the police to find your DNA at a crime scene.

"Even if you weren't involved in the crime, you could get charged. For your own good, if you see something, report it. The police aren't perfect, so sometimes we charge innocent people with crimes. Even if you're not guilty, a murder charge will ruin your life. If you apply to college, admissions people will look you up and find your name in the paper. Future employers will do the same. You don't want them to see we suspected you of a murder. Do you understand?"

He blinked. His mouth opened and closed, but no sound came out. Finally, he cleared his throat.

"Are you charging me with murder?"

"No, but if I had found your fingerprints at a crime scene, I would have turned your life upside down. You wouldn't have liked that."

He nodded.

"Am I in trouble?"

I took a breath and shook my head.

"I'll overlook the weed, but only if you talk to me now. Tell me what happened."

He rubbed his hands together. His mom gave me a tight smile, approving of my attempt to scare him straight.

"Some friends and I were at the warehouse smoking weed. Nobody goes out there, so it's quiet. You don't get caught there."

I nodded and jotted down some notes.

"Were you in a car? Were you on foot? What were you doing?"

"My buddy drove, but we were walking," I said. "We parked two blocks away."

"Your buddy have a name?" I asked.

Demetrius said nothing, so I repeated the question.

"If he wants to come forward, that's his business. I won't make him."

If this lead panned out, I'd have to get his name. For now, I could let Demetrius keep his friend's privacy.

"Okay," I said. "You were smoking weed with some friends. What happened?"

"We were doing mushrooms, too," he said.

Gina closed her eyes and shook her head as she sighed. Since he had already admitted to smoking weed, I knew he had been intoxicated. The mushrooms didn't change that.

"Jesus, Mary, and Joseph," said Gina.

"That's okay," I said. "Your friends were out doing drugs, and you saw something. Tell me about that."

"So we were smoking," he said. "We were just hanging out, you know? Then this gray SUV showed up. We threw down our cigarettes and hid behind a dumpster. We didn't want to get caught. I figured it was, like, a cop or something."

The gray SUV was a good detail, one we hadn't released. It sounded like Sallianne's car. I turned to a clean page on my notepad and got a pen.

"Do me a favor and draw the parking lot for me so I can understand where you were."

He looked to his mom. Gina nodded, so he took my pen and drew a series of squares on the paper and explained that was one was a dumpster, one was Sallianne Cantwell, and the other was the warehouse.

"What happened next?"

"A woman got out of the SUV and started taking pictures with her cell phone. Then an old pickup truck showed up. It had rust on the doors. Two guys got out of the truck, and they talked to her. Then the girl ran, and one guy hit her in the head with a bat. She fell down, and they dragged her to the back of the pickup."

I nodded and waited for him to continue, but he seemed done.

"So you think this was a murder? It wasn't just an assault."

"She bled a lot, but maybe she was just hurt," he said. "I don't know."

"And how do you know it was Sallianne Cantwell?"

Demetrius licked his lips but said nothing. Gina crossed her arms.

"Show her, Demi."

He reached into his pocket and pulled out a driver's license.

"She had a little purse. It fell."

He handed me Sallianne's ID. I clenched my teeth before speaking.

"You had this, but you didn't go to the police?"

Demetrius said nothing. Gina leaned forward.

"My son made a mistake," she said. "He's trying to rectify that now."

I shook my head and sighed.

"Where's the purse now?"

"I don't know," he said, his voice low. "We took the stuff out of it and tossed it. We traded the phone and wallet to a guy in Greensboro. I kept the license. I don't know why."

Part of me wanted to tell him he had done something cruel by keeping this information to himself, but that wouldn't have helped the situation. I still needed his cooperation.

"What happened to her car?"

"I don't know," he said. "After we saw them put her in the truck, we stayed hidden. Then the truck drove off, and we ran. I don't know what happened after that."

"Okay," I said, putting the license on my desk. "You go home. I'll check out the warehouse and see if I can find evidence that fits your story. We'll go from there."

The three of us stood, and I escorted them to the lobby. Before leaving, Gina turned to me.

"My son is a young man, and he made a mistake," she said. "He's trying to make it right."

"I wish it were that easy," I said. "You seem like a good mom, so make sure he learns a lesson from this."

"I will," she said. Before she left, I got her contact information and then watched as she and her son drove off.

Demetrius probably wasn't a bad kid, but he had made a big mistake. In an ideal world, he'd learn from his mistake and move on and nobody would know. In our world, though, a murderer's defense attorney would probably all but accuse Demetrius of Sallianne's murder to establish a reasonable doubt in his client's guilt. The bigger the case became, the harder his life would get. Demetrius deserved a kick in the ass for what he did, but he didn't deserve to have his fifteen minutes of fame in the middle of a murder trial. That was out of my hands, though.

I got directions to the Miller Furniture warehouse from Charlotte Matthews and drove. Miller Furniture must have been a thriving company at one time because its warehouse was a beautiful building with ornate brickwork and big leaded glass windows. In a larger city, a developer would have turned it into condos for doctors and lawyers. Here in Cloverdale, it was a derelict monument to the town's prosperous past.

I parked on the street out front and walked around the building, orienting myself to the drawing Demetrius had given me and making sure I was alone. True to the kid's story, I found an empty dumpster near the building. At night, the warehouse's overhanging hip roof would have cast a shadow along the base and around that dumpster, concealing everyone beneath a blanket of night. Also true to the story, I found cigarette butts and the remnants of two joints on the ground.

I snapped pictures, but I left the evidence on the ground for a better trained technician to deal with. Then I started walking in the direction Demetrius had said Sallianne had parked. The asphalt had cracked with age, but I found a dark brown spot on the ground. It could have been a rust stain, but I suspected it was Sallianne's blood. The kid's story checked out.

I took out my phone and checked my purse for Agent Gray's business card. He answered on the third ring.

"Hey," I said. "This is Detective Joe Court with the Cloverdale Police Department. You need to come out to Cloverdale. I think I found the spot where Sallianne Cantwell was murdered."

40

I walked back to my car and called Chief Tomlin to let him know what I had found. Unfortunately, his phone went to voicemail, so I had to leave him a message. Then I sat in my car and waited. About an hour later, Agents Corbin and Gray arrived with a team of forensic technicians. I briefed them on my interview with Demetrius and showed them around the area. Agent Gray took over the crime scene and supervised his evidence technicians while Agent Corbin went to find Demetrius.

They had things under control, so I called the boss again. This time, he answered.

"Joe, hey," he said. "Where are you?"

"I'm at the old Miller Furniture warehouse," I said. "Did you get my message?"

"No."

I filled him on the events that morning, but when he heard Agents Gray and Corbin were at the scene already, he cut me off.

"Let them have that case," he said. "We'll talk about it later. For now, we've got problems of our own. The maintenance man at the Methodist church on Cedar Avenue found the body of TJ Macon on the picnic table behind his church. I'm there right now."

I furrowed my brow.

"TJ Macon, as in Nicole Johnson's ex-boyfriend?"

"Yeah," said Tomlin. "He's dead. Somebody tipped

off his mom and dad, so his dad's on the warpath and is looking for Nicole Johnson. He thinks she killed his son."

I stood straighter.

"Do we have evidence to support that?"

"I don't think he cares about evidence. Either way, we've got a body. I need you out here."

"All right," I said. "I'm on my way."

He thanked me and hung up. I found Agent Gray and told him my department needed me elsewhere with a homicide. He wished me luck, so I got in my car and drove. When I reached the church, I found two police cruisers, a black SUV, and a minivan from the state medical examiner's office in the parking lot. Chief Tomlin jogged toward my Volvo the moment I parked.

"Body's in back," he said. "You're in charge here. I want to track down TJ's mom and dad before they go after the Johnson family."

I nodded and wished him luck and walked to the rear of the church. The building wasn't large, but it had a big playground and a covered pavilion out back. Officers Lorna Windstead and Lenny Henderson stood beside a picnic table beneath the pavilion. They stared at TJ Macon's body. The medical examiner stood nearby.

The moment I saw TJ, my shoulders slumped, and a heavy feeling began growing in the pit of my stomach. Murder was always wrong, but the murder of a young person was just plain evil. TJ was just a kid with his entire life in front of him. Already, I could feel his death weighing on me. After a moment, I sighed and looked up.

"Okay," I said, my voice soft. "What have we got?"

"A dead young man," said Lorna.

That wasn't the most helpful answer, but thankfully, the medical examiner chimed in. She estimated TJ had been dead for somewhere between eight and twelve hours. Someone had shot him in the back twice, but little blood spotted the table or surrounding ground, leading her to believe the church was just the dump site. She and her team would take him to their morgue and perform an autopsy. I thanked her and then got to work.

Lenny, Lorna, and I spent the next several hours knocking on doors and collecting evidence. Unfortunately, we didn't have much. The picnic tables were rough wood that didn't hold fingerprints, there were no witnesses to the body dump or tire tracks in the parking lot, and there were no surveillance cameras anywhere near the church.

TJ's body was our best piece of evidence, but that didn't say a lot. Hopefully the medical examiner would find something. We needed to talk to Nicole Johnson. I didn't know whether Nicole had killed anybody, but she had a lot of very difficult questions to answer. I also planned to talk to Hiram Ford about this. I couldn't tie him to any crime yet, but he was up to his neck in this shit, too.

By two in the afternoon, Lenny, Lorna, and I had done everything we could at the church, so I dismissed them and drove to the station to start filling out paperwork. The moment I sat at my desk, though, my phone rang. It was Ann. I answered before it could go to voicemail.

"Hey," I said. "What's up?"

"We need to talk."

Ann's voice was taut with emotion. I sat up straighter.

"Are you all right?"

"Do I sound all right?"

"Are you in physical danger?"

She paused.

"No. I'm at my house. I need to see you."

"Okay, I'm on—"

She hung up before I finished speaking. Ann had a good head on her shoulders. If she was this upset about something, she had good reason. I hoped she was okay. I turned off my monitor and jogged toward the front door, my throat tightening and my gut flip-flopping with every step. My old Volvo didn't have lights or a siren, but I drove as quickly as I could, anyway. When I reached the house, the lights inside were off. The trees beside the home cast dark shadows on the exterior.

I parked in the drive and hurried into the courtyard. Roy lay on the grass, but he jumped up when he saw me. Ann emerged from the house wearing a white top and jeans. She looked as if she had just come home from work. Her eyes were red, and the skin over her throat had taken on a pink hue. She practically fumed.

"What's going on?" I asked. Ann closed her eyes and drew in a slow breath. Her hands formed fists at her sides.

"Do you know someone named Darren Rogers?"

My back straightened, and I drew in a sharp, surprised breath. Skin all over my body tingled as a heavy feeling began growing in my gut. My chest rose and fell with every breath.

"What happened?" I asked.

She closed her eyes and shook.

"Please answer my question," she said, her voice tight. "Do you know Darren Rogers?"

I nodded.

"Yes. He was a county councilman in St. Augustine, where I used to live."

Ann drew in a slow breath and nodded.

"Did you murder a woman named Sasha Ingram?"

My breath caught in my throat. Ann crossed her arms but said nothing, giving me a moment to think of how I wanted to respond.

"I've never murdered anyone," I said, "but I shot and killed Sasha Ingram. I was a police officer on the job, and I defended myself. It was a righteous shooting."

Ann looked to the ground.

"Before you shot her, did she try to kill your brother?"

I knew where this was going, and anger began replacing my discomfort. For about thirty seconds, I held my breath so I wouldn't snap at her.

"I don't know what's going on, but this isn't your business. We're friends, but I don't talk about these kinds of things even with my friends. And I'm not interested in having this conversation if you plan to accuse me of murder."

"We're not friends," she said. "Pack your clothes and your dog and get out of my house."

My mouth popped open, but I didn't otherwise move.

"What the hell is going on?" I asked. "Talk to me."

Ann's face grew even redder. She looked as if she would explode, but then she brought her hand to her mouth and closed her eyes tight as her body shook. I gave her a minute to compose herself before speaking.

"Has someone hurt you?"

She trembled but said nothing. Then she looked at me with black, hate-filled eyes.

"Please talk to me," I said. "I can't help if I don't even know what's going on. If you don't want to talk to me, I can get somebody from my station."

"They took Cora," she said.

My stomach tightened, but I nodded and reached into my purse for my phone. My heart pounded.

"I'll call this in," I said. "Try to remember any details you can. We'll find her. Don't worry."

Before I could dial, Ann scoffed.

"A social worker with Child Protective Services took her. I'm not even allowed to talk to her until we have a formal hearing," she said. "This is your fault. Jeremy filed for an emergency order of protection after receiving a letter about you from Darren Rogers. You told me you left St. Augustine because you were tired of small-town politics and that you needed a break. You didn't tell me your boss accused you of murder."

My fingernails dug into my palms as I squeezed my hands into fists.

"I didn't tell you because it was none of your business and because the accusation was complete bullshit. My boss had wanted me gone for years and took the first opportunity he had. I made a judgment call while working a complex murder investigation. That judgment call protected me and my fellow officers. Afterwards, multiple government agencies investigated and cleared me of all wrongdoing.

"I left St. Augustine because I was tired of the bullshit. So, yeah, I killed Sasha Ingram. If you want the truth, I've killed a lot of people, and all of them deserved it. Trained investigators cleared me in every single shooting. If I had to make those decisions again, I'd pull the trigger every time."

Ann opened her eyes wide.

"You're a goddamn sociopath," she said, her voice trembling. "I should have known after those college kids came after you, and you barely reacted. It was another day at the office for you."

I looked down and sighed but said nothing.

"Get your stuff and get out of my house," she said. "Please."

I wanted to defend myself, but this wasn't about me. Ann's ex-husband was an asshole, and I didn't understand the situation he had just put her in, but I recognized the anguish in her voice. The best help I could give her was to do as she asked. Her lawyers would figure this out.

So I left the courtyard and packed my bags. The carriage house had come furnished, so I only had a couple of duffel bags' worth of clothes alongside Roy's dog food and toys. I threw everything in the back of my Volvo and went back to the courtyard. Ann was sitting at her table.

"I'm sorry for whatever's happened," I said. "If there's anything I can do, please tell me. If you need me to write a letter or go to court, I will."

Ann balled her hands into fists again and closed her eyes.

"I could lose my daughter permanently because of this. You have no idea what it's like to lose a child. Don't talk to me. Just get the fuck out, Joe."

My throat tightened, and I felt almost dizzy, but I had spent a lifetime hiding my feelings from those around me. She didn't need to know how much this hurt.

"Do you have a copy of the letter Darren Rogers sent?"

She drew in a slow breath through her nose and then reached for a pile of papers in front of her on the patio table. She pulled out a typed letter and slid it toward me.

"My lawyer gave me a copy. Take it and go."

I took the letter from the table but didn't read it yet.

"I'm sorry," I said. "Cora's a well-adjusted, healthy little girl. I grew up in the foster care system, so I know what it's like. You'll get her back soon, but she's strong. She'll be okay."

She looked up at me.

"You have no idea what this is like," she said. "This is

326

the worst day of my life. I lost my daughter because of you. If you ever cared about her or me, you'll leave right now."

I nodded, swallowed hard, and left without saying another word. Roy followed and climbed into the backseat. If I had planned this, I would have put a harness on him and slung the hammock over the backseat. My chest felt tight, my hands trembled, my lip quivered, and a heavy feeling grew in my belly. I felt nauseated. I wanted to scream and cry and curse and hit something, but I could barely breathe. The dog would be fine for a little while. I needed to get out of there before I hyperventilated.

I thought about driving to a hotel, but I couldn't think straight, so instead, I drove to a public park to which I had taken Cora on numerous occasions. Technically, the park had closed an hour before sunset, but no one had moved the bar that would have closed the parking lot. I pulled into the darkest corner of the lot I could find, and then I cried, knowing I had cost a friend what she loved most in the world.

41

Roy and I stayed in the car together for about half an hour, but then he started getting agitated. I dug through my belongings until I found his harness and leash and took him for a walk around the grounds. As I walked, I took out my phone and started searching for hotels nearby that would accept pets, but I didn't call any front desks. Instead, when I tried to dial a number, I called someone else, someone I should have called days ago. The phone rang twice before somebody answered.

"Dad," I said, my voice wavering. "It's Joe."

Doug Green, my adoptive father, paused.

"Honey," he said, his voice soft. "You okay?"

"Yeah, I'm fine," I said, forcing my back to straighten and my voice to sound stronger than it truly was. "Is Mom there? I need to talk to her."

He didn't hesitate before responding.

"Sure, hon," he said. "And thanks for calling me Dad again. That means a lot to me."

My lip quivered again, and I wiped my nose.

"You've always been my dad even when I've called you something else."

He paused and cleared his throat.

"Thank you. I'll get your mom."

I thanked him and waited a moment before Julia answered.

"Joe?" she asked. "Is everything all right?"

I tried to tell her yes, but my throat was so tight I couldn't speak. I closed my eyes and took a breath.

"No."

"Are you hurt?"

I swallowed hard.

"No, but I hurt a friend of mine."

"What happened?" she asked, her voice soft.

My eyes felt moist, so I blinked and wiped away a tear that threatened to fall before sucking in a deep breath.

"I shouldn't have called. I'm sorry."

Julia said nothing, but she didn't hang up.

"Are you going to say anything?" I asked.

"It sounds more like you need someone to listen."

My stomach flip-flopped, and I sucked down a deep breath as my gut tightened. Then, it almost felt like something broke inside me. It was like cracking a door just enough to let the light inside. My fingers trembled, and I blinked rapidly as I ran my thumbs across the callouses on my palms.

"I thought I could do this alone, but I can't." I paused to take a breath. Julia said nothing. "When I left St. Augustine, I was hurt, and I needed that to stop. I thought if I just pushed everybody away, I wouldn't hurt anymore."

"Okay," said Julia.

No judgment entered Julia's voice. I wanted her to say something, maybe even to yell at me. She didn't, though. I looked around for somewhere to sit, but the park didn't have benches or tables, so I walked to a tree and sat and leaned against its trunk. Roy lay beside me, and I petted his side. Then I drew in a deep breath.

"You're my mom, and I love you. Right now, I'm in a little town called Cloverdale, North Carolina, and I have a temporary job as a detective with the local police department. I've been accepted to graduate school at the University of North Carolina. I'll study social work and plan to work with kids in the foster care system."

Julia said nothing. I cleared my throat.

"You can say something now," I said. "It's okay."

"Then I'm sorry about your friend," she said. "I'm proud of you, and I know you'll succeed at whatever you do. And I'm glad to know where you're living and that you're safe. I hope you're happy, too. You deserve to be happy."

"I don't know what I deserve, but thank you for saying so."

We settled into an easy silence for a moment.

"I hurt my friend," I said. "I didn't mean to, but I did."

"You want to tell me about that?"

I didn't want to tell her anything, but I did anyway. Julia listened to me ramble for almost ten minutes straight. Then she said she loved me, which was what I needed to hear. After a while, I felt a little better, but then something else weighed on me. I twirled Roy's fur between my thumb and index finger.

"I'm mad at you," I said before swallowing hard. "I thought time away would help me move on, but I can't get over it. You hurt me."

"I'm sorry," said Julia.

"It was my last case in St. Augustine," I said. "I was looking for Sasha Ingram. I didn't know her name, but I was looking for her. She was a murderer."

"I remember. I'll never forget her."

I nodded and swallowed.

"She wanted to hurt me, but she couldn't come after me without getting caught, so she came after Ian and Dylan," I said. "She went to Ian's school and shot his vice principal, and she went to the country club where Dylan worked and seduced him. She used him to send a message to me. She wanted me to know she could get to the people I cared about."

Julia drew in a slow breath.

"I remember."

"Do you remember what you said to me after you found out what happened with Dylan?" I asked.

She paused.

"No."

I looked down at the grass.

"You said you'd never forgive me if your son had died. That was how you said it. You didn't call him Dylan, and you didn't call him my brother. You called him your son, like he was different than me."

She paused.

"I'm sorry. I didn't say that well."

"The problem wasn't just the way you said it. Dylan's an adult, Mom," I said. "Sasha Ingram came to the country club where he worked and hit on him. She was a complete stranger, but he followed her across town for sex. Sasha never would have known his name if not for my investigation, but Dylan never would have gotten hurt if he had thought with his head instead of his dick. Still, you blamed everything on me and then told me you needed time away from me."

Julia sighed.

"I didn't realize I had done that."

My face grew warm.

"You did, and it hurt," I said. "After shooting her, I lost my job, my family, and my boyfriend. I needed you, and you told me to go away. So I did."

Julia said nothing for almost thirty seconds.

"I'm sorry," she said, her voice so soft I could barely hear.

My hand stayed on Roy's back.

"I'm not looking for an apology. I'm telling you this because I get it now. Dylan and Audrey are your kids. I'm not," I said. "It took me time to understand that, but I do now. You're not the one with the problem. I thought we were something that we aren't. I'm sorry. My mom left me a long time ago. I had no right to try to replace her with you."

Julia said nothing, but it sounded as if she were crying. Then the line went quiet.

"Stop, Joe."

I waited a moment, expecting her to speak.

"It's okay," I said. "I made the mistake, not you."

Again, the line went silent.

"You are my daughter as much as Audrey is," she said. She paused again, but this time I didn't speak. "I blamed you for Sasha Ingram, and that was wrong of me. You're everything I could want in a daughter, Joe. When you came to live with us, you were so independent. You had seen the ugliest sides of the world, but you kept going. You were a fighter."

I shook my head.

"No. I wasn't strong," I said. "I was broken and too scared to show anybody."

"You were stronger than you realize," she said. "You're also smart and kind and wise beyond your years."

I shook my head.

"Cynicism doesn't make me wise."

"Maybe it doesn't, but you've seen parts of the world your brother and sister haven't," she said. "Because of that, I hold you to a different standard than I do them, and that's unfair. You played a role in what happened with Sasha Ingram, but your brother played an even bigger role. You are my daughter. Never think otherwise."

I tried to respond, but my voice caught in my throat. Then I coughed.

"Are you sure?"

"I've rarely been this sure in my life."

My throat tightened again.

"Thank you," I said, my voice small. Julia and I talked for another few minutes about Dylan. I hadn't talked to him since leaving Missouri, so it was nice to hear he was enjoying college. After a while, our conversation quieted, and I cleared my throat. "I hate my past. I never meant to hurt anybody, but a friend of mine lost her daughter because of me today."

"You said that," said Julia. "Your friend didn't lose her daughter because of you, though. She lost her daughter—temporarily—because her ex-husband is a son fo a bitch. He deserves to get kicked in the balls every morning for the rest of his life."

I smiled and nodded.

"I'm pretty sure Ann would be willing to deliver the punishment if a court ordered it," I said. Then I sighed. "Darren Rogers didn't have to send that letter. I left town. He won. I just wanted to start over."

"If anyone deserves the chance to start over, you do," said Julia. She paused. "St. Augustine's changed since you left. George Delgado lost the sheriff's election."

Delgado was my former boss. At times, he had been a decent supervisor, but at other times, he had been a vindictive, petty tyrant.

"Good," I said. "The county's better off without him."

"I don't know about that," she said before pausing. "How did Darren Rogers know where you lived, and how did he know enough about your life to send that letter to your friend's ex-husband?"

I paused and shook my head.

"I don't know," I said.

"You should find out," she said. "And I hope your friend gets her daughter back."

"Me, too," I said.

334

Julia and I spoke for another few minutes, but we both had work to do. After we hung up, I leaned back against the tree and looked down at Roy, thinking. Mom was right: I needed to find out how Darren Rogers knew where I was and why he knew enough about my life to send a letter to Jeremy Pittman. Something was wrong there. Somebody had tipped him off. If I had to guess, it was Hiram Ford.

Ann had warned me about Hiram. She said he was dangerous, and it seemed she was right. By attacking me at home, he had distracted me and thrown me off the case for a while. Maybe he even thought that'd make me run. It wouldn't work. He had hurt someone I cared about. A better person might have forgiven him, but I had never aspired to virtue. Mr. Ford would regret pissing me off.

But for now, it was getting late, and I had to find a place to stay now that I had lost my home.

42

Nicole's eyes snapped open to the sound of footsteps upstairs. Since Greg and Wayne had captured her, she had learned much about the men who lived in that house. They thrived on consistency.

At six AM every day, Jalan and Bryan—Nicole had yet to meet either of them—woke up, showered, had breakfast, and left for work somewhere in Cloverdale. Shortly after that, Wilmar and Wayne—she hadn't seen Wayne since he first captured her near the drying barn—had breakfast and checked the property. Kevin and Greg slept in until eight most mornings, but they came down and checked on her right away.

All the men made different sounds as they walked, and she could almost tell them all apart by the tap of their shoes alone on the hardwood floor. Greg walked on his heels, so the sound was sharp and heavy, almost a thud. The floor joists creaked whenever Bryan walked, so he must have been larger. Wayne's feet barely left the ground when he walked, so his footsteps were more of a shuffle than anything else, while Kevin danced across the floor with light steps.

Tonight, it sounded like Kevin and Greg were out for a stroll. To their faces, the other guys called them the Lovebirds. Behind their backs, they called Greg the screaming soprano and Kevin the anxious alto. Based on the context, Nicole surmised the nicknames came from the noises coming from their bedroom.

She sat straighter on the futon as the door at the top of her steps opened. Greg and Kevin came down. Kevin held her backpack, while Greg held a paper lunch sack. Nicole opened her mouth to ask what was going on, but Greg held a finger to his lips, stopping her.

"Hush, honey," he whispered, kneeling in front of her. "Hiram Ford sent word that we've got a problem. A detective found some of his fields and called the DEA. A helicopter buzzed the property earlier, and we think they found us. If it were up to me, I'd keep you here forever, but the helicopter forced a vote, and it didn't go your way. We're selling our product early. Hiram's coming to pick it —and you—up tomorrow morning."

Nicole nodded and swallowed.

"If you give me to Hiram," she said, "he'll kill me. You'll be murderers."

"I know," said Greg. "That's why Kevin and I are here now. You need to run. Your money, keys, and phone are in your backpack, but we already got rid of your gun."

She pulled her legs off the bed. She wore flannel pajama pants and a T-shirt, but both of the boys turned their heads as if she were naked.

"What'd you guys do with it?" she asked, looking through the pile of clothes at the foot of her futon for something clean. She pulled out some jeans and a white top before looking at Kevin and Greg.

"Sold it to a guy in Charlotte for cash," said Kevin. "Apparently, that's legal if the buyer has a permit from the local sheriff."

Nicole nodded and walked to the bathroom to change but kept the door cracked.

"Did you guys give him your contact information?"

"Just my email address," said Greg. "Why?"

She threw on her clothes before stepping out.

"I shot a cop with it," she said. "You don't want it tracked back to you is all."

"Oh," said Kevin. "I kind of wish you had told us."

"Don't you judge me," she said. "You've got several tons of weed hanging in your barn, you've been holding me prisoner, and you took a vote on whether to turn me over to a drug dealer who's likely to let his goons rape me over and over before murdering me."

Greg looked to his fiancé before focusing on Nicole, his mouth open.

"Would Hiram do that?" he asked. "He always seemed like a nice man."

"He already did it to some other girls that worked for him," she said. "Now let me out."

They stepped aside, and she climbed up the steps. The house was neat and empty, just as she expected. Greg and Kevin walked up behind her and led her to the back door.

"Your best bet is to go to the road and walk to town," whispered Greg. "It's eight or nine miles, but you should be able to make it before the sun comes up. After that, you're on your own, but I'd get out of town if I were you. Hiram wants you, and he usually gets what he wants. Kevin packed you some breakfast. It's just two hard-boiled eggs and toast, but it'll get you through the morning. Sorry we met like this. You're a nice girl."

"And you're nice guys," she said. "Thanks for not murdering me, and good luck with your wedding. You'll be a beautiful groom, Kevin."

He smiled.

"Thanks, sweetie," he said. "We'd invite you to the wedding, but that wouldn't go over well with the other guests."

"No need to explain," she said. "See you later, guys."

They wished her well, and Nicole tiptoed off the porch. The night was quiet, dark, and cooler than she had expected. She wished she had asked what time it was, but the boys had already gone back inside, so she headed down the driveway, staying in the shadows cast by nearby trees. The boys owned a lot of property, so it took a good three or four minutes to reach the blacktop. Then she headed to town.

Nicole had driven that road dozens of times and never noticed the boys' gravel driveway. It was strange to think West County could still surprise her. Nicole had been born and raised in Cloverdale and rarely left. Her world was small but complete. She had always planned to leave, but she'd miss it.

When she hit the street, she headed toward town, knowing she had a long walk ahead of her. Tonight was the first cool night of the season. When the breeze blew, she almost shivered. For all their kindness at the house, it sure would have been nice if Kevin and Greg had given her a jacket. Nicole brought her arms across her chest and rubbed her sides. That helped a little, but it'd be a long, cold night unless she could find shelter.

After her extended stay in the boys' basement, she no longer had a plan. She didn't even know whether TJ or her daddy were alive. As she walked, Nicole's heart grew heavy, and her eyes grew moist. Eventually, headlights appeared in the distance. Then she heard the deep rumble of a truck.

Nicole stepped off the side of the road and waved, hoping the driver would stop. Instead, he gunned the engine and roared around a curve so close to the side of the road, Nicole felt the wind shoot past her as he rocketed past. She fell into a ditch beside the road, stunned. It happened so fast she didn't even have time to react.

Then, her heart started thumping, and tears came to her eyes. She stayed there for a few minutes, crying and feeling sorry for herself. Then another car came past. The driver probably didn't even see her in the dark. After a few minutes, she picked herself up and started walking again, knowing how stupid it was to walk alongside a dark road in the middle of the night. Half the drivers who passed were probably drunk.

After a while, the woods beside her thinned until she saw a field through the tree line. At the edge of the field, she found a wooden deer stand on stilts. It looked like a kid's clubhouse, but it'd give her shelter until daylight, so she walked toward it and climbed the rickety ladder. The wooden walls and floor blocked most of the wind, so it was more comfortable up there than it had been on the road.

She sat on a mat on the floor and brought her legs to her chest. For a while, she just sat there, but then her eyelids grew heavy. She fell asleep and then woke when the sun started peeking over the horizon. Her back and side hurt, but at least it was daylight. Her perch in the deer blind gave her a clear view of the road and the field. No one was around. She took her backpack and climbed down and started walking toward town again.

A quarter of a mile down the road, a minivan pulled over ahead of her. A middle-aged woman opened her door and looked back. She looked worried.

"You okay, honey?" she asked.

"Fine," said Nicole, forcing a tight smile to her lips. "Just walking to town."

"I'm taking my girls to school," said the woman. "How about you hop in the front seat? I'll give you a ride. These roads are dangerous in the morning. You can't see somebody on the side of the road."

Having been nearly run over twice, Nicole knew the truth of that. She hesitated but then walked to the minivan and sat in the front seat. Two little girls sat in the backseat. Nicole had babysat for half a dozen families in town and knew dozens more, but she didn't know this one. Thankfully, the woman didn't ask Nicole why she was on the road that early. Probably, she didn't want to know the answer, which was fine with Nicole.

She dropped Nicole off in the parking lot of the grocery store and wished her luck. Nicole thanked her, and then the woman drove off. It was a simple act of kindness, one that had saved Nicole several hours and kept her from being hit by a car. Hopefully, one day, Nicole would get the chance to repay that kindness with an act of her own.

She sat on a bench beside the road. In bigger cities, that bench would have been a bus stop, but Cloverdale didn't have public transportation.

Nicole didn't have time for strategy. She didn't even have time to formulate goals. Once Hiram and his men showed up at the boys' farm, they'd start looking for her. Detective Court and the police would search for her, too. As much as she wanted to find her dad and TJ, she didn't have the means. She had to focus on survival, and that started with getting out of town. To do that, she needed a car.

She looked at the parking lot. Cloverdale had a few businesses, but none thrived like the grocery store. The lot held about twenty cars. Somebody was bound to have left the keys inside. Nicole closed her eyes and drew in a breath.

"God, please give me just a little luck."

Then she stood to search.

43

Roy and I slept at a crappy hotel on the road out of town. At first, I tried a little bed and breakfast, but the proprietor took one look at Roy and said no. Then we tried a chain hotel down the street, but they refused us, too. Finally, I tried the local no-tell motel. The clerk made me give him a hundred-dollar deposit, but he didn't have a problem with Roy staying as long as I promised to keep him quiet and to take him outside to use the restroom. That I had to make that promise said volumes about the motel's usual clientele.

My phone woke me from a dream at a little after seven the next morning. Roy slept on the floor beside the bed—I didn't think he liked the chemical smell of the sheets—but he raised his head as I rolled over to get my phone. It was Annabelle Macon, TJ Macon's mom. Chief Tomlin and Lenny Henderson had notified her of TJ's death, but I had figured she'd call me, eventually. I sighed, sat upright, and forced a smile to my face as I wiped sleep from my eyes.

"This is Detective Joe Court," I said. "Is this Ms. Macon?"

"I'm Annabelle Macon," she said. "I understand you're investigating my son's death."

"Yes, I am," I said. "First, let me say I'm sorry for your loss. I know you hear that ten times a day, but it's true. I will do everything in my power to support you and to find out what happened to TJ."

"Thank you," she said. "Chief Tomlin asked us to call you. Tom, my husband, talked to him this morning."

She paused. I waited for a ten count, but she said nothing.

"Okay," I said. "I understand."

"We haven't been able to find TJ's cell phone," she said. "So we assume he had it on him when he died. He had an iPhone, and it has an app on it that lets us track him. We used it this morning. The phone is moving."

Any trace of sleep in my eyes disappeared.

"It's moving?" I asked.

"Yeah," she said. "I just thought you should know. Somebody has his cell phone."

"Where is it?" I asked.

"By the grocery store."

I tilted my head to the side to hold my phone to my ear as I put on a pair of jeans.

"Thank you for your call," I said. "I'll check out the grocery store and see if I can find the phone. If possible, I need you to monitor it and let me know if it moves again."

"I can do that," she said.

I thanked her and then changed shirts before pulling my hair behind my head with a tie. Within two minutes of the call, Roy and I were in my car, and I had called my station. Unfortunately, nobody answered at the front desk, and the voicemail message told me to call 911 in case of emergency. I had worked in a small town my entire career, but this place was getting on my nerves. If we couldn't even man the phone, we had no business calling ourselves a police department.

I sighed and tossed my phone to the seat beside me. The grocery store wasn't far, so it took little time to get there. I reached for my phone to call Annabelle Macon again and ask whether TJ's phone was still nearby when I saw a familiar figure crouching between two vehicles.

"Oh, you have got to be kidding me," I whispered. I looked to make sure the aisles were clear before accelerating hard. If I had lights and a siren, I might have put them on, but my quarry was so intent on breaking into a minivan that she didn't notice me until I slammed on my brakes. Then she looked up.

"Fuck."

I didn't hear it, but I saw her lips move. Before she could go anywhere, I opened my door and jumped out of the car.

"Nicole Johnson, stand up and put your hands on the minivan where I can see them."

I didn't raise my pistol at her, but I removed it from the holster. She turned toward the vehicle.

"Haven't you bothered me enough?" she asked. "I didn't do anything."

"Put your hands on the minivan," I said.

She scowled but did as I asked. I holstered my pistol, handcuffed her right wrist, and pulled it down to her side.

"Lower your left arm and put your palm on your rear end with your thumb positioned to the right."

345

She did as I asked again, but this time she sighed.

"Why are you arresting me? I didn't do anything."

"You have TJ Macon's phone on you?"

I secured her wrists and turned her around to face me. She rolled her eyes and nodded.

"Yeah. I've got TJ's phone. I picked it up at his house by accident the last time I was over there."

"TJ's dead," I said. "Somebody shot him in the back. You're under arrest for his murder."

Her eyes opened wide, but she said nothing. Then she started blinking as her eyes, face, and neck grew red. She fell back against the car behind her.

"TJ's dead?" she asked. A tear slid from the corner of her right eye and down her cheek. I nodded, and she blinked as fresh tears fell. When she spoke again, her voice sounded strained. "Is my daddy dead, too?"

"Not that we know of," I said, putting a hand on her elbow to lead her to my car. "We're going back to my station, and we're going to have an honest conversation. I don't know what's going on, but if your dad's in the same trouble as TJ, you need to come clean. It's not too late to save his life."

She nodded and walked with me toward my car. As I helped her to the backseat, she looked at me with tear-filled eyes.

"You think I killed TJ?"

I blinked but tried to keep my face neutral.

"You've got his cell phone."

She nodded and looked to her left at Roy, who sat on

the seat beside her. He grinned. Then she looked at me.

"I'd like to exercise my Fifth Amendment right against self-incrimination and my Sixth Amendment right to counsel."

I closed my eyes, sighed, and slammed the door shut in her face before she could say anything else. Then I drove her to my station, where I put her in the holding cell. Chief Tomlin and the county prosecutor's office could decide what to charge her with later. For now, I booked her on larceny charges for stealing her ex-boyfriend's cell phone and let her stew.

She wasn't going anywhere, so I walked Roy to my desk, where he lay down on the ground and yawned. Apparently, he hadn't slept well on the motel's floor. Since the boss wasn't in yet, I called Brady Maddox.

"Brady," I said. "It's Joe Court. How's the investigation into Rory McDonald going?"

He grunted.

"Poorly," he said. "Like you suggested, I contacted Newman-Rothschild's IT office and asked if anyone had used their network to learn how to make homemade napalm. They told me they'd look into it and then called me an hour later to let me know they didn't find anything. If Rory learned how to make napalm on the internet, he didn't use university computing resources."

It had been a long shot, so I nodded and sighed.

"I wonder if the library would help us," I said. "Maybe they checked out a book with the recipe in it."

"I considered that, but the library refused to tell me

who checked out what," he said. "And I didn't think we had enough probable cause for a court order compelling them."

"That's good initiative," I said. I paused. "You have any other ideas?"

"I do," he said. "These guys are full-time students, so they've got to go to class sometime. I figured, maybe, there's a chemistry class on campus that might teach them how to make explosives. It'd be like that TV show *Breaking Bad*. The lead character was a chemistry teacher, and he used the stuff he learned in college to make meth."

"Okay," I said, nodding. "What'd you find?"

"Nothing in the chemistry department, but I looked up napalm and Molotov cocktails online, just to see what we were dealing with. I found an article about the history of the Molotov cocktail that said fighters in the Spanish Civil War made them with alcohol, soap, and gasoline— just like the one used to kill Susie and Dean Hillerud.

"That made me look at history classes. Dr. Serge Bissette is teaching a class on the Spanish Civil War this semester. The college refused to tell me who was in his class, but I've got Dr. Bissette's home address. It's about an hour away. I had planned to visit him this morning."

I considered and then nodded. Nicole could wait.

"Let's go."

44

Charlotte Matthews was working the front desk that day, so I asked her to look after Roy. She was a dog person, so she said yes right away, which I appreciated. Then Brady stopped by the station on his way out of town to pick me up. The drive was easy, and we reached Dr. Bissette's house—a log cabin deep in the woods—at a little before 8:30 in the morning. There were two cars in the driveway, an old red Saab and a neon green pickup truck. Brady nodded toward the truck.

"That's his," he said. "Looks like the professor's home."

"Good," I said, opening my door. I unhooked my badge from my belt and walked toward the cabin's covered porch. It was cold that morning, making me wish I had put on a sweater before leaving my motel. Before Brady or I knocked, a man opened the door. He was about forty, and his head lacked a single hair. He wore a gray zip-up cardigan, a light blue T-shirt, and gray slacks. Something about his bearing made me suspect a lot of coeds had crushes on him.

"Dr. Bissette?" I asked. He nodded and looked to Brady. "I'm Detective Joe Court. This is Officer Brady Maddox. We're here to talk to you about Molotov cocktails."

He smiled but then cocked his head to the side when neither Brady nor I returned the grin.

"Good to meet you, detectives," he said. He had an accent I couldn't quite place. It was European, but it was faint. Maybe Spanish. "I'm not an authority on incendiary devices, but I'll tell you what I can."

"Have you ever made one?" I asked.

He considered me and then Brady.

"Do I need an attorney?"

"It's always your right to have an attorney with you when speaking to the police," I said.

He drew in a breath as he considered. For a moment, I thought he'd tell us to leave, but then he crossed his arms.

"Is this about Rory McDonald and Trystan Silvester?"

I glanced at Brady.

"Why would you ask that?" he asked.

"They're two of my students," he said, nodding and covering his mouth. Then he lowered his hand to his side and crossed his arms once again. "My contract with the university requires me to direct all requests for student information from the police to the school's office of general counsel."

Neither Brady nor I said anything for a moment. Dr. Bissette looked down.

"Did Rory and Trystan hurt someone?" he asked.

"We believe they were involved in a series of robberies in West County. In the most recent robbery, two of the robbers threw a Molotov cocktail that ignited automotive supplies. The building burned, trapping a mother and her son in the office. They died."

"Did the Molotov cocktail contain ethyl alcohol, laundry soap, and gasoline?"

I straightened and nodded. Dr. Bissette swore before lifting both of his hands and running them across his scalp as he sighed.

"Okay," he said. "Forget my contract. I inadvertently taught them how to make a Molotov cocktail while teaching a unit on the Spanish Civil War."

I crossed my arms.

"How do you inadvertently teach your students to make incendiary devices?"

"I teach history, but the books and lectures don't always keep my students interested, so the professors in my department throw in experimental days each year. We try to do something fun."

I nodded.

"And you did an experimental day involving Molotov cocktails?"

He closed his eyes and nodded.

"We had read accounts of guerilla fighters defeating tanks by throwing Molotov cocktails at the exterior and then shooting the tank crews as they evacuated. We wanted to see if a Molotov cocktail could produce enough heat to force a crew out, so we had our maintenance team weld together a metal box for us. Then we put a digital probe thermometer inside and poured a mixture of ethyl alcohol, gasoline, and laundry soap on top to simulate a Molotov cocktail."

"Did it work?" asked Brady.

"Oh, yeah," said Dr. Bissette. "The probe burned out at eight hundred degrees." He paused for a moment and then cleared his throat. "Rory and Trystan are both bright young men with big futures, but they're lousy students. This was the only thing they exhibited a single iota of interest in all year."

I looked to Brady.

"Did you search Max Linsenmayer's room?" I asked. He nodded. "And did you find laundry soap, ethyl alcohol, or gasoline?"

Brady considered and then reached into his pocket for his cell phone. He had taken dozens of pictures of the things he found, but he held just one toward me. It was a basket with laundry stuff inside.

"He had boxes of borax and washing soda and two Fels-Naptha bars."

"But no laundry soap?" I asked.

Brady shook his head, but Dr. Bissette cleared his throat.

"Borax, washing soda, and Fels-Naptha, when combined, form laundry soap."

My heart started beating faster. We were getting somewhere.

"Did you find ethyl alcohol?"

"Kid had a lot of booze," he said, sliding his thumb across the screen to bring up new pictures. Max, apparently, had a full bar in a trunk beneath his bed. He also had an empty bottle of 190-proof Everclear grain alcohol in his trash can.

"I don't suppose you also found gasoline," I said. He shook his head, but that wasn't a problem. They could have gotten gasoline anywhere. I thought for a moment and then reached into my purse for a business card, which I handed to the professor. "Thanks for your help. This has my contact information if you can think of anything else. If we need further information, we'll be in touch."

The professor nodded and pocketed the card before heading inside. Brady and I got in his cruiser.

"We've got four names now," said Brady. "You want to try to talk to Trystan Silvester?"

I shook my head.

"Not yet. I want to talk to Max Linsenmayer first and let him know what we found in his room. He might be a little more talkative if he knows he's facing the death penalty." I paused and looked to Brady, who was already putting the cruiser in reverse. "And good work with the search. You broke the case."

He smiled.

"Just doing my job, ma'am."

I nodded, and we drove back to Cloverdale. Max Linsenmayer was still in the West County Jail, but we only had one shot to break him. We needed to get it right, which meant we needed to plan so we could maximize the pressure on him. The moment Brady and I sat down in the station, though, Chief Tomlin came out of his office with a thick white mug in his hand.

"Morning, folks," he said, nodding to Brady and then

focusing on me. "I've got a bunch of lawyers in my office. We need to talk."

I put my feet flat on the ground.

"That doesn't bode well."

"It's the prosecutor and Nicole Johnson's attorney. Ms. Johnson has information about Sallianne Cantwell and various other happenings around town, and she's looking to make a deal."

"Good," I said, standing and looking to Brady. "We'll work on Max Linsenmayer when I'm back. In the meantime, print out those photographs of laundry supplies from Max's room."

He nodded and said he would, so the boss and I went to his office. The room was crowded but workable. The West County prosecutor, Linda Collins, stood beside Chief Tomlin's desk, while Nicole Johnson sat in an upholstered chair in front. Her attorney, a man I had never met, sat beside her. The chief sat behind his desk, but I remained standing.

"Morning, everybody," I said. Then I focused on Nicole. "You need anything, Ms. Johnson? Food, water, a restroom break?"

She looked to her attorney before shaking her head.

"I'm fine. Thanks."

"Okay," I said. "I'm here. What's going on?"

"Ms. Johnson has just signed a proffer agreement with my office," said Linda. "She says she has information about Sallianne Cantwell's death and would testify in exchange for a deal."

I nodded and looked to Nicole's attorney.

"Okay, counselor," I said. "Looks like this is your show."

The lawyer nodded and looked to Nicole.

"Before my client speaks, I want to remind everyone in the room of one fact: Nicole Johnson is sixteen years old. She's not even old enough to buy a lottery ticket. Bear that in mind when she discusses her actions."

I nodded and looked to her. She cleared her throat before speaking.

"So, as you know, I'm Nicole Johnson. My mom was Sherry Johnson, and she's dead. A cop who provided security for Hiram Ford's marijuana-growing business murdered her. I shot him with my daddy's pistol. Hiram had Sallianne Cantwell killed because I told her about the marijuana growing.

"Oh, and I worked for Hiram. I was one of his growers. He hired a lot of girls and a lot of cops. He had said he had cops in every police department in the state, and based on what I've seen, I don't think he was exaggerating. And Hiram pimped out his employees to those same cops. One cop who worked for him is named Michael Grant. He and a buddy of his got drunk and raped my friend Monica Davis. That's what started this whole thing. They also had sex with Jessica Feagin. She's on the dance team at my high school. They didn't rape her, but she screwed them both for money. Other girls may have slept with them, too, but they didn't do it at my garden.

"I contacted Sallianne so she could bring in the cops. I would have just called the cops myself, but I didn't know who worked for Hiram and who didn't. Sallianne was a journalist, and she knew a lot of cops. Michael tried to rape and murder me, too, but I stabbed him in the leg. I didn't kill him, though."

She paused.

"I think that's everything," she said.

The room went quiet. My skin tingled as adrenaline started flooding through my system. Then I cleared my throat.

"Okay, Nicole," I said, nodding as my heart pounded. "Let's start over and go slow."

45

For the next two hours, Nicole told us a story that left me slack-jawed and sick to my stomach. Nicole—and a lot of other young women from the community—grew marijuana for Hiram Ford. Then, one day, Hiram brought Jessica Feagin to Nicole's garden. Jessica tended a small garden patch, but mostly she was kept on staff to sleep with Hiram's security team. They, according to Hiram, needed a morale boost every now and then. Jessica seemed willing, so Nicole kept her nose out of it.

Because Nicole's plants grew well, Hiram brought other girls by to see what Nicole was doing. One day, one of those girls—Monica Davis—was there when Michael Grant and a highway trooper came by. They were drunk and said Hiram was supposed to bring a new girl for them. Since Hiram hadn't shown up with their expected girl, though, they dragged Monica into the shed. She fought back, but they put her in handcuffs and assaulted her.

When the cops came out, they warned Nicole against telling anybody what she had seen. She agreed, but only because they would have shot her if she said otherwise. Nicole found Monica naked and crying in the shed. She cleaned Monica up as well as she could and drove her home. Then she called Hiram and told him what happened. He said he'd fix things. In his mind, that meant paying Monica a bonus.

After that, the job changed. Nicole was afraid Michael and the other cops would attack her, but she suspected Hiram would kill her if she stopped working. She went to Sallianne Cantwell, thinking Sallianne knew enough cops to help. Shortly after Nicole contacted her, though, Sallianne disappeared, and everything just went to shit.

Hiram and Michael Grant then came out to the garden while Nicole was working. Michael Grant took her to her shed and tried to rape her. She stabbed him in the leg with a gardening knife and ran home. By the time she reached her house, Hiram's goons had abducted her father. Then a cop on Hiram's payroll showed up at her house. That cop killed her mom, and Nicole shot him to protect herself. Then she ran to TJ Macon's house, where she found her boyfriend with another girl.

She stole TJ's phone and ran again. Eventually, Hiram's men caught TJ. Nicole didn't know what happened to him, but she had been running ever since.

The story was wild, and she had clearly held things back, but I doubted she had made it all up.

"Did you ever find your dad?" I asked. Nicole shook her head.

"If he's alive, Hiram has him."

I nodded and looked to my boss and then to Nicole and her attorney.

"If you'll excuse us for a minute," I said, "I need to talk to my boss."

Nicole nodded and looked down. Chief Tomlin and I

stepped out of the office. Brady stood from his desk and held up a stack of photographs, but I held up a finger, asking him to give me a minute, before focusing on the chief.

"What do you think?" I asked.

The chief opened his eyes wide.

"It's quite a story," he said.

"Hiram showed up at my house and threatened me," I said. "I think he also contacted my former department to dig up dirt on me."

The chief furrowed his brow.

"If he threatened you, why didn't you arrest him?"

"He wasn't explicit enough," I said. "Nicole's story fills in a lot of blanks in my investigation. She's not telling us everything, but I doubt she's lying."

The chief nodded and crossed his arms.

"What do you want to do, then?"

I tilted my head to the side.

"This is bigger than Cloverdale can handle, but I'd say we need to find her dad and Hiram Ford. We need to keep Nicole talking, too. She knows more about this than she's let on."

"I agree," Tomlin said. "We'll work out a deal with her for testimony and information. She gets on well with you, so I'd like you to stick around and question her again once we've got the documents signed."

I looked to Brady. He held up his photographs again. I nodded and then focused on Chief Tomlin.

"That sounds fine, but first Officer Maddox and I

need to go by the West County Jail and interrogate Max Linsenmayer. We've got new information about the convenience store robberies, and I think we might be able to convince him to roll on his friends."

"Okay," said Tomlin. "Just come back here when you're done."

I told him I would and wished him luck with Nicole. Brady and I then drove to the West County Jail in separate vehicles. Brady had called ahead and let the watch commander know we were coming, so Max Linsenmayer and his attorney were waiting for us in an interrogation room when we arrived. Unlike the last time we met, Max now wore navy blue jail coveralls, and he had bags under his eyes.

Before I could say anything, Max's lawyer gave me a humorless grin.

"Morning, Detective," he said. "I'm Dale Amantea, and I'm Mr. Linsenmayer's attorney. I've spoken to my client, and he's uninterested in any deal you present him with. We consider his arrest to be pure harassment.

"The day you arrested him, my client was in a vehicle driven by a friend. We will not be giving you that friend's name, but that friend lost control of his vehicle, which jumped the curb. He then slammed on the brakes. My client then opened the rear door of that vehicle to apologize to you and anyone he and his friends might have scared, but before he could, your dog ran toward him.

"Fearing for his life, my client fired a pistol at your

dog to scare him off. You then fired on my client and his friends, striking one. Fearing for their lives, they left. At no time did you identify yourself as a police officer, and at no time did you give my client a chance to surrender. The shooting in Cloverdale was an unfortunate and preventable accident. Your recklessness endangered my client and every civilian on that road."

I opened my eyes wide, but before I could speak, the lawyer held up his hands.

"We're not unreasonable. Mr. Linsenmayer fired his weapon at a police officer. The circumstances are complicated, but we are prepared to plead guilty to misdemeanor assault. Otherwise, this will go to court."

"Cool," I said. "I'm not here to talk about that steaming pile of bullshit. I just wanted to let you know my partner searched Mr. Linsenmayer's room and found borax, Arm & Hammer washing soda, and Fels-Naptha soap. These three ingredients, when combined, form laundry soap. When laundry soap is added to ethyl alcohol —which we found in abundance in his room—and gasoline, it forms the thickened, flammable substance that burned down a gas station in Cloverdale.

"Rory McDonald and Trystan Silvester learned how to make the incendiary device from Dr. Bissette at school. Max made the device, and Kit Jameson drove the getaway vehicle. We have forensic evidence tying your client and his friends to every element of this crime."

Mr. Amantea looked to his client and then to me.

"We have nothing to say."

"Good," I said. "I'm not here to talk. I'm here to tell you what's going on. We will amend the charges against Mr. Linsenmayer to include two counts of capital murder. I also intend to charge him with multiple accounts of assault, assault with a deadly weapon, multiple counts of armed robbery, multiple counts of armed criminal action, and animal cruelty."

Max leaned forward.

"I never hurt an animal."

Mr. Amantea held up a hand to stop him from speaking.

"You shot at my dog, but that's the least of your concerns. You will spend the next ten to fifteen years of your life at Central Prison in Raleigh. Once you've exhausted your appeals, the state will pump poison through your veins and kill you for the deaths of Susie and Dean Hillerud. You're fucked. I'm here because I wanted to see your face when you heard."

Max opened his mouth wide and lowered his head to the table. That was satisfying. As I turned toward the interrogation room door, Mr. Amantea cleared his throat.

"Assuming my client has information that could clear up this misunderstanding, is there room for a plea deal?"

I looked to Max.

"For the right information, maybe," I said. "It'd have to be a lot to make up for burning a mom and her kid to death, though."

"It was Trystan's idea," said Max. "We didn't know they were in there. He told us the store was empty, but he knew it wasn't. He's the murderer."

Mr. Amantea closed his eyes. His shoulders slumped, and I smiled.

"Looks like you guys have something to talk about. Good luck," I said. "I'll tell Linda Collins, the county prosecutor, that you're interested in a conversation. Unless there's anything here, though, I've got stuff to do."

He said he'd be in touch. As Brady and I walked away, my partner smiled a little.

"Was that business or personal?"

I slowed a step and then drew in a breath.

"He burned a mother and her child alive. Then he showed up on my street while I was talking to a friend of mine and her daughter. A stray round could have hit either of them," I said. "It doesn't matter if it was business or personal. It's over, and unless he answers every question we can think to ask, he'll die in prison."

46

It was a busy day. I called the West County prosecutor and told her Max Linsenmayer was looking for a plea deal in exchange for providing information about the robberies and about his accomplices. She said she'd send an attorney out as soon as she could, so I left Brady in the jail to deal with the lawyers and then drove back to Cloverdale. By the time I reached my station, Nicole Johnson and her lawyer had worked out a plea agreement with the prosecutor's office that would keep her out of prison.

Nicole and I talked for about an hour, and in that conversation, she apologized for ripping my shower curtain and for dripping water all over my bathroom floor. I appreciated that. I appreciated even more that she gave us a list of sites that Hiram used in his marijuana business. Chief Tomlin called the West County Sheriff's Department and the State Bureau of Investigation for assistance and sent officers to check the locations out.

Meanwhile, I went by the high school and picked up Monica Davis and Jessica Feagin, the two young women Nicole had mentioned by name. Monica broke down the moment I started questioning her. She told me what had happened to her and confirmed Nicole's story. Jessica, at first, refused to answer my questions, but I was pretty good at talking to young women. Once I helped her understand she wasn't in trouble, she, too, confirmed Nicole's story.

Once I had those young ladies on the record, I called the State Bureau of Investigation. Their special agents arrested Michael Grant for first-degree forcible rape and various drug-trafficking charges. At first, he was smug and said some nasty things about Nicole, Monica, and Jessica, but he changed his story when we showed him the clothes Monica had been wearing when he assaulted her. Nicole had persuaded her to save them. After that, he shut up and asked for a lawyer.

And that's how the afternoon went.

Investigative work was like rolling a boulder up a hill. It was slow and ponderous at first—and sometimes the work was downright Sisyphean as the boulder would slip and roll right down the hill to the starting line again—but then you'd crest the hill, and momentum would take over. A judge signed a warrant for Michael Grant's phone, and that let us see text messages between him, Hiram Ford, and half a dozen other police officers across the state. SBI agents picked the officers up for questioning. Most of them refused to cooperate, but that was fine. We had probable cause to search their phones, homes, cars, and bank accounts. Each of them would spend significant amounts of time in prison.

Within three hours of Nicole and her attorney signing a plea agreement, SBI agents had arrested nine officers with six different law enforcement agencies. They also searched every location Nicole had given us. We found two drying barns, a warehouse, and several fields, but no sign of Hiram.

At a little after six in the evening, we got a break when SBI agents showed a Highway Patrol trooper a picture of Monica Davis and asked whether he knew her. The trooper broke and said he wasn't going down alone.

He admitted to putting handcuffs on her so Michael Grant could assault her in a shed beside a marijuana field. He admitted to taking bribes from Hiram Ford, and he admitted to hiding the body of another Highway Patrol trooper who had tried to kill Nicole Johnson. That must have been the cop who shot Nicole's mom. More importantly, he told us Hiram had a bug-out location—a trailer in a mobile home park—that we hadn't known about. A West County sheriff's deputy checked it out and found Hiram's truck parked out front.

At that point, my job was done. I had limited tactical training, so I let the more experienced officers plan the assault. They'd surround the trailer so Hiram couldn't run, and then they'd break down the front door and go in with guns drawn. Hopefully Hiram would give himself up.

As the team planned, I filled out paperwork, but my mind kept going back to Hiram Ford's marijuana-growing operation. We had found two drying barns, a warehouse, and five fields, three of which had plants. Nobody had measured the fields, but the search teams had taken pictures. The largest field was half an acre. Three fields couldn't justify two separate drying barns and a warehouse or the salary of multiple police officers and growers. Hiram had to have more somewhere. Hopefully they'd turn up.

Since I didn't have a lot to do with the raid, I took Roy for a walk around town. Then, we went to a park where I tossed him a stick a few times. He never had much interest in playing fetch, but a mom and her two little boys came and petted him, which he liked a lot.

After that, we drove to our hotel, where I napped fitfully and then woke at midnight when the alarm on my phone rang. Our team planned to hit Hiram Ford's mobile home somewhere around one in the morning. This was my case, and I wanted to be there, so Roy and I drove back into work.

Since our police station was close to the target, the various teams involved in the raid used our parking lot as a staging area. The night had cooled off. We didn't have to worry about ice yet, but my breath came out in a faint wisp of frost. I hugged myself and wished I had brought warmer clothes. Roughly two dozen men and women stood in the lot, talking and drinking coffee. Roy and I stayed by my Volvo.

At a little after one, Chief Tomlin, the West County sheriff, and an SBI agent in a navy windbreaker emerged from the station. The chief walked toward me while the SBI agent whistled to get everyone's attention.

"Morning, boss," I whispered.

"Hey, Joe," he said, before looking down to Roy. He reached out a fist, which Roy sniffed and then licked. Tomlin stroked the hair on the dog's neck. "And hey, Roy."

The crowd quieted. I looked toward the SBI agent.

"Okay, everybody," said the agent. "We've got arrest

warrants in hand. You know your jobs. We are arresting a man accused of multiple counts of murder, assault, drug trafficking, and assorted other crimes. As part of this investigation, we have arrested nine sworn law enforcement officers with six different departments. Let that settle in for a minute. Nine of our fellow officers debased themselves and this state for money. None of us are paid half as well as we ought to be, but that embarrasses me. It's time to put this embarrassment to bed.

"You know what to do. Let's get to work."

It wasn't a pep talk, but it got people moving. The chief and I took separate cars and drove at the rear of a long caravan. We didn't need this many officers to pick up one cantankerous old man, but with nine corrupt officers in custody already, we didn't know what we'd face at his trailer.

Hiram had hidden in the middle of a large mobile home park. It was a neighborhood complete with families and even a small convenience store. If Hiram or his employees started firing, we needed enough officers there to put him down fast before he hurt an innocent person inadvertently.

The drive didn't take long. A split-rail fence surrounded the mobile home park, separating it from the fields and woods around it. I parked on the road outside the complex—alongside every other law enforcement vehicle—and waited by my Volvo. Chief Tomlin stood beside me as the teams got into place.

Then, I jumped as a deep thud reverberated through the complex.

"Police officers! Lay on the ground!"

The shout was several hundred yards away, but it carried throughout the complex. I held my breath, my shoulders tense, as I waited to hear shots. None came.

"Fan out. He's not here. Get the paramedics."

I swore under my breath. Our hunt continued, it seemed. The search teams began running through the rows of mobile homes. We had the entire complex under surveillance, so he couldn't have gotten far. After about five minutes, an ambulance arrived, and the SBI agent in charge of the operation came toward us. Roy pulled on his leash, so I told him to sit.

"We found Trevor Johnson inside the trailer tied to a chair," said the SBI agent. "He's dehydrated and missing a finger, but he's not in critical condition. Mr. Johnson said Hiram climbed out a window about five minutes before we arrived on the scene. He apparently had a video camera down the road that streamed to his phone, so he saw us coming. I've called in a helicopter to assist our search, but I suspect Hiram's in the wind. He likely had a car waiting."

Roy whined beside me and pulled on his leash again. He rarely did that, so I put a hand on his back and petted him.

"Hush, dude," I said, looking down before focusing on the SBI agent. "How far out is your helicopter?"

"Fifteen minutes. It's coming in from Greensboro,"

he said. "Mr. Johnson's asking about his daughter. He wants to make sure she's okay."

I smiled and nodded.

"She is," I said, taking out my phone and making sure I had a connection. "We've got her in custody, so I'll let her know we've got her father."

"I'm sure they'd both appreciate that," said the SBI agent. He sighed and looked over the trailer park again. "Okay. I'll keep you informed if we find anything."

Roy whined again, and I looked at him. He stood with his back straight and his nose pointed across the street to a rolling field that had been left fallow for the season. Long grass undulated in the slight fall breeze, while a lone tree in the middle of the field cast a long shadow in the moonlight. A hunched figure loped across the landscape. He looked as if he were dragging something heavy.

"I think you can cancel the helicopter," I said, reaching down to Roy's harness. I unhooked the leash. He looked at me with his tongue hanging out. I checked to make sure the street was clear and then patted his back. "Go, buddy."

He sprinted across the road with his tongue hanging out. When Roy had moved in with me about a year ago, he had just flunked out of a cadaver-dog training program. He could do everything required of him, but he didn't like the work. My dog was born to be my friend. He was sweet and gentle, and once the pressure of work dropped, he became playful and friendly. As I later learned, in his mind, everyone who ran from him secretly wanted to be chased.

I jogged across the street after Roy. The dog bounded through the tall grass as if it weren't there and reached Hiram well before I arrived. Roy had bite training, but he'd only attack if he was threatened or if I told him to. Hiram didn't know that, though. The old man pumped his arms and legs even harder than he had before. Roy loped alongside him and then ran in front of him before barking and diving into a play bow.

"I'd stop if I were you, Hiram," I called. "You'll have a heart attack way before he tires out."

Hiram slowed and then stopped and unslung a duffel bag from his shoulder. I unholstered my firearm in case he did something stupid. Roy sat in the grass, his tongue sticking out of his mouth as he panted. I reached him a moment later, and Roy snapped to my side. Hiram glared at me but said nothing. About a quarter of a mile away, Chief Tomlin and two uniformed officers walked toward us and waved.

"I've got Hiram," I called out, petting Roy's side. He looked up at me with a big doggie grin. "Good boy."

"I should have shot him when I had the chance," said Hiram, leaning forward and resting his hands on his knees as he gasped.

"If you had, you wouldn't be breathing," I said, petting the dog and smiling down at him. Then I caught Hiram's glare. "You're under arrest, by the way. Murder, kidnapping, assault, sexual assault, child prostitution, drug trafficking…basically every felony in the state of North Carolina. Get on your knees."

Hiram straightened. He was panting, but he looked ahead to the field as if he wanted to run again.

"And if I refuse?"

"I'll tell Roy to rip your balls off. Your choice, but you're not getting away."

He looked me up and down before lowering himself to his knees.

"Fuck you, lady."

"I've heard worse," I said, looking up to Chief Tomlin, who now was about twenty feet away. "Can you cuff him, please?"

The chief nodded to one of the sheriff's deputies behind him. As they secured Hiram, I unzipped the duffel bag he had been carrying to make sure it didn't contain anything dangerous. The bag weighed fifty or sixty pounds —a lot of weight for a slight man like Hiram—but I could see why he wanted to keep it. I waved the boss over and pushed back the top to expose what was likely several million dollars in hundred-dollar bills.

"Wow," he said.

"Good news," I said. "With Cloverdale's share of the forfeiture, I bet you can hire a full-time detective now."

47

For a week, Roy became the most famous dog on the Eastern Seaboard. Newspapers and websites across the state ran his picture and described him in almost mythic terms, while donations of dog treats, food, and toys flooded the station. We gave most of the stuff away to local animal shelters, but Roy got a new chew toy out of it, and Cloverdale got some good publicity.

Hiram Ford had a rougher go. We arrested him for over a dozen serious felonies and put him in a private cell in the West County Jail. Within hours of his arrest, a corrections officer found him hanging from an overhead light by the laces in his shoes. The jail staff rushed him to the nearest hospital, but he was DOA. At least he'd never hurt anyone else.

Michael Grant pleaded guilty to the second-degree forcible rape of Monica Davis, assault with a deadly weapon, and half a dozen corruption and drug charges. He'd spend thirty years in prison without the possibility of parole. The other officers who worked for Hiram pleaded to similar charges and received sentences ranging from five to forty-five years, depending on what they had done.

According to multiple accounts, TJ Macon had died while trying to escape from Hiram's cabin. Hiram shot him in the back twice and then had two cops dump his body at the Methodist Church in Cloverdale. Sallianne

Cantwell was murdered at the Miller Furniture warehouse. At the time, the security team that killed her didn't know who she was, but they stored her body in a commercial freezer at Hiram's house. Then they dumped her in the Haw River and set things up so she looked like a drug dealer who was hit by a car while walking alongside the road at night.

When Special Agent Chase Gray with the SBI proposed that theory, it had fit the evidence. I hadn't realized he had planted that evidence for that purpose. Agent Gray would spend the rest of his life in prison. His partner, Agent Corbin, had no idea the man she worked beside was a dirtbag.

Monica Davis and Jessica Feagin both grew marijuana for Hiram, but the prosecutor declined to charge either of them with a crime. They had been through enough. The case still had loose ends, but I planned to take care of those.

The convenience store robberies were much easier to close, mostly because Max Linsenmayer, Kit Jameson, and Rory McDonald all turned on each other. Max pleaded guilty to six counts of robbery with a dangerous weapon, assault with a deadly weapon that resulted in significant injury, and two counts of involuntary manslaughter. He got fifteen years in prison without the possibility of parole. Kit Jameson, because he was just the driver in most of the robberies, pleaded to six counts of armed robbery and got a four-year sentence. Rory McDonald pleaded to the same charges as Max, but since he acquired the sulfuric acid used in one of the robberies, he got seventeen years in prison.

Trystan, their leader, refused to talk to us. We charged him with two counts of capital murder, six counts of armed robbery, assault with a dangerous weapon, and a host of smaller charges. With the witnesses we had against him and the evidence they had led us to, he'd die in prison.

Technically, my time in the department was up, but Chief Tomlin extended my time with a badge by a week. I spent that week filling out paperwork, writing reports, cataloging evidence, reading documents, and requesting additional documents from Hiram Ford's attorneys. The work was dull but important.

Roy and I walked into Cloverdale's police station for the last time on a Friday morning at eight. Lenny, Lorna, Charlotte, Bobby, Wayne, Brady, and Chief Tomlin—the entire department—waited for me in the bullpen. Charlotte had made cupcakes decorated with little icing dog bones, and Brady had brought in orange juice and donuts.

"You guys didn't need to do this," I said.

"It's mostly for Roy," said Brady, winking. "He's a hero."

The dog panted and looked around happily when he heard his name. We all chatted for a minute, but then Chief Tomlin cleared his throat and looked at me.

"Nicole Johnson, her father, and her attorney are in my office to fill out some paperwork. I assume that was your doing?"

I smiled at him.

"Yep," I said. "You should be in there with me."

He considered me and then slowly nodded.

"Okay," he said, his tone more curious than wary. "Happy to help if you need me."

I stopped by my desk to pick up a file folder and to drop Roy off. He lay down on the ground and panted. He'd be okay for a while.

Then Chief Tomlin and I walked to his office. Brady Maddox followed, just as I had asked him to earlier when we spoke. The chief's office was neat but crowded. The chief sat behind his desk, while Brady stayed near the door. I walked to the side so I could see everyone.

"Morning," said Nicole's lawyer, looking to Chief Tomlin. "There are a lot of officers here to fill out paperwork."

The chief looked to me and raised an eyebrow.

"This is your show, Detective Court. What's going on?"

I looked at everyone before clearing my throat.

"You're right, counselor. This isn't about paperwork. I've spent the past week filling in holes and gaps in our case against Hiram Ford. As you guys know, we've found three fields in which he planted marijuana so far. We estimate those fields would have produced seven hundred thousand dollars' worth of illegal drugs. Based on what we've found in his accounting books, though, Hiram spent almost two million dollars this year on security alone. That's a problem."

No one responded until Nicole's father, Trevor, cleared his throat.

"He must have had fields you didn't know about."

"That was our assumption, too," I said, nodding and looking to Nicole. "You worked for him, Nicole. Did you know if he had other fields or girls?"

She shrugged and tilted her head to the side.

"I only know what I told you," she said.

I nodded and reached into my pocket for a clear plastic evidence bag that held a prepaid cell phone. Nicole closed her eyes and slumped forward.

"Oh, fuck," she said. I nodded.

"TJ Macon's parents hired a service to clean his room. They found this phone in the vanity in his bathroom. It looked like a nice phone, but TJ's parents didn't know who it belonged to, so they gave it to me. You recognize it, Nicole?"

She said nothing, but her lawyer sighed.

"Detective, I'd like a moment alone with my client."

"In a minute," I said, opening the bag. I ran my finger across the phone to power it on and then turned it toward Nicole. "The phone only unlocks when the camera sees its owner's face."

I held it toward her and tapped a button. The phone unlocked with a soft beep. Nicole closed her eyes.

"Okay, so you found my phone," she said, holding out her hand. "Can I have it back now?"

"No," I said. "And it also unlocked with your high

school yearbook photo. It's not the most sophisticated phone in the world."

Nicole stared daggers at me. I smiled at her.

"I'd like to invoke my Fifth Amendment right against self-incrimination," she said. "And I need to talk to my attorney."

"As I said earlier, you'll have plenty of time to talk to him, but you're not going anywhere," I said, picking up the phone. "This was the phone on which you and Hiram Ford conducted business. You were Hiram's lead gardener. He even paid you extra. How many gardeners did you supervise?"

Nicole crossed her arms and looked down.

"Since you don't want to say, I will," I said. "Nineteen. They came from Cloverdale, Siler City, Greensboro, and even Chapel Hill. You were industrious. You didn't tell us that earlier."

"Is there a point to this conversation?" asked the lawyer.

"Yes," I said. "Nicole is a liar. She wasn't Hiram Ford's employee. She was more like a non-equity partner. Under her supervision, nineteen girls tended twenty-nine separate gardens, each of which contained somewhere between two hundred and five hundred marijuana plants. She knew the location of his fields and who tended each field."

Trevor looked to his daughter.

"That true, Nicole?"

"Don't answer," said the lawyer. "I need to talk to my

client.'"

I nodded and let them stand before reaching to my folder for a printout of her text messages.

"Hiram: 'Need to talk, girl. Security price is going up, so I've got to drop wages,'" I read. Nicole stopped moving, her back rigid. "Nicole: 'Got an idea. We'll talk later.'"

I looked up at Nicole. Her eyes locked on mine. She slowly shook her head, almost pleading with me.

"You want to tell your dad about your idea, or should I?"

She said nothing, so I continued reading.

"Nicole: 'Offer the cops free sex instead of higher pay. Pay Jessica Feagin a hundred bucks a go. She's up for it. She already sleeps with her English teacher for money. That's how she pays for her car insurance. I bet other girls will go for it, too.'"

Trevor brought a hand to his mouth. I kept my eyes on Nicole.

"To your credit, you were genuinely upset when Monica was raped," I said. "Instead of going to the police, though, you called Sallianne."

Nicole looked down.

"You gave her a list of eight locations to check out, three of which were fields with marijuana—including the one you tended. You wanted Hiram and his men to pay for what they did, but you held back twenty-six active fields. Why?"

"Three was enough," said Nicole. "I didn't want to

overwhelm her with information."

"Bullshit. You wanted to keep those fields for yourself," I said, reaching to my folder again. I leafed through pages before finding one that showed a group text between Nicole and her gardeners. "Nicole: 'You're going to hear some shit soon, ladies. Keep working. We'll harvest together. This is our chance to make some real money. Hiram's going to jail. This is our world now.'"

Nicole drew in a deep, controlled breath.

"I have no comment," she said.

"That's fine. I wasn't done talking," I said. "You're a smart girl, and you realized that Hiram in jail is just as dangerous as Hiram out of jail. That's why you had a plan for him, too."

Nicole crossed her arms and gave me a petulant look.

"I don't know what you're talking about."

"Hiram's dead. He didn't last a night in jail."

Nicole raised her eyebrows.

"I was in custody. You can't blame me for his death."

"But I can," I said. "He was murdered by Wade Sanders. He was a corrections officer at the West County Jail. You hired him for ten grand. He's already confessed."

Nicole crossed her arms.

"Sounds like you think you know everything."

I tilted my head to the side and shrugged.

"I didn't know everything, but I know enough," I said. "This entire week, I wondered why you didn't leave town. I know you wanted to save your dad, but that couldn't have been the real reason. If you really wanted to save him, you would have talked to me. Not to brag, but I've got a decent track record."

She said nothing.

"Your whole life turned into a horror movie," I said. "Your boss killed Sallianne, he tried to kill you, and you didn't know who to trust. Your sins created a monster, and you had to run. It's a classic horror movie trope. Only, you didn't run. Because Hiram was never the monster. You were. You brought down Hiram Ford, sent his security team to prison, and kept the location of the bulk of his business secret. I underestimated you. Everybody did. You could have made millions if you had just been a little more careful with your cell phone."

I nodded to Brady. He unclipped handcuffs from the back of his utility belt.

"Nicole Johnson," he said, "you're under arrest for soliciting the murder of Hiram Ford."

Nicole's father stood quickly, shaking his head, but her lawyer put a hand on his shoulder.

"Nobody say anything," he said. "Nicole, we'll talk later. Mr. Johnson, go to your car. We'll sort this out."

I didn't know what we had to sort out because we had her dead to rights, but I said nothing as Brady led Nicole away. Trevor Johnson and the lawyer left after that, both looking shell-shocked. When we were alone, Chief Tomlin leaned back in his chair and opened his eyes wide.

"You got any other surprises in store?"

I smiled at him.

"Give me a minute," I said. He blinked and crossed

his arms but said nothing. Brady returned about thirty seconds later.

"Lorna's processing Ms. Johnson right now," he said. "You have any other cell phones we should know about?"

He smiled, but I couldn't return it.

"No," I said, looking to the chief. "Gentlemen, we've got a problem. Chief Tomlin, in the time I worked here as a detective and the time I volunteered here as a reserve officer, I never saw you make a single arrest. Brady, you're a great cop. Sometimes you need a kick in the ass to get going, but you show initiative, intelligence, and ability I don't always see in my colleagues. I couldn't have solved those convenience store robberies without you."

The chief narrowed his eyes at me, and Brady looked away awkwardly.

"Thanks," he said, hesitatingly.

"That's the crux of our problem," I said. "We arrested nine cops from across North Carolina who worked with Hiram. Whenever their stations or departments received tips or reports about Hiram's operations, they made them disappear. How likely is it that Hiram didn't have an officer in his hometown?"

Neither officer said a word.

"Chief Tomlin, I looked up your record. You were born and raised in Cloverdale, but you left after college and became a detective in Raleigh. You're a good investigator, and your former colleagues spoke highly of you. Brady, you're even better. You cleared almost every murder you worked in Charlotte. How did you two gifted investigators end up here?"

Tomlin leaned back and sighed.

"I think it's about time for you to go, Joe," he said. "You've overstayed your welcome."

"I'm on my way out," I said. "Don't worry. Just indulge me for a moment longer. You're here because you were recruited by the town council. Hiram Ford ran that council. Didn't he?"

"Go ahead and make your accusation, Joe," said Tomlin. "Assuming you've got the guts."

I nodded.

"Okay. In the past six months, this station received over four thousand calls. Two of those calls came from a homeowner who found a marijuana field on his property, a third call came from a hiker who came across a marijuana field on property he suspected was owned by the forestry service, a fourth call came from an arborist who found a marijuana field on his company's property, and a fifth call came from a man who found a field of marijuana while playing with his new drone."

"Your point?" asked Brady.

"They found fields controlled by Hiram Ford and called them in," I said. "You two claimed every report was unsubstantiated."

Neither man responded, but then Brady gave me a tight, humorless smile.

"The chief asked me to check out a bunch of fields in the middle of nowhere, and I didn't want to go hiking. I lied on a report. If you were my boss, you could write me up, but you're not. You're a civilian."

Chief Tomlin sighed.

"Thank you for bringing this to my attention, Ms. Court. Officer Maddox's actions are an internal matter that I will deal with appropriately." The chief paused. "You sure like burning bridges, don't you? I thought you would have learned based on your experiences in St. Augustine."

"I did learn. And you're not the first person to bring up my work in St. Augustine lately. Hiram did, too."

Brady scoffed, shook his head, and pointed toward the door.

"It's time to go," he said.

I sighed and nodded.

"We know Hiram recruited you to work in town and that he paid you both off. We've got the financial records that prove it. I came here to give you an opportunity to come clean. Sorry you didn't take it."

I pulled open the door. Special Agent Corbin with the North Carolina State Bureau of Investigation stood outside. Behind her stood Lorna, Wayne, Charlotte, Bobby, and Lenny—every officer in Cloverdale's department who truly deserved their badges. Brady's shoulders slumped. Tomlin sighed and shook his head.

"This isn't over," he said. "I'm going to fight this."

"I thought you would," I said. Then I looked to Agent Corbin and my other colleagues. "Thanks for letting me try. I'm done."

I stepped into the hallway, while the special agent entered the room.

"Bryan Tomlin and Brady Maddox, you're both under arrest. You have the right to remain silent, but anything you choose to say can be used…"

I tuned her out as I left the hallway. My former colleagues followed me to the bullpen, shell-shocked. Lenny shook my hand. Charlotte gave me a hug. We wished each other luck, and I got Roy from my desk and left the building.

I didn't know what came next for Cloverdale, but it had good people. With Hiram Ford gone, the town could become the cute, quaint town it always should have been. Or maybe it wouldn't. But either way, the townspeople could now make their future without a drug trafficker mucking things up.

As Roy and I walked to my car, I found a familiar woman leaning against it. She waved at me. My chest tightened, and my footsteps slowed.

"Hey, Joe."

"Hey, Ann," I said.

She smiled and looked down. Neither of us spoke. I stuck my hands in my pockets so she wouldn't see me work my fingers together. My heart pounded, but I ignored it and cleared my throat.

"How's Cora?"

"She's good. She's at home with a babysitter. I got her back once you moved out. " She paused. "I'm nervous for some reason."

I smiled and breathed out a long sigh.

"So am I," I said before pausing. "You're my friend. I

don't have many friends to lose."

"Neither do I," said Ann. "And you're not losing a friend."

Neither of us spoke for a few seconds, so I cleared my throat.

"I'm glad you got Cora back. And I'm sorry you lost her. If I had known your ex-husband would use me against you in a custody suit, I would have rented a place in Chapel Hill. I never would have come to Cloverdale."

She looked up and gave me a half smile.

"I'm glad you came. I needed a friend, and you were a good one," she said, looking into my Volvo. "Looks like you're leaving, though. Your bags are packed."

Some of the weight left my shoulders.

"Yeah. It's time for me to move on."

She tilted her head to the side and started to say something but then stopped herself.

"Are you going to Chapel Hill now?"

I shook my head.

"The School of Social Work at the University of North Carolina received the same letter about my exit from St. Augustine that your ex-husband did. They rescinded my admission to their program. They didn't think I had the moral fitness required by the profession."

Ann covered her mouth.

"Did Hiram do that?"

"I think so," I said. "It doesn't matter, though. He's dead now."

She stepped closer to me and squeezed my shoulder

gently.

"I'm sorry. I know school was important to you. For what it's worth, my lawyer called your old department to verify the letter Darren Rogers sent Jeremy. A woman named Trisha Marshall called her back. She told my attorney about your old boss, Sheriff Delgado, and Darren Rogers."

Trisha was a uniformed officer in St. Augustine, but mostly she worked the front desk of our station. I had lost touch with her after I left, but she had been a friend, one of the few I had in St. Augustine. I missed her.

"I assume she only had nice things to say about them both," I said.

Ann smiled and slowly shook her head.

"She gave me context about your last couple of days in St. Augustine," she said. "Darren Rogers is a bastard. I'm sorry."

"Yeah," I said, nodding. "Rogers is a bastard."

We settled into silence, but it didn't feel as heavy as I expected. Then Ann sighed.

"If I could, I'd offer to let you stay in my carriage house, but I can't," she said. "The letter Darren Rogers sent is bullshit, but Jeremy would still use it in court to take Cora from me."

I smiled at her and nodded.

"I know."

"Where are you going to go?"

I looked down to Roy and smiled a little.

"Until a few minutes ago, I had planned to drive to

Jacksonville, Florida, with Roy," I said. "The city's supposed to have a great park system, and I always thought it'd be fun to live on the ocean."

"What changed?"

"I arrested Cloverdale's chief of police and a uniformed officer for drug trafficking. They were working with Hiram Ford."

"Oh," she said.

I nodded, considering what else to tell her. Then I figured I might as well be honest. This was her home, after all.

"For a week, I've been looking into Hiram Ford. He blocked land deals that would have brought a furniture factory to Cloverdale, he bribed officials, he used his influence to shut down attempts to build a new school on property donated by a timber company...he did everything he could to keep this place economically disadvantaged. I think he was afraid that a prosperous Cloverdale wouldn't need him or the shitty jobs his little drug empire provided."

"But you stopped that," said Ann.

I nodded.

"I did," I said, blinking. "There are a lot of people like Hiram out there, though."

"You going to arrest them all?"

I smiled and shook my head.

"No, but I've got a few particular ones in mind."

"Well," said Ann, raising her eyebrows, "Cora and I will miss you. You'll always have friends here if you come back."

I smiled and felt my throat and chest tighten.

"That means more to me than you realize."

"To me, too," she said, holding her arms out. I hugged her and wished her well and asked her to give Cora a hug for me. Moments after that, I was in my car, pulling out of the lot.

Roy stretched out on the backseat in his hammock. My throat felt tight as I drove, but I was making the right move. About an hour after I left Cloverdale, I hit I-40 West. I'd be on that until I hit Nashville. Then I'd head northwest. Roy and I had a long drive ahead of us, but first, I had somebody to call.

Julia, my mom, answered her phone on the second ring.

"Joe," she said, her voice bright. "I didn't expect to hear from you."

"I didn't expect to call," I said. "Roy and I are in the car. It's been a long morning, but we're heading home. I wanted you to be the first to know."

She paused.

"What do you mean you're going home?"

I cleared my throat.

"We're going to St. Augustine. I have some unfinished business to take care of."

Did you like *THE GIRL WHO TOLD STORIES?* Then you're going to love *THE MEN ON THE FARM!*

Nearly a year ago, Detective Mary Joe Court left St. Augustine County to find herself. Now she's back home and back on the job to fight for the things she believes in.

Unfortunately, there's no rest for the weary. There are bodies on the ground at a local farm. It looks like a family fight that got out of hand.

But it's not.

The family's teenage babysitter is gone. So is their youngest daughter. The girls were taken.

But why would anyone abduct a little girl and her babysitter?

Joe knows there's more to this case than she realizes, and to get the girls back alive, she'll have to utilize every ounce of ability she has. Even then, that might not be enough. Because the people she's hunting are dangerous…and closer than she could ever realize.

THE MEN ON THE FARM is the eighth thrilling novel in New York Times' bestselling author Chris Culver's Joe Court series. This is a great series. Check it out from the beginning!

The book will be available on June 17, 2020!

Enjoy this book? You can make a big difference in my career

Reviews are the lifeblood of an author's career. I'm not exaggerating when I say they're the single best way I can get attention for my books. I'm not famous, I don't have the money for extravagant advertising campaigns, and I no longer have a major publisher behind me.

I do have something major publishers don't have, something they would kill to get:

Committed, loyal readers.

With millions of books in the world, your honest reviews and recommendations help other readers find me.

If you enjoyed the book you just read, I would be extraordinarily grateful if you could spend five minutes to leave a review on Amazon, Barnes and Noble, Goodreads, or anywhere else you review books. A review can be as long or as short as you'd like it to be, so please don't feel that you have to write something long.

Thank you so much!

Stay in touch with Chris

As much as I enjoy writing, I like hearing from readers even more. If you want to keep up with my world, there are a couple of ways you can do that.

First and easiest, I've got a mailing list. If you join, you'll receive an email whenever I have a new novel out or when I run sales. You can join that by going to this address:

http://www.indiecrime.com/mailinglist.html

If my mailing list doesn't appeal to you, you can also connect with me on Facebook here:

http://www.facebook.com/ChrisCulverbooks

And you can always email me at chris@indiecrime.com. I love receiving email!

About the Author

Chris Culver is the *New York Times* bestselling author of the Ash Rashid series and other novels. After graduate school, Chris taught courses in ethics and comparative religion at a small liberal arts university in southern Arkansas. While there and when he really should have been grading exams, he wrote *The Abbey*, which spent sixteen weeks on the *New York Times* bestsellers list and introduced the world to Detective Ash Rashid.

Chris has been a storyteller since he was a kid, but he decided to write crime fiction after picking up a dog-eared, coffee-stained paperback copy of Mickey Spillane's *I, the Jury* in a library book sale. Many years later, his wife, despite considerable effort, still can't stop him from bringing more orphan books home. He lives with his family near St. Louis.